ADVICE FOR ITALIAN BOYS

ANNE GIARDINI

ADVICE FOR ITALIAN BOYS

HARPER
PERENNIAL

Published by Harper Perennial, an imprint of HarperCollins Publishers Ltd.

First published by HarperCollins Publishers Ltd in a hardcover edition: 2009
This Harper Perennial trade paperback edition: 2010

HARPER ● PERENNIAL®
is a registered trademark of HarperCollins Publishers

HarperCollins books may be purchased for educational, business, or sales
promotional use through our Special Markets Department.

HarperCollins Publishers Ltd
2 Bloor Street East, 20th Floor
Toronto, Ontario, Canada
M4W 1A8

www.harpercollins.ca

Library and Archives Canada Cataloguing in Publication
Giardini, Anne
Advice for Italian boys : a novel / Anne Giardini.

ISBN 978-1-55468-032-0

I. Title.
PS8613.I27A64 2009a   C813'.6   C2009-905763-8

Printed and bound in the United States
HC 9 8 7 6 5 4 3 2 1

For my husband

'A fantasia 'i l'omu esti chhjù povara assai d' 'a verità
Imagination is only the poor relative of truth

CHAPTER ONE

I truoni 'e marzu risbìglianu i cursùni," Nicolo's nonna often said to him. The rumbling thunder of March awakens the snakes. This is one of her more enigmatic, impenetrable sayings, and she delivers it in that way she has, leaning forward, intimate but oblique, with her head inclined to give emphasis to the words' precautionary rhythm, and with a slanting gleam in her eye. Nicolo has always understood this to mean that there are times when a warning or threat may be needed to ensure that we stay on the proper path.

Nicolo's nonna, Filomena Giuseppina Pavone—born Filomena Giuseppina Spina in the larger of two rooms at the back of a cold stone house in Arduino, Calabria, in late April 1930, twelve days after the date the midwife had

advised her parents that she should be expected to arrive—
had dozens, perhaps hundreds of these aphorisms, small,
quasi-medicinal admonitions that she had carried with her
from the old country when she came out to join her son
Massimo twenty-six years ago in the early spring of 1975.
She brought with her Paola Bisceglia, Massimo's seven-
teen-year-old promised bride—a girl of tractable temperament, neat and silent and watchful, still in mourning for
her parents—and very little else: a change of clothes, a tin
that her neighbour Rudolfo Sasso had soldered shut that
held several litres of olive oil that sloshed at her side on the
journey like a small green fragrant ocean, and the papers
that evidenced her right to passage on the *Colombo I* pinned
inside the deep pocket of her gathered skirt.

Although she knows that *i sogni su' menzogni*—all dreams
are lies—Nicolo's nonna dreams often of Arduino, and over
the years the Arduino of her dreams has become how she
now remembers it—its white-yellow sun that so saturated
the air that the streets and fields seemed as heavy and as
textured as the brushstrokes of an oil painting, with light
and shadows of varying depths and intensities; its people
and animals and vegetation, all constructed sturdy and close
to the ground, made from and for dust and labour; its houses
pressed up close to each other like huddled sheep and folded
against the ridge of the hills that breach ever higher toward
the east, becoming, at the horizon, a corrugated rise of mountains; its stones of all sizes, from the minutest flecks of basalt
in the thin soil that the farmers work at with their few, often-
mended tools to worry out a harvest, to massy boulders that
would be too large to roll through the cathedral doors in

Catanzaro if anyone had ever attempted such a thing; its rich summer scent of dry earth and lavender. She dreams of all of these, but she never dreams of the single long journey of her life. She was terrified every second of the voyage and during the three-day train ride that followed, but she hid from Paola her certainty that they would be wrecked or would perish or suffer in some other unimaginably worse way, and so this is a memory that has been so completely submerged that it finds no outlet, even in the untidy nighttime images that her brain concocts from almost everything else in her history.

Nonna referred to her store of lozenge-like adages as *proverbi*, but Nicolo, the quietest of her three grandsons, understands them to be the old timers' way of administering advice, like a poultice applied in advance against trouble. After all, *"uomu avvisatu mienzu sarvatu."* A man advised is already half-saved. It is easy for Nicolo to imagine them, all the nonne and nonni before her, generations of them, reaching back to the days long before the Romans first set out, remaking the world in their image—the grandparents dressed in their homespun trousers and aprons, at rest at last after decades of unceasing work, sitting on wooden chairs or on stone benches set in a spot shaded from the scouring sun in a piazza in the middle of town, watching the young people go by (heedless that they too one day will be old), and passing their *proverbi* back and forth in much the same way that Nicolo and his brothers used to share a wad of chewing gum when they were small. The brothers weren't even certain themselves, back when they were growing up, that they weren't all somehow the same boy. They looked so much alike—black haired, quick limbed, brown eyed—and were always entangled in games or challenges and were treated interchangeably by their parents and by Nonna; they would all be punished for the crime of one, to save the energy and time that a proper investigation would have required and to make sure that the vice, whatever it had been, didn't spread.

Nicolo has an older brother Enzo and a younger brother Enzo, both two years removed. His older brother (a modest enough man, but hopes have always been banked in him like fervid coals) is named Lorenzo Marco, although their mother, Paola, perhaps sensing his ambitions, sometimes calls him *Lorenzo il Magnifico*. His whip-smart youngest brother's full name is Vincenzo Serafino and his mother alone calls him Vince. Their father, Massimo, says *"eh, guagliú"* (which sounds, by chance, almost exactly like "hey, all you") when he talks to all three of his sons. Everyone else, even Nonna, has always called both of Nicolo's brothers Enzo. Which Enzo is meant is usually made clear either by inflection or by context, if clarity is necessary.

Nicolo has always tried to pay attention to Nonna, even though she is sometimes hard to understand, especially when she slips mid-sentence into the old dialect, one that almost no one speaks any more, which has in it vestiges of the languages of the many populations that colonized Calabria in the past— Latin, Greek, Arabic and Albanian, and who knows what else. She speaks the dialect thickly in the roof of her mouth, and her words resound with clattering *u*'s and abruptly shortened consonants that are thrown up from the back of her throat so that her sentences sound more like an engine sputtering along than the kind of language a mother might coo to settle a restless child. Nicolo is often the only one who hears her.

Nicolo's older brother Enzo moved out of the house on the afternoon of the day that he got married to Mima. His brilliant younger brother Enzo was still living at home in the first wintery days of 2001, but he was in his first year of law school and paying for his tuition and books by working part time at a factory that made packaged mixes for cakes, bread and cookies. His mother doesn't listen to Nonna any more. "She's outlived my patience," she has said about her mother-in-law when Nonna isn't nearby, and sometimes when she is. Nicolo's father finishes the *proverbi* for his mother when he hears her start on one, to get it over with faster. He knows them all forward and backward and he recites them with his hands rising in the air, his square palms turned up to the sky in a gesture that appears to entreat the old, capricious, personal gods.

Many of the *proverbi* made sense even here, thousands of kilometres from where Nicolo's nonna grew up in the mountains of southern Italy. *Cunti allu spissu, amicizia alla longa.* If you keep your stories short, you'll be more likely to keep your friends for a long time. Or *chi simmina spini si pungi li pedi.* If you sow thorns, they are bound to pierce your feet. But some of them are much more difficult to follow. *"A gente senza figli nun chiedere nu sordi né cunsigli"* means don't ask for either money or advice from someone who hasn't had children. Nicolo could see the reasoning behind the part about advice, but wouldn't someone without children be more likely to have money to lend? Nonna only produced her thinnest smile and patted his cheek when he asked her to explain.

"You will understand in time," she said, and she assumed that inward-turning expression that she has so often, as if she knows more than she is saying although he sometimes perceives that this might be her way of avoiding having to admit to the many things she doesn't know. She had only three years of school, after all; in the early part of the century, when she was a girl, that was all that Arduino had to offer unless fees were paid and uniforms that would need to be washed and ironed and starched were purchased. Nicolo believed for a long time, for many years longer than his brothers did, that his grandmother knew and saw and understood everything there was to know about the doings and wrongdoings of the world and the people in it. Only recently has he appreciated even a part of what she gave up to come here—not only her country but her language and her gods—and how widely she has had to cast her handful of *proverbi*, like the weights attached to a fishing net, trying to encompass a world for which they were never intended.

Nicolo was working in midtown at Caruso's Gym, a bustling and thriving, half-modernized enterprise that occupied the entire long, fir-floored, high-ceilinged top level of a three-storey building that had been built a hundred years earlier of bright yellow brick, with leased stores on the main floor (Vera's Women's Fashions, Alberto's Cigar and Novelty, Cross-Town GroceryMart, Avondale Gifts & Stationery), and with Talbot's School of Business, Accountancy and Computing on the second. Nicolo had started out at Caruso's during the summer after his last year of high school, around the time that old Battisto Caruso's astute daughter Serena finished her MBA and perceived that it might be possible to reinvent the old men-only gym, open it up to younger men, and to women, and provide the new clients with a range of classes beyond boxing and weightlifting. Nicolo's first role was as a sub for another instructor when he went on holiday. Serena noticed almost immediately that Nicolo had a knack for it, a skill for engaging his students' interest, making them work harder, take greater interest, and he was soon given classes of his own to teach. He had been working full time now for just under five years. He began with the basics—aerobics and stretch and fit classes—but after a year he branched out into power yoga and kick-boxing and core strength training. Then, in the last year, he had begun to provide one-on-one training sessions. That was enough, thought Nicolo, on top of the classes he was teaching, his basketball and softball and hockey games, his obligations to his family, and his plan to take an evening course at the new distance-learning branch campus that had opened up in a low, stuccoed building around the corner from the Vaughan Bakery where Nicolo met his friends Paul, Mario and Frank for coffee every Saturday morning.

Not that this was what Nicolo had planned.

Nicolo's father Massimo had wanted all three of his sons to go to university, to study hard, and to rise up in this new world to become professionals—*maestri*. But Enzo and Mima got pregnant over the Thanksgiving weekend when Enzo was in his second year at North Bay College and Mima was in grade twelve, and that put an end to any possibility of further study for Nicolo's older brother, who considered his options, which were limited, and went to work in an electronics store at one end of a strip mall three blocks southwest of Nicolo's parents' house, where he sold cell phones and home security systems, both of them cheap enough up front, but with pricy monthly maintenance fees. That was where the money was made. He was second to the sub-manager now, but the work was unsatisfying and sometimes dispiriting. At least half of the buyers didn't really know what they were getting into when they filled out and signed their contracts in triplicate.

Only Nicolo's younger brother, the accomplished Enzo, the family's ascendant star, seemed likely to fulfill or even exceed his father's hopes. Enzo's marks had kept him on the honours list at Our Lady of Perpetual Help Catholic High School. His atheism, which he announced with blunt assurance when he was nearing the end of grade eleven, was viewed by the school's principal, Father D'Onofrio, as more of an experiment or adolescent bid for attention than a firmly settled state, and so Enzo made a ready transition to university, first completing a degree in political science aided by several of Our Lady's more generous scholarships, and then starting first-year law school. Enzo was invited back every September to speak to those of the Our Lady graduating class who were considering higher studies, to urge them to strive as he had done to bring honour to their family, community and school. He did this in an appropriately semi-humorous, self-deprecating way, attributing his own success not to personal qualities but to good luck and support from his family and community.

Nicolo had higher than average marks in almost all of his high school classes as well, which was surprising because he was not generally forthcoming about his views and he didn't often participate in class unless singled out. In fact, during those years Nicolo wasn't confident that he *had* any opinions of his own. His older brother Enzo had a few fixed, unshakeable ideas and a gift for dogged industry, like a reliable, well-built family vehicle. Younger Enzo was more of a sports car, nimble, with excess power under the hood; he could size up and analyze pretty well any situation quickly, with no more than a glance at the facts and people involved. Nicolo couldn't think what kind of car he himself might resemble, except, perhaps, one still under construction. Even grown, working, semi-independent, he sometimes felt himself to be as unformed as ricotta, and open to persuasion on most matters.

As a teenager, Nicolo played every sport that he could—basketball (although he wasn't tall), volleyball, soccer, hockey, rugby, even badminton and table tennis. He was something of a star in track and field, especially in the hammer, discus and shot put, and had gone to the provincials in three of his high school years and brought home several shelves-worth of medals, gilded statuettes and acrylic trophies that were kept in the basement and dusted semi-monthly by his nonna. Nicolo had learned from his younger brother Enzo the trick of paying close attention in class, and writing down what was said with fidelity—you're there anyway, was what Enzo told him, so you might as well make it worthwhile—and so he was able to absorb most of what he needed to know without having to put in many additional hours studying. An evening's review of his notes and the textbook at the kitchen table before a test or exam was usually enough to ensure an A or the better sort of B. He and younger Enzo both had a knack for writing out what they had learned in their exams and essays, staying close enough to the material to be accurate, but using their own words and with something of a spin, evidence that what had been learned had also been understood, to demonstrate, but without any flash, the sturdy, capable machinery of their minds.

Nicolo was generally content through his high school years. He enjoyed the anonymous but privileged feeling of being among the teenagers, many of them first- or second-generation Italian Canadians like himself, who thronged Our Lady of Perpetual Help's generous, glossy halls and filled its many high-ceilinged classrooms over which banks of fluorescent lights played their part in the elucidation of the next generation of Marias, Marcos and Anthonys. Nicolo had a gift of insight and he knew by comparing his life with what he had heard about life in Arduino from his parents and his nonna that he was lucky to be sitting virtually idle at a desk, studying equations and French verbs and the trading systems of ancient Mesopotamia instead of breaking his back trying to coax vegetables to grow in some *padrone*'s rocky fields, a destiny he had missed by the sheer chance of a few years and a continental shift by his father and then his mother. But it was in the Our Lady of Perpetual Help weight-training room, a dim, cool cube at the north end of the basement of the school, with its three high windows that filtered dusty sun in the fall and spring and were almost entirely blocked by grey-blue banked snow in the winter, that Nicolo felt most as if he was doing something to become, create and shape the person he might be intended to be. He spent hours there with his friends Paul Felice, Frank

Cecci and Mario Santacroce, whenever they weren't playing hockey or basketball or training for a game or tournament, doing sit-ups, step-ups and bench presses, curls, crunches and calf-lifts, pulldowns, pushups and pec decks. This was the centre of his life outside of his family home; this place of blunted, echoing noises, male sweat, modulated intimacy, brief exchanges of advice and observation. The four of them spotted one another on the major lifts, lean flesh leaning into flesh. They wore last year's gym strip and, since their mothers all used the same detergent—Sunlight, with its readily recognizable yellow box—they looked and smelled much the same, and they had many of the same thoughts and feelings. They talked about everything except girls; they felt toward women then, at age fifteen and then sixteen and seventeen, a kind of respectful, mystified awe that inspired the occasional silent reverie. These were not the kinds of feelings that could readily be compressed into the short, declarative words appropriate for a gym.

Sometimes, when Nicolo was working out alone, he recited aloud inside the small room the lines he had memorized back when he was in grade one. He was not ashamed of this. The questions and answers had an admirable rhythm and they filled the mental space that the levers and weights left empty. They pulled the separate parts of his day toward a strong, central, mysterious place located somewhere between his mind and his body. He breathed in on the questions and out on the responses as he pushed and pulled and hoisted.

Do you know who made you?
God, the Maker of all things, made me.

Out of what did God make all things?

He made them out of nothing.

How were they made?

God spoke, and it was done.

What did God make on the first day?

He made light.

What did God call the light?

He called it day.

What did God call the darkness?

He called it night.

What did God make on the second day?

He made the waters and the sky.

What did God make on the third day?

He made the land and water.

What did God make on the fourth day?

He made the sun, moon and stars.

What did God make on the fifth day?

He made the fishes of the sea and birds of the air.

What did God make on the sixth day?

He made horses, cows, sheep and many other animals.

What else did God make on the sixth day?

He made man.

What was the name of the first man?

His name was Adam.

What was the name of the first woman?

Her name was Eve.

What did God tell them not to do?

God told them not to eat of the fruit of one tree.

Did they obey God?

No, they did not. They ate the fruit that God told them they must not eat.

Did God punish them?

Yes. He forced them to leave the garden.

Nicolo sweated and pressed and pulled the weights so that they rose and fell, and he wondered what would have become of Adam and Eve if they had followed God's advice instead of the serpent's propositions. Would he, as one of their descendants, be living still in Eden with his brothers and parents and nonna? Nicolo knew little of the art of the narrative, but even at seventeen he had felt that generation after generation sheltered in a garden thronged with godly, obedient people would be an unsatisfactory tale, and that a story that follows a straight path, with no deviations, was likely to be no story at all. Nicolo also wondered if there was a connection between the expulsion of Adam and Eve from the garden and his nonna's word for snake, *cursùne*, which seemed infinitely more ancient than the English word, or even the Italian, *serpente*. The word *cursùne* still retained to his ears the echo of the ancient malediction that was invoked beneath the limbs of the fruited tree. Everything turned, it seemed to Nicolo, on the snake and its sibilant misdirections, which had sent Adam and Eve, defenceless, out into the world to make their own way.

CHAPTER TWO

The Pavone boys had all worked since their early teens and had avoided most of the fiscal indulgences of their peers. Nicolo's friend Frank Cecci had poured his money into a succession of recently painted ten-year-old sports cars that had leaking cams and suspiciously soft suspensions. Mario Santacroce had squired a series of indulged girlfriends with high-pitched voices and a fondness for leather jackets, beaded purses, perfume and dinners out in good restaurants. Paul Felice had given full vent to an early fondness for well-cut clothes and shoes imported from Italy. But not the three Pavone brothers. Aside from transportation—they bought gently used cars and babied them—sports equipment and unexceptional clothes, all of their needs were met and their wants were kept under control.

Older Enzo's money was gone now, of course, sunk into the four-bedroom, faux-gabled house, with its honey-beige siding and dark brown trim and an attached two-car garage on Alpha Avenue just south of Major Mackenzie Drive, where he and Mima lived with their children Zachary and Isabella. And almost all of the younger Enzo's savings had been spent on university tuition and books. But Nicolo's account at the Maple Credit Union still had in it almost every cent he had earned since he was twelve years old and was paid a dollar an hour to help Mr. Ariani down the block stake and weed and harvest his vegetable garden, plus what he had earned in interest and a few cautious investments. It wasn't Mr. Ariani who had paid Nicolo, but Nicolo's nonna, who knew that Mr. Ariani lived alone on his pension and was almost blind from cataracts and too proud to ask for help from anyone. Nicolo was directed to profess that it was his desire to learn about gardening that carried him down the street to knock on Mr. Ariani's door. This became an increasingly difficult pretense to keep up as Nicolo grew to thirteen, then fourteen, and the dollar Nonna paid him was decreasingly enticing. Mr. Ariani died (in his garden, in his chair, under his hat) early one spring evening a few days after Nicolo turned fifteen, and a week later Nicolo's nonna arranged for Alviero and Giuseppina Rossi, who owned the small grocery store across the street from the Vaughan Bakery, to hire Nicolo, and that part-time job—carrying boxes, stocking shelves, organizing produce, washing floors—lasted him until he was hired on full time at Caruso's Gym.

Alviero did the ordering, stocking and receiving. Giuseppina ran the store and maintained control over the customers and the profits. She taught Nicolo how to keep orderly books of account. Giuseppina recorded the accounts in the proper manner, in wide flat ledger books that were arranged by date under the counter at the front of the store, going all the way back to opening day on October 12, 1959. It took a long time before she permitted Nicolo to handle the money or make the entries, but she insisted that he watch her so that he would learn, and she showed him how to make the count at the end of the day, sorting fives, tens and twenties into neat stacks, and pouring the change into a machine that, when you turned the handle, jostled the coins into funnels that fed them into tubes that held them in perfect stacks. Nicolo learned how to wrap paper covers around the columns of coins and twist the papers closed on each end like a sausage skin. Nicolo eventually was trusted to handle the paper money as well as the coin-sausage machine and, later, to make entries into Giuseppina's books, carefully emulating her pencilled numbers, which lined up as tidily as the coins in their paper wrappers. The books balanced to the odd dollar and would have been faultless except that occasionally, despite Giuseppina's vigilance, cans or boxes disappeared from the shelves into pockets and purses, and, even more rarely, coins fell into the cracks between the wide wooden floorboards or rolled under shelves and could not be retrieved even by Nicolo fishing with a bar magnet taped to the end of Giuseppina's battered wooden yardstick.

"Self-reliance. That's what's most important," Giuseppina often advised Nicolo. "*Fiducia in issu stessu.*" She tapped her chest with her fist. "You need to be responsible for yourself. Never make the mistake of counting on anyone else. Everyone will disappoint you sooner or later. Let them look out for themselves. *Un fhare male ca è peccatu, 'un fhare bene ca è sprecatu.* To act badly may be a sin; but good deeds—bah—good deeds are a waste."

By age twenty-four Nicolo had, in this manner, and out of his steady earnings at Caruso's, and through prudent and sometimes providential investment, accumulated slightly more than forty thousand dollars, a remarkable sum. The mothers and fathers in his neighbourhood had an intuition for financial worthiness, a highly attuned, quasi-mystical sense for it, almost as if they roamed the streets dowsing with unseen forked sticks for dollars instead of water, and those of them with unattached daughters of approximately the right age—anywhere between seventeen and thirty-four—would lie awake in their beds at night figuring out how it might be possible to put their daughters in Nicolo's way. Nicolo had had enough to do with girls and women over the years to take most of the air out of any possible rumour that he might be, just possibly, because here he was at twenty-four still living at his parents' home without wife or fiancée or girlfriend, a *finocchio*, not entirely a regular man.

His first date, as it happened, although also his last for almost two years, had been with Jessica Santacroce, Mario's only, younger sister. It was Nicolo's mother's idea that he invite Jessica to the graduation dinner and dance that was held in June at the end of his last year at Our Lady of Perpetual Help. Nicolo had planned to go alone and meet his friends there, but his mother caught him by the elbow on his way out the door to a pickup softball game one evening late in May. She had seen that he, unlike his brothers, had not made his way toward girls on his own and she thought that this might be natural, but that it was also somewhat unsatisfactory. He had grown up in a houseful of brothers and he could need persuading that girls wouldn't bite. His mother had already talked with Jessica's mother and the two of them had agreed that Nicolo would fetch Jessica in his father's old brown Thunderbird after the afternoon graduation ceremony, which only family attended, about an hour before the celebration dinner was to start.

Nicolo had at that time the straightforward ways of a middle child, and he had no strong feelings about Jessica one way or the other, so he twisted his neck inside the collar of his shirt, said, "Okay, Ma," and kissed her in the golden middle of her soft and giving cheek as he stepped past her and through the door.

An image—a bright vision—drifted into his mind as he walked down to the patchy field of grass behind Corelli's six-bay service station, of himself in a light blue suit and Jessica in some dress or other, white or pink or yellow, frothy at the neck like the foam at the top of a cappuccino, and of the two of them together, dancing the old-fashioned way, one of his hands resting lightly on her waist, the other pressed against the bare skin of her back. The vision brought a spread of itching heat behind the zipper in his jeans, but the warmth and the daydream both dissolved into the bright evening air in the instant that his bat made contact—solid, square, true—with the ball, which soared up into the sky at an angle that made it disappear into the beaming late-June sun. Impossible to catch a ball like that, errant, lost in the sun, on its own unknowable, arching and triumphant trajectory, and Nicolo ran easily, lightly, safely under that sun around all three bases and then slid into home in a shower of dust and grass.

On the night of the grad, as soon as the Thunderbird reached the end of the long, curving block of orderly houses where the Santacroce family lived, Jessica sent a glance back over her right shoulder, then reached down and pulled her scoop-necked, long-sleeved white lace shirt up and over her head. She tossed the shirt free of her dark hair with two craning motions of her head, first dipping right, and then left, scrunched it up and launched it into the back seat of the car. Then she manoeuvred her legs underneath her lap, kneeled up, wriggled her bottom and slid her long black knitted skirt down her legs. She rearranged herself in her seat, kicked the puddle of black fabric up with the toes of one foot, caught it and pitched it over her shoulder to join her blouse. Her thick, beige pantyhose followed, and next her flat, black polished shoes. Jessica was left with bare, gleaming legs, shoulders, arms and feet, and had exposed a second layer of clothes that had been concealed beneath the first. She was wearing a white halter top that was shot with silvery, shimmery threads, and a glossy black, pleated, very short skirt. Nicolo watched this transformation with darting sideways glances. Jessica's writhing and shedding reminded him of a nature program he had watched on television with his nonna, in which, in an extended time-lapse sequence, a drab mud-coloured snake had worked itself free of its old dull skin, revealing a new, taut, shining surface that glistened with its bright hatched pattern.

19

Jessica opened her purse, took out a pair of high-heeled silver sandals and hooked these onto her feet. She jabbed enormous hoop earrings hung with banks of pink transparent discs through her earlobes, fished for a lipstick and painted a glistening kiss-shape the colour of a ripe plum onto her mouth, dropped the golden tube back into the purse, snapped the clasp of the purse shut, stretched her long, white legs and arms, groaned and wriggled her toes. Her toenails were slick with purple lacquer. She shook her head, tossing her long hair around the car.

"God, I could use a cigarette," she said.

"I don't smoke," Nicolo offered, inadequately it seemed, since Jessica sighed heavily and turned away from him to examine through the window the passing view of garages with houses appended and strip malls each with an almost identical arrangement of 7-Eleven, video store and hairdressing salon.

Jessica was only a couple of years out of middle school. As a peripheral player in Nicolo's life to date, she had seemed a safe enough candidate to accompany him to the grad dance—a simple, comfortable and undemanding companion, likely to be thrilled to be asked and readily impressed by his gift of a pink carnation backed with camellia leaves, ribbon and tulle netting fixed to a fabric-wrapped pin, and by an Italian-style hot-and-cold buffet served in the staff room of Our Lady's, followed by a dance to canned music in a crepe-paper–decorated gym.

Jessica drummed her fingers on her purse, which was black and gathered into thick leather folds; it rested in her lap balefully, like a pug dog. When Nicolo pulled the car into a parking space a block from Our Lady's, Jessica sat forward and assessed the number of cars parked on the street ahead of them.

"We're early," she declared, slumping back in her seat. "Let's go get some smokes and then come back."

"We wouldn't be able to get as good a parking spot," Nicolo said. He glanced at her feet. "If we go and come back you might have to walk a few blocks in those shoes."

"You could drop me off at the front door," Jessica countered. "That would be the gentlemanly thing to do." The word *gentlemanly* emerged from her shiny mouth with a slick coating of something, mockery or irony or an unnameable quality in between. Nicolo shifted one shoulder and then the other under the grey suit jacket that he had borrowed from his older brother, and then turned to look squarely at Jessica.

"Look," he said. "Smoking isn't good for you. You're what, sixteen years old? I'm supposed to be responsible for you. I am not buying you cigarettes."

Jessica frowned. She gave Nicolo a hard, considering look.

"Okay, but we'd better not be the first people here."

No more than a dozen people were in the staff room when they got there, mostly caterers and teachers and parents and student council members moving tables and setting out chafing dishes and stacks of plates and cutlery. The room was stiflingly hot. One or two other early couples hovered uncertainly near the doors. Nicolo saw Carmina Vitale, the chair of student council, struggling to untangle the legs of a table. "I'll be back in a minute," he said to Jessica, and he went to help Carmina. Moments later, Sandra DiNardo came up and asked if he could figure out the system of ropes and pulleys that opened the upper bank of windows to let air into the room. When Nicolo got back to where he had left Jessica, she had disappeared. He reflected for a moment on where she might have gone, and then walked along the main corridor to the east end of the school, to the door where student smokers congregated. Jessica was there with a half-dozen boys and girls, dragging hard on the last inch of a cigarette. A lively conversation stopped and several sets of eyes fixed themselves on Nicolo.

"Hey, Nicco," Jessica said. She waved her right hand toward him, trailing a plume of blue smoke from between her first and second fingers. "I'll come find you in about half an hour, okay?" she proposed.

Nicolo nodded. He was still struggling to think the best of Jessica; it was possible that she had joined the group at the side door out of an overdeveloped sense of social obligation and that she would come to spend the rest of the evening at Nicolo's side after spending a requisite few minutes with her friends. He went back to the staff room, where rectangular stainless-steel containers of pasta and meatballs and sausages and potato gnocchi and broccoli were being set out over gas warmers.

He located Jessica three times more during the evening, once when he took her a plate of spaghetti and wilted salad and a glass of warm pink punch. She was sitting on the same steps where she had been smoking an hour earlier, talking intently to a skinny, short-haired boy Nicolo didn't recognize. An hour later, Nicolo pulled her by the hand into the gym and they danced together without exchanging a word to "I'll Be There" by Mariah Carey, and to Eric Clapton lamenting about "Tears in Heaven." Two dances were enough, apparently. "I'll be outside," Jessica breathed into his ear, and she pulled herself out of his clasp. Her skin was soft and damp and she smelled of some perfume sweet as bubblegum, and of sweat and cigarette smoke. Still later, when all the food had been eaten, and the banners and crepe ribbons had begun to droop, and it was time to go home, Nicolo found her on the same back steps, with the same guy, although this time Jessica was sitting on his lap, her round rump nested into his faded jeans, nuzzling at his thin neck, her pink tongue sweeping her lips, and murmuring who-knows-what into the boy's ear.

"I told your mom and dad I'd have you home by eleven," said Nicolo into the smoky air above Jessica's glossy head. He felt stiff, parental, ridiculous, but he was determined to play by the rules, unsure, in fact, what he could do differently. His brain had begun to trace the beginning of a connection between Jessica and certain customers who came into the Rossis' store, the kind who pressed their thumb too deeply into the peaches and then either complained about the damage and asked for a reduced price, or pushed the bruised fruit to the back of the pile and selected something fresh and unhandled from the front of the display.

"You *see?*" said Jessica to the unknown boy. But she stood up, smoothed her skirt, and ran her right hand several times through her hair, which made a dismissive sound as it swished through a loop she formed from the fingers and thumb of her hand.

She walked to the car alongside Nicolo, a disdainful half-armspan distant from his right elbow. On the drive home, she reversed the process she had gone through earlier, reconstructing her second, more-modest layer of clothes. As

Jessica wriggled in her seat, Nicolo couldn't help observing several brief exposures of bare skin the colour of late-summer cream, a red lacy bra and matching thong panties. As they got closer to the Santacroce house, there came into Nicolo's mind, as perfectly formed as a photograph, a picture of Jessica being spanked, hard, with an open hand, his hand, on her taut miniskirted bottom. He could feel the smack of contact, how his palm would tingle with it, how the air in the car would resonate after the strike, and he could imagine the result—a brilliant red hand-print emblazoned on Jessica's silver-rose skin—a compelling, repellent image. He blinked rapidly, flexed and then tensed his fingers around the steering wheel, and concentrated on driving steadily along the quiet, dark streets.

"You're a nice boy, Nick," Jessica said when he pulled up in front of her house. Gloom or disappointment or something else tugged the pitch of her voice an octave lower.

She surprised him then by inclining toward him, raising her wide face and pressing a kiss full onto his right cheek. Her eyelashes were trimmed with clots of black stuff and spangled with pearls of moisture, and her lips were wet and cold and rough. Jessica's kiss had the sharp, quick, inevitable sting of a mosquito bite, one that both extracted a taste of blood and injected a virus or germ.

"Just wait here until I get inside, okay?"

At home, it took Nicolo many swipes with the soapy corner of a wet towel to remove all traces of purple lipstick from his skin, and it took longer, several years, to get over the shame and horror of that kiss, his first from a girl, bestowed in something like pity. *Bacio di bocca spesso cuor non tocca*, his nonna might have said. A kiss from the lips may sometimes leave the heart untouched.

In the same instant that Nicolo, mortified, infuriated, white-faced apart from the purple smear near the hinge of his jaw, was passing through the front door into the house, Nonna was in her bed, being tossed by the winds of a dream.

A half hour earlier, in the kitchen, before they went to their separate beds, she and Paola had been discussing Nicolo.

"He shouldn't be out so late. When I was a girl, people understood that young people are better off under their own roof than out in the streets."

"You don't need to worry. We know where he is and who he's with."

"And with a *girl*. I can't understand why her parents allow it."

"It's only little Jessica Santacroce. He's played with Mario and Jessica since they were babies. It's good for him. Good for them both."

"When I was young a girl was kept in her parents' sight until it was time to get married, so there could be no doubt that she was *honesta*."

"That may have worked then, but times have changed. You have to let them make their own mistakes. That's how they learn, from their own experiences, not from ours."

Filomena doesn't hear the door open and close as Nicolo comes home. With age her eyes have softened and dimmed, while her dreams have become more vivid. They are now more sharply detailed than any of the hours of her waking world. She falls into her dreams headlong, eager for the places they take her—far in distance and in time—and open to the insights that they sometimes bring. Tonight, in her dream, she is a girl again, fifteen or sixteen, supple and slender as a birch sapling, with her neck as broad and white and fine as a dove's, wearing a full grey skirt, and a yellow blouse tied, loosely, by a string so that it falls open an inch lower than her collar bone. She is slowly walking along one of the narrowest streets of Arduino, Via Arnaldi, a passage that winds lazily west and south, in the direction of the communal well and wash-troughs, and then past them, connecting to the old road north of the village. She allows the backs of her fingers to trail lightly against the stone walls of the houses to her right as she walks. If she wished, she could stand in the middle of this narrow cobbled lane and reach out and touch with her fingertips the wooden window boxes filled with dusty geraniums on two facing houses.

Filomena recognizes every house, and she can name the people who shelter in them. Here the Brunos: Domenico, Giulia, their three daughters, gentle Eva, simple Franca and sharp Luisa. Next door, old Serafina Cornucci, who lives alone, her back so bowed with years and a lack of vitamins and protein as a child, and since, that her chin is almost level with her waist. Across the passage, the Fortunati family: father Rafaele, mother Marta, Marta's parents, and their seven sons, including little Angelo who will die soon of an earache that will travel like a blindly burrowing worm from the uncaring world fatally into his soft, defenceless brain.

The health-care worker that Mussolini sent to Arduino at the start of the war was on an extended vacation of six months when Angelo fell ill, and he said afterward (alarmed that his unapproved trip to Milan might be found out by his superiors) that he could not be blamed because he had not been there to oversee the child's care, although in fact he would have counselled the same treatment: warm mineral oil poured into the ear, and a candle held close enough to the boy's head to singe his hair in an attempt to draw out the infection. Poor Marta, who had already lost her only daughter at seven months when she returned from the fields and fed the hungry baby too quickly. The milk in Marta's breasts was overheated from her labours and baby Pina never woke up from the heavy sleep the hot milk induced.

Filomena extends her fingers and runs her fingernails gently against the coarse stones, smoothing the edges, which are jagged from a morning spent weaving linen under the exacting scrutiny of her stepmother Annalaura. Later she will try to steal a little olive oil from the bottle in the locked cupboard in the kitchen to rub into her hands and cheeks and brow to keep them smooth. *Pane vietatu genera pitittu*—forbidden bread sharpens hunger. She is famished lately for forbidden things—olives, scraps of cheese, under-ripe tomatoes. She has learned the knack of opening the lock with a hairpin, having taught herself one afternoon when she was home minding her father's and Annalaura's three large-toothed and unobservant sons. Filomena is gleeful that she has deciphered the trick of it; she feels joyous, victorious, each time she thrusts the prongs of the pin past the tumblers to the back of the chamber, and then draws them forward so that they click into place and the hasp of the lock falls heavy and free into the bowl of her criminal hand. If this happens on a day or week when her stepmother had been short-tempered or demanding, Filomena takes care to dribble one or two drops of the oil on the ground near the side of the bed where Annalaura sleeps. Spilled oil makes a stain of bad luck that can be undone only by tossing an equal amount or more of salt on the mark and making the proper sign with one hand—the first finger and baby finger outstretched. Annalaura has a squint. She won't see the mark and so will not know to take the necessary precautions to undo the hex of Filomena's ill will.

Filomena's dream carries her now past the bread ovens, which smell of yeast and charcoal and faintly of the sweat of thousands of long mornings of hot labour, Arduino's women pressing and kneading the dough into submission, and then past the bare, wide raked-gravel yard where barrels and cartwheels are taken to be mended, and along the road that runs beside the woods, which are sparse at first, and then dense and dark. The road passes through a row of Lombardy poplar north of the cemetery and into a stand of much older, crooked cedar trees with their flat, pale green needles, and their branches scaly and gnarled like the hands of old women. She is meeting Orlando here, the eldest of the Fortunati sons. He asked her if she would like him to teach her how to kiss and she told him yes. She believes that this information will be useful to her, not with Orlando, whom she has no feelings for—he is handsome but stupid—but for someone else whom she hasn't met yet, a stranger, someone from another town, maybe even another country, even though she has been advised by Arduino's older women that she should choose, when the time comes, from among the boys of her own town. *Figghiola non d'amari furesteri. Ca su comu le genti di passaggiu. Oi le vidi e domuni li spedhi. Ogn' unu s'indi va pe' lu soi villaggiu.* Young girl, don't waste your time in love of outsiders. They are like birds of passage. Today you see them and tomorrow they will have fled. Everyone goes back sooner or later to his own village.

She is humming a tune to herself as she walks, in this dream, which feels more and more like a memory and not the usual nighttime concoction of scraps of sense and nonsense.

Giuvanottellu no lungu e no curtu.
Giuvanottellu fatt' a voglia mia.
Quandu cammini tu tremma tutu,
Peggiu di na folgia a menz' a via.

Young man, you are neither too short nor too high.
Young man, you are made exactly to my desire.
When you walk, everything you pass is knocked askew,
And I tremble like a leaf that has fallen onto the avenue.

She reaches the first gravestone, looks over her shoulder and then steps off the road. She passes several trees and then stops and presses her shoulders and the small of her back against the bark of a broad cedar trunk. She raises her nose into the air trying to catch its scent, but cannot distinguish its sharp, clean odour. The season is spring and the air is vivid with the teeming scents of vibrant, opportunistic growth. At her feet green things that have no name, or at least no name she has ever learned, are sprouting and spreading rampantly and tiny flowers are pitching out of the dirt, shoulders first, with their bell-heads hanging like shamed children. She is young and green herself, and more tender than the first shoots of the chicory that Annalaura sends her out to gather in the mornings from the cold spring soil.

She turns and puts her arms around the tree, embracing its solid waist, opens her lips and runs her tongue lightly against its folded bark, which surprises her by tasting like nothing at all. She had thought it might taste like mushrooms or apples or sawdust. Then she feels Orlando's arms reach around her, enfolding her between the trunk of his body and the tree. The long curls of hair on his forehead fall forward into her eyes. *Capiddhi luonghi e mentalità curta—* long hair but not too bright—Filomena thinks. But he will do for this purpose. Orlando uses his rough chin to push the fabric of her blouse lower on her neck and he kisses her there at the top of the long ridge of bones that divides her back. His lips move up her curved neck and into her hair. They feel like a warm, suckered creature crawling along her skin, trying to make its way into her tingling skull. This, this is more memory than dream, as clear as broth in the soup of her dream. Orlando's mouth feels hotter on her skin than the sun when she is in the fields, and the pressure of his lips and the probing sweep of his tongue and the spiced moisture of his breath sends a shock coursing through her, like the first splash of icy water from the basin on a winter morning. She draws in a breath that expands her chest against her shirt, and she opens her lips wider and forces her tongue into a crevice in the thick skin of the tree. Orlando, who is not much taller than she is but has impressively broad shoulders, whispers something that she doesn't hear—he has chosen the ear that was left damaged after she had measles and a three-day fever when she was eight years old—and then he takes her earlobe between his teeth and tugs so that her head is tipped up and to the side.

"Prisoner," he teases her. "Slave. No one can see us. I can make you do whatever I want and there would be no witness."

He slides his hands from her shoulders up to her neck; he presses against the soft skin under her chin and his thumbs push and rub against the base of her skull.

I am young and green, Filomena thinks, staring up into the maze of needles that shift and settle and fret against one another above her head, making a noise like fabric against the skin of the sky.

Orlando moves in closer; he plants his feet in the soil so that they bracket her feet and his thighs press against hers. All four limbs are bare and dusty from the dry road. He nuzzles around her like a calf forcing its mother's milk and she feels as liquid as cream and as soft and yielding and full of salt as newly pressed white cheese in its woven willow basket.

CHAPTER THREE

Nicolo's muscles look pumped up and vigorous even when they are at rest. When they are working, they function as smoothly as the wheels and gears of machinery shown in Soviet art from the 1930s, in which rounded, rolling cogs and gaskets pull and push together with commanding ease and inevitability. Nicolo wears a suit uncomfortably; his body is too sprung and sprocketed for wool, however finely spun, cut, pieced and tailored. His neck feels constricted in a tie, and his thick calf muscles wear away the elastic on high socks after a few wearings. He is most comfortable in the gym's logoed shorts and a laundered T-shirt smelling of sun and wind and pollen and grass from being hung out to dry on the line in the yard behind his family's house. He was not, for a long time, at ease, even alone, when he was wearing nothing at all.

What Nicolo likes about working out is the sense of incremental, purposeful progress. He is not apprehensive of pain; in fact he welcomes it, invites it every time he adds a new set, or notches the load that he is lifting upward by another kilogram. His aches, which are more or less constant, are real but shadowy; the pains in his muscles and tendons live in the background of his life, like the flat, painted scenery behind the action in a play. In the foreground are pleasure, satisfaction, even exhilaration. When Nicolo strains to shift a weight for the tenth or twentieth time, he experiences—usually all at once and unexpectedly, he can never predict it exactly—a sharp responsive surge from some specific, favoured, unnameable point in his body. This throbbing buzz comes rushing to him as a reward, as pure and true as heavy coins dropping into a metal coffer, quickly filling it to overflowing. The pain is the immediate, resounding affirmation of years of effort and ongoing achievement, a building up, a putting together, like the pieces of a puzzle, the construction of a person. His goal is to attain complete mastery over his corporeal machinery. He is not seeking what many of the other men and women at the gym are striving for, a flawless body, but rather a useful one, one that is quick, reliable, solid, strong and flexible, one over which he has complete and sole command. He has absorbed from his father and mother the idea that the body is like soil, to be used and worked and made productive, and that the soul thrives best when its owner is too busy working to have energy left to wander or be led astray.

One or more students usually linger behind after his classes. Some of those who stay to help put away the mats and weights and balls do not do so out of a sense of volunteerism, but because this provides them with an opportunity to exchange a few words with Nicolo. Usually they start with a comment about the class, most likely some self-deprecating reference to the difficulty of the crunches, or to the pain they expect to feel the next day.

"You just about killed us today, Nicco," one might say with an exaggerated expression of pain. "I'll barely be able to walk tomorrow."

This is only a lead-in, however. What the loitering students really want from him is advice.

"It hurts right here behind my knee when I do those deep lunges. Do you think that's normal? Should I see someone about it? A doctor or physiotherapist? Or do you think it's just age? The knees go first, right?"

"Would it help to build up my stamina if I went to Roberta's stretch classes? Have you heard if they're good for someone like me who's just starting out?"

"No matter how hard I try, I just can't get my hamstrings warmed up properly and I get these cramps, real sharp, like shooting pains, right here. Any ideas what causes that?"

"Could you show me again how to do that kick? The one that starts like this? I get lost when you do that half-turn and then I end up a step behind."

Nicolo may be in a hurry to get to his next class, or to go home, but he almost always pauses and takes whatever time is necessary to consider these questions and to try to answer them. He listens, considers, and pulls from somewhere in his brain's accumulation of whole, half and partial truths something that suits or can be adapted to suit the circumstance. He is not, as it happens, qualified to give some of the advice he is asked to provide. He knows, for example, next to nothing of nutritional supplements, diets, massage therapy, racing hearts or torn ligaments. But he comes from a culture in which to be asked for an opinion is a sign of respect, and in which giving counsel does not depend on any particular expertise or education apart from having lived one's life in such a manner that one is seen as successful or fortunate or resilient. Nicolo has absorbed an understanding that the well-off and the lucky, the people who come from solid families, have something approaching a duty to provide their insights to others faced with difficulties.

One of his students, a short and tightly wound woman named Monica Faye, was the first to ask Nicolo to provide her with one-on-one training sessions. Monica came to Nicolo's nine-thirty boxer-fit classes on Mondays, Wednesdays and Fridays, to his Tuesday and Thursday ten o'clock Pilates classes, and to other classes as well, trailing the odour of organic deodorant, buttered toast and hot chocolate. Monica appeared to have been put together from random scraps of her ancestors' mismatched genetic material. She had abbreviated legs that were fat at the calf, square at the knee and thin as a sapling through the thigh, a short, rounded, can-like torso, long, graceful, freckled white arms—the arms of a dancer—blunt hands with perfect oval nails, a theoretical waist and cello-like hips. Her bottom was narrow and flat, her neck extended and as supple as a goose's, and her breasts almost unmanageably large. Her pale, broad face ended in a sharp point at the chin and she had a widow's peak at her brow; the overall impression was of a lacy, freckled cartoony heart. When she was at the gym she pulled back her thick, curling hair—brown mostly, with a few arbitrary strands of red and orange—with a leopard-print hair band, and she wore bright-coloured stretchy leotards and tights instead of the more common shorts and a shirt. It was her habit to march up to the front of the studio to comment to Nicolo on his classes as soon as they were over. She would approach him while other students were putting away the equipment and provide him with a few minutes of feedback, her hands balanced on her hips, fists turned out, her flat-planed face tilted to one side like a comic valentine. The other students always fell away deferentially. Monica had, despite her lack of height, the weighted presence of a general and the mien of a commandant.

"I need to get in shape quickly," she told him at the end of an hour-long kick-boxing class early on a cold November morning.

Both Monica and Nicolo were breathing heavily, and triangles of sweat showed under their arms and at their breastbones.

"The thing is, my ex-husband Gordon is getting remarried in May and I'm supposed to be going to the wedding with the children—I've got two children—to act the role of the gracious ex-wife, and so I'm going to need to look terrific. I want to look as if I'm in perfect shape, or at least as perfect as possible, considering, you know, considering everything. Considering what we have to work with, I mean, and the kids and all of this, this transition phase. I know whatever we can achieve will be superficial. Fundamentally not much is going to change, and not for very long, but sometimes superficial is all you can really manage, if you know what I mean. If you take me on, I promise I'll come to the gym as often as you think I need to, and I'm willing to work very hard." Monica paused and pressed her locked hands against her damp chest at the level of her diaphragm. "I need you to help keep me focused. I am famous for losing focus; anyone you ask can tell you that. Famous. I've been working really hard already though, and there is no way I can risk slipping backwards. I really need you to help. Please say you'll do it."

Nicolo checked with Sarah and James, the yin and yang administrators who worked in the small office and staffed the front desk—Sarah, tall and angular, lank-haired, square-jawed, blue-skinned and diffident, and bullet-headed James, a fat five-foot-five of roseate, crew-cut, pugnacious taciturnity. They told him he was free to provide personal training sessions to the gym's clients if he wanted to. A portion of his fee would be kept by the gym to pay for the use of the facility and equipment and overhead, and in return Sarah and James would help him with scheduling and with collecting and processing the payments. Nicolo updated his resumé, and his older brother Enzo arranged for the photographer two doors down from the store where he worked to take a series of black-and-white photographs of Nicolo. One of these, in which a trick of framing and lighting and the angles of the room in which the picture was taken made Nicolo appear taller than he was, but that otherwise captured him reasonably well—strong and patient in a white T-shirt with the gym's emblem on his chest, arms crossed over his chest, his biceps sculpted in light and shadows—ended up in an informal blue binder of photos and bios through which members of the gym could browse when they were considering a personal trainer.

At Monica's request, they met first with a nutritionist who worked part time at the gym. The nutritionist, a yellow-haired woman named Sue Hopewell, went over a form that Monica had completed, on which she had been asked to write down everything that she had consumed over the past three days. Sue leaned forward and gave Monica a computer printout that showed, in comparative numbers and columns and pie graphs printed in primary colours, whether she was eating too much, too little, or the right amount of various vitamins, minerals, calories, and other "food values," as she referred to them.

"You are deriving a third too many of your calories from fat," she advised Monica. The corners of her mouth turned down as she pointed to a graph that compared kinds of oils and fats.

"See here. You're getting too much of the wrong kind—saturated. Polyunsaturated is the kind you need, not that you need much of that kind either. And you're not getting enough from fresh fruits and vegetables and whole grains. You need five full servings of fruit and vegetables a day. Those giant bakery muffins you've been eating every morning are going to kill you. They have far too many calories and they're full of corn syrup and refined flour as well as loads of saturated fats. All that kind of thing does is throw your whole system out of whack and set you up for an entire day of cravings for salt and sugar and oil. Okay? Understood? Are we agreed?"

Sue slid a stack of colourful brochures and several photocopied pages across the table—food and nutrition guides, a shopping handbook, a calorie counter, menus and recipes. She pressed them into perfect alignment and then leaned forward, opening and explaining each one in turn, pressing the pages flat and then closed, pointing to highlight the information that she most wanted Monica to remember.

"Overall, I have to say that there's not too much you really need to change, if you're careful and if you pay attention," Sue summed up. "It is more a matter of some tweaking here and there. I teach a cooking class on Tuesday nights at seven, if you're interested. We cover how to cook the same kinds of foods that you're probably making already, but how to make them with more fibre, and with a lot less fat. You can replace the oils for example in many cakes and other desserts with unsweetened applesauce, which you can make yourself and purée in the blender. Not many people know that. There are dozens of little tricks that are easy to put into everyday use once you know about them. If you use fresh ingredients and take a little care, most people can't even tell the difference. They just feel better, and they have more energy. It's a win-win all around."

After Sue had packed up her printouts and charts and folders, Nicolo and Monica went over another form that Monica had completed, one that described Monica's current fitness activities and her goals.

"I don't want to kid you, Nicolo," Monica said, attaching her gaze to his. She hitched up her sweatpants, which in the absence of a waist tended to drift lower on her hips. "My only aim is to look as great as possible by June nineteenth. That's the day when my ex is getting married again. But the day after the wedding I'm going back to how things are now. Not perfect, but good enough. Low maintenance. Comfortable. Relaxed. I know myself really well, and when you get right down to it, this is how I want to be."

"You're already in good shape," Nicolo said.

"Yeah, I know that," Monica said. "This new person Gordon has hooked up with is supposed to be a bit of a pampered brat. The kind of woman—well, she's a girl, really, she's twenty-four, a baby when you think of it—who manages to get looked after all her life. I want to look good of course, that goes without saying, that I can take care of. But I also want to look confident and competent, the opposite of someone who needs to be taken care of, independent, self-reliant. I've thought about it very carefully and I've decided that is what's important to me. This is what it's going to take to get me through this. Can we do that, Nicolo? In less than six months?"

"I think we can do that," said Nicolo. That Monica was so clear about what she wanted to achieve would make progress easier to measure and should help him to keep her on task.

"We can work on your arms today and get started on the ab muscles next time. It's going to hurt, you know that."

"Pain I can do," said Monica. "As long as it gets me to where I want to be and as long as I know it's not going to last forever. I was in labour with Sarah for seventy-two hours and everyone was amazed that I wasn't begging for an epidural. What's a few months of a little extra effort compared to that? This'll be over before I know it and then it'll be mission accomplished."

Nicolo was selected next by a couple, Alden and Clarissa O'Brien—a judge and a local television anchorwoman—to work with them both three times a week. After them came Patrick Alexander, a lean, hyperkinetic, tightly sprung man in his mid-thirties with a mobile, rubbery face, a broad-hinged, dark-shadowed jaw and an active Adam's apple. Then Phil and Bella Fell, dark, slim, tall twins, new members at the gym on the six-month Bring a Friend trial plan, asked if they could see Nicolo early mornings on Mondays, Wednesdays and Fridays.

Alden and Clarissa O'Brien came in together after work on Wednesday. Alden was a tall man in his mid-fifties. His upper back was beginning to curve forward into a studious stoop. He had a round stomach, thick arms and legs, a ropy neck, a substantial head of greying hair and a face deeply etched after years of close reasoning into a permanently shrewd and competent expression. He plunged his large, smooth hand forward to enfold Nicolo's in a solid grip when he introduced himself, adding quickly "Call me Alden," to put an end to any question that Nicolo may have had about the correct form of address for a judge. Judge O'Brien? Your Honour? Your Worship? M'lord? There was no way of knowing. Even Enzo hadn't been certain when Nicolo had consulted him on this point of protocol. Alden's handshake was a double up and down, strong and authoritative.

The clasp of Clarissa's long, freckled hand was considerably gentler. She was twelve years younger than her husband, and very slender. Her face—pale skin, wide-set eyes, strong nose and chin, elaborately furled lips, and a high brow winged by thick dark waves of hair—seemed familiar to Nicolo, likely from some TV show or other, Clarissa suggested, and she named six or seven programs she had hosted that he might have seen. Nicolo had heard of none of them. "A billboard maybe," she concluded, and she raised her shoulders, making it clear that both she and Nicolo knew that TV programs and billboards were ridiculous. Her smile hung in the air for a long moment, a curved and complicated bracket.

Partway through their orientation tour of the gym, Clarissa hung back while her husband walked ahead. She rested one of her hands on Nicolo's forearm.

"I bought these sessions with you as a birthday present for Alden," she said to him. She spoke in a low voice and inclined toward him, her manner direct and complicit. "The trouble is he works too hard and spends far too many hours at his desk. His oldest friend died a year ago and since then he doesn't even get out to play tennis any more. He needs to get some exercise, move around a bit, or he'll end up like Bruce with his heart attack. I have to confess to you that I only signed on to keep him company. I hope you don't mind that I'm telling you this. It's easier for him to have me do this with him."

Alden caught up with Nicolo at the end of the tour, after Clarissa had returned to the women's locker room to change out of her workout clothes. "It is important for you to know that my wife is not strong," he said. "She will want to push herself, but she can't do as much as she would like. I made up my mind to go along with this scheme of hers only so that I could make sure that she paces herself. There's nothing serious, don't get me wrong, but she had a close bout with an eating disorder, anorexia nervosa, a few years ago, a year before we were married, and I want to make sure she doesn't head down that path again. It still holds temptations for her. So we can't let her overdo it or get too fixated on any of this. Do you understand me? We'll watch her together, both of us?"

The judge thrust his hand into Nicolo's and pumped it up and down, once, twice, making the bargain physical, manifest, and Nicolo felt that an enforceable pact had been made between them.

Early on Thursday afternoon, Patrick Alexander gusted into the small room where Nicolo met his clients. He was almost half an hour late, and he emitted explanations and apologies like nonna's watering can, which leaked and streamed and sprayed where it would. A long and utterly boring meeting had run hopelessly, fruitlessly late. Dreadful people—he was sure Nicolo knew the kind: demanding, grudging with money, quick to judge, but slow to make any kind of decision. Certain Nicolo understood but terribly sorry nonetheless. Simply not possible to break away. Dying to be here. And then the direst traffic possible. Every intersection clogged with pedestrians. Who walks these days? With this weather? Sheer idiots all of them, in those stupid puffy jackets and tuques. Drove like a maniac. Miracle hadn't crashed or killed someone or gotten yet another ticket. Hoped he hadn't thrown an absolute wrench into the schedule. Ready as soon as he changed.

Patrick was a whirl of chatter and confessions. He emerged from the men's change room after another five minutes wearing very short white shorts with a dark green stripe down the sides, a lime-green tank top of a synthetic woven material that clung to his skinny chest, black socks with a subtle pattern of chevrons running along the outside of his ankles, and black lace-up leather shoes.

Nicolo looked down at Patrick's feet and cleared his throat. Patrick was bouncing at the knees and swinging his arms forward and backward to loosen his shoulders. He gazed expectantly at Nicolo. Nicolo hesitated. He could let the shoes go, but they were likely to mark up the floor and, more seriously, they didn't provide the kind of cushioning and support he advised his clients to have when they exercised. Patrick's feet looked to be about the same size as his own, nine and a half, although not quite as broad.

"Would you like me to lend you a pair of training shoes?" Nicolo offered.

Patrick looked down at his socks and shoes and smacked his forehead with his right palm. Nicolo must think him an absolute idiot. Always in too much of a rush. Hadn't been thinking. Mind somewhere else completely. Too many things going on to try to keep track of them all. Sure he understood. New project keeping him up all day and half the night. Sheer madness of people to try to get an entire product launch done in under two months. So sleepy during the day, completely drained. Too tired to think straight. What an utter nuisance he must be. Would not be a minute. Three shakes of a lamb's tail.

Patrick reappeared minutes later wearing fine-spun lime-green socks that slouched around his ankle bones, and thin-soled lemon-yellow tennis shoes. Nicolo decided to make allowances in light of the unavoidable crisis in Patrick's professional life, and, although they were a good twenty minutes late getting started, gave Patrick the full allotted hour, which was devoted almost entirely to Patrick's single stated goal: abs. Abs as solid and ridged as wet sand on the beach, abs to die for, was how Patrick described what he wanted. Deadly, killer, suicide-inducing, mouth-watering, knuckle-gnawing abs.

The brother and sister pair, Phil and Bella Fell, arrived more than promptly at ten minutes before seven on Friday morning, the start of a dark day in which snow hung heavy in the cold, pregnant clouds. They were not identical but close to it, slope-shouldered, narrow-chested, twenty-nine and a half years old, both of them sales associates at Vit@lity, a rapidly growing computer parts and software manufacturer in an industrial park east of the city. Both were tall, thin, grey-eyed and slightly stooped. Their inturned shoulders bracketed their chests. Phil wore his hair long, and Bella wore hers short, and their hair, which was fine and formless, fell in a similar way around both narrow skulls, in limp ferny fronds over their pointed ears and sloping brows. Their skin had a yellow cast over a darker underlayer, like a cheaply made metal alloy. They had similar quick, tightly sprung mannerisms: a flat-line, flickering manner of smiling, a rapid series of irregular, darting eye movements when they were thinking and after they had spoken, and a tic that involved raising their shoulders in half-circles around their necks, lifting first the left, front to back, and then the right. The air around them smelled damp and electrically charged.

And their goals were . . . ? Nicolo enquired.

"They ssay we need some exercise to help us deal with stress," Bella hissed.

"Ssomething physical to relieve the pressure." Phil's words followed quickly behind hers as if he were finishing a sentence that she had started. He had the same curious lisp.

Each of them blinked and raised first one shoulder and then the other, while their thin lips stretched into identical brief, humourless grimaces.

"What do we have to do to sstart?"

Nicolo looked from one to the other, uncertain which of them had spoken, unsure how to respond. He was beginning to understand that working with people alone or in pairs would be considerably more difficult than he had anticipated.

CHAPTER FOUR

After dinner one December evening, Nicolo sat down in a chair at the kitchen table to work his way through the course outlines that had arrived in a large brown envelope from the university. He hooked his feet behind the chair's metal legs and leaned forward into the task. He had been thinking along the lines of accounting or investment management, something to do with finance that would help him make good decisions about the money that was building up in his bank account. His mother had more than once suggested that he buy a house and start planning for the day when he would have a wife and family. His father, he knew, would like him to quit the gym and go back to school for a degree. Nicolo didn't know whose advice he should follow. He felt that his work, his savings, all the many different things he was learning, the advice and views of his parents and brothers, even Nonna's *proverbi*, all of these were or could be important, and that he was reaching the point in his life, close to a quarter-century, when he should be putting them together somehow toward an end. But so far, no picture had emerged, no image or map or solution or key to his life or to its purpose. Occasionally he imagined that he had been granted the shortest possible flash of insight, but these revelations were clear for only an instant. They flickered into his mind and then out before he could take in more than a fleeting impression, like the striking of a distant match. There was so much to consider and the context was vast. The world was chaotic; that was clear. And it was unfair: some people were lazy and grew fat, while others worked hard and still starved. He could see that. Everywhere there were people who made mistakes, or acted wrongly, deliberately or in error. He wanted to become a purposeful adult. And although so far his purpose, the reason for his existence—the son of Massimo and Paola, the brother of Lorenzo and Vincenzo—remained without form, it had begun to occur to him that the answer might have something to do with providing clarity and order and with helping people get what they wanted most. He had also a concept of service. At least, that was the impression he had from time to time. Beyond that, he had no certainty. But he liked to believe that the rest, the details and timing, the who, where, when, why and what, would be revealed to him in time. If he was patient. If he was ready.

Enzo came into the kitchen and poured two short glasses of their father's homemade wine, which was almost as purple and rich and rough as the *musto* from which it was made every fall, and which had the sweet odour of decaying roses. He slid a glass of wine across the table to Nicolo, sat down, pushed a long strand of hair behind his ear, and pulled one of the course descriptions toward him. He began to read through them with his characteristic focus, his hands curled around his brow to concentrate his gaze. Nicolo drew a sip from his glass, circulated the wine around his tongue and into the roof of his mouth, and then swallowed. The wine had a familial taste, warm and sweet and strong. He had already divided the courses into two piles, in and out, and was working on reducing the most likely pile to one or two. Enzo reached across and ran through the subjects that Nicolo had eliminated. After a few minutes, he pulled out a piece of paper and pushed it at Nicolo.

"This one," he said, and stabbed with his forefinger at the title of the subject he had selected. "Psychology 101." He pushed a strand of hair back from his face.

"Why psychology?" asked Nicolo. "I was thinking of a first-year accounting course or something about investing."

"You work with people. You'll be better at it if you understand how your clients think. What motivates them. How to recognize and get them beyond avoidance tactics. Let's face it. People don't like to exercise. We're lazy really, most of us; we want to take shortcuts. That's why they can sell so much crap on TV, those diet pills and miracle exercise machines and drinks that are supposed to speed up your metabolism. People are going to be paying you to make them do something they actually don't want to have to do. The reason they hire you is to help them to succeed despite themselves.

You're going to need to know what kinds of strategies you can use, not to manipulate them exactly, that won't work for long, but to manoeuvre them into working harder so they can get what they want. People often unconsciously sabotage their own good intentions. I'm sure you see it all the time. Learning how people think and what will make them work will help you understand why people do the things they do. Anyway, once you get rich you can always hire an accountant or an investment adviser."

Nonna came from the living room into the kitchen, silent as a shadow on her slippered feet. She must have fallen asleep in her armchair in front of the television; her short, dove-coloured hair fell in disarray, like ruffled feathers, and one side of her face had the white and crumpled appearance of unironed linen. She turned her head and blinked slowly at her two grandsons as they sat with their heads together at the table, conferring in low tones over their glasses, and then she shook her head severely. She turned in her thumb and the two middle fingers of her right hand and waggled the first and smallest fingers like two horns at Nicolo and Enzo.

"*Alla cira si vidi lu core*," she said in an admonitory tone. On the face the heart may be seen. It must have seemed to her, perhaps from their complicit expressions, that they were plotting misdeeds, as they had sometimes done as boys, and she thus warned away any possible harm their discussions might engender. Nonna switched on the stovetop, which burst alight with a brief hiss, and a red-orange flame with a halo of blue, into the still air of the kitchen. She filled the kettle with water, placed the kettle on the burner, and turned and shook her head emphatically at the brothers, *tsk*ing under her breath.

Then she made her way back to her chair in the living room. The heat from the gas flame made the drops of water on the outside of the kettle spit and burst. The kettle groaned and then slowly began to exhale a moistly rising sigh.

"Okay," said Nicolo, who was in that instant suffused with a strong sense of the absolute and fundamental unknowability of each one of us to anyone else, even our closest family members. He shrugged and let his weight fall against the back of his chair. "Psychology. Maybe it's not such a bad idea. It's somewhere to start anyway."

"Come on up to my room," said Enzo. He stood and gathered one or two of the brochures in his hand. "We can register you online right now, before the class fills up."

They left their empty glasses sitting on the table. Over the years they had learned to take care to leave or create enough work for both their mother and their nonna to feel sufficiently needed within the small household. Deliberate divisions of labour had been created in the household, watertight compartments of work. Their mother cooked their meals and planted and kept up the garden. Their nonna washed and ironed the clothes. Paola made bread, sauce, pizza and pasta. Nonna made their beds and dusted and tidied their rooms. When Nonna took sheets from the line after washing and prepared them to be put away in the cupboard in the hall, she always folded them first widthwise, and once when she saw him watching her, she explained to Nicolo that she did this to divert any lurking bad spirits away from the household, for the dead lie in their final linens lengthwise and it would be unwise to invite misfortune into the house through the carelessness of seeming to prepare for a death.

Everyone in the family was used to the odd, totemic piles of stray objects that Nonna created as she worked. Because she had a limited frame of reference, Nonna was sometimes unable to separate the important from what could be jettisoned. A shirt button, a business card, a flyer, the plastic cap from a ballpoint pen, a single cufflink, three linked paperclips and an insole might be gathered together and left neatly folded inside a handkerchief in the top drawer of the dresser. She would leave on the windowsill the cap from a can of shaving cream in which she had placed a golf tee, several bank withdrawal receipts, the stub of a pencil, a tie clip and the empty transparent holder for a roll of tape. The boys understood that these symbols of their lives outside the houses were mysterious to their grandmother. They cleared away these collections periodically, and this gave Nonna the opportunity to create new inexplicable groupings from different materials—bottle caps, twist ties, mateless socks, cheque books, nail clippers, ticket stubs, coins, the minute metal clips that had held a new pair of socks together at heel and toe, toothpicks, wrapped mints from restaurant counters, tokens, stamps, maps, pens, envelopes and tags— all manner of unrelated items bound together only by their peculiar, quotidian gravity, which Nonna had no means to measure or to weigh.

Within three days of signing up for Introduction to Psychology on Enzo's desktop computer, Nicolo received, via Enzo's Hotmail account, an e-mail with an attachment that confirmed his registration and listed details about the location, dates and times for the course. He was pleased to see that the classes included three lectures on motivation and emotion, and another on stress, coping and avoiding. He was beginning to see Enzo's point, that an understanding of all of these might be useful to him in his work at the gym. He asked Enzo to pick up the textbook at the university bookstore downtown, and Nicolo began to work his way through the first chapters at the kitchen table in the evenings after work.

Nicolo had learned that his new clients came in an assortment, ranging from least to most difficult, although each presented an individual challenge. The O'Briens were the least demanding and seemed to be the easiest to please. Clarissa always deferred to Alden, allowing him to set the pace. Alden's progress was slow because he didn't like to be moved on to something new until he was certain that he had completely mastered whatever Nicolo had been teaching them. On the first day they came, Nicolo started them in one of the smaller weight rooms, one that held the simplest machines, the kind that were adjusted by pressing buttons that increased or decreased the level of resistance by adjusting the air pressure in shiny cylinders. Nicolo had intended to rotate the couple in their one-hour session through several of these machines, then move on to spend a few minutes on free weights, then the bicycles or treadmills or stair climbers for some aerobic exercise, and then finally over to the mats to stretch, but the entire first hour was spent showing the O'Briens (really only Alden; Clarissa caught on quickly and then Nicolo could see that, although she remained close beside them, her attention drifted) all of the possible positions and levels of difficulty of two of the leg-press machines. During the second session, they focused on an extended biceps curl, except for the last ten minutes, which Nicolo insisted they spend stretching on the mats. Alden was taken with a back stretch that Nicolo had adapted from a yoga position called the cobra, and they spent, it felt to Nicolo, five minutes on every one of Alden's seven cervical and twelve thoracic bones. The hour ran late, but Alden took evident pleasure in the machines and in the stretching, and Clarissa seemed to be happy enough that Alden was content, and so the time passed easily and without conflict.

Monica Faye was next in difficulty. Monica's conversation during the hours she worked with Nicolo was almost exclusively about her ex-husband and his imminent remarriage.

"I dumped him like a sack of hammers," she told Nicolo during their first workout session together. She was lying on her back on a blue mat, her hands locked behind her head, straining her way through the second of eight sets of crunches. "I dumped him like a sack of hammers three times in a row and each time I turned around and took him back again like an idiot, once for each of the other girlfriends, at least the ones I know about. First, little Carley with the curly hair. Then weird Wendi. She was tall and bony and disjointed, sort of like Olive Oyl in the old Popeye cartoons, you know? Then that ridiculous Suzanne, not a brain in her head. I'm sure there must have been—urrrgh—others, because that's just the kind of guy Gordo is. None of them worked out very well for him—well, they wouldn't, would they?—and he always seemed so sweet and contrite and untended and rumpled and unhealthy and tragic afterward. So then, what happened was, the fourth time, I dumped him for good. I've always been a fan of Brigitte Bardot—you know the French actress? against furs and seals?—and what she said was, Always leave first; be the one to decide. But that was the one and only time that he finally didn't come begging like a puppy for me to take him back. That one was Hayley. I said, yes, please God, when he asked me for a divorce. I wish her—unngh—well. He hasn't a clue, though. Not the remotest, foggiest notion of a clue. He's used to having me around to come running back to, to reassure him and pat him and fix everything and sweep up the wreckage. She's a cute little thing, only twenty-four and sweet and not too bright. She really can't have any kind of idea what she's getting into husband-wise, although I tried one time to tell her. They felt they had to—ahhhhh—invite me because they want the kids to come and because I've been such a good sport about it all. Well, why wouldn't I be, it's not as though I want him back. Lexie's going to be the—urgh—flower girl. Well, she's maybe a little old at twelve and with her growth spurt she's not exactly what you might call dainty—how am I going to find low-heeled pink shoes that aren't like boats in a woman's size eight?—but she's never—huhh—been one before, so here's the big chance, eh? That's got to be eighty at least. I don't know how you can listen and keep count at the same time."

Monica wanted results faster than they seemed to be coming. She weighed herself at the end of each session on the scale against the wall outside of the women's change room.

"I need to be no more than a hundred and thirty pounds, one thirty-four or -five at the absolute, outside, top, top max," she said, joggling the weights on the scales to see if she could get the right-hand end of the lever to move a fraction lower. Nicolo was impressed, as he always was, by her clarity of purpose and the specificity of her goals, but he was beginning to believe that their relationship might provide him with an opportunity if not an obligation to suggest more personal, longer term goals. He began to try to derail Monica when she set off on a description of her ex-husband and his impending marriage, and to encourage her to talk about her children or her plans.

"Do you think I should take that cooking class that Sue recommended?" Monica asked Nicolo at the end of one session. "Or there's this new diet. Have you heard about it? All steak and cream and butter, but no carbohydrates. It doesn't make any sense at all, but I've heard that people swear the weight melts away like magic. Carbs are just like poison, that's the theory. If you stop eating bread and pasta and white flour, your body will start to eat into your own fat reserves. The cave people didn't eat carbs and we shouldn't be eating them either. Or something like that. Maybe it was the Neanderthals. Were they the ones that lived in caves? In the south of France? And made those paintings? Anyway, you're supposed to get really bad breath as your body starts to feed on itself, but apparently that only lasts for a while, and then your body adjusts."

"Try the cooking class," Nicolo replied. This was not difficult advice for him to give. Sue's class couldn't hurt, and it might give Monica something to think about, a distraction from her weight and her ex-husband. He thought sometimes of what he understood medical students were taught about their chosen profession: Above all, do no harm.

Nicolo thought that Enzo, who had already completed four years at the university and half of his first year of law school, might have some advice on how to deal with

Monica. Beginning at age nine or ten, around the time that the boys had first begun to differentiate themselves from one another and to take on more distinctive personalities, Enzo had become a reliable source of information and then adviser to his older brothers. He absorbed facts effortlessly, quickly discerned patterns and trends, was swift to acquire new terminology and was shrewd at deducing motives. Enzo was modest about his abilities around his brothers, however; Nicolo had the keenest moral sense, he said, and older Enzo was the most tenacious. Nicolo described Monica to Enzo one weekend afternoon when they were turning the compost pile in the backyard.

"Ah," said Enzo. He grunted and pushed his heavy fork through a frozen surface layer of earth. They were in the deepest corner of the yard, using a pair of ancient, rusting, wood-handled pitchforks that, although they seemed venerable enough to have been brought from the old country, in fact had been bought with the house, abandoned by the previous owner and found leaning together like a long-married couple, along with their near relatives, a shovel, a hoe and an edger, all of similar vintage, in a dim, cobwebbed corner of the garage. A steamy emanation rose up from the softly stewing underlayers of leaves, grass and kitchen peelings as they were turned, and a rich, mushroomy odour filled the air.

"Neurotic," Enzo said as he lifted his pitchfork with its load of peels and eggshells and coffee grounds, and he explained the meaning of the term to Nicolo, who had heard it before but had not understood how to match it to a set of human behaviour.

"There are greater and lesser degrees of neurotics," said Enzo, stopping and shaking his head so that a hank of his hair fell forward across his brow and into his eyes. He pushed it away with the back of his hand and then rested for a moment and leaned into the handle of his fork. "This sounds like a milder case. But still to be taken seriously. Neurotics are interesting people, and can be great friends when life is going well, but when things go badly you will find that they tend to try to assign blame. Generally they are loyal to the people they trust. Better overall to stay on their good sides."

Up a notch from Monica in concern were the brother and sister, Phil and Bella Fell, although so far it was difficult for Nicolo to explain to Enzo why he felt this way. They were almost entirely passive, trailing Nicolo from machines to weights to bikes to mats without questioning his intentions or his plan. Neither of them ever made suggestions or demands. They stood together, side by side, slowly blinking, heads tipped, fingers clenched into loose fists, during Nicolo's explanations, and they followed his instructions precisely, if mechanically. Their form was good for beginners, but Nicolo found that they lost heart quickly. They tended to turn to him after only ten or fifteen reps, in a single motion, as if with one thought, and their compressed expressions indicated, clearly, *What next?* They had no small talk, even between themselves, and so Nicolo laboured alone under the effort of providing conversation, which he had come to learn moved the hour sessions with his clients along more efficiently—an encouraging word or two to smooth out the transitions between stations, a few distracting comments during any task that was strenuous or repetitious, a joke or bit of gym news toward the end. The Fells almost never responded to his comments about sports, the weather or front-page news. Nicolo had once had his hearing tested in a thickly soundproofed booth, a small dark room in which the walls and roof were covered with what looked like hundreds of black Styrofoam egg trays. Inside, with the door tightly closed, his words fell heavily from his mouth without any reverberation or echo from the surrounding walls. Speaking to the Fells was like that. His sentences were flattened by their blank impenetrability. His words didn't seem to reach any farther than the outer edge of his own lips.

In addition, the Fells seemed incapable of feeling encouraged or discouraged.

"Is everything okay?" he would ask. Or: "Do you think you can do that?" Or: "Shall we move over to the free weights?"

"Yes-s," they would reply almost in unison, words almost overlapping, at different inharmonious pitches, their heads tilted. There was seldom any request for more information; they followed his directions exactly as he set them out, without question, deviation or improvisation. They were always impeccably neat—they didn't even seem to sweat—but Nicolo had learned to turn his head to the side when they spoke. They both had breath that reminded him of the compost heap in the backyard, a warm, acrid and repellent smell like eggs that had turned.

And then there was Patrick Alexander, who was becoming a steadily increasing challenge. Nicolo had not yet fixed on any system to manage Patrick or to predict what he would do next. Patrick's faults varied wildly from day to day. If it were just that he was late, or had forgotten his gear, Nicolo could have planned around these shortcomings. But Patrick sometimes didn't arrive at all, or he came on the wrong day, or he came an hour early, or on time and on the right date but without his gear, or at the right time and with the right equipment but completely distracted and unable to follow Nicolo's instructions. Patrick seldom demonstrated any memory or understanding of what had been thoroughly shown and reviewed and reinforced during the prior sessions. Patrick was always charming and apologetic throughout. He motioned toward the heavens. He struck his forehead with the flat of his hand. He smacked himself a glancing whack at the back of his beautiful haircut. He wrung his hands as if they were damp towels. He made deeply chiselled expressions of dismay. He bowed. He cringed dramatically. He explained, exclaimed, declaimed and apologized. He all but wept. He was eminently forgivable, every time, and Nicolo did forgive him, even grew fond of him. He made room for him in his schedule if possible when he appeared, and filled in his absences with other work. No harm of any duration was ever done, and Patrick paid for all of his sessions even if he missed them. He wafted his golden credit card in front of whoever was on cash at the front desk, crying "Pay poor Nicolo! Double! Triple! Whatever it takes!" But Nicolo was beginning to dread the sessions with Patrick. He wasn't running out of patience—he seemed to have been born with an infinite store—but his time with Patrick left him feeling exhausted and with a mounting sense that he was failing to provide whatever it was that Patrick really wanted from him.

At dinner one evening Nicolo described his problems with Patrick to his parents and Nonna. Enzo had eaten early and had already gone to work. His father got up from the table to return to his basement workroom.

"What can you do?" he shrugged as he departed.

"*Cosa pensi, Nonna?*" Nicolo said. His mother stood up and began to clear the table. What do you think?

"*Chine è natu quatru 'un po' morire tunnu,*" she said.

"Yeah," Nicolo said. He nodded once, slowly, and then again. "Yeah, I know that, Nonna. What is born a circle won't die a square."

CHAPTER FIVE

On Saturday morning, Nicolo drove to Vaughan Bakery with his new psychology textbook beside him on the passenger seat of his car. He carried the book into the wide, bright store, which sold Italian groceries and small household goods as well as coffee and bread and pastries, and he propped it on the table up against the blue fluted bowl filled with paper-wrapped sugar cubes behind his cup of cappuccino with its monk's hood of chocolate-flecked foam. He read through a page while cracking three packages of sugar lumps against the side of his cup so that the sugar cubes spilled like dice into his coffee, and he continued to read while stirring the froth and coffee and hot milk and sugary grit together.

Nicolo came to the bakery every Saturday morning a half hour before the ten o'clock time that he and the others had agreed on. He liked to watch the customers as they flowed through the doors and carried out an efficient series of straightforward and gratifying transactions. Each Saturday morning, Nicolo bought a dozen ricotta-filled cannoli, and he and Frank, Mario and Paul would eat three each directly from the pastry box, balancing them over their coffee cups. If someone didn't show up, as happened occasionally, Nicolo took the extras home for Enzo and his father. The bakery had served for years as a meeting place for Italians in the area. As well as breads and sweets, it sold brands of tomato sauce, pasta, meats and cheeses that were difficult to find in the regular stores and it was a useful source for news and rumours—who was marrying or having another child, who to vote for or against in the upcoming municipal elections, the degree to which the region's plans to close the landfill were advancing or stalled.

Marietta, the owners' granddaughter, who had played around the counters and tables as a child, and who now served pastries and sometimes prepared the coffee in the enormous red sighing Gaggia with its banks of stainless steel valves and indicators and black dials and intermittent blasts of steam, had grown up observing Nicolo and the other three every Saturday, among the stream of customers and visitors. Nicolo has become aware of her gaze. What he cannot know, however, is how Marietta sees them: Mario foremost, the handsomest of the group, with his thick head of hair that cascaded across his forehead in shiny black rings like carved, coiled snakes, his dark skin, with, on Saturday mornings, a beard in threatened eruption around his long jaw, his wide, brown, swimming eyes, his dark lashes, thick and curled at the outer edges like a woman's, his strong, straight nose, his cleft chin, his thick neck. Mario wears clothes that are neither new nor old, but the exact right place in between—black jeans, a close-fitting white T-shirt, a jacket cut from soft, cinnamon-coloured calfskin. He smells—she has occasionally manoeu-vred herself close enough to him to take in his scent—like starch and musk, with a slightly acrid edge of tangy male-ness. Even the memory of his scent makes her mouth water. He moves through her yearning vision as if under water, like a great fish, slowly and with a surfeit of grace and without any evident consciousness of the way he refracts the light. He is as without flaw and as remote as a cloud or mountain or god. It makes Marietta weak to gaze at Mario for longer than a moment, and she tests herself every Saturday. Standing behind a wire shelf with its display of pasta and canned Roma tomatoes, she stares at Mario until she feels the tips of her fingers begin to tingle. Then she rests her eyes on the dark blue boxes of Barilla penne rigate, which she pretends to straighten on the shelf although they are almost always already in per-fect order. She has, in this manner, memorized every word on the Barilla box, and the phrases printed on the box have taken on a deep, Mario-tinted significance: COTTURA 11 MINUTI. N° 1 IN ITALIA. There are for Marietta no words more charged with romance in any language of the world than these. COTTURA 11 MINUTI. N° 1 IN ITALIA.

Once Marietta has soaked up as much of Mario as she feels she can bear, and if she is not too busy serving other customers, she might watch Paul for a while, since he is infallibly splendid, although not nearly as good looking as Mario. Paul's jeans and colourfully striped button-down shirts are always crisply ironed, his boots polished, his black leather jacket stiffly assertive, his belt buckle almost aggressively large and glistening. He sometimes wears a black cashmere scarf loosely knotted around his neck. Marietta has sometimes thought that if Mario were to dress as Paul does, he would be too much to endure, and she is grateful that Mario sticks, on Saturday mornings, to jeans and T-shirts.

Marietta pays no attention to Frank, who is shaped like her father—short, with a mild face, rounded torso, and a humble walk with no bravado or swagger. Frank works on Saturdays, and comes in for coffee during his break, dressed for work in blue canvas overalls with the name CORELLI'S AUTO BODY stamped on the breast pocket. She hasn't ever seen Italian paintings or sculpture, and so doesn't know that Frank has a classic, slanting Roman profile, the profile of a nobleman, a silhouette surely intended for coins and for marble busts rather than the muddy, greasy undersides of cars.

Marietta knows Nicolo best, in fact Nicolo is the only one of the four she has ever spoken to, since she often takes his orders, but he has always treated her like a child—she is sixteen—and so she assigned him many years ago to the category of adult. As a result, she now perceives him to be middle-aged and therefore entirely beyond any possible romantic significance.

That Saturday morning, Frank was the next to arrive at the bakery. He slid into the chair across from Nicolo, the seat closest to the high glass counter with a good view of the parking lot, his usual place because it allowed him to keep an eye on his car, a sherbet-yellow 1988 Corvette, to make sure no one placed a foot on its bumper or leaned on its hood or came too close to its recently waxed surface in manoeuvring through the constricted parking lot.

"Hey," he said to Nicolo. "Whatcha doing?"

"Reading," Nicolo replied. He folded the covers of the heavy book closed. "It's for a class I'm starting."

"Look at our good wittle Nicolo, weading his book." Paul had arrived. Except for Mario, who had recently completed a real estate course, none of them had studied after high school; they had all fallen into work that they liked well enough and that provided the advantage of reliable pay without requiring diplomas or degrees.

"Yeah," Frank said, mugging, widening his eyes and mouth into an expression of foolishness. "You know, now that I think about it, I remember I read a book once too. It was red, about this size. Some kinda title. Fulla big words. Didja ever read it?"

"Yeah, yeah," said Paul. He sat down and shot his cuffs. "Yeah, sure, I remember that one. Red cover, real thick. You gotta like a book that's got lotsa pages, 'cause then you really get your money's worth. That's the most important thing with books; you gotta make sure you get your value."

"A short book," Frank said. "A short book is hardly worth your while. You might as well not even bother with a short book. You're done before you've even started. Two covers, a couple of pages, a few words in the middle. Nothing to it. Sneeze and you've missed the whole plot. Where's the challenge? A book for girls. Now this, this here is a book." Frank seized Nicolo's psychology text and held it up. "You could kill someone with this thing. You know? It's more of a heavy, blunt object than a book. And the beauty of it is, is you can carry it around right out in the open without even you gotta get a licence. Could come in useful, if you get me, eh? In a certain kind of situation."

"Idiots." Nicolo removed his book from Frank's hands and placed in on the floor beside his chair.

The glass door of the bakery opened and Mario came in on the heels of an older couple. Nicolo watched the little Gerussi girl slip away from the counter and take up her usual spying post on the far side of the pasta aisle. Two boxes of penne rigate were moved a finger's width apart and he saw a slow-blinking brown and glistening eye appear between them.

The four of them ran through their usual topics of conversation: soccer or baseball or hockey, depending on the season, work, cars, family, neighbours, anyone who had done something unusual or of interest, bought a house, moved, married, separated, divorced, gone bankrupt, met with unexpected fortune or success. Nothing unusual that Saturday at all, except that, after they had drained the last of their coffees, set the cups with their grainy residue of sugar askew in their saucers, as they were rising to leave, Mario held up his right hand in a signal for the others to wait for a minute before heading off into the rest of their Saturdays; he had something to say.

"We decided. Well, Angie decided. No, we both did. The other night after, um, dinner. We both decided that we should ask you guys to help us out. At the wedding. I need to have six whatdyacallem, best men or attendants or something, because Angie wants six bridesmaids, her two sisters and a bunch of her friends. So can you do it? The first Saturday in June. We're going to ask Angie's brother Joe and her cousins from Vancouver, Nick and Guido, as well, and with her brother and with you guys that makes six. Okay?"

This was the first Nicolo or any of the others had heard of a wedding.

"Yeah, sure," they all told him, clapping him on the shoulder, leaving overlapping powdered cannoli sugar outlines of their hands on his jacket.

"We'll be there, man. We're there for you," said Paul.

Nicolo slipped a glance to the little Gerussi girl behind the pasta, but the brown eye had been withdrawn. Poor Marietta was on her bottom on the floor. COTTURA 11 MINUTI. N° 1 IN ITALIA floated in the sparkling blackness that swirled in front of her blinking eyes. COTTURA 11 MINUTI. N° 1 IN ITALIA. She twisted and tugged the silver ring that she wore on the fourth finger of her left hand as a place-holder, but it resisted her efforts; it twisted and dug into her plumply upholstered knuckle and, unlike her tender pink heart, refused to be moved.

Mario had parked his cosseted Mustang beside Nicolo's black Civic, and Nicolo felt that the few moments when they were walking together across the lot toward their cars should include some acknowledgment of Mario's announcement.

"So," he said. "Angie, eh? She seems like a good kid." Nicolo had met Angie once or twice. He thought he remembered that her family lived in one of the suburbs to the west of the city, Brampton, or maybe Rexdale, not as far out as Oakville. She was thin, large busted, with thick blonde hair teased and sprayed into a curling mass. She wore several jangling bracelets on each arm, and large gold hoops swung from her ears. Not a calm woman. Quick moving. Quick talking. Take charge. Smart.

"Yeah," said Mario. His breath puffed thin and blue into the cold morning air. "She's got a good job at the bank, management track even, it looks like, and now that I have my licence, we thought, you know, get a house and some proper furniture of our own, maybe think about beginning a family even, start to live like grown-ups. You know?"

"Yeah," Nicolo replied. "Big wedding too. That's good. I'm really happy for you. For the both of you."

"She's okay, Angie," Mario said. He stopped and turned toward Nicolo.

Nicolo could hear more than a trace of self-persuasion in Mario's voice. Which was only natural, he thought. Getting married. What could be bigger than that? He wondered too what would make someone take that leap, commit to someone else for the rest of his life. It would be like deciding to go on an uncertain trip with a stranger instead of staying safely at home.

Nicolo and Mario stood for another half-minute, facing each other but not talking. Nicolo kept his gaze near Mario's shoulder, which he thought about punching lightly, but that seemed not quite right. Nicolo stubbed a booted toe against a ridge of ice on the pavement. A companionable silence, easy as breathing, was broken finally when Mario said, "I guess I should be . . ." and Nicolo said at the same time, "So, I'll be seeing you around . . ." Nicolo threw his book into the front seat of his car and they each slammed their car doors and drove away in separate directions, their quick minds already moving on to the next thing that the day held and the next thing after that.

CHAPTER SIX

After Jessica, Nicolo successfully avoided even the possibility of romantic humiliation for two full years. He had decided after several weeks' deliberation that he needed to be wiser, more attuned, more fully on his guard before he could hope to be able to engage with women on anything like equal terms. His mother may have known more than she let on about the humiliations of his graduation dinner and dance, because she didn't mention Jessica Santacroce again, even in passing. And it wasn't much longer before the family was overtaken by the need to make wedding plans for Nicolo's older brother Enzo and his girlfriend Mima. Mima's family, the Bonfiglios, had six daughters, of which Mima was the third, as well as the third in four years to have disclosed during her last year of high school that she needed to get married. Enzo, who was twenty, wasn't given much choice in the matter; as far as Nicolo could tell, no one had even asked Enzo how he felt about a marriage. Instead, immediately after Enzo and Mima had disclosed the situation to their two sets of parents, the mothers had taken over; they hurried the young pair in for an urgent talk with the priests from the families' churches, and then took turns telephoning around to the local banquet halls to ask about cancellations. Within three days, a small wedding was scheduled and planned for early August, and printed invitations were ready to go out to two hundred guests.

"What are you going to do?" Nicolo overheard Mima's father, Joe Bonfiglio, say to Nicolo's father at about ten o'clock in the morning on the day of the quickly organized wedding, his voice an aural shrug of fatalism. Nicolo walked into the kitchen and saw Joe sitting with his back straight as a plank of wood in a chair that had been pulled back from the kitchen table. He had one of Paola's aprons, which was printed with deep purple poppies on olive-coloured sway-backed stems on a black and yellow background, tied around his wide, red neck, and his head was tipped forward so that his chin was cushioned by a folded band of rosy flesh at the top of his wide chest. He spoke carefully from one side of his mouth, avoiding any unnecessary movement. Massimo was standing behind him in the small space between the table and the refrigerator, scraping errant hairs from Joe's neckline with an ancient and freshly honed straight razor. Nonna had prepared espresso in a battered wasp-waisted pot, and from time to time one or the other of the two fathers sighed, contemplating his scapegrace son or daughter, and then brought his cup close to his lips, blew short cooling breaths across the dark surface rimmed with minute white bubbles, and took a small sip. Nonna set the blue-flowered sugar bowl on the table and then turned to slice one of the heavy, crusty loaves of bread that she had made the day before. She placed two of the slices carefully into the toaster, which she did not trust. It had once given her a shock that coursed like a *serpente* up her arm from her fingertips to her shoulder when she used a fork to try to free a piece of bread that had been cut too thin and had curled in the heat and got caught in the wires. Nicolo reached over and pressed the lever down for her, while she rummaged inside the refrigerator for a jar of the blackberry jam she made every August, each jar kept this side of too sweet with a fat paring of lemon peel.

"Kids these days. They got too much time on their hands. They flock around each other like flies and honey. And the way they dress. Boys and girls both. Tattoos. Earrings everywhere, even in their noses and stomachs. Tight jeans. Those little shirts. Legs and arms and boobs and belly all out for everyone to eyeball like the vegetables outside of a grocery store. Nothing left for the imagination. No wonder they get themselves into trouble—who wouldn't? But, then I think to myself, after all, I mean, we got to remember that they would be married by now already if we were still living back in the old country." Joe reached out to take a noisy slurp from his cup. "And anyways, you can't lock them up any more or we'd be up on charges for child abuse."

"Aspirin," said Massimo, snipping his scissors for emphasis in the empty air above Joe's ear. "We should of gotten them to take aspirin. That's my advice."

73

"Aspirin? I don't get you." Joe twisted his head around to look at Massimo. "Aspirin's for headaches, not for getting knocked up."

"It works."

"I never heard of that. How many they got to take?"

"They don't take them. They just hold them." Massimo finished his coffee in one swallow and held his empty cup out toward Nonna, who hurried over with the espresso pot in her hand. "Between their knees."

The two men laughed while Joe repeated the punchline, savouring it, wondering how he could work it into the speech he was going to give at the wedding reception. "Between their knees. Yes. That's good. Between the knees. Couldn't hurt, eh?"

Nicolo carried his toast, and his coffee which Nonna had diluted for him with milk heated in a small pan at the back of the stove, into the living room. He fell onto the sofa and switched on the TV with the remote. A wedge-shaped formation of women—three with blonde hair and three with dark—were demonstrating aerobic exercises to the rhythm of a thumping, repetitive soundtrack. The women kept broad lipsticked smiles fixed on their faces, and their six sets of eyes gazed into the camera, but none of them seemed to be getting any enjoyment from the workout. The manner in which they bounced and stretched and reached made exercise appear like a necessary evil, something to be concluded in as short a time as possible, perhaps so they could go and relax on the beach, of which a simulacrum could be seen in the distance behind them. Nicolo ran through the channels but ended up at the first program again. The pace of the music had slowed, the throbbing beat replaced by the breathy tootling of pan pipes against a background of rippling harp chords, and the women were now sitting in formation on pink and blue mats. Their legs were propped opened in wide leotarded Vs, and they reached and strained their torsos in synchronized arcs toward their toes. Nicolo winced at the way they forced their lean bodies and outstretched arms forward. The woman at the front, the only one with her hair cut short, was relentless, with the manner of a drill sergeant. "Four more! Three more!" she barked, and the women behind her complied cheerlessly, their glistening expressions undented, their arms and legs in perfect alignment. The sharp angles of their hard bodies glinted under the lights.

Enzo came into the room, dropped heavily onto the couch next to Nicolo and reached to take a piece of toast from Nicolo's plate. He stretched his legs out and let his shoulders fall back into the cushions.

"You look like a wreck," Nicolo said.

Enzo didn't answer. He chewed Nicolo's toast and stared at the absurdly smiling women on the screen. He was unshaven and unshowered. His hair lay around his head in tufts and valleys and his expressionless face looked rumpled and colourless.

"Coffee?" he grunted, without taking his eyes off the television screen.

"I'll check," said Nicolo, but before he could get up from the sofa, Nonna appeared at the doorway carrying a cup for Enzo, a flowered, gold-edged cup with a saucer, taken from the cabinet of never-used best china in one corner of the dining room.

"*Sposa bagnata, sposa fortunata,*" she announced, holding the coffee out to Enzo ceremoniously. A wet wedding is a fortunate wedding.

Nicolo and Enzo turned their heads and looked out the window behind the couch. The clouds were breaking and scattering and had begun to surge southward like a defeated armada of ragged ships. Patches of blue-white sky were breaking through where the clouds were retreating. Thin streams of pale sunlight breached the gaps as they opened and light shone down onto the wet houses and hedges and cars of their street. Enzo shrugged and accepted the cup. Nonna gave a satisfied smile and headed back toward the kitchen. Soon she returned with a large piece of St. Honoré cake on a plate with a fork balanced beside it, the last remaining from the rehearsal dinner two nights before. She gave the plate and fork to Enzo. The women on the screen finished their toe stretches and switched to sitting cross-legged on their mats, breathing in and out in rhythm and rolling their heads from side to side as instructed by the leader, who held her own head high like a border collie's and continued to call out commands. Enzo ate his cake, scraping the fork against the plate to get the last crumbs, and drank down his coffee.

"Today's the day," Nicolo tried again.

A grudging but unrevealing sound emerged from deep inside Enzo's chest.

"You're all right with this?" asked Nicolo. "You're okay with marrying her—Mima?"

Enzo didn't reply. Nicolo reached and pressed the button to turn off the TV.

"Hey. Earth to Enzo," Nicolo said into the silence, without turning his head.

"What do you want me to say?" said Enzo. He shrugged, and his plate and fork and cup bounced and rattled on his stomach.

"I want to know. What's it like?" Nicolo persisted.

"Well," said Enzo. "If you want to know the truth, I don't love her, if that's what you mean. I don't hate her, but I don't love her. She reminds me of Ma a bit, you know? She's bossy; she knows how to do things; she means well; she's organized. She told me she couldn't get pregnant, that she had taken care of things, but she hadn't done anything at all. It's hard not to feel like I've been made a fool of, you know?"

"Does she love *you?*" Nicolo asked. He wasn't sure where the question had come from, but, after all, wasn't love supposed to go with marriage? He turned to look at Enzo. This conversation wasn't one he had expected or planned for.

"She says she does," said Enzo, who was staring at his cup. "But she doesn't, not really. I am the kind of person she wanted for a husband. That's all. She wanted to get married young, like her mother did, and her sisters. Eat what you kill. That's the Bonfiglio motto. The girls all figure it worked for their mother and it'll work for them too. Mima wants to have lots of children. She wants a big house. She wants to cook. She doesn't want to have to get a job or work. I fit into this picture she has of how things are supposed to be, and I'm going to be the one who supports it. Do you think I really wanted to quit university and sell car phones for a living?"

"Are you going to be okay?" Nicolo asked again. He felt an intense need for the story of his brother to make sense, for his brother to love Mima, for Mima to love his brother, for their child not to be born because of random grapplings and guile but because he or she was destined to be born, of these two parents, at this time, in this place.

"What would you do if I said no?" Enzo asked. Obstinacy had been one of his traits since early childhood.

Nicolo considered. "I guess I wouldn't know what to say," he answered honestly. "I don't know what choices you have, not now. A baby. It's a big deal, you know. A big deal." As he said this, it came to him for the first time that he would be an uncle. To a pink infant with eyes shut tight and its crooked thumb in its mouth. A fat toddler swaying on unready feet. A boy in striped shorts and yellow and black striped socks and scuffed shin pads kicking a soccer ball around a muddy field on a cold Saturday morning, or a girl with long dark curls and tiny gold earrings and a hand reaching up to his. Uncle Nicolo. Zio Nicolo. What wouldn't he do for this child?

Enzo turned suddenly so that he was looking directly at Nicolo. He spoke in an urgent, appealing tone. "Ma could raise it. Did you ever think of that? Mima wouldn't have to if she didn't want to. It might be a girl. It's probably a girl. All her sisters have girls. Ma always wanted a daughter; you know that. She's got a name picked out and everything. Pa told me once. It's not impossible. It could be the right thing. For everyone."

Enzo gripped his hands into fists as if they might be of use, as if he could use his hands to keep hold of his independence, and his plans to finish a degree, and then, and then— he wasn't sure, couldn't be certain, but his mind's focus shifted to a semi-transparent manifestation of his aspirations, a vision of his life to come as he had only half-imagined it so far. His goals and desires and acknowledged limitations spun and twisted inside his head and his heart like a cloud before the arrival of a storm, and then they coalesced and were transformed, this vision, the one he had never quite been able to bring into focus, of his autonomous future. It took on a more concrete, but still not quite solid form, of a well-lit tunnel with encouraging markers and road signs, a tunnel that broadened generously at the far end where it was drenched in a warm and hope-inspiring light. He tried to describe it to Nicolo: he wanted . . . he wanted a job at a local business, light manufacturing or distribution, one that he did well at and that would lead over time to a solid position in middle management and then a business of his own. A successful business. And volunteer work. Membership in, and then an executive position on one of those semi-secret clubs run by men much like him who once a year ran an appeal, some sort of "athon," that raised money for an urgent cause—a wing for the children's hospital, a cure for one of the more compelling diseases, support for a languishing segment of the highly deserving poor. And, after a few years, maybe a run at and then election to city council, as an alderman or reeve, isn't that what they were called? A wife, of course, at his side, attractive, but definitely not Mima. A woman not remotely like Mima. His wife would be someone whose family had for generations owned a cottage in Muskoka furnished with battered antiques. Someone with a natural head of straight, mocha-blonde hair, deftly feathered at the tips. Someone with a wardrobe of sweaters made of that soft wool, merino or cashmere, and navy tailored pants that zipped up at the side and shoes made of the best leather, and smooth golden thighs. The Breck girl's twin or cousin or next-door neighbour. Enzo poured out all of this, or as much as he could put into words, and then he groaned and with his teeth worried a loose scrap of skin at the edge of his thumbnail.

The need Nicolo felt to be fair to Mima, whom he had known all his life, together with his wish for a more or less logical unfolding of events, swamped his loyalty to Enzo. Nicolo felt as if he, perhaps alone, could picture it, how Enzo's life would actually be, and the pattern of Enzo's life began to come together in his mind and gather substance, like a hologram, in the air between the couch and the television. It was a vision that didn't differ very much, in fact, from Enzo's, except that Mima was central to it and there was no cottage or parson's tables or sisters-in-law named Debbie and Becky. Nicolo almost believed that he could, by imagining it, call it into being for his brother—although at eighteen, he had no thought that any of this image might ever apply to himself. What he foresaw for his brother but could not have articulated was an early marriage to a clever and devoted wife, three or four children, hard work, watchful stewardship of a modest but steadily increasing store of resources, the acquisition of a small block of apartments in town that Mima could manage once the children were in school, no more than the usual number of disagreements, and the growth, like the twisting tendrils of vines, of an infinite number of bonds—thick and slender—and unspoken accommodations slowly maturing over months and years, all leading to a fiftieth anniversary party in a community hall or the ballroom of a suburban hotel, organized by their children and grandchildren, at which Enzo would speak briefly, white-haired, moist-eyed, moved by the genuine warmth and domestic harmony of all that he and Mima had engendered. A well-lived, useful life, better than most.

Nicolo was overwhelmed by this vision. He had no means to express the way he felt. "No," was all he said, speaking around Enzo's moan. "This is your daughter. Or your son. And Mima's. It isn't Ma's. It isn't anyone else's. So long as you're the father, marrying Mima is the right thing to do. We know her. We know her family. I don't think you two will have any worse chance than anyone else has starting out. Ma and Pa didn't even meet until the day before they got married. They've worked it out. You guys will too. That's what people do."

"You're not the one who's got to get married," countered Enzo. He scowled and pushed his fist hard against his chin and rubbed the rough stubble until his knuckles hurt. The bright tunnel of his future was narrowing and darkening, finally, inexorably. There would be no burnished lights, no dinners on tastefully mismatched family china on reclaimed pine tables, no lakefront cottages with a collection of battered canoes and small sailboats in the boathouse, no civic honours or inherited riches or bursts of unearned glory.

"What are you afraid of?"

"It's not what I expected," said Enzo. "This wasn't what I had planned."

"It *will* be different from what you expected," said Nicolo. "But it could be better."

"It'll be worse," Enzo lamented. He rubbed his whiskery face hard once more and his elbow struck the remote control on the arm of the sofa.

The television flared into life. The weather channel. A woman wearing a close-fitting, short-sleeved knitted top the colour of milky coffee, her light fine hair pulled smoothly away from the ledges of her cheekbones, was crisply announcing a sixty-percent chance of rain that afternoon. Enzo rested his elbows on his thighs. He leaned toward her, and Nicolo felt how keenly he longed to fall through the screen, so close, so transparent, so tantalizing, into another world. She was— Nicolo could see this—perfect, and as unattainable to Enzo as the sun and the moon and the stars. Nonna came into the room on her silent slippers with her coffee pot in one hand and the little pot of warm milk in the other and leaned over to refill their cups, first Enzo's and then Nicolo's.

"*Sposa bagnata,*" she said, and pointed through the window to the skies in which the morning's undecided clouds were gathering and thickening into grey, doughy mounds heavily weighted with the absolute certainty of coming rain.

Nicolo turned his head and saw that Enzo had tears in his eyes.

CHAPTER SEVEN

Every Sunday, Nicolo's mother and father get up and go together to the earliest Mass at St. Francis of Assisi parish church over on Stevens Street at the corner where it crosses Lyon Avenue, the break-of-dawn Mass for the few most fervent, die-hard congregants. Nicolo's mother is out of bed first. Yawning in her once-white terry slippers and with her ancient pink quilted housecoat with the pilling cuffs and fraying hem belted snugly around her waist, Paola pads to the kitchen and makes coffee for the two of them, Canadian coffee, measured with a brown plastic cone-shaped scoop from a large red and green tin with a snap-on plastic lid. She uses the electric plug-in coffee maker that sees service only on this one morning of the week. This is the start of the weekend for Nicolo's father; he switches off the twirling red, white and blue pole outside of his barbershop on Saturday evenings, and on Tuesday mornings he starts it up again, giving a polish to the chrome knobs at the top and bottom with a chamois rag. On Sundays Massimo wears his good pants—the crease pressed crisply during the week by his mother, who wields the iron like a weapon—a clean undershirt and suspenders. He pushes his feet into the rubber boots that he keeps just inside the side door, and carries his mug of coffee, which Paola has splashed with cream, outside where he conducts his weekly survey of the perimeter of the house. He checks, depending on the season, for an accumulation of leaves in the gutters, for flaking paint, for snow packed into the basement window wells, for any sign of incursions by weather, mice, rats, raccoons, or neighbours' children or pets, anything that is or soon may be in need of his ministrations. He hitches his pants fractionally upward with his free hand as he rounds each corner of the house, and his gait is stiff, such is his swell of pride in his well-tended domain—his fruit trees planted on the south side of the house blanketed at the roots with rich mulch, his eight staked garden plots, two rows of four, or four rows of two, depending on how you count them, his sweet compost pile steamily rotting and caving in on itself, his tightly lapped pressure-treated siding without open knots or warp or wane, his sturdy garage with its two sash windows, one to the west and one to the east (he cleans the panes weekly with vinegar and handfuls of crumpled newspaper), his padlocked garden shed, in which his tools hang on a pegboard, waiting for his hand, and, on a wide workbench that he made himself out of the discarded boards of a fence torn down by a neighbour, rows of nails and screws and other bits and pieces sorted by size and function and stored in the red and green coffee tins that Paola passes on to him when empty, his neatly stacked woodpile, a half-cord or slightly more of wood that he buys from a place north of the city from species that burn well without too much spark or smoke or ash—maple, beech, ash and larch—wood that has been cut and trimmed and split by his three strong, grown sons, his lawn and the ancient push mower that keeps the grass in submission.

His own father had nothing compared to this, had only fettered and entailed title to a small stone house pitched on the dark side of the road that ran uphill into the mountains, two rooms, unheated, no water, a privy over a fetid hole out back—there was nowhere left to dig that hadn't been used and reused for generations—two ancient iron pots, a patched tin pan and a half-dozen chipped, mismatched dishes, rope-strung bed frames for the two beds, a few rusted tools, a patch of rocky earth to till a kilometre away by foot, often no shoes or boots or else a pair or two to be patched, shared and handed down, a bitter morning drink made with ground and roasted chicory roots and consumed on the doorstep in the thin early morning sun while the smell of real espresso imported from Brazil drifted over from the Gagliardis' expansive three-level house two doors up and across the street; the village had been too small for the rich to keep themselves separate from the poor.

Nonna sleeps in on Sundays and her snores contain a rattle of reproach against her ostensibly devout son and daughter-in-law. She had a noisy breach with the priest at St. Francis of Assisi ten years ago and in its aftermath stopped going to Mass as a matter of pride and principle. *"Preti e cauci 'nculu, vijatu chi ni tena,"* she said. Priests and kicks in the backside, blessed is he who has neither one. And *"Piscia chiarru e 'ncuuo a lu miericu!"*—one of her *proverbi* that has no possible translation, but having the sense, roughly, of the expression "piss off" directed in particular toward one's so-called betters. She made exceptions only for weddings, funerals—especially funerals—and baptisms, although she hedges against the potential peril to her eternal soul by sending Nicolo twice a year to make an anonymous donation of five ten-dollar bills drawn from her tiny war widow's pension. She has managed to convey to Nicolo as she silently counts out the money into his palm that although he is not to mention her name, he is to leave the priest (the third successor to the role since the one whose reproach about Nicolo's younger brother Enzo's non-attendance led to Nonna's dramatic departure) in no doubt about the identity of the donor.

On Sunday mornings Nicolo's mother and father carry out their routines in peaceable silence. They drink their coffee without more than the briefest of exchanges, although their fingers may brush together when Paola hands Massimo his cup to carry outside and in this passing contact is enfolded the whole of a conversation of which they know every tone and nuance. The house is warm and silent. They place their empty cups, rinsed once quickly under a brief stream of water from the tap, on a folded dishcloth in the sink. They dress with careful attention. Paola sheds her soft, faded, fraying housecoat and puts on satiny underpants and bra, both of a matching mocha hue. She drapes and fastens one of her two good dresses, the navy blue one with the slim self-belt, or the red one with a wave of gathers at the waist from which the fabric drops in a slimming cascade as fluid as falling water around her hips. She pulls on stockings and places her black shoes beside the front door. She combs and pins her hair in a heavy knot behind her head. Massimo wears his black pants, and a white shirt that has been ironed and starched by Nonna and hung on a wooden hanger in the closet that he shares with Paola. He knots a careful tie under his chin. At the door wait his solid black brogues, the ones the boys bought him a few Christmases ago, so sturdy that no one in the family would have been in any doubt at all, had the question been raised, that, with Massimo's customary care and frugal use, these shoes will be on his feet when he is laid out in his coffin—even the shoelaces are barely worn.

Massimo can never look at these good shoes without seeing his own father's brown, callused feet with their thick nails, ridged, dented and black-edged; his father, Peppino, had not worn shoes until he was ordered at age nineteen and a half to go north to the town of Tarsia to help guard two thousand rounded-up Jews at the Ferramonti internment camp. Afterward, near the end of the war, out of fear of reprisal, he had thrown the shoes and uniform that he had been issued into the river Crati. It was the morning of the day that the camp was liberated by British and Canadian troops—strong boys who advanced in confident ranks, long-legged, pale-haired, red-skinned—and although he had longed to keep the shoes, which had thick soles and strong laces, instead he had walked home barefoot, a journey of five days, mostly at night, wearing civilian clothes he stole from a pile behind the camp laundry in order to blend in with the local citizenry who thronged to the camp to watch the tall soldiers arrive. He kept his homeward steps on pace with a silent song.

Filomena mia, fammi nu vutu,
Fammillu no mi vaiu pe surdatu.
Fammillu no mi vaiu pe surdatu.
Mi vaiu a Catanzaru e m'u m'indi votu.

Filomena mine, say a prayer for me,
So that I won't have to go to be a soldier.
Say it so that I won't have to go to be a soldier.
I'll go as far as Catanzaro and then come back to you.

Peppino's bare feet bled at first, and at night he dug soft, powdery clay from the riverbanks and applied it to his cuts and blisters to draw out any infection. His feet got blacker and coarser and tougher as he trudged closer to his wife Filomena, with few stories that he could ever bring himself to tell her except that the prisoners had taught him, an unlettered peasant and their jailer as well, how to read, starting with the backs of cigarette packages and then moving up through scraps of old newspapers to books, real books, including parts of the Bible, but only the older stories. For some reason the Jews' Bible had in it nothing from the gospels of saints Matteo, Marco, Luca or Giovanni, or from the letters of Paolo to the earliest Christian flocks right there in Italy, up in Rome where everything, as he had thought, had begun.

He had not owned shoes of his own after that, except for the local style of sandals with thick leather soles, until he died, aged fifty-one, of a twisted, septic bowel, in agony, but relatively quickly, which was a sure sign of God's kindness and mercy, everyone told Filomena, who listened to these reminders of God's grace with her head bowed to conceal her expression, and closed her hands into tight fists in order to feel the pain of her fingernails digging into her palms. Her acid silence made her tongue swell inside her mouth. She acquired during the week following her husband's death a hard-edged ball of disappointment and thwarted sensual longing that settled in her chest and had never thereafter been dislodged or dissolved. Having no one else to blame, she had laid her loss at the feet of the bungling, ineffective God of southern Italy.

Shortly after, she began encouraging Massimo to leave. She knew that her only son would send for her once he was settled, and after that, the God who had not lifted so much as a finger to take care of her good, devout husband could look for her all over Calabria as hard as he wanted, she would not be there to be found. At the last minute she took Paola with her. Paola was not the most beautiful of the neighbourhood girls, but she had been left with no one—her father gone first, of black lung from his years working in the Belgian mines, and her mother not six months after, of a broken heart—and Filomena saw that she might do for Massimo.

Dressed, brushed, polished, Paola and Massimo leave the house as quietly as possible. They pull the door softly, softly shut behind them. They do not want to risk waking any of the house's sleepers and they want even less for anyone to express a desire to come with them. This is one of the few times during the week when they are alone together. They close the door behind them with care. When they walk down the path to their car, Paola rests her hand on the warm sleeve of Massimo's jacket. Massimo opens the car door for her, and he cradles her elbow as she slides her bottom into her seat. Paola's scent (shampoo, face powder, a lingering suggestion of coffee) mixes with Massimo's (aftershave, deodorant, shoe polish, fresh air) inside the rumbling car that conveys them the eight blocks to the church. Paola inclines slightly toward Massimo's shoulder as he negotiates the car around a right-hand turn. He swells taller, larger, with pride in her, his own, attractive, competent, steadfast wife.

They are young, after all, younger than you might imagine. Paola was only eighteen when their first son was born. She is forty-four now, and Massimo won't be fifty for three more years. Paola knows of someone, a near neighbour, a few blocks to the east, in one of the smaller houses east of the old mill pond, who gave birth a month ago to twin boys at age forty-eight. She hasn't seen the babies, but she has heard reports of their birthweights—five and six pounds—and complexions—fair like their mother. Almost anything remains possible for Massimo and Paola, even this.

Massimo's hair is still black and thick and it has receded from his forehead by no more than the breadth of his thumb, and although Paola's waist has expanded by several inexorable inches, her breasts are almost as high and full as the day she was married. Massimo still interests her, thrills her sometimes. Her own heart can surprise her, spilling like an overflowing glass of wine without warning some mornings when she looks at him. Her emotion rises sometimes like a flush into her throat, where Massimo has observed it pulsing. In bed, Massimo can't gaze on his wife's naked, unguarded face without perceiving her affection. He makes love to her in the night under the blankets, beneath her cotton nightgown, in full darkness, his hands on her large brown nipples, to keep his great fortune doubly and triply safe and secret. He falls asleep at night with his head in the deep valley between the tenderest inner slopes of her wonderful breasts and he hears the ocean in her heartbeat. She lies against his back with her fingers threaded in the curls on the thick skin at the nape of his neck, her thighs tucked inside the hot crook of his legs, and feels like a fragrant pink shrimp floating snug inside its tough and resilient shell. Her three sons. Her husband. Her heart is almost entirely filled with them.

Nicolo doesn't go to Mass on Sunday mornings. He wakes up hours later, usually after nine o'clock. What pulls him from sleep is the scent of Nonna's strong, dark coffee hiccuping in the espresso pot on the front of the stove, and the clattering noises she sends forth from the kitchen. He can also hear his parents talking to each other. They have returned from Mass—unburdened of their trivial sins, forgiven, shriven, blessed, renewed—and they are lifting the heavy oak dining room table between them and ferrying it to the far side of the room underneath the lace-curtained window. "Careful." "Watch your foot." "Hold it one more minute while I . . ." "We can put it down here."

Nicolo hears the doors to the stereo cabinet pulled open, the snick of the magnetic clasp being pulled apart, a reverberation of the doors of the veneered wooden cabinet as they reach the outer limit of their hinges. The sound of hands fumbling with a record or tape. And then the music begins. Waltzes mainly. Foxtrots. Quicksteps. Sambas sometimes. Occasionally a rumba, or the exotic to-and-fro of a tango. The sounds of a weekly hour that begins slow and ends with something fast-paced and difficult—salsa, mambo, merengue or swing. This is what Nicolo and his brothers think of as classical music, the music they heard on Sunday mornings when their parents came home from Mass, shriven and sinless, and, still in their church clothes, cleared an open space in the dining room, the largest room in the small one-storey house, and danced.

Massimo and Paola begin with the most sedate of waltzes, moving in small circles in the centre of the oval hooked rug, arms around each other's back and waist and neck, her hair or cheek occasionally brushing, accidentally in passing, the skin of his shaved jaw. Massimo holds his left elbow high and uses it much as a yachtsman uses a rudder, steering them both through the dining room in more or less the same area that is occupied during the rest of the week by the large circle of lace that sits on the table weighted down by a white china soup tureen with its matching china ladle. They get bolder as they go, venturing outside the circumference of the lace tablecloth, their orbit expanding. The music gives a charge to the blood in their veins. Their tendons loosen. Their bones rock and their muscles swim. One of them reaches over to the stereo and turns up the volume. Massimo pulls Paola closer, enfolding her progressively nearer to his chest. Paola adds a flourish with one leg. She kicks up the heel of a shoe. Her eyes and hands and ankles move and slide around him. She sends him glancing sideways looks of comic-book love, or turns away false-haughty, teasing, enticing. Massimo pulls and then spins her from him to the end of his grasp, to his fingertips, and then reverses to pull her back again into his embrace. He changes direction, light as a moment on his feet, and her feet reflect his steps so closely that it is impossible to tell that they are not following a single, shared inclination. All the atoms in the room and in their liquid bodies are spinning end on end. When their hour is done, on the last note, Massimo dips a trusting Paola backward through a sphere of space. They trace together a final large, sweeping parabola. Then, briskly, they release each other, pull away, smooth their clothes.

They lift and carry the table back to the middle of the room, where it belongs. They unroll and smooth the rug. One of them switches off the stereo and closes the cabinet doors, and they both go to change into work pants and housedress to take up the afternoon's tasks. Nothing is left over from the dancing; no expression or gesture gives them away, except perhaps, if you are watching for it, the faintest trace, like atomized mist, of contentment, of serenity, of something essential having been accomplished.

The boys sometimes used to peek at their mother and father through the doorway, and there was a time, even further back, when they would sit cross-legged on the floor under the dining room table and watch. But as soon as they were old enough to sense that Sunday dancing was something between their parents only, and perhaps more hallowed than the Mass that preceded it, they began to find something to do other than watch their parents behaving so strangely. Sometimes when they were younger, Nonna would give them cookies to eat to distract them, or even allow them to sit in front of the television and eat bowls of sweet *canadese* cereal drowned in milk.

In grade eight, Father Santino taught Nicolo's class that the first proof of God's existence as laid out by Thomas Aquinas was that nothing can move itself, that the first object in motion needed a mover, and that the first mover, the unmoved mover, is called God. Listening, Nicolo felt that this was something he already knew and understood because he had been a witness to this fact since his earliest years. His mother and father, his first childhood gods, his *genii loci:* it had always seemed to him that they set the world in motion, wound it up like a watch, from the very centre of the household, not the hearth or the stove, but from the area created when the dining room table was lifted and displaced, a central, crucial, fundamental space in which constancy, goodness, decency and ardour dwelt, and in which shelter, safety, beauty and love were created and recreated over and over every Sunday morning from the beginning of time without cease forever.

Massimo and Paola were strangers on the night of their afternoon wedding, and Massimo, who had been taught as a boy to waltz by his uncle Rudolfo, a small-town dandy with polished two-tone shoes and a thin moustache waxed to twin tips pointing northeast and northwest, taught downcast Paola the three-step between the hours of ten and twelve, after which they fell asleep with several modest centimetres between them in a double bed in a small room. It wasn't until weeks later that Paola conveyed an invisible signal to Massimo that he had earned her trust and Massimo parted the folds of her embroidered nightdress and discovered with his hands and then the rest of him her secret places—her warm, giving softness formed into ridges like sand carved by wind or water, flesh laid down unstintingly over bone that fit into his palm like a shell, his fingers reaching inside his wife as if he were a sailor and she were the warm, glossy, eternal ocean—and they began the process of creating Enzos and Nicolo.

Dancing took the place of birth control in their marriage, which they both felt was undertaken under Roman sanction and scrutiny and therefore was to be practised according to its exacting rules. Their three sons were judicially spaced over a span of fifty-seven months by means of many Sunday afternoons spent dancing in the dining room, supplemented by the occasional midnight session when Massimo, in ardour, would pull Paola out of bed, sleeping, laughing, protesting, and take her in his arms and spin her on the bedside rag rug, humming into the thick waves of her hair as her head grew heavier and heavier, trusting, dozing, contented and warm on his shoulder. The daughter that might have arrived three years after their third son simply had never appeared, although Paola is still, after all these years, attentive to any possible signs that God might not yet have completed his promises to her. She believes that her daughter is waiting, floating in some small and fluid place inside her belly, a miniature of her future self, wise and pink and, while perfectly formed, not yet animated, delicate, curled up in the shape of a seahorse, eyes and ears and mouth closed as tightly as small new buds on the earliest day of spring. Paola counts the days between one month's ever-advancing flow of blood and the next—this month it arrives on the fifth, the next month on the third, on the cusp of the next— ready for and alert to the subtle changes that may yet come. She dreams sometimes of her daughter, a girl she has provisionally named Sofia Rosa (the first name for wisdom and the second name for her grandmother, Rosa Catterina Spina, remembered still back in Arduino for her unparalleled goodness, modesty, charity and kindness), as she will be one day when she is finished, unfurled, sparked with life and born at last, the weight of her on Paola's lap, her sleeping eyes swelling under their lids like almonds and fringed with blackest lashes. The scent and colour and texture of this daughter come to her in her dreams as well. Sofia Rosa is poppy seeds and flowers and grapes, she is pinker and creamier than gardenias. She smells of honey and yeast and lavender. She is as warm and heavy in Paola's waiting arms as new dense bread pulled fresh and salty and sweet and soft from the oven.

Although Paola loves her grandchildren Zachary and Isabella, they have not replaced Sofia Rosa, nor has Enzo's wife Mima. Mima and her small children live almost exclusively in the constant, feverish, hectic dramas of the Bonfiglio family, which now has, in addition to its six handsome daughters, five sheepish sons-in-law and thirteen grand-children (with a fourteenth grandchild and sixth surprised son-in-law pending), and so Zachary and Isabella, although they live only a few blocks away, seldom visit, and, although Paola and Nonna are often invited to the enormous and complicated events at Mima's house—engagement parties, wedding showers, baby showers, baptisms, first communions—Paola realized long ago that she is surplus to the Bonfiglios' requirements, whether for dramatic actors, chorus or audience, which are more than met by the Bonfiglios themselves. Also, she has tired of the boasts of Mima's mother, Augusta, which chiefly concern how well settled all of her daughters are, but also include frequent mentions of how close her bond is to Enzo and Mima's children. Augusta never fails to mention that she is the only person Mima trusts with them, the broad category of persons not to be trusted including, by implication, Paola herself. Paola has come to understand some of the reasons Mima and her sisters might have been so eager to get out of Augusta's house and into homes of their own, and she feels as if she understands why her eldest son comes by so often to help Massimo with the heavier chores—taking down storm windows, mending the back fence, splitting wood—and why he usually stays for an hour or two longer than strictly necessary, drinking coffee or a beer at the kitchen table and talking to Massimo about the plans he still has to go into business for himself. He has looked at a chicken sandwich franchise, a brew-your-own-beer outlet, and an organic grocery store, but so far he has not settled firmly on one thing or another.

What Paola can't know, but what Massimo intuits, is that Enzo is happier with Mima than he predicted. Mima had surprised him. Stole his breath. Cemented his love. After their wedding, after his early morning denials of her, after she had, before the priest and a few moments following Enzo's hesitant, unsteady "I do," responded in the clearest, most assured of tones "I do" (to the amusement of the congregation, none of whom older than twelve were in any doubt as to how things stood), at the reception, hiked up the skirts of her drop-waisted wedding dress, released her hair from the constraints of its pins and the too-tight, pearly tiara that pinched and threatened to give her a headache, downed a glass of her Zio Giovanni's wine, led Enzo out onto the floor and danced with the passion of a flamenco dancer. Her smouldering assurance carried over into the hotel suite where she made love to him against the wall of the bedroom, in a cloud of steam against the cold tiles of the shower, in a surging sea of bubbles in the bathtub to the sound of eight roaring jets of hot water. There was no part of her body that she withheld from him—her mouth, her belly, her hair, her feet, the warm, scented bounty of her breasts—all the while making it seem as if she were an emanation, a creation of Enzo's most fervent wishes and fantasies, like a genie released from a bottle that he had accidentally brushed, until Enzo ached with confusion and pleasure and astonishment.

Younger Enzo, although he is only five years junior to older Enzo, because he has gone to university and has travelled a bit—east to a debating competition at Dalhousie at which his team came in second nationwide, west on a high school ski trip to Lake Louise (where, although he had never skied before, he deftly mastered the relatively simple art of falling to one side while controlling the pull of gravity with bent knees, a trick that might, he thought at the time, be something like arguing in court, using the weight of precedent to pull the decision to one's side of the argument)—because of these experiences, and because of his hopes and plans, younger Enzo existed in a different world, one in which one-night or only slightly longer relationships were possible, even desirable, and unexpected babies are not, in which virtually all hazards were banished through atheism, chemistry, prophylaxes, diligence and a cost-benefit analysis that included the danger of jeopardizing a chance at a clerkship at the Supreme Court of Canada or, failing that, at least the Court of Appeal. Nicolo's younger brother had never yet had a sexual adventure that wasn't planned and strategically negotiated by both parties. He was satisfied with this; this is not the part of his life in which he has ever wanted to take any risks. He had a woman friend, Nandita Dasgupta, in her final year of the accountancy program at the university, who slept with him once or twice a month, in order, as each said to the other, not to fall completely out of practice, much like now and again running the motor of a car that is not otherwise taken out of the garage. So efficient are they at this task that Nandita seldom takes the time to undo her long braid, although when she does so, Enzo is weakened, like the inverse of Samson in the Bible story, destabilized, disarmed inside its glossily swishing tent, which blurs the light and smells of soap and tea and licorice.

Nicolo has had a somewhat more complicated sexual life than either of his brothers so far, although not, perhaps, as fraught as his client Patrick's, which is chaotic at best.

Patrick made his living in a random and occasionally frantic catch-as-catch-can manner as a reviewer, editor, script development consultant, assistant assistant producer and the like, being generally useful in a vaguely creative/organizational way, the kind of person likely to be brought into a flagging project after a very late-night meeting near the end of which someone would toss the stub of a cigarette into the scummy, pearly pool at the bottom of a cardboard coffee cup and suggest in an anxious but not unhopeful tone that perhaps Patrick might be asked to lend a hand—did anyone know what he was doing these days, didn't everyone agree that Patrick, if asked, might have a solution for that portion of the project that had gone off the rails?

Patrick has been smitten, bitten hard by love, and Patrick impassioned is a hundred times worse than Patrick between his frequent, intensely felt, ephemeral affairs. He arrives these days to his sessions with Nicolo with alarming punctuality, but, once attired and presented to the equipment, he moons and droops and swoons.

"Ah, Nicolo," Patrick sighs. "I can't tell you how I feel. It's impossible. No. Yes. I do have the word. *Exalted. Exalted.* That's what it is. *Exaltation.*" He turns away from the rack of free weights and he grasps Nicolo's shoulders fervently. "Do you know what I mean? Have you ever felt like this?" His eyes burn raw and elemental as embers. "I ache!" he declaims. "It hurts all over." He pedals on the elliptical bicycle like a maniac for five or ten minutes, and then drapes himself over the bars, his hands and head dangling, moaning.

"What am I going to do?" he asks, shaking his head, addressing the floor. "I love him far more than he loves me. It is hopeless. He'll see that I am old and boring and ugly, and give me up. I like to stay in. Timothy likes to go out. He likes dance parties. I like dinner parties. He's been dragging me out to clubs and restaurants at all hours and I have been trying and trying to keep up with him. I'm not a kid any more. I'm exhausted. My head hurts. My joints ache. I have a hangover every morning. I can't keep it up. What can I do? I am addicted. I am addled. I am lost and bewildered and doomed. Advice! I need advice!"

Something is called for, it seems. Anything.

"My grandmother always says '*Chi nasce tondo non può morir quadrato,*'" Nicolo told him. "It's a saying, from the south of Italy where my family comes from. What it means is that something that is born a circle can't die a square."

Patrick gazed up at Nicolo damply. It appeared something more was expected. Nicolo took a breath and thought hard.

"I think what it's saying is that we all have our own natures," he said. "And I think it is trying to tell us that it is important to accept what we are, instead of trying to be someone different. When we are teenagers, we like to be with people like ourselves. But, when we are older, we learn to understand and even start to like the fact that we are all different. A circle stops looking for other circles. It might find a square more interesting. Even if that doesn't happen, the circle can't try to become a square. It isn't in its nature."

Patrick shook his head slowly. "What's that again? Ki nashay tondo non . . . ?"

"*Chi nasce tondo non può morir quadrato.*"

Patrick nodded slowly. "Yes, you might have something there. I'll have to think about it."

"Let's go and do some stretching," Nicolo suggested.

Patrick disentangled himself from the bicycle and, his long arms hanging freely from his shoulders, followed Nicolo meekly through the crowded gym to the mats.

CHAPTER EIGHT

Nicolo arrived ten minutes early for his first psychology class. The availability of university courses in the distant northern suburb where Nicolo's family lived was a phenomenon of recent years. Over the past decade, in a bid for new sources of revenue, although not without misgivings, the city universities had begun to cast off some of their former aura of exclusivity and to engage in experiments at delivering "modules" of learning, like educational spores, beyond the borders of their historic campuses, first in carefully selected downtown locations, and then, confronted with growing competition from community colleges and institutions, many of which were offering all kinds of alternatives to students—courses by correspondence, classes on the Internet, movable classrooms in portable trailers—in parts of the city that some of the university faculty had never visited, except, perhaps, when they drove along one of the highways on their way to their northern cottages. Nicolo walked over from his parents' house, allowing himself extra time in case he was waylaid by a neighbour and also in order to see whether the pleasure of walking to school was recoverable after a gap of several years—it was, but with some self-consciousness. He felt overgrown and not entirely sure of himself, returning as an adult to a formal classroom with its neat rows of desks. He was carrying his textbook and a new silver-grey laptop, which was thinner and lighter than the textbook, in a sports bag slung over his shoulder.

"Make your notes directly onto your laptop," Enzo had advised him. "Highlight the key concepts as you go. You can sort and search through them more easily when you're getting ready for the exam. And scout out the kind of person you might want to have in your study group. The good ones get taken early. A good study group is practically guaranteed to add four or five percentages to your final mark."

Nicolo was the second student to arrive. Already in the room was a young woman with a broad back and solid arms and a thicket of short bristly hair cut into a geometric wedge above her neck. She had selected one of the tables at the front of the room and was busy arranging in front of her a stack of new notebooks, a plaid-printed plastic pencil case with a zipper, her textbook, a one-litre bottle of water, a metal box of geometry instruments and a small clear-plastic package of tissues. Nicolo chose a desk at the back of the room.

Over the next ten minutes, a dozen other students arrived, most of them younger than Nicolo. Only one or two were clearly older, including a man who looked as if he might be retired—he wore tan-coloured slacks, a loosely buttoned red cardigan, and a beneficent expression that he bestowed on everyone as he entered. He was the only other student who had come equipped with a laptop, a matte black rectangle that he held in his outstretched hands with obvious pride. At the last minute, a woman of approximately Nicolo's own age, with long flat brown hair, darting eyes and slightly shaking hands, slid into the chair next to him. She was empty-handed. She leaned toward him.

"Do you have any paper I can borrow?" she asked.

Her voice was low and grainy and pleasing; it reminded Nicolo of a toy instrument from his kindergarten class, two ridged sticks that were played by being dragged rhythmically against each other. Nicolo tore a few sheets from the pad he had brought with him and slid them over to her.

"Thanks," she said. "Carla."

"Nicolo."

"Got a spare pen?"

Nicolo took one of his extras from his jacket pocket and handed it to her.

At exactly seven-thirty, a thin man dressed in professorial clothes—khaki trousers, beige shirt, tweedy jacket, unpolished loafers—strode through the door and up to the front of the class. He kneaded his hands together and cracked his knuckles, then ran his fingers through the strands of ginger hair on his brow, lifting them a centimetre above the top of his head and then patting them back into place.

"Welcome," he exhaled. Then, more strongly, "Welcome, all of you, to an adventure in higher learning."

Nicolo glanced sideways at Carla. She met his gaze and shrugged.

"O-kaaay," she said from the side of her mouth, her voice sandpapery. "Because we live out here, he thinks we're a bunch of dummies."

The thin man turned and began to write with a marker on the whiteboard that was fastened to the front wall. He spoke slowly, sounding out the syllables as he wrote.

"I am Pro . . . fess . . . or . . . Wern . . . er. Pronounced *Vvverner*, not *Wwwerner*. Professor Werner." He turned back and looked somewhat challengingly at the class.

"Any questions? Good. Let's get started then. You will need to read chapter one of our textbook, *Introduction to Psychology: Voyages in Understanding*, before our next class in one week's time. What we'll be doing today is laying the groundwork for some of the ideas and lessons in that chapter."

Professor Werner turned and wrote CH 1 FOR NEXT WEEK and GROUNDWORK on the whiteboard. He underlined each word twice.

"Any questions? Good."

"There's a textbook?" Carla whispered.

"Yes." Nicolo raised his book and tilted it to show her the front cover. "You can get it at the university bookstore."

"Can I see it for a minute?"

Nicolo passed the book over to Carla and then trained his attention on Professor Werner.

"Wouldn't you know it?" Carla muttered after another moment. She held up the book, and inclined her chin toward the front cover. "'Chapell, Strang and *Werner*, eds.' And you paid a hundred and ten dollars for it? Some kind of a racket they got going, eh?"

Nicolo lifted his shoulders and let them fall, recognizing the gesture as one that his father made frequently around the house, signalling a kind of resigned acceptance of the generally wicked and inexplicable ways of the world. *Eh bene.* Oh well. What can you do?

Professor Werner erased the words on the whiteboard and drew in their place a pyramid shape, which he then divided with lines into horizontal slices. He wrote underneath it: MAZLOW'S HIERARCHY OF NEEDS.

"What is our most basic need?" he asked.

No one in the class spoke.

"What could we absolutely not do without?" Professor Werner prompted.

"He thinks we're a load of idiots," Carla whispered. She put up her hand.

"Food and water," she said.

"Very good," said Professor Werner.

"Food and water. Unless you have both of these, you won't last longer than a few days." He wrote the words FOOD AND WATER in the lowest level of the pyramid, and then drew a circle around them.

"This is existence at its most basic. With food and water alone, you might be able to attain the barest minimum level of subsistence. You exist but you are not exactly living. What do you think comes next?" He rapped with his marker one level up on the pyramid.

"A place to live," the woman in the front row suggested.

"Excellent." Professor Werner wrote SHELTER and then drew a circle around the word.

"Shelter. Safety. Warmth. Protection from the elements and from animals. A cave or hut or tent or longhouse or igloo or hut. Add a safe place to store, preserve and prepare food and water and you are getting a bit more out of life. You have sustenance and you have security. Nothing to sneeze at, but still pretty minimal. Once these needs are met, what do we need next?"

"Family?" came a suggestion.

"Good," Professor Werner encouraged. He wrote BELONG-ING on the pyramid, one step up. "A family or tribe or gang that accepts you or at least tolerates you. Some group to be a member of. Then what?" Four rungs remained blank above those that had now been labelled.

"Television."

"Education."

"Transportation?"

"Sex."

"Beer."

"Who said education?" Professor Werner held up a hand, palm forward, to stem the cascade of suggestions. "Education may be closest to what I am looking for in the next two categories. We all have a fundamental need to achieve—for self-esteem, to have a sense of self worth and to acquire and hone our skills and understanding."

He wrote ESTEEM in the next slice of his pyramid, and KNOWLEDGE in the one above that.

"What about beauty?" he prompted. The class remained silent.

"What about art?" Professor Werner's hand hovered in the upper third of the triangle.

"Art?" a woman repeated, turning the word into a suggestion.

"Yes, yes." Professor Werner's voice took on a cast of impatience. "Our need for art, for symmetry, for order."

"Aesthetic," Nicolo said quietly. Then more loudly. "Aesthetic needs."

The truth is that he had seen the word when he was reviewing his textbook and had asked Enzo what it meant, and had paid attention to how Enzo pronounced it, and so he felt that the professor's glance toward him, in which he could read a subtle but plainly recognizable upward reappraisal, was dubiously earned. Professor Werner wrote AESTHETIC NEEDS in the next level of the pyramid.

"And at the top?" Professor Werner asked. "What is it that we strive for, and yet so seldom achieve?"

His face took on an ambiguous expression, one in which Nicolo thought it might be possible to discern that even Professor Werner, with his textbook, his precisely calibrated clothes, his vaguely and possibly faux East Coast accent, his degrees and honours and classes and students, even Professor Werner may have yet to attain all that he longed for.

No one spoke and Professor Werner didn't prompt them. Instead, after a long minute, he emitted a long slow breath and then reached forward and wrote in looping letters, a change from the block capitals he had used below this, in the peak of his triangle, the word *Self-actualization*.

"The need to be fulfilled," he said. He spoke quietly, as if he were speaking to no one in particular. "The need to be integrated, to fully realize our inherent human potential. That is what makes it all worthwhile, this gathering of food, hunting and storing up of provisions, building or buying a house, raising a family, getting educated, making or hanging art on the wall. This is the goal. Self-actualization. Achieving the goal of becoming the fullest possible person we can be." Most of the students nodded and bent to write *Self-actualization* in their notebooks or on their laptops.

At the end of the class, Nicolo packed his computer and book into his bag and nodded to Carla, whose untidy notes, he saw, filled less than a quarter of a page. Her handwriting varied in size, starting small and growing larger, and it sloped down the page. She nodded back and jammed the pages containing her notes into the pocket of her navy-blue peacoat.

"Thanks for the paper," she said, and then twisted her mouth in a manner that suggested a wry self-awareness. "See you next week, I guess," she added, and she reached and touched Nicolo's jacket just above his wrist once, lightly. She was close enough for Nicolo to smell her scent—like bread and flowers. There was something in the set of her head and shoulders that made her seem brave.

Nicolo walked the six blocks back to his parents' house, taking long strides through the thin, cold air of the dark January night, his computer bag bumping like an awkward companion against his side. He could smell a mass of snow in the northeast, yellow-toothed, unwashed and unruly, and he could hear the coming force of the storm worrying already like an advance scout through the skeletal branches of the trees that bordered the street—maple, oak, ash, poplar, beech. The heavy branches of the trees swayed in the swelling wind and the few dry leaves and seed pods that remained from the fall were stirred and tossed together, whispering and rattling, the percussion section of a reedy orchestra warming up. Dried stalks of last summer's grasses rustled and sighed near Nicolo's striding feet. Beside the walkway, massed banks of shrubs huddled like dark sheep butting heads against the forward eddies of the wind. Every forty or fifty feet, a cement path led away from the sidewalk straight up past banked snow to a modest front door with a half-pie window inset at eye level. Some houses still had their Christmas lights up and lighted—white, red, green, one house done up in startling pink.

Nicolo swung his arms and as he lengthened his stride had a sudden sense of how free he was, compared to the fixed immobility of the rooted plants and paths and houses and even compared to the frost-encased cars—domestic, worthy, faithful—parked along the quiet curb. He walked down the avenues, and brittle ice and rime cracked underfoot, smashed by the tread of his boots into islands and continents that would reform and refreeze all through the long hours of the night. He could feel his warm blood coursing in his swinging arms and hands, and his heart stir—every physical part of him weighted, tested, dependable—against the gravity and chill of the late, late evening. He heard and felt his own pulse throbbing to the steady metronome of his heart. He felt a sense of joy, of membership in, even a feeling of ownership over this still, northern slice of the city, these streets settled by people who had come from a sunny, dry, hot place, a new geography turned by their naive and faithful labours into something useful and enduring. He passed a small row of stores, paused, turned his head and blinked. The sign for Catanzaro Grocery was no longer lit. It had been turned upside-down in its frame, signalling the failure of the business, an unexpected reminder of the fragility of all human endeavours.

When he reached the corner of Ross Avenue and Emerald Crescent, Nicolo stopped again. He could see his house toward the far end of the block. The hour was late. His parents had gone to bed. Their bedroom window was dark, the lights out, their curtains drawn. Enzo's car was missing from the driveway; he would have come home from school, eaten dinner, got in a few hours of sleep or study, and then left for the factory where he worked three nights a week from eight in the evening until three in the morning. Nicolo let himself into the silent house, put his bag and keys on the desk in his bedroom, and went into the kitchen with his psych textbook under his arm, drawn by the dim glow of the yellow light that could just be seen through the small, fogged, heat-etched glass window in the oven door. On the centre rack of the barely warm oven was a dinner plate covered with a damp linen towel, and under the towel was a plate of pasta with garlic and bread crumbs cooked in olive oil, fava beans and braised fennel. He turned off the oven and set the plate in the centre of a placemat that had been left out for him, with fork and knife, on the kitchen table. He sprinkled the pasta with several spoonfuls of grated cheese from a metal container in the fridge, and he read ahead into the next chapter while he ate his dinner, chewing slowly. Suddenly too tired even to let the water run cold, he filled a glass and drank and then he placed his dishes in the sink and went down the hall to clean his teeth. The furnace rumbled companionably and warmed air rose silently from floor grates toward the ceiling. Food. Water. Shelter. A sense of belonging. What else would a person need to be able to climb from these up the steep slope to the apex of Professor Werner's triangle?

Inside her bed, down the hallway, Nonna is asleep and dreaming. Her dreams are liquid and lucid and they have the heavy weight and swelling undulations of the ocean. In her dream, her grandmother Rosa Catterina has died and the women of Arduino have laid out the thin old woman on the battered kitchen table dressed in her long white nightgown and with a blue knitted cap fitted around her head from which all the flesh seems already to have fallen away. They have borrowed four candelabras from the church and have placed them on the floor, one at each corner of the table to remind the mourners to keep their chairs well back in order to leave room for the unseen dead, who are known to be not so unlike us: they rush to visit the newly dead, to pay their own cold condolences and in hope of forming new alliances that might be useful in the afterworld. The flames redden the faces of the mourners, and cast the shadows of giants on the room's four walls. The shadows stretch up to the ceiling and merge with a century of soot.

Nonna is a girl again, three years old, and small and bony as a kid goat. She is not yet Nonna, but Filomena. Her mother calls her Mina-mia—the mother who will die in childbirth in another two months, a stillborn daughter stuck fast behind the bones of her pelvis which will refuse to soften to grant the insistent infant passage. Filomena has crept unseen underneath the table. Looking up, she can see the rough underside, on which the marks of her grandfather's axe are visible, and, extending from one end, toward the fire, her grandmother's feet, narrow and as icy blue as the surface of winter milk. She stretches up one hand to touch her grandmother's foot. She wants to know if the toes are as cold as they look. Why have they left the poor woman's feet bare, with no shoes or stockings? Reaching, she strikes her forehead on the underside of the hard table and bursts into startled tears.

"Hear how the little one mourns," the women all exclaim, a collective, indivisible sound like the throaty, fluttering coos of doves roosting warmly together.

"*Poverina.* Look. See how she grieves. Such a good and loving child."

Nonna's girl-heart swells in protest—no one has remembered to feed her her dinner, no one has come to comfort her, no one understands her. They are confusing her with their praise. Forlorn and misunderstood, she cries harder. Hands reach down all around her, from all sides of the table, offering her consolation in the form of biscotti and sugared almonds and dusky black figs that have been soaked in wine, like small, tough dried hearts reconstituted, and even thumb-sized glasses of *limoncello.*

"Leave off crying," the women say. "*A ciancere 'u muortu, su' lacrime perse.*" Tears for the dead are wasted. "*Dopo il dolce vien l'amaro.*" There will be time for bitterness after the sweets are finished.

But even in the thick cloud of her dream, Nonna under-stands that this dream must be one of her mind's senseless and random excursions and not a true memory. *Dopo il dolce vien l'amaro* is a real *proverbo*, but it doesn't belong in this story. It is something that might instead be said to a young girl at risk of falling for her sweetheart's pressing flattery, at risk of the rancour that will almost certainly follow if she falls for his too-urgently pressed and sweetly fleeting love.

CHAPTER NINE

As it happened, everyone in Nicolo's family went out after dinner on Tuesday night the following week. Massimo played bocce at the Colombo Lodge in one of its five raked basement lanes on Tuesday evenings. Enzo had been called in to work to cover for someone who had phoned in sick with the flu. Nicolo had decided to sign up for Sue Hopewell's cooking classes along with Monica; the classes were starting that night and would run for the next six weeks. Paola surprised everyone by announcing at the dinner table that she had decided to go to a public open house to be held that evening at the community centre to discuss the future of the landfill a kilometre east of the house. She would take Nonna with her.

"An outing," Paola said firmly. "She doesn't get out enough, especially in winter. She's in the house all day. She should be able to understand what's going on in the community, in the city, some of it, anyway. What goes on affects her as well as the rest of us. She lives here too."

Nonna nodded severely and folded her hands in her lap. Before dinner, she had put on her second-best dress and the black shoes that she wore to funerals. Paola had explained to her that they were going out and that they might even have a chance to state their minds. After years of promises that the nearby landfill would be permanently closed, the neighbourhood was humming with rumours that the garbage dump might instead be expanded. Paola's eyes narrowed at the thought.

"It's not just our trash," she pointed out at the dinner table, gesturing with her fork. "The whole city brings its garbage up here, dumps it and then turns around and forgets about it. It suits them perfectly. Out of sight, out of mind. But we've done our part. It's time for some other community to take its turn. Marissa Stefanio down the street was saying that what we should do is take over the highway and force all those trucks to turn around and dump it all on the grass in front of city hall for a few days, and see how they like it when they have to live on top of it like we do." She speared a meatball and pointed it toward Massimo. "It's not right. You know it isn't. But no one's doing anything about it."

Massimo nodded. He had learned as a barber the art of signalling support, even encouragement, without himself committing either way to whatever cause was under discussion.

Sue's class was held on familiar territory, in Nicolo's

old high school, in the large tiled room with its six home-ec kitchens where in grade ten Nicolo had learned how to make chicken soup and spaghetti Bolognese and tea biscuits. Thirty or so students perched on stools in the lecture area, men and women in their early twenties or a bit older, roughly the same number of each. Many of them showed evidence of a lifetime of generous eating; they balanced and shifted on their stools with varying degrees of awkward self-consciousness. Nicolo took one of the few remaining places, near the front of the classroom. Sue was already standing behind the demonstration counter. She smiled at Nicolo.

"Great to see a familiar face," she said.

Nicolo ducked his head and nodded.

Sue glanced at the clock and then walked briskly around to the back of the room to close the door. Monica dashed in just as it was about to close. She hurried to the front of the room and sat down beside Nicolo.

"I couldn't get the kids to settle," she whispered hoarsely. "What'd I miss?"

"Nothing so far," Nicolo reassured her.

Sue had returned to the front of the room. She cleared her throat and began to speak. "As I am certain you all know, there are many ways to pack on weight," she began. "Unfortunately, there's only one way to lose it and that is to adopt a healthy diet and lifestyle, one that will, over time, ensure we attain and then maintain an ideal weight. This is more sustainable than the kind of get-thin-quick schemes that advertisers spin, the ones that tell us all we need to do is modify what we eat drastically but temporarily so that we shed weight rapidly, only to have it all come back as soon as we go off the diet. How many of you have had that happen, lost weight on a diet, and then gained it back again as soon as you revert to your old, evil ways?"

Many hands were raised, and then lowered, Monica's among them.

"Can anyone name a diet they've been on that had this effect?" Sue prompted.

No one spoke.

"Anyone?"

"The grapefruit diet," someone volunteered. There was a ripple of laughter.

Sue turned and wrote GRAPEFRUIT with a marker on a portable whiteboard that she had wheeled to the front of the room.

"The hard-boiled egg diet."

Sue wrote HARD-BOILED EGG on the board.

"The South Beach diet," someone said.

"The Scarsdale diet."

"Fasting."

"Bingeing and purging."

Sue wrinkled her forehead. She did not write this one on the board.

"Dr. Atkins."

"The Hollywood Miracle diet."

"G.I. diet."

"Jenny Craig."

"Weight Watchers."

"The caveman diet; you can only eat what you're willing to kill yourself with your bare hands."

Everyone laughed.

Sue wrote these suggestions on her whiteboard.

"What we are going to try to do is forget about diets and focus instead on eating properly by preparing a few wholesome meals together," she said. With her marker, she made a circular motion, a gathering lasso in the air, as if pulling everyone in the classroom together. Sue picked up a stack of photocopied pages and began to hand them around the room.

"Here are today's recipes. You'll see that we're going to make cheese and vegetable–stuffed tortillas, peach-blueberry crisp, apricot-ricotta muffins, and decaf mocha lattes—the kinds of foods and drinks that you might make for a breakfast or brunch with a few of your friends on a weekend get-together. Please divide yourselves into groups of four or five at a workstation, and you will be able to follow along with me as I demonstrate. You'll find all the ingredients and other materials already set out for you. Everything should be labelled, just in case you've never seen a manual egg-beater before." Sue held one up and spun its handle vigorously. "If you are missing anything, any equipment or ingredient, or have any questions or run into trouble, just call out and I'll come over to your workstation."

In his group, Nicolo was assigned the task of grating cheddar cheese, slicing dried apricots, measuring rice and grinding coffee beans. He tried to imagine his mother or Nonna making any of Sue's colourful, balanced, up-to-the-minute recipes, but he could not. Would he be preparing food like this—wholesome meals in modest portions, meant to be quickly made and swiftly eaten—if he was living on his own, or married? he wondered. Both possibilities were blanks in his imagination, at best vague and generic, not unpleasantly imprecise but mysteriously evasive.

Several blocks away, at the Future of Our Community Landfill meeting, Paola and her mother-in-law were also, as it happens, watching a kind of cooking lesson. A brisk woman with her hair in a ponytail and a matching swinging, jaunty manner—she had something of Sue's upbeat energy, but tuned to a higher pitch—had just introduced herself as "Cara Cooper, Certified General Public and Government Relations Consultant."

Cara started by inviting the fifteen "interested citizen participants" who were gathered in rows in folding chairs to take turns introducing themselves. When each of them stated his or her name, Cara wrote it on a name tag with a bright blue border preprinted with "Hello! My name is _____," and then she pressed the sticky tag onto the citizen's chest. "Paula" she wrote on Paola's name tag, and then turned to Nonna.

"Mrs. Pavone," Nonna said.

Cara hesitated, but capitulated without argument. She wrote "Mrs. Pavoney" on the tag. Nonna took the tag from her and applied it firmly upside-down on the sagging front of the black cardigan that she had put on over her dress.

After ensuring that everyone had a name tag, Cara went to stand behind a large table covered with bowls and bags and packages. "Next," she said. "I thought it might be useful to provide you with an overview of what a landfill actually is and the way in which it is put together. I think you will find that this little demonstration will answer many, many of the questions you might have had."

Cara reached into one of several large plastic shopping bags.

"We have here all that we need to make our very own working landfill demonstration model. One pre-made pie crust. Four pudding cups, two caramel, two vanilla. One bottle of chocolate syrup. A bag of licorice twists. Spearmint candy sticks. A package of chocolate cookies that I've already crushed into crumbs. A bag of green sprinkles." Cara assembled these on a table.

Paola exchanged glances with her mother-in-law. She was baffled herself, not sure where this was all leading, and curious as to what Nonna was making of this.

Nonna nodded toward Cara, stiff-necked, and reset her shoulders almost imperceptibly. Her name tag began to curl inward from the top edges.

"Now, we will have to use our imaginations here just a little bit. We are all going to try to think of the pie shell as representing the bottom of the area where the brand-new landfill will go. Specially trained engineers, graduates from top universities around the world, prepare the entire area carefully, and then they line it with clay in a process that is a bit like when you put a pie shell into a pan in your own home." Cara placed the pie shell in a glass pan. She pressed it down on all sides.

"So that any groundwater underneath our new landfill will be safely protected, the engineers line the clay shell with a special thick layer of heavy plastic. I am going to cover our crust with this chocolate syrup and that will represent this special impermeable plastic liner."

Paola glanced sideways at Nonna, who leaned back in her chair and folded her arms across her chest while Cara squirted chocolate noisily out of the bottle into the pie pan.

Nonna's name tag peeled away from her sweater, rolled itself into a sticky cylinder on her lap, and then fell to the floor. Better without it, thought Nonna, who noticed more than most people believed. Names should not be shared before trust, only afterward.

"As material is added to a landfill, a kind of juice is created as rain and moisture percolates through the deposits of material inside. This liquid has a special name: leachate. Leachate can't get through the plastic liner or the clay, but it has to go somewhere, so pipes are put in by our team of engineers and these pipes collect and pump the leachate to the surface, where it can be whisked away in special container trucks. As you can see, these black licorice sticks that I've brought are hollow inside. They can be our collection pipes." Cara snipped the licorice into shorter sections with a sharp pair of scissors, and arranged the pieces on end inside the pie plate.

Nonna's expression changed from guarded to bewildered—a garbage dump made of candy and sugar?

"Over time, through natural processes, the material we bring to the landfill begins to break down, and a side effect—an added bonus if you like—is the production of gas. Methane gas. Your neighbourhood landfill, you'll be pleased to know, is completely state-of-the-art, and so this gas doesn't go to waste. Instead it is carefully vented and collected and used to produce power, many megawatts of natural electricity, which the city uses for the benefit of all. How about if we use these long stripy spearmint candy sticks to represent our methane collection pipes?" Cara arranged the candy carefully, and then pulled the covers off the pudding cups and dumped the pudding into the pie shell on top of the chocolate syrup, licorice and candy.

"This pudding represents the material we bring to the landfill in trucks every day. It really doesn't look very attractive, does it." Cara stood back so that everyone could see.

Nonna's eyes widened and she began to chew on her lower lip.

"But, not to worry; it doesn't look like that for long! A thick layer of good, clean topsoil is placed over our waste, in layers, like a cake. I'll sprinkle these cookie crumbs on top and smooth it down like so." Cara patted a thick coating of crumbs evenly across the pie dish.

Nonna wasn't able to watch any more. She closed her eyes and pinched her lips together.

"When the landfill is full—and that can take many, many years—another plastic liner is placed on top. This prevents water that occurs naturally in the environment—rain and snow and sleet and hail—from leaking into the site and making more 'juice' or leachate. We'll use another coat of chocolate syrup to cover the top of our landfill to protect it from the elements."

Paola reached over and patted Nonna's hands, which were now clenched together in a single fierce knot in Nonna's lap. A rare gesture of solidarity between them.

"The last part of the landfill is the grass that is planted on top. These green sprinkles"—Cara shook a container of candies over the top of the accumulation of chocolate and candy —"represent our approach to the final stage in the life cycle of a landfill. Contouring and landscaping is the finishing touch and is all that is needed to turn our neighbourhood landfill into an attractive, useful community park available to all."

Cara reached into her front pocket—she was wearing a pale blue smock-like garment over her sweater—and pulled out a handful of small plastic figures, which she placed on top of the sprinkles. A pink mother holding a white baby. A brown-skinned, black-haired father with a pipe. A blonde girl in a red dress holding a skipping rope. A curly haired boy with a black-and-white spotted dog at his feet. Cara pressed down firmly on the top of their rigid heads so that their feet were held fast in the pudding and sprinkles.

Nonna turned, her mouth close to Paola's ear. "You do. You say something," she said. Her elbow pressed into Paola's side.

Paola rose to her feet. She was shaking.

"What about the birds, eh?" She opened her mouth again, but no more words appeared to be willing to be spoken. She closed her mouth and sat down, heavily, and the hinges of her chair squeaked.

Nonna glared at her, disappointed.

"Yes, there will be birds, of course," said Cara. "And many other forms of wildlife too. You will find that after the eventual closure of any landfill the entire spectrum of flora and fauna and animals and plants will be represented."

Paola stood up again, surprising herself. "No, I mean now." She could feel the burn of Nonna's white-hot thoughts and something of Nonna's outrage spilled over into her as well. Such a thing had never happened before. There were more words and they came tumbling out. "There are hundreds, no, there are thousands of them. Seagulls. They're like rats, dirty, grey, and they're everywhere. Worse than rats. All over the neighbourhood. Why do you think are they way up here? So far from the water? They come for the garbage." She had more that she wanted to say. She wanted to convey the fullness of her indignation. She was riven with frustration that her words were so few and so feeble. She had no official title and no swinging ponytail and no props. At her side Nonna nodded.

Cara frowned. "Yes," she said. "Birds of all kinds are a natural part of the eco-system that springs up around a landfill."

"And there are actual rats, too."

Thank heavens. Someone else, a man at the back of the room, had spoken. Paola fell into her chair. Cara folded her arms across her chest.

"And the smell," said a woman. "It's everywhere. It's foul. The smell of rotting garbage. You can't get away from it. It gets into everything. The clothes on the line. We can't sit in our garden. We have to keep the windows shut. Even in the summer—*especially* in the summer."

"Every region should have to deal with its own garbage. That would be fair."

"Many measures are taken to manage and diminish the risk of undesirable odours," said Cara. "And in fact, recorded complaints are down by well over one-hundred percent from five years ago."

"What is the effect of this stuff, this leachate or whatever it's called, on the groundwater?" asked a man. "Where does it go? What's in it?" Cara's face wore an expression of determined patience.

"And what about our children? The seagulls scavenge at the dump and then dive-bomb them in the schoolyard. My daughter had one land and peck on the ponytail holder in her hair. They're filthy, vermin. Like the woman said, nothing more than rats on wings."

"We've taken the city's garbage up here long enough. We're fed up."

"When is this thing going to close for good?"

"We've all heard the rumours. It's not going to close, is it. Is that the plan? Is that what this is all about?"

"We bought some bottles of wine two years ago to celebrate closing this place for good. That wine will be vinegar before we ever get to drink it."

Nonna stood up. "*Tuttu 'u munnu è paise,*" she said.

Cara turned and stared at her. "Pardon me?"

"*Tuttu 'u munnu è paise.* Is all one and is all the same country." Nonna spoke firmly. Then she nodded once to indicate that this was all she had to say.

Paola opened her mouth to explain, but closed it again without speaking. She knew what Nonna meant—that it was important to treat the entire world with the respect due to one's hometown—but there was no simple way she could think of to convey this message to the others. Once again, she felt thwarted and baffled, and she realized, looking at Nonna, how much more frustrating this must be for her mother-in-law, who had almost no one left who could understand her, to whom she could make her needs and wants and fears known. She reached her arm around Nonna's shoulder, surprised at how much frailer the woman felt than she appeared. Nonna's flesh was soft on her bones, and her bones felt insubstantial, as if the years were hollowing them out, making them ready for flight.

Cara clapped her hands together, once, twice, her expression intensely pleasant. "I think," she said, "I think that you are all ready for the second stage of this citizen's orientation and information program. I would like now to extend a personal invitation to each and every one of you to take a real-live tour of the actual landfill in operation. Tours are being offered to interested participants completely free of charge for a limited time only. For your convenience and at your option, fully guided tours will take place on various dates, all of which are listed on the sign-up sheets at the front of the room. Please have a look at the list on your way out, and put your name, telephone number and address on the sheet beside the time that suits you best. Please rest assured that all of us here at the transfer station will endeavour to meet all of your scheduling needs."

Paola signed her name and Nonna's on the schedule, and then took Nonna by the elbow and guided her outside to the car. After Paola started the engine, she had to crank down the window and clear the windscreen, which was partly obscured by sheets of paper that had managed to escape over the chain-link fence from the landfill into the parking lot. She glanced at them—someone's printed resumé, scrawled with handwritten editing comments in red ink, grimy from contact with who-knew-what in the landfill and with the powdery outline of the sole of a boot on the back of the last page. She didn't like to drop the papers back outside onto the pavement, so she folded them together and dropped them onto the floor in the back seat.

"*Sporchezza,*" sniffed Nonna. Filthy.

CHAPTER TEN

Although Nicolo's psychology textbook is large and heavy, it has developed a habit of travelling in the house to odd spots. He has found it in the basement powder room that no one uses, on the floor beside the rubber plant in the living room, and beside the wood bin on the small covered porch at the back of the house. On its cover is a deeply shaded picture of a striking young person, although the image has been created so that it is difficult to tell whether it is a man or woman. His or her hair has been cut short or pulled back, and the features and clothing are shadowy and indistinct, so the sex is impossible to discern. This person's large, red, stylized heart is shown, as if it has been scooped out of the chest and pinned on to the front of the black, velvety textured, collarless shirt like a medieval blazon, and it is divided like a puzzle or heraldic shield into irregular quadrants, which are labelled via a dim dotted line *a*, *b*, *c* and *d*. Due to some transparency in the way the artist has depicted the person's brow, the brain can be seen as well and it is also divided into segments, marked *i*, *ii*, *iii*, and so on. No key, however, is provided. The image might be symbolic, Nicolo suspected, of how psychology seeks to understand the human heart and brain, but he had not quite resolved this, and he still believed that it might be possible that more advanced students could, if asked, tell him the names of the divisions in the picture and their function. Nicolo understood too, although not yet clearly, that his own heart and mind were divided in a not dissimilar manner, and that he was sometimes one thing and sometimes another. An example of this is how he felt about still living at his parents' house in his early twenties.

Living at home signified, within his community, that he was a dutiful son to his parents, a good grandson to his nonna. But he is teased about it at work. James at the front desk calls him not "Nicolo" or "Nick," but "Momma's Boyo," passing it off as a nickname and not ill-intended, but there is more than a lick of malice in the way he says it. Nicolo sees that there is something stunted in James, not just his height, but something else, something he reads as a historical, irredeemable lack of being treasured when being treasured was important—and when is it not?—and so Nicolo doesn't rise to James's derision, but pretends to take it as casually as it is ostensibly offered. His client Clarissa teases him too about living at home, but gently and kindly. She is genuinely curious about how this must be for him.

"What if you want to bring someone in, you know, at night at the end of a date?" she asked him one day. "Isn't that awkward? Could she come down afterward, in the morning, and have coffee at the kitchen table with you and your parents and share the newspaper and eat some toast and talk about the weather?"

Nicolo laughed. "I can't imagine that ever happening," he said. "I just wouldn't do that to them. My mother would probably be okay. I think she'd just pour out another cup of coffee. But my dad would be stunned. He wouldn't know where to look or what to say. And my nonna would rush out to find a priest, drag him in by his collar and have us married off right there in the kitchen. You can't imagine the drama."

"So how do you manage, then?" Clarissa persisted.

"You remember, honey, how they did it in Italy." The judge had finished his dogged twenty minutes on the recumbent bike and, mopping his neck, joined them on the mats. "We saw all those young people in Florence, remember how it was, along that road up on the hill beside Fort Belvedere?" He sat on a mat and stretched gingerly in the direction of his toes while describing to Nicolo a walk that he and Clarissa had taken during their two-week honeymoon after their mid-September marriage. An evening stroll had taken them past a long line of cars parked at the side of the road—small, older-model Fiats, Alfa Romeos and Lancias—many with newspapers taped over their rolled-up windows, some of them rocking gently from side to side or back and forth, the closed windows humid with breath. He and Clarissa had smiled at each other and blushed. He had wrapped his hand around hers, had drawn her slender hand deep into the pocket of his new brown suede jacket that she had helped him choose in the market; he had never bought anything before from a market stall. He remembered that he had been grateful for the support of the high, firm bed in the middle of their overpriced room with a pizza slice of a view of the old city, a *letto matrimoniale* but a little envious too of the young couples hidden from sight behind the newspapers and tape, wistful for their supple, valiant, semi-public exuberance. He recalled also the steady warmth of Clarissa's hand inside his jacket pocket; he had been so lonely before meeting her, although he hadn't known it until she spoke to him at a dinner party twenty months after his wife Linda passed away of a cancer that had worked quickly and ruthlessly—it was only three months, ninety-one days from a diagnosis delivered in a manner that left no doubts and no possibility of deliverance, to the dimmed hospital room in which Linda's long breaths slowed and then fell into silence. At this party, Clarissa had been seated beside him, and as he fumbled with his hosts' good cutlery, their excellent silver fork and heavy knife, over lamb and roasted parsnips, she turned her face like the sun toward his and reached over and touched his wrist, and asked him not what he did, but how he did it, how he could ever bring himself to decide, how he determined which actions deserved censor or reward, what punishment to mete out and for which crimes, to whom he would give the benefit of a second or third or fourth chance, how he knew who had done what, how he managed to live with any mistakes that might have been made. He hadn't understood how frozen he had become, how hoary, how crusted over in that soul's chill, that enduring winter, before she turned her beams toward him at that party, where everyone was chatting and where his friends' wine and food were plentiful and excellent, and he began, right there, in the centre of that noisy, candlelit dining room, first to speak and then miraculously to thaw into this belated, unlooked for, luminously redemptive spring.

In bed sometimes, embracing this new, prized wife, he summoned up images of the Italian couples in their parked cars. They were shorter, overall, the Italians, he had noticed. Maybe natural selection had somehow favoured the genes of those who could disrobe and accomplish the act and then recompose themselves within the confines of compact places. His mind would float, trying to determine how they could possibly manage it: front passenger seat tipped back, accordioned across the back seat, kneeling? Who crouched over whom, breasts or penis or stomach or buttocks suspended? If you could make it work, it could be, perhaps—he could almost appreciate this—quite thrilling. The accommodating give and take of the suspension of the vehicle, the scent of leather, perhaps, in the better class of vehicles, the belts and constraints and compromises could be . . . And at this point his concentration was usually lost in what he felt simultaneously as both a dark implosion and a bright explosion. Small in scale, of course. He had few illusions of the range and likely effects of his aging love craft, but obvious nonetheless to Clarissa, who would pull him closer to her and whisper "My darling, my love" into the greying margins of his hair. He would rise afterward and stride into the bathroom to urinate, and his body, out of pride, out of joy, would produce what it otherwise could not, a loud, thick, ringing stream, as thick as a rope, as warm as his heart and as fragrant as straw, resounding inside the bowl like the pealing of a church bell on the day of resurrection.

Now Clarissa creased her elegant nose and laughed. "Not Nicolo," she protested. "Not our Nicolo. He would never do anything like that."

She had, as it happened, made love many times in the back seat of a very small car with no heater and few comforts during her last year of high school, and she remembered the inconvenience of it, never quite knowing how to arrange her limbs or his, cracking her head or knee or ankle bone against glass or metal or gearshift, the murmured requests—"if you could just"—and apologies—"oops, sorry"—and the difficulties when the act was finished: wrinkled, disordered clothes, no ability to wash, no place to stretch out and luxuriate if all had gone well. Afterward, a sock or panties would always elude discovery, only to be shaken out of a pair of jeans or from the sleeve of a sweater at home that night or a few days later.

She had fewer romantic illusions than Alden did. She had been the only child of a single mother and had had no father nor husband nor son before Alden, and so he was everything to her. She tried to keep this from him because she didn't want him to be unduly burdened by the component of her love that was hunger, that was pure need. He had fallen in love with her and she recognized that his love had cured her of something that she couldn't describe. It wasn't simply that she had been lonely before she met him. It had been something deeper than loneliness, more fundamental, an ache in her bones. She felt when she looked back as if she had been starving for him.

Nicolo's first understanding of the anatomy, the plumbing, the tubes and protuberances of sex had come from a series of drawings his older brother Enzo learned at recess at school and reproduced, inaccurately, out of scale, in crayon on scrap paper for his two younger brothers at home. Five-year-old Enzo paid no attention at all; he saw only scribbles. Nicolo at seven was entranced. He watched Enzo draw a line like a forking branch inside an arching heart-shaped outline.

"What's this?" he challenged, and Nicolo correctly read from Enzo's grinning excitement that this was a sort of illicit riddle.

"A bare-naked woman bending over," Enzo announced without really waiting for Nicolo to try to guess. He spat in his excitement, his mouth wide.

Nicolo, caught up in his brother's giddy glee, rolled around with him on the floor giggling and repeating, "A bare-naked woman." "Bending over." "Showing her bare bum."

There were others, drawings of long fried eggs with three yolks of different sizes that were really "between a woman's legs," and many variations on fatly inflated sticks, raised up like hammers overtop of paired bulbous circles, or plunging into the curious fried eggs.

"This is how they do it when they do it!" cried Enzo.

He almost shuddered beneath the weight of all that he knew, at the splendour of his drawings, and at his generosity, he at nine imparting to Nicolo, who was entirely undeserving, such expansive knowledge of these, the greatest mysteries of the grown-up world. He himself hadn't had access to such opportunities at Nicolo's young age.

And then, several weeks later that same spring, the boys were outside knocking a fraying tennis ball around with their hockey sticks when a yellow dog came loping along their street, a stray with bony hips and matted fur and no collar. They had never seen it before and didn't see it ever again afterward. The lone dog came toward them and then, nervous of the sticks the boys held, hurried its pace, veered wide and galloped past, but not so quickly that the boys missed seeing clearly a swollen purple object, its *thing*, knocking against the hair and bone of its hind legs.

A store of new words was learned over the next couple of years, schoolyard words, street words, rude words, acquired from dubious sources, known to be not allowed, not even half understood. But the discovery by Nicolo and his brothers of the magazines at the back of Massimo's beloved and carefully kept barbershop, concealed under the sink behind a stack of towels, was vastly greater in scale than any of these. The boys were eleven, eight and five or so, and they had been left at the closed, locked store for a couple of hours during a snowy Sunday afternoon while their parents visited a neighbour who was in hospital following surgery, her head shaved, black-edged stitches showing the place where an as-yet-unanalyzed polyp had been removed from behind her ear—certainly not a sight to which the boys should be exposed. To keep them occupied and out of trouble, they had been given soft rags and paste, and told that they should dust the baseboards and polish the chrome of the barber chairs and the stainless-steel taps and sinks. The three of them made a cursory job of this chore and then began an unsatisfactory game of hide-and-seek. The shop was small and there were too few places to hide. Only younger Enzo could fit in the cupboard that concealed the pipes underneath the sink at the back of the store, and when he was pulled out by the collar of his shirt, the magazines came sliding out with him.

Young Enzo took no interest in the magazines; he was in the thrall of the comics that were kept in plain sight on a table at the front of the shop. There were a dozen or so of them and the boys had leafed through them so often that the comic books were as soft and limp as cotton. Enzo had committed to memory the main action, and was now studying the background details: the licence plates on the cars, the clothes that the parents wore, the books on bookcases with their indecipherable titles, the signs on stores, and the shape and colour of the food dished out at the school cafeteria or at the restaurant where the characters went for milkshakes and hamburgers.

Nicolo and older Enzo were, on the other hand, keenly interested in the magazines from under the sink. There were ten or a dozen of them, every page filled with drawings and cartoons, almost all of which had naked women in them, surrounded by jokes and stories and letters. This was another world entirely, one in which women seemed to exist solely so that they could display their ample breasts and thighs, and plunge plumply into bed with any man that happened to be near—their neighbours, bosses, co-workers, and with mechanics, dentists and—especially—door-to-door salesmen. These women wore tight sweaters and short skirts, or bikini tops and cut-off jeans, and they had eye makeup and lipstick on even when they were doing something normal, such as washing the dishes or shopping or driving a car. All of these activities led to the same thing—*it*, in bed or in the back seat of a car or on couches.

For the first half-hour, Enzo and Nicolo read two or three magazines together, side by side on their stomachs on the floor. But then Enzo complained. "You're too slow," he said. He was the faster reader, and didn't seem as interested as Nicolo was in puzzling out the more mysterious pictures.

Enzo took one of the fatter magazines and climbed with it up on to one of the high swivelling barber chairs.

After another half-hour of reading, Nicolo began to feel an ache in his stomach, as if he had eaten too much candy. His eyes felt raw with gazing on bras and panties and breasts and legs and hair. When he closed his eyes to rest them, he saw the same images against a spangled black background: women in all positions enticing the attention of the cartoon men and of himself, Nicolo, surely at best an unintended viewer.

He pulled himself up and returned the magazines in a jumble to the back of the cupboard from which they had fallen, hearing in the same moment the rhythm of familiar voices and the dull sound of approaching footsteps.

The bell above the front door of Massimo's barbershop jangled sharply, once, twice. Nicolo slammed the cupboard door shut and slid in his stocking feet toward the front of the store. What had Enzo done with the magazine he had been reading? Nicolo looked and could see its outline pressing against the striped pattern on the inside of Enzo's T-shirt.

His parents and nonna noticed nothing unusual, it seemed; they were preoccupied by Marcella's illness, and by the late hour and the need to get the three boys home and fed and to bed. Younger Enzo knew enough not to say a word about what his brothers had been reading, or perhaps his blissful hour in the pastel streets and homes and school grounds of Riverdale had displaced any memories of the pictures he had glimpsed in those other magazines; it was even possible that their seedy quality had escaped his notice. The magazine that had been stashed hurriedly inside older Enzo's shirt found a permanent home rolled up inside the heat register in his bedroom, attached to the underside of the metal slats with two wide yellow rubber bands.

Massimo had acquired earlier that year a new fellow barber at the shop. Vito Greco, the cousin of a cousin, had been sent out from Italy when word reached Arduino of the loss of Guido Bianco at age forty-eight of a heart attack no more than twenty minutes after Friday evening dinner with his wife. (She had cooked his favourite meal: polenta baked in a slow oven with cheese, tomato sauce made from their own tomatoes, and slices of hard-boiled eggs, a salad of onions and bitter escarole from their garden, several slices of rosy melon and a few overripe black figs recently rescued from the predations of wasps and birds, a small post-prandial glass of wine sweet enough for the communion table and a handful of anise-flavoured biscotti;

when he drew his last, abruptly broken breath, Guido Bianco was sated, drowsy and contented.) Guido had been Massimo's partner from the earliest days of the shop. The two of them, thin, young, confident, too green to know any better, opened Continental Barber in the first year after they arrived from Italy. Their business thrived from the start and both were able to send for their families the following year. Language had never been an impediment. Their clientele was so close to one hundred percent Italian immigrants that it was almost exclusively Italian and Italian-accented English that could be heard above the sound of snipping scissors and buzzing razors.

Guido was Massimo's partner for over two decades. They spent close to seven thousand days working within two paces of each other, treading the same linoleum, swapping combs and scissors, razors, and rare bits of advice that were offered and accepted with mutual esteem. Massimo had the obdurate business sense that Guido lacked, and Guido had what Massimo did not, the gift of endless, fluid, ready conversation. Guido greeted everyone who entered the store with exuberant joy, strangers and friends. He teased and cajoled and bantered and debated, not just with his own customer in the chair before him but also with Massimo's customer, and with whoever happened to be waiting in the L-shaped arrangement of seats at the front of the shop. Guido's voice was the background music for the shop; it rolled and rumbled like that of an organ grinder, a percussive counterpoint to the cadence of the work that kept them on their feet, hands hovering above heads, from Monday mornings through Saturdays at five, filling the rare empty mid-afternoon half-hour, easing the passage of the many hours when the two chairs were so busy that the next man sat down on a seat that was still warm from the buttocks of the last and Massimo and Guido sometimes sprang into action without even waiting for instructions. Guido's effusiveness gave them energy, kept them in temper, and kept them moving; it provided the pacing and the tempo for the tending of head, beard, moustache, brow and even the furtive, coiling nasal hairs that were attacked and quelled quickly with a neat, curving swipe of the smallest of the shop's assortment of electric clippers. Other shops installed radios or television sets that were always kept tuned to news or sports, but at Continental Barber the commentary, sports, news, near news, frank gossip and personal interest stories were almost all delivered and moderated by Guido. Their customers came as much for this as for the haircuts, of which there were in truth no more than four or five elemental variations. The men enjoyed the unstintingly convivial atmosphere of the store. They felt a kind of privilege, understanding that Guido's rumbling eloquence, which had no apparent start or end, was provided entirely for their benefit. Even the youngest child of three or four in for his first haircut could see that Guido's loquaciousness was sustained and reinforced by Massimo's silence, which was broken only now and again by the briefest response, a "no" or a "sì" or the barest suggestion of a vowel-less syllable, seldom more, since only rarely was anything more needed.

Massimo and Guido both cut hair, but only Guido gave shaves, and he administered them the old-fashioned way, with scalding hot terry-cloth towels applied first and then shaving cream made from bar soap frothed lavishly in an earthenware bowl and applied with an ancient badger-hair brush. The shaves were administered with a Pearlx-handled straight razor that Guido sharpened on a carborundum hone and polished on a leather-and-linen strop that hung ready to hand from a swivelling hook on the wall.

Massimo had a trick he liked to play, when—and this happened rarely, so there was no risk that the joke would grow stale—Guido accidentally nicked a customer's neck with the razor's sharp blade, the smallest over- or under-calculation, from which a tiny, glistening bead of blood would emerge with Guido's reflection trembling in it, carmine, upsidedown. The customer would blanch and sit tremblingly still, or jump from the chair and launch into real or jocular curses, depending on his temperament. "Go, go get the poor guy a glass of water," Massimo would cry out to the other customers—his one, his only joke. "We got to check him out to see if maybe the water leaks out through the hole."

Guido's loss was more than a setback for Massimo. It called into question the future of Continental Barber itself, which had always been just the two of them. Guido had built the plywood counters and cabinets, fitted and painted the sliding cabinet doors with white enamel paint that had yellowed only slightly over the years, cut, placed and glued the pale blue melamine countertop, and bent and nailed in place the grooved metal band that edged the countertops. Massimo and Guido had chosen and laid the tiles, and had selected and paid for the two swivelling chairs with their red vinyl upholstery and nickel levers and knobs that moved them up and down and back and forward, as well as the electric red-white-and-blue striped barbershop pole that rotated out front and the lighted sign over the door. There was nothing in the store that Massimo had done alone or without Guido's counsel.

Three desolate weeks passed, during which the regular customers continued to come, although there were some who had to be turned away because there were too many for Massimo to handle alone and those who made it into the chair could get their usual trims and haircuts but no shaves. The shop had no jokes or music or teasing on offer, only the small, tragic percussion of a single pair of steel scissors snipping in the vast white noise of Massimo's disconsolate sighs. In the late afternoon of the third Saturday, Massimo finished the last customer an hour late, shook his head, switched off the lights and the sign and the pole, turned the faded red OPEN sign around on its chain to display the blue CLOSED side, went home and told Paola that maybe it was time for him to close out the lease. For a hundred and fifty dollars a week he could rent a chair instead at Joe's Custom Hairstyling four blocks down and across the street. None of his sons would become barbers; there was no good reason to preserve the business that he and Guido had built up.

Guido's widow Gianna was called on the phone and she came right over, pulling her black cardigan close across her chest with her left hand on which Guido's gold wedding band spun loose at the base of her fourth finger, inside her own, closest to her heart. She was adamantly against this proposal.

"I couldn't stand it, to see Continental gone," she told Massimo, her eyes dark and wet. She twisted her hands together. "It would've killed Guido to've known it would just close like that if he went. And you know what he thinks of Joe's. A clip joint, that's what he always called it. You've heard him yourself. A clip joint. He wouldn't't've wanted to see you there. You know he wouldn't't've."

She suggested instead that he give Vito a try—this young cousin of a cousin of a cousin she had heard about back home in Arduino. Vito was up to date, she said, on all the newest styles, and he was single and restless in his late twenties. An engagement had fallen through suddenly for unexplained reasons; the girl had been lovely apparently, and pure as the snow and from a good family and willing, and Vito was, as a result of this event and the fact that the girl had several brothers, anxious to get away. And so it was arranged. Vito's papers were expedited by younger Enzo, who was able to convince the immigration officials that Vito's unique tonsorial skills were not otherwise available in Canada. Trained in Milan, the fashion capital of the world, he said, stretching the truth by a few hundred kilometres. Several months later, as promised, Vito arrived at the store—very tall, very thin, his stomach carried forward like a young girl's, his Adam's apple prominent like a half-swallowed stone in his throat, his long black hair combed back and formed into ridges and furrows with gel, shadow-jawed, all quick dark angles—on a Friday in February (the darkest, wettest, coldest month) at nine-thirty in the morning, delivered to the glass front door of the barbershop by Gianna, who had offered him a bed and his meals until he could get on his feet. She had no children and had hopes that Vito might help diminish the emptiness of her house in a way that seemed otherwise entirely beyond her.

Vito lived up to Enzo's sales pitch. He was a skilful, meticulous barber. He had learned the craft in one of the alleys that reach out like the ribs of a fan from the harbour in Naples, where he had gone on his own at age sixteen to apprentice. He had started sweeping thick piles of hair from the floor made of yellow-veined, cracked marble—women of the neighbourhood would come and ask for a few fist-fuls of the sweepings, to sprinkle around their tomato plants to discourage the city's feral cats—becoming next a soaper, wetting and soaping customers' cheeks and necks for a senior barber to shave, and so on up through the strata from insignificant to second barber. Vito brought with him to Continental Barber his own long-bladed scissors, which he sharpened himself with a palm-sized whetstone, and a bur-nished aluminum comb for flat-top styles.

He proved to have the knack of it. He could smooth tight curls and mould them into sleek, shiny pompadours. He could contain the thickest head of hair into a formal, tidy shape, with properly squared-off sides and back. He adopted Guido's abandoned straight razor and delivered shaves with surgical exactitude. But Vito was brusque with the custom-ers, showing no inclination to engage with them or get to know them. He limited his attention strictly to the hair and whiskers that sprouted above their necks. He had no small talk or thoughts or opinions that he cared to share. Massimo thought at first that Vito was getting used to a new place, and then that he might be bored by the shop and its clientele and possibilities. He noticed that Vito's eyes seemed always to be darting toward the window, to the sidewalk and road outside where people and cars passed.

The only time Vito became animated was when the shop was visited by the sales representatives who peddled shampoos, conditioners, oils and soaps. Vito invited them in, all of them, offered them small glasses from the collection of bottles of bitter grappa and sweet anisette that he had installed in a cupboard under the sink at the back of the shop, tested creams and lotions and salves on the skin on the underside of his wrist, rolled up his sleeve and tried out multi-headed electric razors and super-sharp shears on the dark hair of his forearm or on his own thick, black moustache. Massimo and Guido had always turned the travelling sales reps politely away, declining even the samples they offered at no cost and no obligation. Both of them had been suspicious of anything that purported to be free and they had stayed loyal over the years to the original companies that had helped them start out by providing easy credit terms and lots of advice. Massimo worried too about the fact that the bylaw governing barbershops, which Paola had read closely and had summarized for him, expressly prohibited serving food or drink on the premises. However, he kept this concern to himself.

"Be patient with him," Nonna counselled Massimo at the dinner table at the end of Vito's first week. "*Nessuno nasce maestro.*" Everyone has to learn.

CHAPTER ELEVEN

Mario's fiancée, Angela Trapasso, invited Nicolo's mother and nonna to her wedding shower. The invitation arrived at the house in a pink and white envelope addressed to Filomena and Paola Pavone. Nicolo opened the envelope when he came in from work and he read the details aloud to his mother and Nonna. Nicolo had already mentioned Mario's engagement to them, but this announcement and summons to a celebration made it official. Nonna studied the envelope and card carefully. She cannot read, really—she is *analfabeta;* she had no school after age eight or nine and almost none before then—but she has an abiding respect for formal *documenti,* for notices, bills, correspondence and announcements that come in substantial envelopes embellished by stamps and labels. She was able to work her way through the names *Mario* and *Angela*, her forefinger tracing the letters as a guide for her eyes. She smiled and made a sign with her thumb over the names, invoking fortune, averting any possible domestic sorrow.

"It is very kind of them to include us," his mother said. "This Angela must be a thoughtful girl." She was leaning over Nicolo's shoulder to look at the invitation as she spoke and in her voice was slightly more than a shade of a suggestion, a reminder that if there were *one*, then it was very likely that there were other thoughtful girls out there. This was, however, offered lightly, not as advice exactly, but with a reticence that happened to be the exact size and shape of the advice unspoken, and at the same time his mother touched just as lightly the whorl of hair that sprang up from the centre of the crown of Nicolo's head. He is, she knows it, they all know it, the child that most fills her heart. *I jirita de' manu 'un su' tutti guali*—even the fingers of her hands are not the same. Not that she loves him more than she loves the others. Her love has no divisions or measures. It is just that her love for him affects her more profoundly. She is weaker in it, tender sometimes almost to the point of tears toward this middle child, this son who seemed just now unruddered, incomplete, when compared to his brothers. Lorenzo with his job and house and wife and two children already. Vincenzo with his studies and achievements and honours and gleaming prospects; Vincenzo would do well, would marry well, there was no doubt, perhaps would even become a judge one day. She delighted in having Nicolo still under the roof of the family home, but she was also concerned about him. She wondered from what direction the wind would come that would convey him forward. She was concerned about both Enzos too, but not so achingly. They seemed to her to have tougher shells, and in some way that she could not articulate, even to herself, less at stake. Most of all, she worried that Nicolo would end up alone. There was something in him that was sealed up, cautious, perhaps some lack of an understanding of his own worth, something that might hold him back from the kind of letting go or falling into trust that a relationship needed as a catalyst in order for it to kindle.

"Who will you invite to the wedding?" she asked, dipping in close to his ear, so close that she felt Nicolo shrug his shoulders in response.

She thought that she had spoken quietly enough so that only Nicolo could hear, but she saw from a small adjustment to the angle of Nonna's head that she had heard the question too.

This was a subject on which the two women disagreed entirely. Nonna had somehow concluded that Nicolo's path would take him alone into a different life, one far from the family, and that this fate would have to be submitted to. This seemed to Paola to be wilful if not cruel. Wilful since even to imagine it would make it more likely to happen. Cruel because the prediction struck at Paola's greatest fear, that one of her children would be lost to her. She had had no brother or sister, and few relatives apart from her parents, both dead before they were forty. Massimo and her sons, even Nonna, were her family in the way that few people understood. They were not her second family or simply the family she had married into, they were all she had and would ever have. She felt that Nicolo's marriage to a girl close by, someone from one of the families of the neighbourhood, could be all that it would take to divert the possible course of Nicolo's life away from Nonna's prediction. This was one of the reasons Paola was dismayed at Nicolo's decision to take a university course, foreseeing that this could expose him to possibilities that she might be unable to deflect. Although she had said nothing, she had begun to tidy away Nicolo's textbook when he left it out, putting it in places in the house where it could not be easily found but could not exactly be said to have been mislaid.

At the bakery on Saturday morning Nicolo brought up the subject of whether he should invite someone to Mario's wedding. He had thought that he might invite Carla from his psychology class. Frank and Paul had other ideas. They mentioned women they all knew, single or newly single women, women they had met at school or through work or in the neighbourhood. "Laura Bartucci." "Rita Tassone." "Tina Fiorino." "*Lahoor-a*," Frank said, using the Italian pronunciation. "She's the one. She's a nurse now. I wouldn't mind being her patient. That hair, those big eyes, those, you know—" Frank mimed Laura's upper figure with his hands. "Kind of quiet."

"I don't know about Laura," Paul said. "I ran into her a while back. She's got kind of heavy lately. You know how that happens? She's on the way to getting a big butt. Remember, her mother's big too. That's what she'll end up like, guaranteed. They always take after the mother, that's what you have to watch for. Rita's more fun, anyway. Not too serious. She's a legal secretary downtown. Someone like us has to grab her before one of those downtown guys gets her."

Mario didn't join in the discussion. His hands were busy, restlessly contorting a small rectangle of paper, the wrapper from a trio of sugar lumps, into a twisted red and white strand. "This stuff going on at the law school—what does your brother have to say about it?" he asked suddenly, changing the subject. He turned to look at Nicolo. His voice had taken on an odd tone.

Nicolo was startled. "What do you mean?"

"I saw something in the newspaper last night. A short article, you know, buried on page five or something like that," Mario said. "It said that a couple of the students out at the law school are in some kind of trouble, were caught putting down fake grades on their resumés. They're supposed to have given themselves As instead of Bs or Cs, something like that. And it said there are rumours other students might have been doing it too but haven't been caught yet. There's some kind of investigation going on about it. I just wondered, you know, if Enzo had mentioned it."

"It can't be Enzo's class," Nicolo said. "They haven't even got any marks yet. The first-year students don't write their exams until April." However, a tentacle of concern began to probe at something in the recesses of Nicolo's mind, a memory from an early morning back at the beginning of December, the sky still dark outside, cold pressing hard against the windows of the house, of coming across Enzo sitting at the kitchen table, studying in that way he had, wholly absorbed, his hands sheltering his brow, under the bright light that hung from the kitchen ceiling—for an exam or important test, it must have been, for that level of intensity. Something must have been at stake. Enzo, who left nothing to chance, reviewed every possible detail before his exams. He tried to remember how Enzo had been behaving lately, but they had been keeping different hours, and it had been several days since they had spoken.

Nicolo looked for Enzo when he arrived home, but Enzo had gone out and his mother wasn't sure where he had gone and didn't know when he would be back. Nicolo had a few free hours before he was due to meet up with friends for a basketball game and he decided to see if he could track Enzo down. He tried the local library first, since that's where Enzo went to study, and found his brother in a study carrel on the second floor, near the collection of bound federal and provincial legislation, peering into the screen of his computer and tapping slowly on the keyboard.

"Hey," Nicolo said.

"Hey," Enzo echoed, glancing up. His expression of surprise at seeing Nicolo transformed almost instantly into anxiety. He half-rose from his chair. "Is everybody okay? Ma?"

"No, no, everything's fine. I needed to find a book for my course and I thought, why not check to see if you were here and wanted to go for a coffee with me."

Enzo glanced at Nicolo's empty hands. "Didn't you find your book? And don't you have a game?"

"It's not until later. Come on. I can get the book anytime. Can't you spare half an hour to spend with your own brother?" He knocked Enzo's shoulder lightly with his fist.

"I'm kind of in the middle of something," Enzo said. He sat down and turned his back to Nicolo, fixed his eyes on the glowing screen of his laptop. "I'll probably be home for dinner tonight, though. Okay?"

"Come on," Nicolo urged. "I need to ask you about something." It seemed to him that Enzo was being unnecessarily difficult.

"You can ask me here."

"No. I can't."

"Why not?"

"You know." Nicolo tipped his head to indicate the people who were sitting in chairs and other carrels nearby. One or two of them glanced back, signalling early-stage irritation and an implied suggestion that the two of them take their whispered conversation farther away.

"Oh." Enzo hesitated, but then he reached to snap his computer shut. He unplugged the electric cord and coiled it neatly into a figure-eight secured at its middle with two taut wraps of the cord. He put the computer into his briefcase, zipped the case closed and followed Nicolo downstairs, out the front doors and into the café next door to the library.

"What's up?" Enzo asked once they had made their way through the queue, picked up their cardboard cups of coffee and found seats outside at one of the café's small tables in a sheltered spot that was only slightly warmed by a thin late-winter sun. He fidgeted. He rolled his shoulders, rattled his plastic stir-stick against the inside of his cup, shifted on his chair and squeezed his cup.

"What were you working on just now?" Nicolo asked. It was difficult to read Enzo's demeanour. He wasn't sure how to start a conversation about a news article he hadn't read about troubles that probably had nothing to do with Enzo.

"Nothing. Things. Studying."

"How's it going at school?"

"What do you mean, how's it going? It's going fine."

"We haven't had much time to talk lately."

"You know, you're making me nervous. Enzo came and found me like this a few years ago, and that's when he told me about Mima being pregnant. He wanted me to help him break the news to Ma and Pop."

Nicolo stirred another packet of sugar into his cup and then raised it and took a sip. The coffee tasted like syrup. He looked down and saw that his hands had created a pile of empty sugar packages, six at least. He set the coffee down again and cracked his knuckles—an old habit, one that his mother had bribed him out of the summer he was sixteen by promising him a new pair of hockey skates. Paola had not been able to break one of Enzo's habits, which he was engaged in now, tugging at the long hair above his brow.

"I wanted to ask you about this thing that's going on out at the law school," Nicolo said, feeling as if he was plunging into cold water. He ripped open another sachet of sugar and dumped it into his cup.

Enzo had not yet tasted his own coffee. His hands were raised in a teepee above his cup. He pushed his lips forward and knit his fingers together. "What about it?" he asked, breathing steadily over his entangled knuckles.

"I heard that some of the students had been caught changing their marks on resumés, or something like that. I heard it second hand, though. It's probably just one of those rumours."

Enzo didn't answer.

"And I heard that there might be others." Nicolo experienced an odd sensation of dislocation, an almost physical shift in the ground under their table. He wrapped his hands tightly around his cup. He had never been his younger brother's confessor or adviser.

Enzo still didn't say anything. He dropped his forehead onto his fingertips and massaged his brow into deep folds. Nicolo noticed for the first time that his younger brother's hair had begun to recede, and he felt a small bolt of pity and concern.

"Well?" Nicolo said at last. "What's going on? You can't be involved in this, if it's even happening. You haven't had any grades yet."

It took a long while for Enzo to speak, and when he finally did, his words came out in a rush. "First-year students do write exams in the middle of December, but the Christmas exams don't count for anything. They're supposed to be for practice only, to get you ready for the real exams in April, the ones that count, so you can get a feel for the way they work. You have to find the issues in the problems, and then pick them apart; that's even more important than solving them. There's a way of doing them, and it takes a while to get the hang of it. But then, the way it happens is, if you decide to apply for a summer job at a law firm after first year, the firms always ask you for your December grades. That's all they have to go on, they say. It's unfair, because the December tests are not supposed to mean anything. There are lots of people who don't do very well and then go on to graduate at the top of their year.

"A group of us were talking about it in class a few weeks ago and the prof asked if we had considered how easy it would be to subvert what the firms are doing. All we had to do, she said, was make a pact that we would give straight As or whatever marks we agreed on to the firms and this would send a message that we don't think it's right to insist on seeing marks that aren't intended to have any meaning and in fact *don't* mean anything. Because it isn't right, what they're doing; it isn't fair. Then some of us got to talking about it afterward, after the class, and we agreed that there wouldn't be any risk because the law school doesn't give transcripts and they don't give out the grades; they won't even confirm or deny them. What you report is supposed to be based on the honour system, I guess. But I've heard that the truth of it is the honour system has been broken for years and the marks are often misreported and everyone knows it, even the administration knows it, but no one has ever done anything about it. They just let it go on."

"What did you do?" Nicolo wished that Enzo would look him in the eye, but Enzo's gaze was fixed on the rim of his coffee cup.

"I asked around about what the others were planning to do, but no one would commit one way or the other. I had got okay marks on the practice exams, better than most—an A, two Bs and the rest were C-pluses—not as good as some of the others got, but not bad either, pretty good in fact. I had already decided that I should apply for summer jobs at some of the medium-sized firms and maybe one or two larger ones just to see what happened. The jobs that pay the best, the ones that pay well, are the ones that want to see the grades. So, what I decided was, I decided that it would be wrong to give myself straight As or anything like that. Even if others did it, I couldn't; it would be too misleading. But I couldn't see how it would do any harm to anyone to make a very small adjustment, to change the C-pluses and put B-minuses instead. It's a very small difference, a matter of a percentage point or two or three, well within the margin for error for the people who do the marking. I worked it out carefully, ran all the numbers. I didn't want to do anything wrong, I just wanted to give myself the same chance as anyone else."

Overhead, a formation of clouds had made a slow passage across the sky and was gathering across the contracted orb of the dim sun. A sharp wind found its way around the corner of the building and crept across Nicolo's scalp under his hair. Another fugitive breeze found a path under his jacket and along his back. He sipped his coffee again, for something to do, and then set his cup down and slid it to the side of the table. He leaned back, folded his arms across his chest and frowned.

"I know. I know. You don't need to say it. It was wrong. But it's done."

Nicolo jammed his hands into the pockets of his jacket. "You mean you did it? You sent the marks out?"

"Yes. The next day. To six firms."

"Have any of them got back to you? Your letters might not have been delivered yet. They could still be in the mail somewhere or in a pile on someone's desk. We just need to figure out how to get them back."

"No, it's too late now. I've already had one or two calls to set up interview times. One of the students did the same thing apparently, or something similar, and then he told a few people, one or two too many anyway, and someone ratted him out to the dean's office. Then, all of a sudden there

were memos posted around the law school on all the bulletin boards to say that anyone caught misrepresenting their
grades could be expelled. They're starting some kind of an
investigation. Maybe it's like Nonna says, you know, '*Chi va
ai al mulino s'infarina.*' When you go to a mill, you get covered in flour. Only this feels more like shit than flour. This
system, it's sick, all of it, rotten. It makes you rotten too, only
it's hard to see that when you are in the middle of it. When
you're inside something like that—it's hard to explain—it
feels almost like just another problem that has been set and
that has to be solved, like in the exams, and it feels like the
smart students are the ones who catch on quickly, play the
system, and the dumb ones, the losers, are the ones who
don't figure it out or think that they're too good, too pure,
to make the system work for them."

For the first time in his life, Nicolo wished that Enzo
wasn't so smart. Some systems, he thought, might not be
worth figuring out if the result would be a temptation to
beat them.

"Pull the applications. You can get a summer job somewhere else, or keep working at the factory. I can always give
you a loan if you need it. I have lots of money saved up. I'll
give you whatever you need. I know you're a good investment. I totally believe in you. There are lots of ways to get
through this. Loans, grants, the bank of Nicolo, and you still
have your scholarships."

Enzo made a sound, a groan that seemed to rise up from
deep inside his body, from the centre of his belly. "It isn't
that simple. These jobs aren't only for the money, although
the pay is a big part of it. It's the fact that they're the right

kind of job. They take you places. Being a summer student at one of the better firms is the closest thing you can get to a guarantee. It's like you've been approved, anointed. After that, assuming you don't completely screw up, you're on the inside."

"I'm not saying that doesn't matter. I'm sure you're right about all of it. But you still need to ask for your applications back if they aren't one-hundred-percent accurate." Nicolo grasped his cup for warmth, but his coffee had gone cold. Then he reached across and wrapped his hand around Enzo's fist.

Enzo shook his brother's hand away and crossed his arms across his chest. His expression was closed and obdurate.

"And even if I did withdraw my applications, that wouldn't be the end of it. This thing is going to get bigger. There're going to be questions asked, a few at least, maybe more. I feel like I'm caught in one of those leg-hold traps and it's only a matter of time before someone comes along to finish me off."

"I know. But it's a start. It's the right thing to do. The only thing to do. We can get started, and work out the rest later."

"I don't even know how to withdraw them now that they've been sent. It's as if I suddenly can't even think straight. I was sitting there, up in the library, staring at the electronic copies of letters I sent out. Thinking, imagining, wishing that if I just deleted the copies from my laptop then they would disappear, that this would never have happened, as if it could all be undone by pushing a button. Do you know, I even started to pray, right there in my chair. Like at confession. 'Forgive me, Father, for I have sinned,' and all the rest of it. I almost got down on my knees right there, as if I were back in grade one, remember how they used to make us do, in the aisles beside our desks? As if there were some kind of almighty, powerful God who would give even the remotest shit about this kind of stupid screw-up."

"We'll call the firms and say there's been a mistake."

"I can't do it."

"You don't have any choice."

"They'll want an explanation."

"If you have to tell them anything, you can say the truth, that your transcripts have a mistake in them."

"Three 'mistakes.'"

"Okay, three, then. It doesn't matter. There's no way around it. You don't necessarily have to give them chapter and verse."

Enzo lowered his head to the table. "I can't believe I was so stupid."

"Okay, so you've done something stupid. You've been to the mill and you're covered in flour. But we can't just do nothing. It's bad, I know, I'm not trying to kid you, but the other way is worse."

Enzo wasn't listening. "We can't make any calls until Monday anyway. And I don't think I can last until then without it killing me. I feel sick. Maybe I *am* sick. Everything hurts. All my muscles. Even my bones hurt. My brain hurts."

"We'll send e-mails, then. Right now. Let's go home and get it done."

"And then what?"

"One thing at a time." Nicolo infused his voice with more confidence than he felt. "We'll work out the next thing later."

He rose and tugged at Enzo's shoulder. Enzo stood up and followed him, clasping his bag to his chest, radiating misery.

They drove to the house in their separate cars, Enzo following behind Nicolo. Nicolo kept checking in the mirrors to ensure that Enzo was still there, almost as if he expected him to bolt—but where could he possibly go? In the house, on their way past the kitchen to the stairs, they could hear Nonna half-speaking, half-singing under her breath as she spread fresh, damp pasta strands to dry over linen towels draped on the back of kitchen chairs. She gently patted each row of the waxy white pasta, as if they were the hairs on the head of a small, attentive child.

"*Un morire ciucciareddu meo c'a vena maio e t'ingrasso.*" Don't die, my little donkey, because May will come and I will fatten you up.

CHAPTER TWELVE

"Come with me. Please? Would you?"

"Sorry? Come with you where?"

"Come with me to my husband's wedding. My *ex*-husband's. You know, Gordon? I've been meaning to ask if you wouldn't, if you couldn't, if you would please agree to at least think about coming along with me. It's at the end of May. I think I've told you that. I've thought a lot about it and I'm really going to need to have someone there. It would mean everything to me, having a friend along for moral support and all that. Don't worry. I don't have any designs on you or ulterior motives or anything like that; I'm a married woman. Well, I'm not, but you know what I mean. I might just as well be. I have no interest in that kind of thing any more; that part of my life is a closed book, done, *finito*, you know how it is? It might even be fun. It will be overdone and tasteless and sometimes that's kind of a hoot. Probably not, but maybe. You don't have to decide right now. You can think about it for a while, okay? You'll think about it? It would mean a lot to me. I know it's a big favour to ask. But promise me that you'll at least consider the possibility?"

"Alden and I can't use our tickets to this play next month. I get tickets all the time at the station, for movies and plays and launches and shows, and we usually try to use them, but Alden has a work dinner that night and he can't get out of it, someone's retirement. So we were thinking that maybe you might like to go. You could take someone with you, we have two tickets. The play's called *Wit* and it's about cancer and I think she dies at the end, which I know sounds grim, but I've heard it is absolutely amazing. It's by a grade-school teacher, I think, her first play, and it won a Pulitzer, which I find completely inspiring because if she can do it maybe I could too if I ever get around to writing a novel or screen-play, which I've always wanted to try to do. Anyway, we both thought that you might like to go. I've been meaning to tell you as well that Alden is so, so pleased at the six pounds he's lost. And don't you think he looks better? Happier even. I think he's happier. He has this new spring in his step when he gets up in the mornings. This is so good for him, this new routine you've created for us to do together. It's been good for both of us. You make it easy. We're both surprised, but we actually look forward to the days we're going to meet with you."

"Timothy finally said he'd come to Las Vegas with me. Did I tell you I have to go out to Las Vegas? I'll be gone for a few days in the second week of April. Frankie's people called me especially at four in the morning, can you believe it? They got the time change backward or a day early or late or something like that. I had just got to sleep after a night out with Timothy and I could barely even find the phone, let alone talk. I was like 'Who *is* this?' I think I dropped the receiver about ten times. It's a complete mystery why they didn't hang up on their end. Anyway, they were calling to ask if I could fly down ASAP to try to fix whatever it is that's gone terribly, dreadfully, horribly wrong with the show. I'm sure you've read about it. In *People?* It's in all the magazines. Frankie Donato? The singer? A disaster, and not the kind that's supposed to build character. It's the other kind, the wrong kind, the kind that can absolutely slay a career, like an enormous, giant wooden stake straight through the heart. The songs aren't right. Or the dance routines. Or the pacing, or the costumes, or the decor or something. They're already into it for millions now, the money people behind it all, and they're getting skittish, so someone came up with the idea that maybe I might have some thoughts how to fix it. If it even *can* be fixed. I've done a few things like this before, worked miracles even, you know? But this one might be beyond even me. I mean, Frankie Donato. Anyway Timothy finally, finally agreed to come with me. I didn't want to go without him. I had to beg on my knees practically. So, anyway, remember you told me that you've never gone anywhere? Well, that's just not right? Okay? You've got to go somewhere before you settle down and have the big wedding and your eight little kids or however many you're going to have. So I got them to put you into the budget as the Personal Trainer to the Creative Consultant—neat title, huh?—airfare, hotel, meals, gym, spa, the works. Second week in April, Friday to Monday. You would be able to make sure I stay on track and maybe keep half an eye on Timothy and also have a vacation. A junket. Think about it, okay? Can you promise me you'll think about it?"

"I ssaw the fax. It's a sure thing, I tell you."

"You can't know for certain."

"I told you. I *ssaw* the fax. It described the whole deal, who's in, the bids, the price, the deadlines, everything. Even the financing's been finalized. The money's been committed."

"Where did you see it?"

"On Brad's fax. He's ssuch an idiot. He didn't check the machine before he went home and there it was. *And* a copy of the confidentiality agreement they made him sign, as if it was even worth the paper it was written on when he leaves it lying around like that. As if Brad isn't going around and telling people anyway. I can't help it if I see something that ssomeone leaves lying around. There's no law against that, is there?"

"The shares will, what, double? Triple?"

"Higher, through the roof. I bought us some calls. A *lot* of calls."

"Will they keep the name Vit@lity? I heard that the value is all in the brand."

"Who knows? Who cares? We've got a few thousand calls. When the news hits the market, the shares will ssoar and we'll be rich. That's all that matters."

"Where did you get that kind of money?"

"Like I said. I borrowed it. From the bank. Leverage. That's what it's all about these days. Leverage. Only ssuckers put their own money at risk."

"Not so loud. Someone will hear us."

"Don't worry. You worry too much. No one here understands this kind of stuff."

"Welcome back, all of you. I am glad to see you back again tonight, and hopefully ready to tackle some new and challenging recipes. You all did wonderfully last time, even the group that burned your muffins, which was a good reminder to all of us to check stove settings carefully. Even when you get the temperature right, broil is *not* the same thing as bake. I've added a recipe that calls for broiling tonight, so that will give us all a chance to get the hang of it. Most of you were doing just fine and in fact I think I may have spotted more than one budding chef. This evening we are going to push the envelope just a little bit more and work with some fresh and healthful ingredients that you might not be all that familiar with. I know you will all try to keep an open mind. What we're going to do is try out recipes that use bean curd, swiss chard, toasted wheat germ and grated unsweetened chocolate. Not all in the same dish—don't worry, I'm not that cruel. Please, as I said, just try to keep an open mind. None of these recipes are too far off the beaten path. As I said earlier, I think you're all going to be very pleasantly surprised."

"I have here a sturdy pair of fail-safe, moisture-resistant paper overalls for everyone, and if you will please have a look over there along the far wall, you should be able to find a pair of safety boots that will fit you. The sizes are clearly labelled and they buckle at the sides—like so—so you'll be able to fasten them tightly. Just roll up the legs and sleeves of the overalls if they're too long—like this. As you see, they have elastic at the waist and cuffs so one size fits all, although I think it is safe to say that no one, including yours truly, is going to win any fashion competitions with these babies on. Today's visit will involve just a little bit of walking, and some climbing too if you happen to be so inclined.

"I also have a box of sanitized paper masks here if you want one, but I can assure you that you won't have to worry very much at all about unpleasant odours. While it is true that odour could be one of the formerly less desirable side impacts of the older, outdated, less-scientific style of landfill, it has all but been banished these days through the many miracles of modern-day innovations in waste management. In fact, some people describe the scent of a modern landfill as musky or sweet or honey-like. One gentleman visitor went so far as to compare it to mead, which is a kind of flavourful wine made from honey that was formerly consumed in England in medieval times. I think, as I say, that you're likely to find yourself pleasantly surprised."

"Hey, Nicco. Come to the wedding shower, okay? A few of us will be getting together in the kitchen over at the hall, just the guys. Come round to the back door and you'll find us. The girls will be out in the front doing whatever it is they do at showers, you know, the gifts and stuff. They won't even know we're around. Come hungry."

"If you open your textbooks to chapter four, you'll see two classic studies on how people can be induced through suasion and pressure to carry out an action that may be entirely against their natural character, such as inflicting torture. We'll be discussing these studies in detail and you will be required to write a short paper—it's due in two weeks; please make a note of the date—about an incident in your lives that has some or all of the hallmarks of the five factors of peer persuasion, or as it is often called, peer pressure, that we will be reviewing next. This will count for fifteen percent of your final mark. You can find more information about the grading structure on the sheet I handed out at the first class. Please stop by to talk to me after class if you need another copy."

"Wait a minute. Let me think. We have to be sure this is the right approach. We can only do this once."

"You're the one who was so sure. And it sounds okay. It says what we need to say. I'm withdrawing my applications; that's the gist of it. Anyway, I think you're right. It's best to get this over with as quickly as possible. If I don't get any offers, then there can't be any harm to me or anyone else."

"I'm just thinking. You know, *nel dubbio, astieniti.*"

"That's what the people in Pompeii said when the volcano began to glow. They decided to wait to see what happened and they ended up baked to ashes in their own homes clutching their gold and silver."

"It's still only Saturday. Whether we send these out today or tomorrow won't make any difference. It's not very likely that anyone will be reading them until Monday morning. Why don't you go to work? I'll try to make my game. We can look at this again in the morning and see how this reads after we've slept on it."

CHAPTER THIRTEEN

Nicolo woke in the early hours of Sunday morning, listening for and then hearing the sound of Enzo's car pulling into the driveway. He fell asleep again, but started awake once more some time later. He could not remember hearing Enzo come down the hall, or the sounds of Enzo getting ready for bed. The house was silent, apparently taking a rest from its usual nighttime symphony of creaks and electronic hums and clicks.

Nicolo got out of his bed and went down the hall to the kitchen, careful to make as little noise as he could as he moved through the house. No lights were on. As his eyes slowly adjusted to the darkness, he thought he could see a darker shape seated at the kitchen table, a shape that coalesced over the space of a few seconds into Enzo. His younger brother sat absolutely still for a long minute, and then raised his hand, which seemed to have something in it, to his mouth.

Nicolo walked slowly into the kitchen, lifting his elbow so that he made a soft, brushing noise against the door jamb as he passed. He could smell Enzo more easily than he could see him. Nicolo took a glass down from the cupboard and then sat down across from his brother, who leaned forward and poured something into Nicolo's glass from a bottle on the table. Nicolo raised his cup and tasted scotch, likely from his parents' large store of dusty, unopened bottles in the lower cabinet in the dining room. The scotch, neat and warm, tasted like furniture polish. The second sip tasted much worse than the first and landed uncomfortably on his stomach, which protested by contracting and then sending a warning tremor up into the base of his throat. Enzo poured more scotch into his own glass. The liquid in the bottle seemed to be down at least a quarter.

"Have you eaten anything?" Nicolo asked.

"Eaten? I don't know." Enzo twisted his face into an exaggerated expression, a parody of trying to remember. Nothing seemed to come to him, and after a minute he gave up and shrugged. "I'm not sure. I don't think so. Maybe. It doesn't matter. I'm not hungry. I'm stupid and I'm sick."

Nicolo got up and opened the refrigerator door, squinting against the white light that shone from inside. He took out a container of eggs, broke three of them into a bowl, added a bit of water from the tap, and pushed everything around with a fork. He set a pan on the stove, poured in the eggs and scraped them away from the bottom of the pan with the fork while they cooked. When they seemed to be done, he turned the pan upside-down onto a plate and pushed the plate toward Enzo.

"Don't want any," said Enzo, but he took the fork Nicolo handed him and prodded the grey mixture with it. He took a swallow from his glass and then put a forkload of eggs into his mouth. He moved the muscles of his face into a cartoon-ish oval of disgust.

"Awful," he said. "You can't cook. Where's the salt?"

When Enzo had finished eating, he pushed the plate away and reached again for the bottle, but Nicolo had placed it on the floor under the table, so Enzo's hand swept through empty air. Enzo reached again, and then seemed to forget what he had been looking for.

"So tired," he said. He dropped his forehead down onto his arms.

Nicolo yawned in sympathy and then sat, his elbows on the table, his chin on his fists, and waited to see what Enzo would do next. He heard his brother's breath rattle once, twice, and realized that Enzo would soon be asleep. Rising from his chair he pushed and pulled his brother by his shoulders up and into the living room and onto the couch, levered him down along its length, and covered him with the crocheted blanket that Nonna used when she napped there in the afternoon. Enzo curled on his side like a child and tucked his hands between his folded knees. He looked unhappy and uncomfortable, and he smelled like sweat and scotch and unwashed wool.

"Cold," he said. "I'm an idiot. Everything hurts."

Nicolo couldn't think of anything else that he could do for him. He carried the bottle of scotch back to the dining room cabinet, rinsed the glasses and left them in the sink, and went back down the hall to his own bed. It seemed to him that he fell asleep the same instant that he pulled his heavy blankets up around his chest.

Down the hall, Nonna is dreaming again and in this dream she is flying over Arduino. Although it is night and she is high above the houses, there is something different about her eyes. She can see in almost every direction. With such vision, perhaps she is a hawk, but more likely she is an angel, since she can see through the rooftops, as if they were made of rippled old-fashioned glass instead of tile and stone. Her gaze takes in whole families who are sleeping, one, two or more to a bed, and a few in the town who are awake. Three sleepless older women drink warm milk, each alone in her house, each one beside her own banked hearth, her feet near the soft, livid ashes. If only they each knew that the others were awake they could gather and chat companionably until dawn. They need the company more than they need the milk. One man, his clothes rumpled and torn, huddles outside the bar under a crumbling archway scrawled with graffiti; his companions had been too soused to bear him home. Nonna glides down low. She comes close enough that she can smell the stale tobacco smoke and grappa in the creases of his clothes and she marvels for a moment—she is certain that never before has a dream included details such as this rich, rank odour. This dream is so much like waking life, but more concentrated, more intense. She moves on and sees through a low window another man, lean and long and dry as a walking stick, who is dying in his bed beside his round and soundly sleeping wife. His breaths are irregular, becoming shallower and further apart. A cancer has weakened him and is hurrying to finish its task under tender darkness, before the sun breaches the crest of the hill to the east. He hasn't complained, this fading man, of his daily pains and loss of vigour—there was too much work to do each day, and there was always a hope that the doctor in Cozenza, consulted in secret, had been wrong, although he had been left uneasy by the fact that the doctor frowned so deeply and refused resolutely to be paid. At the very least, he has thought in these last days, *"na bona morte tutta 'na vita unura"*—a good death will reflect honour on his entire life. On the next day after this one dawning, Nonna knows, her sight extending ahead through the hours yet to unscroll—on that day his sons will place a stoppered bottle of water, a piece of two-day-old bread and a tattered ten-lire note into his coffin before the top is nailed down. Thus, on his trip to heaven, the expired man will have ten lire to give to a poor man in the path, who will step aside and let him pass. He will then meet a hungry dog, which the thick wedge of bread is meant to mollify. His last encounter before paradise will be with a thirsty pilgrim with whom he will share his cool flagon of water and who in gratitude will accompany him on the final leg of that final journey. The two travellers will match their pace so that they step together across the threshold into God's great villa, where food and wine and fragrant tobacco and soft feather beds await. Bonita, the good man's wife, will be lonely, and so will marry again after a widow's year. This confuses Nonna in the midst of her dream—which man will Bonita be reunited with in heaven when her time comes? And then her confusion lifts, and she understands that God has planned for this too. Bonita will be multiplied and magnified in death, as will all good people, so that in heaven they can be children to their parents, parents to their children, wives to their husbands and husbands to their wives.

Beneath the eaves of the closely set houses of Arduino, red and black and golden hens roost fatly, contentedly; they shift, settle and sigh. Many of them are almost ready to be plucked and roasted; between feathers and skin is a nicely built-up layer of fortifying fat intended to crown the soup pot. Carrots swell crisp and cool in the soil of the sloping fields, wheat stirs, its millions of sharp heads rattling companionably in the thin night breeze; goats nestle in a single, undifferentiated heap of bones and wiry hair and moist noses and sharp horns and hooves; cows shift from haunch to haunch and sway their tails like pendulums counting out the seconds until their owners will come to relieve them of their increasing encumbrance of milk; children breathe deeply, their lips fluttering and their eyelids quivering with the emergent drama of their own dreams; dogs twitch against the furtive bites of fleas; moss creeps, slowly enfolding stones and fallen logs; mould burrows a maze of blue veins through linen-wrapped cheeses that are as round and yellow as the moon; earthworms root through the soil and rise to the surface to expel their elegant castings.

If she were to awaken from this dream, and had to hand an enormous sheet of paper and a set of coloured pencils,

Nonna could sketch every stone and inhabitant of Arduino, every crevice in every rock, every hair on every head and every fold on every brow. No more than God himself can she protect them, but, godlike, she can inventory and treasure every atom, every breath. She rises now and soars above the village so the air spills around her like water, and the village shimmers beneath her like a painting or scene in a play.

"Ah," she thinks. "So this is what it feels like to have wings. Lucky birds. Fortunate angels."

Both Enzo and Nicolo awoke to the usual Sunday morning swell of music from the dining room—a waltz that began modestly with an upward sweep of violins, like curtains sliding on iron rings along a rod when they are pulled apart to let in the light, and then a trill of piano notes like running water, with the time marked by shy cello and discreet and sombre viola—and to the sharp, insistent smell of Nonna's bitter coffee heating in the pot at the back of the stove. These pulled Nicolo out of bed and into a shower, and drove Enzo deeper under his nonna's blanket, which smelled to him, now that he was partially, uncomfortably awake and all of his senses switched to high, intensely of her.

Enzo turned on to his back and tried to solve the problem of what to do with his cramped legs by hanging his feet over the arm of the couch, but this made his knees ache. Contrary to Nonna's often-cited promise that *la notte porta consigli*, the night had not, he thought dully through a headache that was swelling, mushroom-like, from the front of his forehead into his temples and sinuses, brought him fresh counsel. He felt stale and thick and slow; his brain, which usually so reliably clicked and pinged along like a continuous game of pinball with its thoughts and ideas and strategies, felt unplugged. He heard next from inside the dim and echoing cave of a half-sleep the abrupt bleat of the telephone ringing, and he struggled to sit, suffused with a sense of culpability, of being caught out, his heart constricting and expanding inside his aching chest like the fist of a pugilist preparing for battle; but someone else answered the telephone, and after a long minute of anxious immobility, he fell backward, curled his legs and arms inside the random folds of Nonna's blanket, and found brief oblivion again in a shallow, open-mouthed, drooling doze.

CHAPTER FOURTEEN

It was Nonna who answered the phone and she passed the receiver to Nicolo without comment. The caller was Pietro Salvatore, one of the community's four most prominent citizens (along with Giulia Crudo, a federal member of Parliament, Angelo Santanove, a Superior Court judge, and Carmine Falucci, who had founded and operated a thriving factory that made modern-style furniture in glass and black lacquer for restaurants and hotels). The idea of consulting Salvatore had come to Nicolo toward the end of his Saturday basketball game yesterday. A scuffle had broken out, a high elbow jab responded to with a sharp jostle, met in turn with a leg sweep, and then the two players fell heavily toward each other, trading insults and each struggling to keep a safe distance from the fists of the other and place blows in any spot that might be vulnerable. They were yanked apart, and then pulled to opposite ends of the court by their respective teammates. Nicolo, observing his own team's combatant, thought of a young boxer slumped in his corner of the ring, shaking his head to clear it so that he could take in the urgent blasts of counsel from his coach. Enzo, it occurred to him, needed someone like that, someone quick on his feet and with a store of strategies and tactics, someone grey-haired, sharp, experienced in the topography of troubles and the ways that a person could be extricated from them.

He found Pietro listed in the phone book (he was surprised at this; he had imagined that someone so illustrious would be harder to track down), dialled and was directed by a recorded voice to leave a message. In a few careful sentences, Nicolo laid out what he understood of the trouble that Enzo might be up against, and left his home number, not expecting to hear from the famous lawyer at ten o'clock the next day, on a Sunday morning.

Pietro asked Nicolo to bring Enzo to see him right away. He would be waiting for them in an hour on the sidewalk at the front door of his office building on Yonge Street, so that he could let them in.

Nicolo felt sorry for Enzo, who protested resentfully at being forced awake and out of the house into the cold air. A snowstorm in the small hours of the morning had dropped a layer of heavy, wet snow on the city. The sky was dreary, the colour of cold dishwater, and the streets were slick with a coating of dirty ice and silver-brown slush. Nicolo drove slowly, careful not to jar Enzo more than necessary. He was uncertain whether he would have been able to persuade his brother to go to the appointment if Enzo's resolve and independence hadn't been weakened by drink and a miserable night's sleep. He had cajoled Enzo into a shower and then into clothes, an old pair of jeans and a sweater, and had forced him to swallow a cup of Nonna's coffee. Enzo would accept nothing more; he glared sourly at the toast and sliced cheese that he was offered and he swung his head from side to side, cautiously but categorically. He climbed into the passenger seat of Nicolo's car, and swayed more than the slight motion of the car warranted as Nicolo steered through the night's new snowfall to Salvatore's office.

Pietro was there already. He was clearing the sidewalk in front of the building with a shovel that had a broad, shiny silver blade and long straight wooden handle. He wore a knee-length tweed coat with a fur collar, a Russian-style fur hat with the flaps turned up and tied at the top, gauntlet-like fur-lined leather gloves and sturdy boots tied with leather laces. He wielded his shovel skilfully, taking short, rapid thrusts, and lifting and neatly tossing uniform loads of snow away from the sidewalk. Pietro nodded to Nicolo and Enzo as they approached, and accelerated his pace slightly. He had completed the span of sidewalk in front of the building by the time they reached him. He straightened then, raised his bright shovel in the air, and sent it plunging blade first into a pile of displaced snow, where it quivered for several moments and then came to rest upright and still. The face that he turned to them was larger than average including his nose, which was prominent and round at the end like a loaf of French bread. He raised his dark, dense eyebrows and then brought them closer together as he turned his gaze first to Nicolo and then to Enzo.

"Well, which one of you is it, then?" he asked.

Enzo didn't answer and Nicolo didn't want to appear to accuse his brother, so a stretch of silence elapsed. Enzo stood still, arms crossed on his chest, head downturned. Nicolo looked upward, swung his arms, brought his hands together and then slid them back into his pockets.

"You, is it then, eh?" Pietro asked. He turned his head to look at Enzo.

"Yes, sir," Enzo answered, raising his head.

Another silence settled over the three men. Nicolo could see that both Enzo and Pietro were breathing heavily; Pietro's breath billowed out around his head like the clouds ringing the peak of a mountain, and Enzo's settled near his lips, forming a fog dense enough to obscure his expression.

"Well, you might as well come upstairs to my office, both of you, and we'll see what it is we can do about all of this."

Salvatore turned. As he unlocked and pulled open the heavy front door of the building, an alarm emitted a warning. When they were all inside, he turned and relocked the door behind them, and then moved quickly halfway down the dim hall. He opened a metal panel and punched in a code that switched off the alarm system, and then Nicolo and Enzo followed him up two flights of stairs—Pietro took them two at a time. They waited, side by side, while he unlocked his office door, disabled a second alarm, and dialled a number on the telephone that activated the overhead lights. Inside, they were directed to sit in two chairs in front of Pietro's broad desk. The tables and cabinets around the office were stacked with papers, and with photographs, some of which showed the lawyer shaking hands with politicians and others both famous and near famous. They waited while he switched on his computer and entered a series of passwords and commands. At last, Salvatore turned toward them, and allowed a long minute to pass.

"You may find this surprising," he said. "But I am not going to need you to tell me what happened. What I am going to do instead is to offer a series of propositions to you, and all you need to do—and here, I mean Enzo only—is tell me whether you can agree to them. You understand me? If you can't or don't agree, you only need to indicate that you don't agree. I am not looking at present for details or for an explanation. Is this clear? You don't need to elaborate or do anything more than provide a response."

Enzo and Nicolo nodded, without, in Nicolo's case at least, fully understanding what it was that Pietro had proposed.

"I am going to start with an example only, so we can make sure you have the hang of it, all right?"

Enzo gave another shallow nod and widened his eyes to signal readiness.

"Do you have the time, by the way?"

"Yes, sir. It's twenty to one."

"No. The right answer is *yes*. You *do* have the time. I need you to give me no more of a response and no less than I ask. Do you see?"

Enzo brought his head down and clenched his jaw.

"Several students enhanced their marks."

Enzo hesitated but looked up again. "Yes. I believe so, yes."

"In fact, many did."

"I don't know," Enzo said apologetically. "I think at least a dozen, maybe twenty. Maybe more. Not less than a dozen. I think more—"

Pietro held up his hand signalling that no more explanation was wanted.

"Yours is not a large class. This is a sizable percentage."

"Yes, at least . . ."

"A *meaningful* percentage."

"Yes . . ."

"This is not one or two renegades."

"No."

"This is serious, but widespread."

"You could *say* that."

"This is not a case of one or two individuals making a bad decision. This is systemic."

"Yes."

"This is serious and pervasive."

"Yes."

"There is something wrong with *the system*."

"I believe so, yes."

"There would have to be something wrong with *the system* if between, say, ten and twenty-five percent of first-year students took this single opportunity to increase their grades."

"Yes, sir. I believe that would be correct."

"If the law school took the trouble to issue official transcripts, none of this would have happened."

"No, sir."

"If the law school had provided students and prospective employers with official transcripts, it would have been impossible for this to happen."

"Yes, sir."

"You prepared your applications on a laptop, I expect. An older model perhaps."

"It's three years old."

"The screen is neither large nor bright."

"No."

"You work as well in places that are not particularly well lit."

"That's true. Mostly either in my bedroom or in the back corner of the library."

"You had no transcript or summary, official or otherwise, to refer to."

"No, sir."

"You relied on your memory."

"I did, sir."

"There are strict deadlines to apply for the summer positions that are open to first-year students."

"Yes, very strict."

"And the process to get those positions is highly competitive."

"Yes. It is."

"It is fair to say that you may well have been rushed, in order not to miss the deadlines."

"Rushed. Yes. I did rush. Especially toward the end."

"There was a deadline."

"Yes."

Nicolo felt as if he were watching an acrobatic performance. Enzo would start to slip, and every time, without fail, Pietro would hold him. It even seemed sometimes that Pietro was letting his brother fall, or even pushing him, just a bit, in order to be able to catch him seconds later. Enzo had always been the one in the family most capable of this kind of acrobatics; he could set arguments spinning like plates in the air above all of their heads, and then resolve them all neatly, presenting ingenious solutions like a bouquet plucked from a magician's sleeve. Nicolo had never seen Enzo in a situation like this, with someone else keeping several deft paces ahead. Pietro kept at it for another two hours, making statements and eliciting responses from Enzo. When he wasn't content with a response, he rephrased the question, refining the words, trying different angles and approaches, until Enzo was able to answer satisfactorily. Every now and then Enzo shook his head violently, as if he were trying to rearrange by force the details of what had happened, of what he had done.

Finally, the counsellor seemed to have finished. He placed his hands flat on the desk and settled back in his chair.

"This will be a challenge, but there is reason to be somewhat optimistic," he said. "I will take your case on. I will send you a retainer letter. If payment is an issue, we can come up with some agreed terms. In any case, you will find that my rate for members of the community, in particular for younger members of the community who may find themselves in some degree of difficulty, is very fair."

"Thank you," said Nicolo. Enzo bit his lower lip and stayed silent.

"Good. As it happens I know Dean Vance well. I'll call him tomorrow morning in my capacity as your adviser. I can ask him what measures he's planning to put in place to ensure that everyone's rights and interests are protected. I believe that I will be able to provide him with a few suggestions for the process that he will find are in the interests of the students and of the school as well. It is important to keep in mind that the reputation of the school is involved here. These kinds of things are seldom straightforward. And the students in your position are, as we have discussed, almost all of them quite young and under a great deal of stress. Everyone seems to have something at stake. It will be critical to ensure that due process is in place in order for justice to be seen to be done. And I believe that your case in particular presents some unique aspects that will, at the right time, need to be brought out and made clear."

Pietro rose and reached his large hand across the desk, first to Nicolo and then to Enzo. "This will be difficult, Mr. Pavone," he said. He kept Enzo's hand in his grip. "I don't want to mislead you or give you false hope. But, however it unfolds, I believe I can assure you that this incident will neither ruin your life nor end your career. You will in the future, however, remember to take every care to safeguard your name and reputation. There is a saying I like very much, one that can be expressed two contradictory ways, but somewhat paradoxically both of them are abundantly true. 'God is in the details' is the way that I often hear it said, and this is perfectly correct. But I have always preferred the other version, the one that reminds us that it is the devil who is hiding in the details. And it is always the devil that we need to take the most pains to avoid. He is always in wait for the careless. This is something we must never allow ourselves to forget, yes?"

CHAPTER FIFTEEN

On the afternoon of the shower, a bright day, a day
that started and remained cold enough that the air
stung the nose and smelled of iron and almonds, and yesterday's spring slush refroze on the streets into slippery
ridges, Nicolo drove his mother and nonna slowly through
the streets, with their scant, dawdling Sunday traffic, and
pulled up at the front of Palazzo Enrico on Bernardi Street
just south of dingy, shuttered St. Clair. They were late;
Nonna hadn't been able to find one of her single pair of
good shoes. Massimo, who was not looking for it, was the
one who found it, in the basement cantina on the shallow
window ledge with a cartoonishly flattened spider adhered
to its sole.

Paola helped her mother-in-law out of the back seat of the car. She had learned over many years that irritation only fed on itself and that an unnecessarily solicitous act was often helpful to put to rest the hot white sparks that sometimes swarmed inside her head like angry hornets. She held open one of the hall's heavy, gilded doors to let Nonna enter, and Nonna nodded left and right as she passed over the threshold like a duchess on a carpet acknowledging her subjects.

Nicolo heard a burst of distinctively feminine noise released into the street when the doors were pulled apart. Talk like a stream, familiar shouting, the calling out of names, comforting, abundant, anchoring, the sound of happy women celebrating a milestone of one of their own. The noise was a thicket, a jungle, a rain forest, made up of dozens of voices, layered, intermingled, excited, high pitched as flutes, with a warm echoing trill like evening birdsong. Was that where the slang term "bird" for young women had come from? Nicolo wondered. Or did it come from the way girls and women seemed so often to dart more lightly than men did from one thing to another?

The doors swung shut, leaving Nicolo in what sounded at first, by contrast, like solitude and silence. After another moment, his ears adjusted to the noise of car engines, brakes whistling, tires spinning against spring slush, the whine of a faraway machine of some kind, and a horn's repeated blasts, territorial and aggressive. Mechanical sounds, in an entirely different impersonal, industrial register from the clamorous celebrations within. Nicolo turned the car right and right again, into the lane behind the building. He parked and found another wide set of doors, poor twins of the ones in the front, and entered.

The corridor was lit only by the red-pink glow of the exit sign above the doors. Nicolo didn't need to wait for his eyes to adjust or to feel along the wall for a light switch. He was guided toward the kitchen by his ears. The clang of pans. The clatter of dishes and cutlery and glasses. Heavy objects being dropped or stirred in tubs or pots or bins. Metal wheels spinning over ringing tiles. A low, churning sound accompanied by bursts of water and steam: the motor of an industrial dishwasher. A larger, broader rumble not unlike gears tumbling together—men's voices. Bursts of laughter, sharp and happy, reminded Nicolo of dogs let loose and barking together. Inviting stripes of light could be seen around the edges of another set of doors, without knob or handle, dented where they had been pushed with carts.

And then he was in the kitchen, and this was what it must be like to be born: an unknowing plummet into moist air and overbright light and a close, dense cacophony of sounds. Two cooks, noble and tall as cardinals, in billowing white hats, stood before a massive stove, manhandling pot after pot in ranks on the stovetop—steaming, boiling, hissing, lids rattling, the cooks' spoons clashing and clanging against them like the clappers of church bells. Two other cooks, with peaked white folded caps like paper boats, were pulling pans from an oven in which an ox might have been roasted with room at the side for pumpkins. Platters on every surface were piled with orgies of seafood, carmine tomatoes cut in rounds and spread in fans, billows of white bocconcini, melon flesh—green, white, peach—sweating in cool crescents, ruby meats marbled with glistening fat sliced thin as parchment, black olives dusted with salt and as deeply wrinkled as prunes, a coronary of artichoke hearts marinated in oil and vinegar, purple eggplant and lime-green asparagus, bowls filled with mounds of pale lettuce, deep green, vibrant and spiky arugula, parsley, peeled curls of carrot and thin strands of translucent onion. Gallon jugs of green-gold oil and of wine vinegar were lined up in rows. The boat-hatted cooks leaned forward, reaching massive hands into shiny rectangular vats overflowing with grated cheese, sliced peppers, chopped onion and garlic, basil, oregano, peperoncini. In musical precision, they swept handfuls of colour—white, green, yellow and red— over platters, bowls and plates. A convoy of two-tiered metal carts moved in both directions, pushed by women, half a dozen or more, strong-armed, red-faced, with their hair in nets, wearing wide white aprons and once-white shoes with silent beige crepe soles. The outward-bound carts were pushed into a dark passage that must have led to the front of the hall. On these rattled food-laden white plates and the platters, with their border pattern of entwined gardenias. The carts rattling back to the kitchen were ferrying plates that had been wrecked, ransacked, plates disordered as a battlefield: sodden crumbs, gnawed bones, brown olive pits, torn edges of lettuce, single slippery strands of pasta, tomato sauce smeared and spattered as if a murder had been committed, the fronded heads and burst tails of giant shrimp, bread crusts on which butter shone in a scalloped pattern where teeth had torn, shreds of onion, crumpled napkins slashed with lipstick and stained with wine.

Several tables had been set end to end down the middle of the kitchen, and a miscellany of chairs and stools placed around it, all of them occupied by men of various ages. Mario was there, at the near end of the table, with Paul on one side and Frank on the other. Mario's father Ugo was seated at the far end, with Mario's uncle Lou, and Angie's father Sal and her brother Joe; and those two skinny teenaged boys over close to the stove were probably Angie's cousins from Vancouver, Nick and Guido—they had the same high brow and square, dark-shadowed chin as Sal and Joe. There were a number of other men Nicolo didn't know and whose shouted names he didn't catch.

Nicolo found a stool under a counter and a place was made for him in Mario's zone of the table, two seats away from Frank. There was a tribal cry of welcome, greetings, introductions, and then enormous platters of meat, fish, chicken, pasta and salad were raised high in the air by sets of arms with rolled-back sleeves, and passed down the table toward him. A squat glass was placed in front of him and amber wine, someone's uncle's homemade, splashed into it. A complicated joke was being told by someone at the other end of the table in a mix of Italian and dialect, about a novice nun and an old priest and a donkey and a hen, and laughter swelled in anticipation of the punchline. The story was met with a roar of approval and then alternative versions and endings were loudly put forward. No, not a hen but a cock! Not a novice nun, but an ancient crone. She has to be old for the joke to work! Paul yelled something to the table as a whole. A one-up on the punchline, it seemed, because laughter and competitive shouting erupted again all around the table.

"*Non è possibile! Non è possibile,*" Frank declared, and the table fell into factions dedicated to one aspect or another of the debate.

Nicolo tried to listen but it was impossible to fix on any single conversation and so what he took in was a medley, while he pushed back his own sleeves and mostly concentrated on eating. He suddenly felt empty, starving. Everything tasted good and there was no end of it. The platters that were passed around the table from man to man to man left his two hands more or less depleted, but came back from one side or the other filled up again. This was living, he thought, this was life perfected. Comrades, food, warmth, talk, laughter. Who would willingly choose anything different?

Because he was at the business end of the kitchen, the cooks and waitresses occasionally brushed against his back as they worked. When a dishwasher was pulled open behind him, Nicolo turned and blinked into a thick bank of steam through which cooks and servers came and went. A section of the cloud thickened, billowing closer to him, taking on substance, coalescing as it neared on its rattling cart into a cake as tall as a schoolgirl, swaying slightly from its large cake hips to its small garlanded cupcake head, enticingly iced in white, with pink and yellow swags, buttons and rosettes. The cart moved seemingly on its own, as if it were being propelled on tracks.

Nicolo rose to his feet on an impulse that he could not define, and followed the cake and cart through the dense dishwasher cloud, out of the kitchen and into the dim corridor. The cart darted ahead, driven forward by a bent figure in white, and once again Nicolo heard the rich abundance of sounds coming from the hall at the front of the building, louder, more raucous, and higher pitched than the voices and industrial noises of the kitchen. One turn, and then another, a shallow rubbery ramp up, and then through swinging doors (metal on his side, red satiny material on the other) into the back of the main banquet hall. The cake surged ahead into the brilliant lights and noise, and Nicolo hung back, hidden from view between a stack of chairs and a piano, behind the deep folds of thick curtains that hung all the way from the ceiling to the floor and smelled of dust and blocked out the light. The dining room was vast; it could have held a hundred tables or more, although only a portion of the far end of the room was now in use, where a dozen or more round tables of twelve women each had been set up near a long table occupied by Angie, her sisters, her mother, and Nicolo's mother and sister.

"You are just in time. I love this part."

A girl's hushed voice below his ear, a hand pressed against his arm just above the wrist, almost as if his arrival had been expected. There was a scent around her that Nicolo could not identify. Vanilla, a flower, orange peel, sweat. Nicolo was not surprised—or rather, all of this was surprising.

A group of women had gathered around Angie, who was being led now to a chair draped in white cloth and garnished with paper lace and curling ribbons and streamers. She wore pale trousers and a yellow sweater and high-heeled shoes. Her hair was piled on top of her head and her cheeks were flushed. Someone dimmed the room lights except for a single bright spotlight that shone over Angie and her throne. A woman wearing a white pantsuit pressed a plastic tiara into Angie's tall, stacked hair, and a woman in a long dress patterned with roses chose a parcel from a skirted table at the side of the room that was piled high with presents and handed it to her. Angie accepted the parcel and balanced it on her lap. Then she carefully removed several clusters of pale purple ribbons that had been cut and curled and gathered together like chrysanthemums, and drew apart the layers of pink wrapping paper.

The gift, unveiled, was announced by the woman in the dress with roses in a trilling, elated voice: "An electric pasta-maker!" The woman in the pantsuit took the pasta-maker and held it high, and then carried it around the room to each table so that the guests could admire it. Many of them reached out and touched it or held it as it was borne aloft. Angie's mother, who was seated beside Angie, took and neatly folded the discarded wrapping paper. Angie's sister stood just behind the chair, using a stapler to attach the ribbons and bows from the present to a very large paper plate. The next gift to be unwrapped, announced and exhibited was a cappuccino machine, and after that a set of white sheets—"three hundred thread-count!"

"The presentation of the consumer goods," said the girl at Nicolo's elbow. Her voice was low, gravelly, amused. "And later they'll make her wear the hat that they're making out of that paper plate. Could any better reason exist to remain single forever?"

Nicolo looked down at the hand on his arm. A small hand, no bigger than a child's, short uneven nails, perhaps bitten. The top of a head of curling hair, the blunt end of a nose, the curve of a cheek, fine scant lashes, a white shirt with a neckline open low to show clavicles that framed triangle cavities deep enough to rest a pair of eggs in, the faint scent that now reminded him of something freshly made in a bakery—lemons, cinnamon, cloves. A scrap of a girl. Nicolo could imagine himself lifting her in the air with one hand, in the way the strongman in a circus in his striped muscle-shirt might raise a spangled acrobat, her stomach balanced in his palm, her head, arms and legs extended and flashing like the rays of a star. The absurdity of the thought made him smile.

"It's ridiculous. It's like you can't be properly married unless you've got half a department store to play house with," the girl said.

"I don't think it's so bad. It's meant to help them get started, to give them some of the things they might need," Nicolo said, remembering Mima's wedding shower gifts, the pots and dishes and towels and cookbooks.

"So you think a bride's chances for a happy marriage are improved if she is launched into matrimony in possession of an electric deep-fryer, a pair of silver ice buckets, china for twenty people and a matched set of thousand thread-count sheets?"

"Some gifts are more practical than that. My brother's wife got—"

"Someone she loved?"

"Well, it was a bit more complicated than that."

"In that case, maybe they needed the consumer goods so that they would have something in common."

"They had a baby in common pretty quickly."

"Oh. I see."

"It all worked out."

"They found they were able to bond after all over the fifty-piece espresso set?"

"I don't think any of that really mattered to them."

"But they didn't skip it, right? They had a shower and hauled in the loot like pirates?"

"Yes, and wedding presents and a few baby showers too."

"So how many years have they been married? Have they ever even *used* the good china?"

"Six or seven years. I'm sure they'll get around to it. They've been pretty busy." Nicolo was annoyed at the girl for understanding none of this, and at himself for feeling so unable to explain. He dipped his head to try to get a better look at her, but she remained mostly in shadows. It was hard to see more than the gleam and shadow of her collarbone and the shimmer of her white blouse, which seemed almost to float on its own in the darkness. "Who are you anyway? A friend of Angie's?"

"Yes, a friend, sort of. Angie's parents were short-staffed and I volunteered to help out. I just dragged in that monstrous cake. What are you doing here?"

"I'm one of Mario's friends."

"Which one are you?"

"Nicolo. And you're?"

"Zoe. Look, I'd better get back. They can't exactly fire me, but they're probably really wishing they could."

Zoe's hand had remained pressed against Nicolo's forearm during their short, whispered conversation, in the way that someone might lean against a tree for support while removing a stone from a shoe, and when she moved away Nicolo felt its withdrawal as a cool hand-shape exactly corresponding to where her warm palm and fingers had rested. A new surge of noise—approval, encouragement, laughter—rose out of the women at the other end of the room. He looked over and watched as an unsteady construction of paper plates and ribbons and bows was tied with pink ribbons to the top of Angie's hair. Angie held her tiara in one hand, and a plate of cake in the other.

He saw Zoe once again when he was back in the kitchen. She was laughing and retying the strings on her apron while being admonished or instructed by one of the flushed cooks. She turned and moved away quickly, and he caught a glimpse, an impression, of a narrow face, thickly curling red-brown hair, no rings or necklace or earrings, and little makeup that he could see apart from a trace of pale lipstick in the centre of her lower lip. She was as slight as a cat. When she turned to pass behind him, Nicolo leaned backward, tipping his stool on to its two back legs. He caught her wrist lightly in his hand. His hand wrapped easily around the bones. Zoe stopped. She turned the upper half of her body toward him. They were the only still figures in the middle of the noise and movement that continued around them.

"They're—we—we're all celebrating. That's why there are so many gifts. This isn't supposed to be ordinary. It's *not* ordinary. It's an engagement and then there's going to be a wedding, a marriage, probably for life because that's how we do it. It's a big deal, and everyone wants to be a part of it. The presents may look like dishes and towels and appliances to you, but they're more than that. You may think that they're for display, to show off how generous someone is being, or because of how they want to be seen, but that's not it either. They're meant to show how people feel. It's like they're a symbol. Not everyone can say what they mean in words. This is how we do it, instead of with words, and then you don't have to say it. It's all understood. That's what it's about."

Zoe paused and then leaned into him, resting her left hand on his shoulder, bringing her lips down to his ear. He could feel her breath moist and warm against his cheek and neck.

"You're right, Nicolo. Of course you're right. But still, you have to admit, it's pretty good entertainment."

A beat of laughter, a drawn breath, her hand pulled from his, that scent like a garden or pastries that lasted only another instant, and then she rushed away, her hands flying into the air to deflect or receive a volley of reproaches and demands cried out by the cooks and other servers.

CHAPTER SIXTEEN

Zoe was shorter and thinner and paler than Nicolo remembered, and more boyish, with only a suggestion of the swell of hips and breasts, although she carried herself extended to her full height as she approached his table at the Vaughan Bakery the next Saturday afternoon. She had pale pink polish on her nails, which were cut short. She wore dark grey trousers, a shirt, as pink as the inside of a shell, that was unbuttoned at her throat, and black shoes, round-toed, with a small, inward curving heel. Nicolo started to rise from his chair, but Zoe moved so quickly that she was seated in the chair opposite him before he had stood up completely. He sat down again.

"Would you like a coffee?" he asked. "A latte?"

"I ordered tea on my way in," she said. "They said they'd bring it over."

Nicolo couldn't understand how she had achieved this; he had been watching the door and had not seen her pass through it.

"I came in through the kitchen," Zoe explained. "I worked here for about three years when I was younger. My first paying job. They've always done their own baking, and my mum thought I might put on a few pounds being around so much temptation, but all that happened is that I was put off *dolci* for life."

She pronounced *dolci* properly, as if she had learned the word as an infant.

Nicolo had obtained Zoe's telephone number from another server at Palazzo Enrico, and had asked her to meet him. He felt intensely curious as to why she seemed both familiar and unusual. She reminded him of the times when he had gone to watch one or the other of the Enzos play hockey. Although the players were all dressed alike, he didn't need to watch the game for more than a minute before he could make out which one was his brother. The bulky padding, the skates, the sticks, the rapid movements—none of these could conceal the familiar set of his brother's head on his shoulders or the angle of his torso leaning into his stride. There was something about Zoe that he recognized in this same way, although he was certain he had never met her before the wedding shower. He would have remembered her hair, which was thick and glossy, like curling, pulled-copper wire, brushed back at the sides and at the front and held in place with a row of the kind of unadorned flat silver clips that he associated in some way with hair salons. He could not have forgotten, if he had ever seen it before, the unguarded appearance of her brow, where the skin was as pale and smooth and plump as the surface of the bread dough that his nonna set out to rise twice every week; he felt as if he wanted to run his thumbs across it to test its temperature and texture. He was drawn by the steadiness of her gaze. There was nothing tentative about her that he had yet seen. She emanated calm, but made him feel an almost overwhelming possessive anxiety. He sensed that she was exceptional, rare in some way that he did not yet understand. And he felt that his advantage—for here she was, sitting across the table from him, giving him her full attention—was likely to be fleeting, that others would soon see what he had seen, and that they, whoever they were, rivals or challengers or usurpers, would inevitably try to displace him, although he could not have said what standing he thought he had or might ever have with her. More truthfully, if asked, he would have had to concede that he had none. All he had, somehow and without any basis for it, was hope.

"How do you know Angie? From school?" he asked. He heard in his voice an interrogatory tone and he stopped to take a deep breath.

"I know it's not obvious, because we don't look anything alike, but we're cousins, more or less. What I mean is that Angie's father and my father are cousins. I was adopted by my parents when I was a few months old. Angie and I are the same age; I am just over a month older, five weeks I think. I'm December of '76 and she's January of '77."

The tea arrived, brought by a wide-hipped woman wearing a white apron on whom Zoe bestowed a quick smile. Zoe poured some of the tea into a cup. She added milk and honey, lifted the cup, and then set it down in its saucer without drinking from it. Nicolo began another question, but Zoe interrupted him.

"Okay," she said. "Here's my story. I don't usually tell it all in one go, but you'll hear it somewhere and I might as well give it to you all at once."

Nicolo nodded. He wasn't sure what story she was going to tell him, but he didn't want to interrupt her as she began.

"My mother was just over seventeen when she had me. She was from Sturgeon Falls, a small town up north of here, about a half-hour drive west of North Bay. She had a boy-friend, I don't know who, and one thing led to another and she found out she was pregnant. She left home before her parents found out, and came to the city all by herself on a bus. She was completely on her own; she didn't know any-one. She'd hardly even been out of Sturgeon Falls before coming here. She worked for a while, waitressing in a res-taurant somewhere, and then eventually I was born. When she went into labour she took the bus to the hospital and checked herself in—I've tried but I can hardly imagine it. Then, three or four days later she was let out with me, and it was the middle of the winter and she was cooped up in this basement apartment that social assistance helped her to find. She didn't have money for a stroller or even to buy a coat for me, and she didn't have a television or books, just a small radio that she'd brought with her, so what she did was she would go out during the day and in the evenings and walk around the city with me wrapped up in her scarf and buttoned inside her coat. She was trying to figure out the city and how it worked, how people lived, where they went for work, what they did with their time, how other people interacted, how they managed their lives.

"She saw my mum out with her own baby, my brother Marco, in one of the parks one afternoon when I was maybe two months old. My mum was pushing Marco in a big, broad pram; you know the kind people used to have—high, and navy blue and shiny and British, with crests, like a boat on wheels? My father had gone out and bought it the day Marco was born. Even then, that kind of thing wasn't usual and it caught my mother's attention. It looked to her as if my mum knew what she was doing. Inside this huge buggy was baby Marco propped up in blankets and pillows in his blue knitted cap and mittens and booties and a warm coat. And then there was my mum, perfectly competent, doting and fussing and checking all the time to make sure that Marco wasn't too cold or overheated.

"My mother followed my mum home that first day, and another few times after that. I think she must have checked it out pretty carefully. The house was in a normal, family neighbourhood, not rich, not poor. No other kids yet, just Marco. A husband. Someone who came home from work every evening about five. Groceries being carried into the house in armloads. Friends and relatives coming and going. Maybe she came close enough that she could smell dinner being cooked at night—sausages, garlic, tomato sauce, baking bread—I don't know. And then I guess she got a bit desperate. She had to go back at the end of every day to that basement, and I think it was worse than you can even imagine. Grim. Depressing. She was still just a girl. She had never had any fun and she didn't have anyone to talk to except her caseworker, who can't have cared, really, and the city was cold and confusing—it ignored her. And having a baby dependent on her overwhelmed her."

Zoe paused, but she didn't ask Nicolo whether he wanted to hear the rest. He felt certain that she could tell from the way that he was listening—attentively, without interrupting—that he did want to hear it. He was watching her as much as listening, observing how her lips formed the words, how her face remained unguarded. Her expression was that of someone not bothered about being judged. He was so determined not to appear to be critical in any way about any of what she was describing that he held himself absolutely still, and he had to remind himself once or twice to draw the next breath.

"So, then, one afternoon in February, early February, about two o'clock in the afternoon, Marco's in his crib napping and mum's in the kitchen cooking and she hears the doorbell and she opens the front door. She sees my mother standing there with this bundle held up in front of her, and she thinks at first that this is maybe a beggar like back in Italy trying to sell her something. My mother pushes this scarf toward her and she says, 'I hear that you're good with babies.' And then somehow it happens that my mum has the wrapped-up scarf in her arms, and I didn't weigh a lot but I was too heavy to be just rolled-up fabric, and so she looks down and the bundle starts to move and unfold in her hands. Now she thinks it's a kitten or a puppy, and she hates animals let alone whatever this woman has dragged in, so she's half letting the scarf unwind and half pushing it away. But my mother takes a step back and then my mum sees that it's me, a baby. I am just waking up, my mum says, but I'm quiet and skinny and not too clean, at least compared to the way she kept Marco. And my mum looks up at my mother and she said that she can just tell. She can tell that my mother has had it; that she isn't able to take care of me at that particular moment. My mum has a new baby of her own, so she knows how much care a baby that age needs. So she makes a decision. She pulls me in toward her, and then she stands there in the doorway while my mother backs away some more. As she's going backward down the steps my mother says, 'I'll be back for her.' And then she turns and walks fast down the street, not looking back, and my mum carries me inside and makes me a bottle from some canned milk and corn syrup and she sits on a chair in the kitchen and rocks me in her lap for a long time. She didn't even know my name.

"I didn't go back to sleep, she said; I just stared up at her. Eventually, she undressed me and checked me all over. Skinny. She said I was skinny—*sciupata*—she still says that about me now—but otherwise, she sees that I'm okay or maybe she would have called the police. She gave me a bath and dressed me in some of Marco's clothes and propped me up in Marco's bouncy chair. She said I didn't cry much and I stayed awake all that afternoon, as if I wasn't used to napping, and so she carried me from room to room on the little chair and I kept my eyes on her while she cooked and tidied."

Nicolo couldn't help himself. He asked, "And your mother never came back?" He realized as he said this that the story couldn't work that way; Zoe knew too much about her mother, more than she would have known if she had last seen her as an infant. He bit his lip.

"No, she did, about ten o'clock that night."

"What did your dad—Marco's dad—say?"

"He got home at his usual time I guess, after work, and he was really upset. He was worried that my mother wouldn't come back for me and he was sure that there was some law that neither of them knew about, that it must be illegal to have a stranger's baby, or that my mother might be crazy and would go to the police and report me missing or charge them with kidnapping me. He would have reported me to some-one, but he didn't know who he was supposed to go to, and he didn't want to involve the police if that wasn't the right thing to do. But my mum was calmer. She convinced him that it would be wrong to get my mother into trouble with-out any real reason. Eventually, she talked him into waiting until at least the next morning, and they decided that if my mother didn't come back by then, they would go together to the priest and ask him what he thought they should do; they were both certain that the priest would know the right thing. They had this perfect faith, you know? And my mum said that she was certain that my mother would come back; she said that she knew in her bones that if my mother hadn't intended to come back she would have said goodbye to me when she left, and she hadn't. While she was waiting, my mum made up a bag for my mother with some clothes for me and some food and a baby blanket, a few things like that. But all that happened was my mother came back that night, fairly late, and said thank you, and took me away along with the parcel that my mum had made for her."

"And then?"

"She did the same thing another few times later in the spring and in the summer, in the same way, leaving me with my mum for a day or a half-day or an evening. My mum tried not to ask her too many questions. She felt that she was doing something that my mother seemed to really need.

"Until July second, which was a Saturday, the holiday weekend, and my dad was home and so he's the one who opens the door—he hadn't laid eyes on my mother before that—and when he sees her, he does the strangest thing, for him, because he's not normally the kind of guy who—he's not usually like this: he sees her there holding me on the doorstep and he sees I think what my mum hadn't really seen, that she's just a girl, and he stretches out his arms to her and folds us both inside, like a hug but longer, more protective, and they stand there a long while with me between them. He said my mother was stiff at first, like a plank of wood, but then she slowly became more and more relaxed until he thought she was almost sleeping, standing there with his arms around her, even though it was the middle of the day. And he thinks that's what made up my mother's mind, that this was okay, that this might be somewhere that I could stay for longer.

"She wouldn't come inside. She never would come inside the house; it seemed to make her nervous. So my dad gets some folding lawn chairs from the garage, and he sets them up on the front lawn, and they sit in front of the house in the shade into the late afternoon and figure out the arrangements. She leaves me with them that time overnight, and when she comes back the next day, he and my mum have been to a local lawyer's office and have had the papers made up, and Bepina and Pasquale from next door come over to be the witnesses. It was simpler back then to do these things I guess, and it wasn't adoption, just temporary custody, and there was no father involved, my mother made it clear that whoever he was he wasn't ever going to be in the picture, so that made it easier, there was no one else whose consent was needed. My mum said she realized she had to make it flexible, so that my mother would feel that she could come and see me, but she also made it clear to my mother that this was a long-term deposit, until I was grown and able to make decisions myself, and that she wouldn't be able to check me in and out like a library book. So that was the deal and it pretty much worked out, give or take.

"Eventually I became a Trapasso too, around the time that they enrolled Marco and me in kindergarten. A name change isn't difficult to get, and it made it easier for people to under-stand and for my parents to fill out forms and enrolments for all of us. They mixed us kids in together and treated us all the same. Like Marco and the others—there's also Tina and Joseph and Emma and Stephanie—I learned dialect at home before I learned how to speak English."

"And did you see your own mother again?"

"She came to see me twice when I was growing up, once when I was six and a second time when I was eleven. Just short visits. A few hours, even though she'd come all that way. She'd moved out west to Vancouver almost right away, and later she moved out even farther, to one of the smallest islands off the coast that you can actually live on, Lasqueti Island, population about three hundred. I took the train and then two ferries out to see her there for a few days during the summer after I finished high school. She sends me parcels once in a while, something that she finds and thinks I might like, books or shells or stones, one time a purple silk scarf that she wove herself on a loom. I mail her cards at Christmas and on her birthday, and I'm pretty certain my mum and dad have sent her some money over the years. She's had a hard time—a few hard times."

"You don't sound mad at her."

"I have been. I was furious with her most of the time I was growing up. I felt like one of those birds, you know, cuckoos, whose parents are too lazy to raise them and so they roll their egg into another bird's nest. There is no point, though. I've long since realized that I can't go through life angry with her. It's just self-pity—and what reason do I have to feel sorry for myself? My mother made a really good choice when she left me, one of the better decisions she's ever made. My job is in child protection. I see the kinds of homes that kids have to grow up in. My mother picked the kind of place for me that she didn't have as a child but that she probably wanted, somewhere she would have been supported even if they didn't understand her. My family is great; I have two brothers and three sisters and my mum and dad are wonderful. I don't think they even remember most of the time that I wasn't theirs from the start, except that, of course, I don't look at all like any of them. It was harder on Marco, sometimes, having me always around, having to explain me, and having me steal some of his thunder. He would have been the oldest if I hadn't come along and he would have had his parents to himself for at least a while longer. That bothers me a bit, that I caused that, although I know there really isn't anything I could have done to fix it; it's something he's had to work through for himself. The only issue I think I still have apart from that is that I can't help feeling that where I ended up seems arbitrary. You know? I could have been brought up Greek Orthodox or Lithuanian or WASP or Jewish. I could have been anything. Why this family, this culture, this place, and not some other one?"

Because, thought Nicolo, surprised himself at the quickness, the intensity of the idea. Because this is what brought you to me.

CHAPTER SEVENTEEN

Massimo didn't allow any concerns about Vito to take root in his mind for the first few months after the boy arrived. He knew it would take Vito a while to settle in. He was still young, after all, and in an unfamiliar country and a new workplace with a new language to grapple with. But frigid February became melancholy, stormy March, and then a long, blizzard-filled, sharp-winded April, followed by the first, still-bitter week of May without any thaw in Vito's approach to his work or the customers, most of whom still continued to come in to the shop, as they had always done, for their trims and their shaves; they were, like Massimo, slow to make changes and willing to suspend unfavourable judgment in the case of a recently arrived *paesano*. Paola had persuaded Massimo to install a television, a black sixteen-inch Panasonic. This had been attached to an angled stand above the waiting area, and it provided noise and colour that moderately compensated for the absence of garrulous Guido. But Vito's silence and aloofness were unalloyed and it was impossible not to read into his manner at least some level of disregard, if not active disrespect.

Then, late in the morning of the first Thursday of an unseasonably slow-to-start May, before breaking to eat the hot lunch that Paola had carried over for him in a foil-covered dish, Massimo, who had just finished cutting Tony Dario's thick helmet of iron-grey hair, left Tony in the chair to make change at the cash register for Dom Cremona, who had dropped into the store while passing by because he had only a twenty-dollar bill and needed change for the bus. Dom, while not suspicious, was cautious about money—he wanted no more and also no less than his due—and it took Massimo several careful counts into Dom's broad palm before Dom was assured that he was leaving with his twenty dollars transformed into coins, with neither increment nor shrinkage. After this small, concentrated transaction, the two men lobbed *ciao*'s at each other and then Massimo turned around to walk the four or five paces to his chair so that he could sweep the back of Tony's neck with a neck duster and unfasten the Velcro closure of Tony's black plastic cape. As he turned he saw, in a disbelieving instant, that Vito had stepped into his place behind Tony's bent head while he, Massimo, had been distracted. Vito's two feet, in their beautiful calfskin loafers, were on the very patch of linoleum from which Massimo's feet had worn away almost every trace of the scattershot pattern, and Vito was just lifting his long, slick scissors and tortoiseshell comb away from the back of Tony's head. Massimo turned and saw Vito standing in his place, and everyone in the shop in that moment held perfectly still—Massimo, Vito, Tony, and even Dom, who paused at the door with his bus fare securely inside his closed fist. For another instant the only movement in the entire store was the silent and minute flurry of just-severed hair that spun toward the floor from the back of Tony's head, shimmering in a sudden beam of light that pierced at that moment, like a godlike pointing finger, through the broad window at the front of the store. Massimo had no vocabulary for what he saw, and nor did Tony or Dom or Vito himself, it seemed, because none of them uttered a word.

Vito took two slow paces backward, retreating in a sliding motion toward his own workstation. Once there, he set down his scissors and comb and leaned toward the mirror, as if scrutinizing his appearance for flaws. He drew the palm of his flat hand along the side of his own hair. Dom went out the front door without saying anything, the bell above the glass and brass door jangling briefly to give emphasis to his departure, and once outside, he gave a backward glance through the window, shook his head, and shifted his shoulders up and down before walking stiffly and rapidly away along the sidewalk. Massimo felt a hot clench in his heart, or lower, in his stomach, or even farther down, in his bowels. Something, somewhere, swelled and boiled inside him. There was a spot at the back of Tony Dario's head that had always given him considerable trouble. Tony had an off-centre swirl of hair there, a seemingly unconquerable cowlick, the hair spinning counterclockwise around an area where his coverage had thinned. Massimo had never managed to trim this problematic area without exposing the bald spot and so he usually avoided the hair just above it, which meant that Tony was left with an elongated and protruding hirsute knob, the shape and size of half an egg, a hand span above his shirt collar. Before Massimo could begin to comprehend what Vito had done, his feet had carried him to his usual spot and his hand had reached out automatically for the horsehair brush on the counter. He began to sweep Tony's neck, taking infinite care. Tony craned forward in order to help with the task. With Tony's head thus extended in front of him, Massimo observed that Vito's quick cuts had been highly effective. The rough area that Massimo had, as usual, left largely untouched, and that Tony had never complained about and perhaps hadn't even noticed, had now been cut by Vito's clever scissors at an oblique angle that neatly solved the problem. The hair underneath was snipped short; the hair on the top lay flat. The thinning spot was completely concealed by the slightly longer layer of overhanging hair. Massimo could see that it was a neat job with, perhaps— given the short time it had taken and the pressure to accomplish it while Massimo's back was turned—even a touch of genius.

Massimo stood, shifting his weight from one foot to the other and then back again, brushing Tony's extended neck with short, careful swipes, and tried to identify the emotions that had seized possession of his body and determine which would prevail. In his bowels and stomach, shame was most evident. It was unheard of, unthinkable, unimaginable, for one barber to knowingly interfere with the work of another. Even more improbable was the possibility of a junior, a *giovane*, a *subalterno*, tweaking his master's nose in such a manner. It had already become apparent that this Vito was furtive in his ways, but no one could have predicted this. *Fidarsi è bonu. Ma non fidarsi è megliu,* he reminded himself. To trust is good. But, he thought, not to trust is better still. There was, at the same time, a small and opposing emotion in Massimo's chest, something that could develop in time into something like pride, that this Vito, whom Massimo had sponsored and then imported from Italy, like a fine wine or silk ties or a sports car, could demonstrate such virtuosity; this attested however indirectly to Massimo's discernment, good sense and sound judgment. His head buzzed with these and other contending thoughts. Tony said nothing, only waited, patiently, while his neck was swept over and over. His skin began to redden, but he did not like to ask Massimo to stop, to point out that the job must be finished. At last, Massimo reached out and he swept the cape from Tony's neck, added one or two more superfluous flourishes with the brush, spun Tony to face the mirror, and then held up a round hand mirror so that Tony could inspect his cut from all sides.

"Is okay?" said Massimo.

"S'okay," Tony replied, and he ducked his head almost imperceptibly in Vito's direction. Tony was not a subtle man, but he was a careful one.

Vito sniffed deeply and turned to the back of the store to rearrange his growing collection of lotions and waxes and creams. At that instant, miraculously, as if summoned or sent in by a stage manager, three customers came in through the door like the cast of a comedy team—one tall and almost bald, the second short and spiky-haired, and the last medium-sized with a halo of corkscrew curls—all needing to be served. At the same time, a noisy talk show came on the television, a popular local program, and it turned out not to be necessary or possible for Massimo or Vito to say anything to each other until the day ended, and even then no words were necessary since they had been busy and had run late and Vito left quickly, apparently having an appointment to keep, while Massimo stayed to close up the store.

That night at home Massimo ate his dinner silently. If he was not more quiet than usual, his silence had at least a deepened and shaded quality, and Paola tried to discover what the problem, if there was one, might be. Something at work, possibly, but the gnocchi she had made that afternoon hadn't risen to the top of the pot as they should have and the cheese that she had grated over them was not as sharp as Massimo liked it, so that could be it too. In any case, Massimo gave her no opening, no clue, and she wondered about it until they were in bed, as close together as a single sheet of origami paper folded cleverly into two nested figures: sleeping husband, sleeping wife. She felt her eyes fill, so concerned was she for this man, for his hidden sorrows whatever they were, and she thought of a rhyme from her youth: *Se vai' a lettu non mi pidghija sonnu. Pensu a' l'amuri e mi ment' a ciangiri.* If I go to bed, I won't be able to sleep. I'll think of love and start to weep. She reached up and pulled her fingers through Massimo's hair, finding and rearranging the few snarls and knots into neat rows of curls, forgiving him for suppressing whatever it was that was bothering him, and comforting herself over not having detected the cause.

Her preening sent chills down Massimo's back, a pleasurable sensation that transformed into heat as it crept lower, a warmth that began to erase the day's tensions. He reached back and pulled Paola's hands so that they were flat on his shoulders. She kneaded his muscles there, and when her hands tired she reached around his chest to embrace him. He turned toward her and tested her in the dark, ran his hands over her arms, shoulders, neck, breasts and waist, overcoming her modesty, until she was warm, giving, willing, and wholly ready to embrace all of him. He folded back his clothes and hers, and came into her, and they rocked together like the tightly joined boards in the keel of a boat afloat in calm waters. The concern that Paola had intuited was worn away, and the moment when Massimo might have told her about what Vito had done slipped by. (He could never have told his mother. *"A ru zingaru 'nsiegni a minare 'u mantice?"* she would cry, blaming Vito. No man should be so foolish as to try to teach a Gypsy how to operate his bellows?) Before he fell asleep entangled with the limbs and unbound hair of his trusting wife, Massimo was reminded of a gesture his sons had sometimes made as children, pressing their lips firmly together and turning the fingers of their right hand before their closed mouth like a key securing a lockbox where a secret would be kept safe forever.

Inside Paola's belly, Massimo's sperm, continuous and countless and relentless as a swarm of bees, coursed toward her womb, where a coy egg, warm and round and luminous and as sweetly evasive as a lone pear overlooked by a hot day's gatherers, awaited suitors in darkness and in silence.

CHAPTER EIGHTEEN

Nicolo had been trying to persuade Bella and Phil to add stretches to their morning workouts. They were both remarkably inelastic, particularly Phil, whose fingers could only just brush through the air in front of, but not near, his own knees when he inclined forward from the waist. Although they were not yet thirty, both Fells were like antique wind-up toys, mechanical soldiers that had not been used in a long time and so had slowed and seized up. They both liked the elliptical machines, however, and would have spent all of their allotted hour on them, if Nicolo had let them, moving their arms and legs forward and back in a martial gait. One early morning before they got started, Nicolo made a rough drawing on a plain sheet of paper on top of his clipboard. He sketched in the muscles in the upper legs, hips and trunk, as well as the hamstring and Achilles tendon, and then added arrows to show Phil and Bella how their muscles were meant to extend and contract when their bodies moved. He demonstrated three or four simple trunk and leg stretches, and then persuaded both of them to lie down on mats, on their backs, face up, legs bent, and he grasped each of their sneakered feet in turn to guide them as they moved their legs first up and then in toward the chest. He showed them how to use a looped skipping rope to gently pull a straightened, extended leg up into the air. Over the following morning sessions he added new leg, neck, shoulder and trunk stretches. Both of the Fells followed his instructions perfunctorily. They made no effort to push themselves to add to their limited, resistant range of motion. After a couple of weeks, Bella said, abruptly, as they were about to get started, that she didn't see the point of these stretches.

"We ssit at our desks all day," she told Nicolo, and as she spoke, she tucked her sharp chin in toward her chest, and then jutted it out several times in a repeated emphatic tic or twitch. "We don't need to be flexible. Sstretching isn't relaxing for us." Beside her, Phil made several sharp, repeated inward and outward movements with his neck and chin that echoed and emphasized Bella's words.

Nicolo felt a bubble of dislike rising up like heartburn from his chest into his throat. "Have you tried yoga?" he asked. He felt an unanticipated rush of heat. His face flushed and he could sense his heart labouring under the skin of his chest, *pump-pump, pump-pump, pump-pump,* like a diesel motor. "Many people find that yoga—"

"Too sslow," said Phil.

"Too mindless," said Bella. "We tried it once." She shuddered.

"No, not yoga," they said almost in unison.

"Pilates?" Nicolo tried again. He drew in a breath that seemed to leak back out steamily through his forehead and ears. "There's a course that you could both take on Saturday mornings with a new German-trained instructor. I hear he's very good. You might want to think about switching to that instead."

Phil and Bella quickly turned to look at each other, and then Phil shifted his gaze to a spot on the ceiling and Bella tipped her head downward, toward the polished wooden floor, so that her words were slightly muffled.

"We can't do that," she said. "We want you to undersstand this. We're used to you now. It would be very difficult for us to change. Neither of us likes change. We aren't adaptable. If you say this stretching is important, we will jusst need to try to do better."

The three of them stood there for a full minute, not speaking. All around them the activity of the gym continued busily and noisily. On the other side of a long glass wall, an aerobics class bounced and lunged to rhythmic, disco-like beat. In the weight room, barbells and free weights were lifted and then dropped with resonating thuds corresponding to their weight. Piped-in pop music swirled above the heads of people on stationary bicycles, stair climbers, treadmills and rowing machines.

Neither Phil nor Bella looked at Nicolo, but he could feel them waiting for him to provide a response. When he opened his mouth to speak, he intended to provide assurances, reassurances, plans, a shared commitment to a sustainable strategy for their physical development. But what he really wanted was not to have to deal with them for a while.

"I should let you know . . ." he said, not certain until he said it what excuse he would give, "I should let you know that I'll be away for several days, quite soon, in Las Vegas, and so I'm afraid I will have to reschedule a few of our sessions." He felt an unexpected bolt of joy, a warm ray that struck somewhere near his solar plexus and then spread out, a small thrill of possibility.

Bella raised her head. "That is very dissappointing for us to hear," she said. "We had been given to understand that all of the insstructors here were very reliable. We checked this carefully before we signed up." She blinked once, twice, and Phil blinked too, an unsyncopated beat behind her. "We will have to conssider this carefully together," Bella said. Phil nodded, and then the two of them picked up their towels and evaporated in that odd way they had, soundlessly, like smoke or vapour, in the direction of the change rooms.

Nicolo met Zoe at seven-thirty that evening on the pavement outside the theatre where the play *Wit* was showing. Nicolo had come downtown from work and he was wearing jeans and a gym shirt and a jacket with the crest of his high school hockey team on it. Zoe was there ahead of him, wearing a calf-length blue dress, a yellow quilted jacket with a stand-up collar and red low-heeled shoes. A small red bag hung from her arm.

"Shoot," she said. "I'm overdressed. You don't happen to have a tux on underneath that bomber jacket, do you? Because if you don't, I am not sure we go together well enough for us to sit next to each other."

"No," Nicolo said. "You're just right. It's me. Work ran late and I didn't get home to change."

There had in fact been time to change, but Nicolo had lingered at the gym instead. Going home and then going out again would have attracted his mother's interest, and his nonna's, and he didn't want to establish expectations, even for himself. He had dated before—not regularly, but enough to wonder about whether he was the kind of person who would ever do what Mario was doing—pick someone, or allow himself to be chosen, and live in an entirely different way, not as a solitary person but as half of a pair, like those birds that mate for life. And even if this was possible for him, Zoe did not seem to be the kind of person who might want this from him. She was more educated than he was, and more serious, not the sort who would fall for a guy who worked in a gym. She had finished a degree in social work and was working for a newly formed charity called The Moses Project, which proposed to set up a system of doors and bassinets on pulleys and levers at the regional hospitals. A baby could be deposited anonymously into this system from outdoors and conveyed inside. The scheme was controversial because it freed the parents from responsibility and robbed babies of the chance to know anything about their identity, and the start of construction had been delayed twice. Zoe was impatient, she told him.

"I don't understand it when people just don't get on with whatever it is that needs to be done. I can't see how hard it would be to just start, and work out any issues that come up later."

They found their seats and Nicolo helped Zoe shrug off her jacket, which she accepted back from his hands without shifting her gaze from the stage, which had been set up as a hospital room. She shook the jacket, folded it neatly, laid it flat in her lap and then began to study the program. Zoe's arm was so close to Nicolo's on the armrest of her seat that he could feel, or at least sense, the mild heat that she radiated. He watched the movement of her flexors and supinators as she raised her arm and passed her program from one hand to the other. When she laid down her arm again, he saw how her extensor muscles rippled smoothly like fabric or water under her skin and then subsided. He observed from the corner of his eye the surface of her cheek, fine, pale, faintly freckled, and he saw how her temple crimped outward and then smoothed flat again when she closed and then opened her eyes. Her bare shoulders shone in the red light of a distant exit sign, sharp bone under pale skin, and her neck inclined slightly forward at an angle that was already familiar to him, although he didn't make the connection, from years of watching his father cut customers' hair. Her lower lip hung slightly open except when she placed it between her teeth and slowly drew it out. She looked as self-contained and still as a pool of water. He wanted with an intensity that startled him to place his hand on hers, to feel the play of bones under her flesh, and the length and strength of her fingers, but he was reluctant to distract her. The play was just beginning.

The main character was a woman, a professor who taught poetry. Her specialty was the work of a long-dead poet named John Donne. She was brave and archly clever, but she was told early in the first act that she was dying of cancer and she spent the rest of the play getting the dying done. The professor told a story about a poem that Nicolo remembered from his last year of high school, in which death was compared to sleep. He remembered as he heard it again the trick at the end, how it mocked death, defining it as only a brief interlude before an eternal afterlife. What he had forgotten, or hadn't realized before, was the defiance of it, like whistling into a hurricane:

> *Death, be not proud, though some have called thee*
> *Mighty and dreadful, for thou art not so;*
> *For those, whom thou think'st thou dost overthrow,*
> *Die not, poor Death, nor yet canst thou kill me. . . .*
> *Thou art slave to fate, chance, kings, and desperate men,*
> *And dost with poison, war, and sickness dwell,*
> *And poppy or charms can make us sleep as well,*
> *And better than thy stroke; why swell'st thou then?*
>
> *One short sleep past, we wake eternally,*
> *And Death shall be no more; Death, thou shalt die.*

The woman told how, as a young student, she had been reproved for using a semicolon in the last line instead of a comma. "Nothing but a breath—a comma—separates life from life everlasting. It's very simple really," she said, standing with one hand holding on to her IV pole and lifting the other, palm upward, in a half shrug. "Life, death. Soul. God. Past, present. Not insuperable barriers, not semicolons, just a comma."

Toward the end of the play, the sick woman died and this scene was one of pain and confusion. A team of doctors tried to restart her heart, and the shouting and barking of orders and what looked like brutalities inflicted on the small body pulled Nicolo's attention fully away from Zoe at last and to the action onstage. In the play's last scene, the actress, in the gentlest of motions, rose and walked away from the medical ministrations. This was the moment of her death, and she had risen out of and shed her own racked body. She stood for a minute, reached up and set aside her hospital gown and the cap that had covered her head, and then walked, naked, bald, toward a strong light that shone directly down on her.

For a few moments the crowded theatre was silent and still. Then someone clapped in the upper balcony, and immediately after, several others joined from below. Like a flock of birds taking off in an expanding flurry, the theatre had poured into it a rising surge of applause. Nicolo glanced toward Zoe and saw a tear, a tracing of a sliding bead, creeping downward on her cheek.

"You cry at plays?" he said. He stretched an arm around Zoe's shoulders, and she lowered her head so that it leaned against his upper arm. He could feel her smooth hair against his chin, and under his arm he felt her heat, the speed of her heart and pulse, the way her breath pushed against and then pulled together the bones of her chest. He had an impression of how active the motor of her entire body was, even seated, and when she turned toward him, he felt that her face was transparent as a crystal and that he could see how her thoughts and feelings agitated inside her head.

"Of course," she answered. "Who doesn't?" She placed a hand on his arm and examined his expression closely. "How could you not? It's tragic. It's not the death so much; we all die in the end. It's the futility. What is life for, after all—getting things, learning things—when it always ends like that? It's heartbreaking if you stop to think about it."

Nicolo didn't know how to answer. He couldn't remember the last time he had cried. He closed his eyes, experimentally, testing, waiting. Nothing came. The play had affected him; his chest had tightened and he had felt in the base of his throat an unnameable ache, but no more than that. Was he defective in some way? Was this evidence of an irredeemable lack of feeling? A sign that he had an unusually stony or obstinate heart?

"It was sad," he said, slowly. "It's a terrible story. But part of me can't let go of the fact that it is a story, with actors."

"I do forget," Zoe said. "I suspend disbelief as easily as that." She held up one hand and brushed her fingers against her thumb. "I've always been able to do it. It only takes a moment, when I read a good book or go to a movie or a play, and then, once it happens, I'm lost, as if I've fallen into a hole. It's funny, but I actually don't mind that, being dropped or pulled completely into another universe. Even when whatever happens makes me upset, it's worth it. It's like getting to live another life for a while. Otherwise you're always stuck in your own. It's a chance to be taken somewhere else completely."

The lights had not yet come up and the theatre was still

dark. They were close to the stage, in very good seats in the centre, a dozen rows back from where the actors had played out their drama. Zoe's head brushed against Nicolo's shoulder and it may be that at one end or the other of their row of seats a door or vent was opened. A thin stream of cold air settled down around them. Nicolo's skin contracted in this abrupt change of temperature, and, for the smallest space of time, he experienced a strange physical dislocation. He felt as if some essence of himself had rushed as easily as a breath out into the room, and then he had an even stranger sensation, of flowing in some unimpeded way into Zoe, as though she had become permeable and he was somehow moving through the receptive pores of her skin. For a moment he could feel her body from the inside, see through her eyes, hear what she heard, breathe as she breathed. He felt how wide and orderly and well-stocked was the calm place in the centre of her, like the shelves of a library surrounded by thick walls that held the world and its clamour and disorder at bay, and how complete and whole she was, not lacking in some important way as many lone people are—one hand soundlessly clapping, a scant pound of flour at the bottom of an enormous sack, a lone cypress tree without its companion Lombardy poplar, the barrel of a bell without its clapper. The experience lasted as long as a blink. He had time for only the briefest impression of a very different geography from his own. The space he inhabited, his own interior self, resembled the rooms and streets where he lived—busy, domesticated, commonplace, conventional. Hers was a more original and mazelike arrangement, and he felt it might take a very long time to work through it. Zoe shifted next to his arm and immediately the experience ended. He was himself, back inside his own head and skin. He felt a sense of marvel but also of confidence and warmth. What a strange sensation, but one for which there must be a rational explanation—the result of having just seen the play, and the darkness of the theatre, and his desire to understand Zoe. Or it was possible that he had fallen asleep; people must doze off in theatres all the time, and a play, after all, so closely resembles dreaming.

"Do you think it might actually be like that?" Zoe was saying. "Do you think there's a bright light and then walking along, through a dark tunnel, and then, I don't know, do you think that then there's heaven?"

"Yes," Nicolo said. "I do. I'm sure of it."

CHAPTER NINETEEN

Nicolo did believe in heaven. His image of it was vague, but if he had been forced to do so, he very well might have described something like the Italy that his nonna spoke of—not the Italy that was, but the Italy that should and could have been, if there hadn't been the wars, if the government had sent doctors and trains as promised when votes were sought, instead of tax collectors, whose complicity could be bought, and unscrupulous police officers. This heaven existed overhead, somehow, suspended by unseen wires or forces in a separate layer, like a stratum in a wedding cake, above the visible sky but lower than black outer space in which bright stars and blue and red and gold planets spun in their orbits. Heaven had gravity, like Earth, and light, but the gravity of rocks and dirt in heaven had less substance and the light somehow had more. Heaven had sideways-slanting hills, deep-mounded earth that forced green shoots up through the soil after the afternoon rains, heavy grapes warm and sweet and so willing to be pressed into wine that they were already half-fermented and loose on their stems under a sun that glowed through the gathered clouds of a second, higher sky. In this heaven, sturdily built stone houses with sound roofs had people inside them who knew exactly where they belonged, a benevolent *padrone* in a *palazzo* overlooking the central, fan-shaped *piazza* where festivals were held—a *padrone* who took every pain to ensure that all wants were anticipated and met before they were felt—fat, gold grain carefully stored in the barns, sturdy milk cows in the fields, cheeses ripening in caves behind the village and turned daily by small boys, the rumbling noise of coffee being ground every morning under every roof, bread baking in hot, banked rows in the communal ovens—every family having no more and no less than what they required. Heaven.

Nicolo's older brother Enzo went to a family Mass at ten o'clock on Sunday mornings with his wife, Mima, and their children, Zachary and Isabella. His parents went on Sundays as well, almost without fail, to the earliest service possible, anticipatory to their weekly sessions spinning in each other's embrace on the dining room rug. Younger Enzo attended only funerals and weddings, and he did so in the manner of a visiting anthropologist—dispassionate, analytical and ironic, making mental notes of items that he could recount later to fellow unbelievers as evidence of the great

distance his rational mind had carried him from his super-
stitious upbringing. Only Nicolo still went several times
most weeks. He had not fallen away from the Catholicism
of his early childhood but had become over time committed
to its familiar rhythms and routines. He had grown aware
that the rituals and ceremonies of attending Mass worked
a transformation on his brain waves, immersing him into
a kind of waking trance in which his thinking was both
slowed and sharpened. He became restless if too many days
went by between visits; he felt the lack of it more intensely
than he felt the need for it. Nothing—not dreaming, not
working out, not sports—took him out of and yet socketed
him into the world in quite the same way, although he was
aware that there were certain parallels between going to
Mass and working with the heaviest weights at the gym.
It seemed to him that taking part in church was a kind of
lifting up of weights too, but exercising his spirit instead
of his muscles, and with the priest as his spotter. He hadn't
deciphered, or even seriously questioned why faith was
important to him. (This was a puzzle he solved years later,
in his late fifties, after his wife's death, after many hours of
talk with his brothers at the coffee shop, and it had to do
with ballast. Belief had centred him then, saved him from
the sin of wanting without cease to be at her side, first in
her coffin, which was too wide and too long for her to lie
in alone, and then inside the space into which she had been
fitted at the mausoleum with the shadowed void at the left
for when his time came—how hungry, how impatient he
had felt, how sinfully, how unforgivably he had ached for
their separation to end.)

Which is not to say that Nicolo was unaware of the many challenges and paradoxes and irrational demands of faith. Believers were called upon to think, but not to question, to worship without idolatry, to seek freedom in discipline, to speak routine utterances aloud and in unison in order to cement a fresh and personal and wholly interior connection to God, to make rote and ritual intense and personal.

Nicolo was vigilantly, almost superstitiously, observant of the practices of faith and he had added to them some of his own. He always walked, when possible, on the left-hand side of the outdoor stairs leading up to the church doors, treading where the stone steps were not yet worn down. He pulled open the right-hand door of the heavy, panelled pair at the entrance. He touched the holy water with the tips of his third and fourth fingers. He made the sign of a cross with his head bowed toward the font, touching rather than tracing his forehead, his chest above his heart, his left and then his right shoulder. He sat in one of the pews at the back, close to the doors. Nicolo had occasionally been invited by the priest to come forward and read aloud from scripture, but he tried to avoid being chosen by keeping his gaze low, toward the tiled floor with its alternating pattern of burgundy *fleurs-de-lis* and yellow diamonds. He did not attend Mass in order to participate, but so that he could be ministered to; he wanted to arrive empty and be filled, with nothing more expected of him than his presence with an attentive heart. He preferred to sit quietly toward the back of the church, in a part of the sanctuary where two soaring columns had been placed close together, forming a kind of grove, a dim and sheltered recess. Here, the shadows never lightened, and the floor and columns gathered and amplified the spoken words and the music so that he could feel his chest respond to the resonance of the solemn invocations of the priest calling on all of the collected celebrants to reflect on their unworthiness and sinfulness. Even if Nicolo were suddenly struck deaf and blind, he felt that if he were brought here and placed in this spot, he would know through the medium of his bones exactly where he was.

When Nicolo intoned the confession with the other celebrants, he spoke the words sincerely, confessing with right and proper candour that he had sinned in his thoughts and words, in his actions and in his failures to act. He sang the Kyrie—*Lord have mercy, Christ have mercy, Lord have mercy*—with a reverent and penitential heart. He recited the creed instinctively. Yes, he believed in God . . . Creator of Heaven and Earth, and, yes, in Jesus Christ as well . . . conceived of the Holy Spirit, born, suffered, crucified, risen again. He believed absolutely in the resurrection of the body, accepting that this was a mystery he would never penetrate, and he believed in life everlasting, those went without saying, but he had much less certainty about the promise of the forgiveness of his sins. The priest who had had the charge of the parish during the years when Nicolo was aged five to fifteen had spoken perhaps more strongly than he had intended, and he had left Nicolo convinced that the weight of a single boy's transgressions might be more than even the most forgiving God could endure. Nicolo kept his eyes closed during the Eucharistic prayer and he felt, every time, even if he did not precisely understand the mystery it invoked, the substantiality of it, the consecration and transformation of the bread and wine into the very body and blood of a sternly loving Christ, that he took inside himself in hope, every time, of enduring grace. He felt precisely and gratefully the moment when Jesus entered his being, and his body and soul were almost always perceptibly lightened. This sense of buoyancy, of weightlessness, carried over until the Mass ended and the congregation was sent out by the priest into the world, but after a day or two it would wear away, like the shine on a new pair of shoes, like the point on a pencil, like the crease in a pair of pants, and he would need to return.

In addition to the deliberate, purposeful service of the Mass, Nicolo liked the tidy, almost formulaic way in which the church's teachings and obligations were enumerated and unambiguously conveyed so that it was possible to believe that they provided a certain road map to grace. What were the seven spiritual works of mercy? To instruct the ignorant. To counsel the doubtful. To admonish sinners. To bear wrongs patiently. To forgive offences willingly. To comfort the afflicted. To pray for the living and the dead. What were the seven corporeal works of mercy? To feed the hungry. To give drink to the thirsty. To clothe the naked. To shelter the homeless. To visit the sick. To visit the imprisoned. To bury the dead. There were seven of each, no more no less, finite and understandable and comforting—even though he knew that it was virtually impossible to accomplish them all and in fact the intent seemed to be to make them just slightly impossible to achieve in order to keep the faithful striving. And some of the works were metaphors. He understood that. He was unlikely to be called upon to physically clothe the naked or bury the dead, but he did make charitable donations that covered most or all of his duties. He also instructed the ignorant, although he tried not to think of his clients using that expression. He knew that he bore wrongs well—he was forgiving by nature, willing to make accommodations for others and to accept excuses for why they might act badly. He didn't counsel the doubtful or admonish sinners, but he felt about those works much the same as he felt about reading aloud in church—unskilled, not fit by nature or otherwise for the task, certain that God would arrange for others to undertake them in his stead.

Nicolo thought as seldom as possible about his sexual sins, but when they did compel consideration, he found that they fell readily into two categories. The first was his irregular habit of touching his sexual parts in bed or while showering, and occasionally at other times when he was alone. There was no way to deny that he enjoyed the way they felt inside his hand: the always surprising textured softness of the skin over muscle and blood vessels, the warmth of them, like ripe fruit in the sun, their purposeful arrangement, as useful as new and well-constructed machinery, as satisfying to manipulate as an efficient lever, as capable and finely balanced as fishing tackle. These parts of his body seemed almost to have been calibrated exactly to his touch, being located where his hands fell naturally, and providing a combination of satisfyingly contradictory sensations against his hard thighs and firm stomach—downy, ridged, warm, cool, loose, tight, at ease, urgent, hard, soft, light, oddly counterweighted. (The first time he ate dim sum in a restaurant, he was astonished at how closely the warm, salty little dumplings filled with shrimp and bamboo shoots that were presented to him in a bamboo steamer-basket resembled the twin bundles that upholstered his penis in colour and texture and even temperature; he placed a dumpling in his mouth with equal parts anticipation and trepidation and was taken aback by their almost muscular resistance to his teeth and tongue.)

When Nicolo was a teenager, Father Xavier had collected the boys of the church together once or twice a year, in the same basement reception room in which coffee and tea were served on Sundays—had gathered them on chairs arranged in semicircles in ranks that became decreasingly ordered over the course of the hour, to caution them that touching themselves and all the rest were as dangerous as having anything to do with girls, and perhaps worse because God had at least designed girls for a purpose. The boys needed to take every care possible to avoid this kind of behaviour; any deliberate exercise of sexuality must be reserved to a regular, approved, sacramental relationship—holy marriage in short, ideally to a faithful girl who understood this too: that the pleasures of the body were to be postponed, suspended and safeguarded for the future and then turned only and always to their proper use. Nicolo had thought, listening to this lecture at age twelve or thirteen, of a brilliant blue and green beetle he had seen on a school trip to the museum. The iridescent insect had been trapped and preserved for the edification of future schoolchildren, intact, immobile and changeless, in a sleek candy-like globule of translucent amber.

Worse than this sin, which was one he could at least contemplate with an endurable level of regret since the weight of it was not overpowering, was the second category—his list of sexual encounters. There had been six of these acts or sequences of unchastity since the age of seventeen. He accepted that they were the consequence of having, on each such occasion, wilfully turned away from the route God wanted him to follow. He had confessed most of these to the younger of the two current parish priests (and he knew that his avoidance of the other, older priest was yet another category of uncategorized and unatoned-for sin, related to sex although not in itself sexual) and had been, in response, exhorted to strive to live a life of the spirit and to resist temptation by means of devotion to the Virgin Mary, regular confession and frequent attendance at mass.

"Evil doesn't exist in and of itself," Father Bem told him. "God wouldn't permit that. No, evil grows out of our inadequate consciousness or mindfulness of God. Evil comes from ourselves alone."

On the night after he had agreed to go with Patrick on his trip to Las Vegas, Nicolo lay in his bed after turning off the light and reviewed in turn these six events of active sexual transgression.

First, a week or two after his seventeenth birthday in the shower of a hockey rink in a more northern suburb—he had avoided playing there ever since—with a soft-skinned boy whose long halo of blond curls almost entirely concealed his face and whose name he had not known and had not been at the time concerned about. This memory made him burn when he considered it, but, on the other hand, he had been taken entirely by surprise, and the interaction was over before he could come up with any thought of, or plan for, demurral.

Second, about two weeks later, in the washroom of a bar, after another hockey game, with someone dark, short and slim whom he assumed the first unknown boy had told since he was approached with such open and ready confidence, and although the boy had departed instantly, he had done so without furtiveness. This second boy had even kissed Nicolo's cheek as Nicolo rezippered his pants closed. A quick, guiltless, efficient kiss on a spot that had prickled ever since whenever Nicolo placed his fingers there. He had time, but only barely, to contemplate violence—a knee to the groin, fingers into eyes, an elbow to the throat. What had held him back was the silken thrill that he remembered from the time before, like being jolted by electricity and then, almost simultaneously, enfolded in satin.

Third, at nineteen, once only, with a woman who worked at the bakery, Talia Carrara, aged thirty or so, near the end of a fourteen-week friendship. She had been fired a week later for being overfamiliar with customers and had moved back to Montreal. Talia had responded to a question that had been left hanging as heavily as a medicine ball: he had found her wiry, muscled body beautiful, including her breasts, like golden oranges, and her ballet-slipper-like vagina.

Fourth, at twenty-one, over the space of a week, with another woman, his own age, Stefania, visiting from Melville, Australia, a sub at the gym. Stefania was the first person who had taken any time at all. She had examined every part of him and told him, in case he was interested, that he was perfect.

Fifth, with Camila, who was younger by a year or two, in a bedroom at a house party at which they met and had too much to drink. Afterward, when they were sitting on the front steps, she cried and began to tell Nicolo that she had issues, father issues, but partway into her story, a girlfriend interrupted and took her home.

And then Stefania again, for three months, when she came back to teach yoga while Barb was on mat leave from the gym.

Sixth, and most recently, rarely but over a longer period, close to an almost-chaste half-year, quiet Francesca, twenty-three years old, who was plump and modest, but who grew even less talkative than usual toward the end of their five and a half months, and who finally told him gently but firmly on the telephone that the widower who owned the garden supplies store where she worked had asked her to marry him and that she had decided to say yes for the sake of his three young children whom he neglected and who needed her.

When Nicolo disclosed this breach to Father Bem, the young Nigerian priest at St. Francis, Father Bem, whose skin was so dark Nicolo could never interpret his expression or mood, asked whether he too intended to marry, a question that Nicolo found impossible to answer. He didn't know, he said. He wasn't sure. Then, in response to Father Bem's furrowed forehead, he went on to say that he thought he might—because, after all, although he didn't say this part aloud, wasn't this what everyone did in the end; how else was it possible to live your life?

"Best get on with it, then," Father Bem counselled, and his tone might have had in it impatience or humour or both. "These bodies that God himself saw fit to give us can be a serious source of trouble unless brought early into harness."

Nicolo thought of this exchange with Father Bem when he went to borrow a suitcase from his older brother Enzo, a black, zippered case on wheels that Enzo had bought for his honeymoon trip to Montreal with Mima. He asked younger Enzo for advice on what clothes to take with him. Enzo looked up the question on the Internet. "It's already hot there. Much warmer than here. Take one pair of long pants and a light jacket in case you get called into any of Patrick's meetings—even if that's not very likely, it's always better to be prepared—a few decent shirts, one pair of real shoes, a pair of shorts, a couple of T-shirts, sandals, a bathing suit. Socks and underwear. A toothbrush and toothpaste. Shaving stuff. That should about do it. I can't think of anything else."

"Statti ccu dui piedi intra 'na scarpa," said Nonna at dinner. Keep your two feet in one shoe—a saying meant to ward off imprudence.

He asked Carla, the woman in his psychology class, if she could take notes from the class he would be missing, and she smiled self-consciously at the request.

"I don't take the best notes," she said. "But I'll do my best and I'll make you a copy. Maybe," she added, and she touched the sleeve of his shirt on his upper arm, "maybe we can get together after you're back, to study for the next test." Nicolo nodded although he felt that Carla was not the kind of study companion that Enzo had had in mind. He would, he thought, be distracted by Carla's mind, which seemed not quite settled, and by her hands, which were red and rough. Her bitten nails were both repellent and fascinating. He had the strange feeling that he could mend them if he held them for long enough between his own.

Zoe telephoned Nicolo to thank him for taking her to the play, and he let her know that he would be gone for three days. He wanted her to understand, although he did not say this, that he would have liked to see her again, if he had not agreed to go. Nicolo told her what Massimo had said when Nicolo told his father about the trip: "*Chine 'un fha pazzie in gioventù, e' fha a ra vecchjaia.*" If you don't do foolish things in your youth, you'll do them when you are old.

"The best advice I ever heard was not to take anyone's advice," Zoe answered. "But for what it's worth, my dad's advice is always that we should try to learn from everything, good and bad. He says that way nothing in life is wasted."

CHAPTER TWENTY

The first sight of Las Vegas at night was startling: uncountable lights throbbing and wheeling below a wide, bare blue-black desert sky. Enormous, brilliantly lit hotels and billboards could be seen through the airplane window, quite close, as if the pilot intended to land the plane on a thoroughfare in the centre of the city. Nicolo thought of what his nonna had told him about the cathedral in Naples, the one time she had seen it, on her way to the ship that took her away from Italy—that she was fortunate that she had heard it described in advance by the village priest since its magnificence could otherwise blind the unprepared eye. The plane banked and then dropped upon the runway at a high rate of speed and with a roar of the engines that seemed to create or restrain stresses that threatened to pull apart rivets and bolts. When the brakes were applied, hard, with another intense throb of noise, the passengers were thrown forward in their seats, and as they fell back again a collection of young women toward the rear of the airplane broke into cheers.

These women surged down the aisle before Nicolo had undone the buckle of his seat belt. They were dressed in short pleated skirts and brightly coloured T-shirts, many of them with slogans and illustrations. *Catholic Girl Gone Bad. Little Miss Naughty. If I Can't Set a Good Example, Then I'll Settle for Being a Warning to Others. If You Aren't Living on the Edge, You're Taking Up Too Much Space.* Two or three of the women slowed when they passed Nicolo's seat and gave him appraising looks. "He'd do," he heard one of them say. Nicolo was left in a cloud of their sharp mingled scents and the echo of the purposeful slap of their sandals against their bare feet.

Inside the airport he followed the signs toward the luggage carousel, passing banks of slot machines, at some of which people were playing intently, hunched close so that the fortune disgorged by the ringing, blinking machines, good, bad or fair, could not be discerned by passersby. He found his bag easily—Enzo had advised him to mark it with a length of yellow twine around the handle. When he turned to search out where he might be able to get a taxi, a sign with his name caught his eye. At the front of a waiting throng, a small, thin man wearing a dark and oversized suit stood holding up a piece of cardboard with PAVONE handwritten on it.

"Are you looking for me?" Nicolo asked him.

"Mr. Pavone? In that case, yes. My name's Mick. Mr. Patrick Alexander from Pure Lane Productions has sent over a car to take you to your hotel. You have all of your luggage already?"

Mick led Nicolo past a slowly snaking taxi queue to a silver Lincoln Town Car. He held open the back door for Nicolo, clicked it closed behind him, and flipped Nicolo's suitcase into the trunk. He left open the sliding window between the driver's seat and the back, and provided observations as they drove.

"First time here? Okay, I'm going to give you all you're ever going to need to know in five minutes or less. A free service that I throw in for the unenlightened and the uninitiated. Take it or leave it. No charge. See, even though Las Vegas means green grass, there wasn't enough water here for a city until they built the dam. That's the Hoover Dam, a make-work project to keep people working back in the Dirty Thirties. Some people go out to see it, but to me it's just a big wall and a lot of water, always makes me thirsty just to look at it. Aside from the dam—and that's outside of town, remember—nobody and nothing here is exactly real. Everything is a replica or a reproduction or a representation of somewhere else, or of some other time in history. Some people get into the back of my car and the first thing they ask is they want me to take them to see the 'real' Las Vegas. They want to know where it is, like there's some secret place where the locals keep the true, authentic place stashed behind all the scenery. But there isn't one. This is it, as real as it gets. The settings are fake and the history is fake, even the grass is fake, most of it. You can have a good time while you're here, but it's all flim-flam, you got me?"

"But what about the people who work here?" said Nicolo. "They must have homes and go to stores and send their kids to school, and get married. Isn't that all real?"

"Well, I don't know about that," said Mike. "I guess that's true, as far as it goes." His tone was dubious, but then he brightened. "Yes, there's something to what you say, but that part, where people live, that isn't Vegas." He stopped the car. "Here we are," he said.

Patrick rushed at Nicolo as soon as Nicolo stepped through the heavy door into the cavernous air-conditioned hotel lobby, in which several dozen people milled. Signs overhead pointed in a dozen directions—POOL AND SPA. BELL DESK. REGISTRATION. RESTAURANTS. CASINO. MEETING PLACE. TERRACE BISTRO. SYBARITE'S LOUNGE. SILHOUETTE BAR. GUEST ELEVATORS. SELF-PARKING. GAMES ROOM. LAUGHING STATUES. Patrick rose up on the balls of his feet and he waved his arms like the blades of a windmill. He was grinning.

"Everyone's up on eleven. We've been at it for a day and a half already, pulling the show apart and dissecting it with tweezers, atom by atom by agonizing atom. It's as painful as having your chest hairs yanked out one by one, but it has to be done, there's no way around it. There's something missing in the show. You know, that thing, *sprezzatura*—artlessness, guilelessness, innocence. It's all too contrived and heavy somehow, like an overweight, middle-aged bride in a corset and pancake makeup. We're trying to figure out how to turn it from a lump of lead into something weightless, effortless—a balloon, a feather, a soufflé, the lightest possible, most fleeting notion, a dream. It would be pure alchemy if we can do it, base metal into gold. There's still no guarantees at this point. I made sure they paid me in advance, if you know what I mean. And, meanwhile, I've got this killer stress headache in a knot at the back of my head, which might be the first signs of a brain tumour for all I know, and tension all through my shoulders, they've completely seized up, so I've booked an appointment in an hour with this masseuse in the spa. I can't tell you how good he is. Hands like absolute Roto-Rooters; he gets into every muscle. It feels like getting worked over by the more vicious kind of debt collector, but it is so, *so* worth it. We'll have to get you an appointment for tomorrow. His name's Dylan, can you believe it? One of those names ditzy parents gave their kids in the seventies. But you'll feel like butter afterward—melted butter. Did I mention he's an Adonis? An absolute feast for the eyes. I promise you'll fall in love with him. And after that, we plan to work late, so you and I will have to get our workout in first thing tomorrow. I'm up at the crack of dawn, nine or a bit later—that counts as early around here. We can get started then. Maybe you can try to chase down Timothy while I'm at the spa. But first, you have to come up. Come up, come in and see where the so-called magic happens. I'll introduce you to everyone."

Nicolo felt—as he often did when he was with Patrick— swept up into the windstorm of his energy and enthusiasm. Patrick was hard to resist. Nicolo followed Patrick into a mir- rored elevator, which took them to the eleventh floor, and then along a hall to the meeting room. The room had a high ceiling and an enormous window with thick drapes, and it held a dozen people sitting around or near two long tables that had been pushed together. On the tables were pens, highlighters, stacks and loose sheets of printed paper, half-filled glasses, and plates with scraps of food—sandwich crusts, fruit peels, shrimp carcasses, broken potato chips. One of the men was drawing intently on a large pad of paper. Over beside the window two women with very short hair were leaning toward each other talking intently. Everyone else was sitting on chairs, not obviously engaged in any activity.

"Nicolo, this is Dawn, Derrick, Leesa, Claudia, Steven M., Steven S., Walt, Marshall, Tatiana and Jean-Pierre, and over there are Marlene and Steph. Everyone, this is Nicolo, my trainer. He's the best there is. He's helped me to see the light. Healthy mind in a healthy body. So trite and yet so true."

Nicolo sat down in an upholstered chair in a corner of the room. Jean-Pierre, the man who had been drawing when Nicolo and Patrick came in, held up his sketch and delivered to the group a short lecture on the importance of vanishing points. Perception and perspective were everything. If tickets were two hundred dollars and up, the audience needed to be visually inundated if they were to feel as if they got their money's worth. The current sets were too small, too monochromatic, too lacking in drama. Patrick entirely, completely agreed with him. Marlene and Claudia were concerned about the music. There was too much reliance on Frankie's old hits from the eighties. For what people were being asked to fork out for tickets, they were entitled to expect something new, even if they were mixed in with the standards. Patrick thought this was a brilliant, and easily overlooked point. Walt was worried about pacing. We can't let the momentum flag for so much as a heartbeat, not for an instant, he warned. Patrick tugged on his chin and looked worried as well. Marlene and Steph thought it might be wise to get Bianca out from New York to jazz up the choreography. Patrick said he would call her immediately to see if she might be able to pop out for a few days. Patrick also shared Leesa's quietly stated concern about the lighting—too dim, too diffuse, too pastel—and was inclined to see the point of Tatiana's much more vocal objection to the use of multiple projected images of Frankie's twin daughters when Frankie sang that song about childhood.

"They're ugly," she shouted. "Why can't we all admit they look like a mismatched pair of pug dogs? We might as well get that little fact right out on the table right now." She slapped her open palms on the table. "It's no use pussy-footing around it. They're like Mutt and Jeff. Someone will just have to tell him. If he won't use those infant models we found, you know, the ones with the gorgeous curly hair from Seattle, then someone will have to talk him into leaving that song out."

Patrick mentioned that he had been meaning to have a word.

Meanwhile, the two Stevens were plugging a tangle of cables into the back of two computers and several matching electronic boxes at the far end of the table. "We're ready. We're ready," one of them called out, and the other sprinted across the room and pushed two buttons on the far wall. One of these activated a mechanism that briskly closed the cream-coloured curtains. The metal cleats sewn to the top slid first, and then the rest followed, with a swish of the long, rich swaths of damask. The other button switched off the overhead lights. Patrick pulled a flying-saucer-shaped module across the table toward him and flicked a toggle that caused a coloured course of active light to beam from one of the black boxes onto a rippled screen formed by the closed curtains. Frankie could be seen on stage, a barrel-chested man in a stiff suit, wearing a high-necked shirt buttoned to the top and a wide, striped tie. An orchestra at his feet started up with a swell of violins and flutes. Frankie waited one beat, two, a third, and then opened his mouth into a perfect O and began to sing. No part of him moved aside from his lips and jaw. He was like a life-sized, wind-up automaton but one with a fabulous built-in sound system and hidden speakers. Occasionally he pressed an inward-turned fist to his chest and thumped himself there twice—a gesture meant to emulate passion. Once or twice he swivelled his hips. Otherwise he held his body immobile. Nicolo thought he might be able to see where the challenge lay: a paying audience would want to feel that they were in the presence of an actual breathing, living star, and not an over-mannered robot.

Nicolo stayed for an hour and watched the group at work. He noticed how Patrick kept the discussion focused, worked the room for support of ideas that he considered valuable, and let other suggestions drift blamelessly away into the air. Patrick had a small black Palm Pilot that he used to send e-mails, and another mechanism, a silvery phone with a short antenna and multiple buttons, that he used to connect others in to the discussion or to convey instructions or leave messages. He kept page after page of notes in a small book and he reached every now and then to check or cross off a task that he viewed as completed. This was all a revelation to Nicolo, who had never considered the possibility that Patrick was capable of seriousness and that he might be good at the work that he did. When Patrick left for his massage, Nicolo walked with him to the hotel gym, and as they walked, Patrick gave Nicolo a description of Timothy—short, dark-haired, muscular, thinner than Nicolo, actually not unlike him overall but with round-lensed, wire-rimmed glasses—and the places he might be: the pool until eight o'clock when it closed, and after that, Sybarite's Lounge most likely, or one of the other restaurants or clubs in the hotel.

Nicolo found his room, which was a smaller version of the meeting room below, but with a bed the size of a tidy suburban garden plot instead of a conference table. He tested the various doors and switches as well as the vast mattress on which were layered not two but three sheets, the top two encasing a light, fleecy blanket the colour of wheat, and over that a white down comforter and then a silky, diamond-patterned pale gold bedspread. There were several doors in addition to the entrance; two pairs of doors opened to two closets and another hid the bathroom. The last door was dead-bolted, but seemed only to connect to an adjoining room. He read the labels on the short, round bottles on the marble counter in the bathroom. The contents each had a distinctive, glimmering colour: lime–mint mouthwash, rose–lavender soap, orange–oatmeal shampoo and lemon–sage conditioner. Bio-Seremic face cream (pale pearly blue) came in a miniature, corked test tube with a set of printed instructions pasted on the side. "Cleanse skin and then apply gently with balls of fingertips around areas that may be prone to lines prior to your habitual beauty routine," it advised. In the top drawer of one of the two bedside tables was a Bible with limp vinyl covers. The book fell open in his hands when he pulled it out. Three twenty-dollar bills fluttered out from between pages 590 and 591 and landed at his feet. A previous reader had highlighted with a yellow marker a passage from the book of Matthew at the top of page 591. "When they had crucified him, they divided up his clothes by casting lots." Nicolo held the money in his hand, uncertain. The right thing might be to turn it in to the reception desk and let the hotel decide what to do with it. Or he could ask Patrick what he thought. Then he remembered what Zoe had said—"The best advice is not to take anyone's advice." He hesitated but put the money in his pocket.

Nicolo ordered a burger and fries from a menu the size of a newspaper in one of the hotel's sixteen restaurants, the first one he came across on the main floor, a brightly lit semicircle of tables under hanging stained-glass lamps several paces from the casino floor. Then he made his way through the entire complex, as methodically as he could, although it was a labyrinth of passages and rooms. He started at the pool, which was about to close, and then visited each of the restaurants and bars, passing several times through the vast, central casino. After an hour and a half, he sat down and drank a beer in the Silhouette Bar, at which the entertainment consisted of two women dancing, apparently naked, behind lighted screens that framed a bar at which the bartenders poured drinks with acrobatic panache, juggling glasses and bottles, and tossing olives and stir-sticks through the air. After that, Nicolo bought a roll of tokens from a cashier for ten dollars and used them to test a few of the slot machines on the periphery of the casino. All of his tokens had vanished within five minutes and Nicolo sat for a moment blinking in the machine's flashing lights and jangling, mystified as to the appeal of this kind of activity. By eleven o'clock he could no longer shrug off a growing sense of the pointlessness of looking for a stranger in all of the hotel's different zones, someone he would be unlikely to recognize even if he did come across him, and who might well have wandered away from the hotel in any event. He went up to his room, brushed his teeth and climbed between the cool sheets of the bed. He left his curtains open and for several minutes watched the cartwheeling lights that were reflected on the ceiling. If he dreamed, his dreams left no residue.

On Sunday, Nicolo woke up early, sprawled across the enormous bed, surrounded by pillows and mounded blankets. He felt almost completely, but not uncomfortably, out of place. He turned on to his back and tried to work out how many nights he had spent somewhere other than his own bedroom in his parents' house. No more than twenty-five, he thought, less than four weeks in aggregate, including camping trips with the Cubs and Scouts and visits to relatives.

His appointment to meet Patrick at the gym wasn't until ten o'clock, which was more than three hours away. He got out of bed, drank two glasses of cold water from the tap, had a blasting shower in the glass and marble enclosure in the bathroom, and shaved his cheeks and jaw by feel inside a lingering cloud of warm, dense steam. When he was ready he rode one of the polished, silvery elevators downstairs, and then hesitated in the almost-deserted lobby. Three women wearing short skirts and shiny tops wobbled in through the front doors and trailed across the lobby toward the elevators.

Nicolo went outside and made his way through the hotel grounds out to the main street. For no reason other than to have something to do, he turned north and walked along a broad sidewalk, past the vast, sprinklered acreages of several other hotels as far as the second intersection, to a street marked Cathedral Way. He could see, a block and a half to his right, two large modernistic triangles that resolved themselves as he approached them into a tall, white steeple astride the shorter, wider blue equilateral of a sanctuary. A concrete and glass sign on the lawn read, Archangel Gabriel Cathedral.

The morning sun had by this time lightened the sky to a blank, lacy white, and the surface of the street and sidewalk had begun to shimmer as they were warmed. The inside of the sanctuary by contrast was dim and cool. The room was expansive and orderly, with chairs arranged in neat rows. A small altar at the front appeared humble under the massive overhead volume of vast, empty space. Nicolo felt at home, at ease inside this space, with its softened, scattered light filtered through tinted windows and its lazy currents of circulating air. He sat down on one of the chairs, in the closest approximation to his usual place at St. Francis—at the back, to the left of the entrance—and waited quietly, in what was closer to a dozing trance than to prayer, until the start of the 8 a.m. Mass. At the first strains of an unseen organ, he was pulled back to alertness. He was surprised to see that almost all of the seats around him had been taken. Could it be that gamblers came to pray for good luck, and, if so, were these the kind of prayers that were likely to be answered?

The priest introduced himself as Father Godkewitsch. He was a very tall man, well over six feet, constructed of bones that seemed loosely jointed. He wore a white robe cinched with a cord at his waist. His sermon was on the eighth Psalm.

> When I consider Your heavens,
>> the work of Your fingers,
>> the moon and the stars,
>> which You have set in place,
> what is man that You are mindful of him,
>> the son of man that you care for him?
> You made him a little lower than the heavenly beings
>> and crowned him with glory and honour.
> You made him ruler over the works of Your hands;
>> You put everything under his feet:
> all flocks and herds,
>> and the beasts of the field,
> the birds of the air, and the fish of the sea,
>> all that swim the paths of the seas.

Father Godkewitsch read the Psalm through slowly, putting an oddly stressed emphasis on the nouns: "When I consider Your *heavens*, the work of Your *fingers*, the *moon* and the *stars*"—and he then lifted up his head and began to speak of his own father, whom he described as a simple farmer in the Midwest, a man who had tended the earth and livestock to little profit, and of his mother, who had ordered, cleaned and replenished a frugal childhood home. Nicolo didn't follow the sermon closely. The reference at the start of the Psalm to the skies being the work of God's fingers had snagged his attention. He recalled reproductions he had seen of the painting on the ceiling of the Sistine Chapel that showed

God as a muscular old man, with the pointing finger of an outstretched arm delivering the spark of life to a man. Adam, it must be. The Psalm reference seemed too solid and intentional to be intended as metaphor. Would God have the other parts as well, or was He disembodied fingers and hands? Nicolo considered where else in the Bible any part of God's body was referred to. He knew there were many references to God speaking, which implied that He had a mouth, and to listening, which implied that He had ears. His feet were mentioned in the Psalm. Speech and listening implied a brain. Hands required arms. Feet clearly called for legs.

The priest was talking now of Moses, an example of a person who had been elevated by God as referenced in the Psalm, and this reminded Nicolo of the very odd story about Moses in the book of Exodus, in which Moses, after speaking several times with an unseen God, asked for permission to see His face. God replied that Moses could not do so and live, but said that Moses would be permitted to conceal himself in a cleft in a rock, and as God passed by he would be permitted to see not God's face but His back. A memory rose up, from years ago, when someone, one of his brothers or one of the other boys, had crowed at this story, "God mooned Moses!" and they had all picked it up for a week or two, in awe at the daringness of the boy who had started it. A fad had sprung up, he remembered now, of uttering as casually as possible, as an expletive or curse, the phrase "God's Bum!" They had all been thrilled with themselves. Aside from that one episode, which passed after several months, Nicolo had never considered that God might have a form and parts decipherably human. A back seemed to Nicolo to absolutely require a torso, because what else could it be the back of? There could not be a back without a front. Would the torso be complete lower down—that of a man or even possibly a woman?—or incomplete—some species of generic, undifferentiated figure? But if God were perfect, would He not be perfect in all of His parts? What would perfection require? And what would God, being unmarried, do with this part of Him? Neither urination nor anything else that humans do with these loose and amiable bits seemed possible. He shook his head, blinked, and glanced at the people sitting on the chairs beside him. There was no evidence that anyone else was contemplating the problem of God's genitalia.

He was grateful that the idea of God's hands returned, displacing his more profane reflections. This time what came to mind was not the elegant image from the painting at the Vatican, but, as clear as any photograph, his father's hands—short, broad, almost square from wrist to fingertip and from side to side, his father's thick fingers holding the scissors over his customers' bowed heads as lightly as the priest was now raising the host toward the soaring ceiling.

Toward the end of the Mass, Nicolo placed the money that had fallen out of the hotel Bible into the collection plate when it was sent from hand to hand around the congregation. He felt as if a satisfactory transaction had been concluded. Maybe, he thought on his walk back to the hotel, this was what people meant when they said that a side effect of travelling was not only to see different things but to see things differently. Nicolo thought of his family, his work—the familiar things that rooted him in place—and of this trip and other risks and chances there were to take, both in the world and at home. It seemed to him that there was no contest between the two—home was best—but it might be possible to perceive it more fully coming back to it from another place.

The workout room at the hotel proved to be another kind of cathedral. The lounge where Nicolo waited for Patrick had large windows on three sides that overlooked a garden, a green and white profusion of trees and flowers, a blue lap pool and half a dozen black tennis courts with the lines crisply delineated in white. He sat on one of two deep orange couches among layers of triangular pink and yellow cushions. Water trickled from several small backlit fountains made of round stones. The side tables were arranged with baskets of fruit, bottled water, and vases of flowers that gave off mingled sweet and musty scents.

At ten-twenty, one of the attendants, a tall woman wearing a matching set of pale blue workout clothes, sleek low-hipped pants and a close-fitting, zippered top, and a white headband that held her long dark hair back from her brow, offered Nicolo a stemmed glass of fresh orange juice and a selection of crisp newspapers. He accepted the juice and two of the newspapers. The speakers over his head were emitting the latest Coldplay song. Just before eleven o'clock, Patrick arrived in his usual rush, but with less than his normal level of effervescence. He croaked his apologies.

"We all worked until late, late, late, and then a few of us

gave up and went out looking for Timothy. We looked everywhere but never found him."

Nicolo shrugged his shoulders to indicate that he hadn't
had any more luck. He rose and took Patrick by the shoulders and steered him toward the mats. Patrick flopped down
on his back, did two straggling sit-ups, and then raised himself up on his elbows.

"I gave up and went to sleep at two or three, and then in
he wafted at ten this morning and folded into bed like a col-
lapsing tent. He'd had a win on one of the machines—seven
thousand dollars on a fifty-cent bet, if you can believe it.
He's always had more luck than he deserved. And so he and
a few of his instant new friends made a tour of the bars. They
hired a limo and kept it waiting wherever they stopped. Lots
to drink, big tips, and the last thousand dollars coughed up
for someone's sob story, a dog at death's door or something
like that. He's got nothing to show for it now but a big, fat
headache and horrible pains in his stomach." Patrick leaned
forward and peered at Nicolo. "Really, you know, when I
really think about it, the way I really feel is, I was pissed
that he didn't tell me where he was going, and pissed that
he didn't take me with him, but I wouldn't have liked it if I
had gone, and I am more of a Cabernet Sauvignon kind of
person than someone who could drink something made out
of tequila and coconut and animal fats. So, what am I doing
with him, really? Look how low love's brought me."

The piped-in music ended and for some reason nothing
came on to replace it. All that could be heard was the whirring
and clicking of exercise machines and, in the distance, the lav-
atory-like sound of water falling from the unseen fountains.

"I can't tell you what to do. You know that," Nicolo said.

"Okay then, what would your grandmother have to say about it? She seems to have a maxim for everything."

"Well, it's hard to know for sure, but what she might say is, '*Falla cumu la voi, sepre è cucuzza*': Cook it any way you like, it'll always be a pumpkin. He's what he is. He's not likely to change very much. So the question is, is this what you want?"

Patrick let his elbows fall forward onto his raised knees. He rested his chin in his hands. "If I'm fed up with pumpkin," he said, "do I still have to keep doing these stupid sit-ups? There really isn't any point, is there? No one's going to see my abs or care about them one way or another. No one."

"You'll care. I'll care. Let's get through our hour, and then you can go and get a coffee if you like. Caffeine's worth working for, right?"

"Half an hour."

"One hour. You'll feel much better at the end of it. Guaranteed."

Patrick fell backward on the mat again, sighed, and then pulled himself forward. "*One,*" he began. "You're going to kill me, you know that. Kill me. It'll be on your conscience. You'll be doing penance or saying novenas or whatever until you're a hundred." He fell back and pulled up again, struggling against gravity and depleted spirits. "*Two.* Actually, make that *four.* I did two before we started counting."

Nicolo was able to keep Patrick working for forty-five minutes, and then released him to go on a quest for the strongest latte in the city. Nicolo spent some time on the weights in the gym, an hour in his room studying his psychology textbook and notes, and then walked slowly through the casino, watching as men and women lost, and less often won, money at blackjack, craps and roulette. A group was forming around a roulette wheel edged with flashing lights. A bulky woman wearing pink pants and a pink hooded jacket was on a winning streak—seven wins in a row so far, someone told Nicolo. Several of the onlookers made suggestions each time she placed a bet: "Inside." "Outside." "Corner." "Split." The woman cheerfully stacked and slid her chips in response to the general trend of advice, and the developing crowd watched and cheered encouragingly as the large wheel was spun and a small white ball released in the opposite direction. Each time it was sent on its orbit, the ball, initially a solid blur, became, as it slowed, a dotted line, the white dashes growing shorter in length until it came to rest. Three more times the ball landed in the woman's favour. She bounced excitedly, unzipped her jacket and tossed it behind her. Another woman caught it and folded it respectfully over her arm. The onlookers pressed in closer to the roulette table, shoulder to shoulder, watching intently, shouting their approval of each successive win.

Nicolo felt a flash of perception, an unexpected insight into the appeal of this odd, counterintuitive activity, which seemed to him almost exactly like tossing money into a whirlwind. This must be the attraction, or one of them: the experience of a shared euphoria, a group celebration of a win or series of wins against the odds, or at least the potential for a victory. Looking out over the room, he saw the way in which the various activities—cards, slots, whirling wheels, games of luck and chance—made of the participants and onlookers a tribe, a group who understood the rules and took pleasure in their logic, even though, or maybe even *because*, the probabilities were so unfavourable. Not his tribe, and not his pleasures, but he was pleased that he had worked it out, as if this was a puzzle that he had been set.

The woman's luck turned. She lost four times in a row.

"Quit while you're ahead, honey," the friend holding her jacket counselled her. "There's never no sense in chasing your losses. They ain't never gonna be caught up with."

The gambling woman shook her head. "I guess you're right. It's time to throw up the sponge," she said. Her voice was soft, with an appealing foreign burr. She raised her shoulders and let them fall again and then accepted a bar-coded winnings ticket to take to the cashier.

Patrick had made an appointment for Nicolo with his massage therapist at two o'clock. A woman wearing white pants and a pale blue smock greeted him at the entrance to the spa and directed him to a change room, where he put on shorts and one of the spa's thick robes. When Nicolo emerged, she led him to a small room in which everything was snowy or gold: blond wood floor, white table and cabinets, white walls and sheets, beige towels, white and gold light fixtures.

"We have you booked with Dylan today," she murmured. "It will be on Mr. Alexander's tab." She directed Nicolo to take off his robe and arrange himself flat on the massage table. "You can leave your shorts on or take them off, as you choose." She handed him a sheet to cover himself, and then exited and closed the door silently behind her.

Nicolo kept his shorts on. He hung his robe on a hook and arranged himself face down on the table—there was a recessed area at the top for his nose and chin and forehead to rest in. He reached around and pulled the sheet up over his legs and back. Noise trickled down from overhead speakers, a rushing and flowing sound that Nicolo identified after several repeated cycles as that of waves surging onto a shore.

After another minute, the door opened. Nicolo turned his head for a quick sideways glance. He saw first Dylan's loose-fitting white pants, and then a white tunic with the spa's logo embroidered on the yoke. Dylan had a strong, unshaven jaw and ski jump cheekbones. His straight, very shiny blond hair reached his collar. He matched the room perfectly. He was almost unsettlingly beautiful.

"Sage or lavender?" Dylan asked.

Nicolo couldn't imagine what response he was intended to provide.

"Massage lotion?" Dylan clarified.

"Oh. Lavender, I guess." Sage was something his mother put in chicken stuffing.

"Do you have low blood pressure?"

"No. Normal."

"Because lavender can lower your blood pressure, so I really don't advise lavender if your blood pressure is already low."

"No. It's fine. It's good."

"On the other hand, if you do have low blood pressure, the good news is that you'll live forever. Ninety or a hundred at least. Especially if you remember to drink eight glasses of water every day."

Nicolo could hear Dylan rubbing his hands back and forth slickly, warming the massage cream. For some reason the noise made him want to urinate. Dylan leaned over, pulled the sheet down to Nicolo's waist, and began to push and pull against the muscles of his shoulders.

"You're tense," said Dylan.

"I guess I am," said Nicolo. He was in fact tense and getting tenser. In response to, or in apprehension of, Dylan's touch, his penis had begun to stir inside his shorts like a restless animal confined for too long inside a small cage. *Down*, he willed.

The muscles of his abdomen tightened and his scrotum gathered itself into a snug anticipatory bundle. *No*, he urged.

He shifted his hips from side to side in an effort to quell the insurrection, but this motion only accelerated a relentless expansion. Dylan lathered more massage cream onto his hands, making the same slippery sound, and then moved to work on Nicolo's upper arms. This was better, since it felt more impersonal, and Nicolo began to think that he might be able to master the situation, but after several minutes Dylan began to massage first his right hand and then his left, bending and folding the fingers, pressing the pads at the base of each of his fingers and smoothing the webs between them. This was *intensely* personal. Nicolo's face reddened, and he could feel sweat erupt on his forehead, under his arms and along the palms of his hands. His groin felt moist.

"You're warm," said Dylan. "This is normal. Lavender heats the blood. It is a relative of the mustard plant. To sweat is good. This will help to release the toxins."

The concept of toxin release was a welcome and distracting thought. Nicolo imagined poisons seeping out of
his pores under the pressure of Dylan's manipulation. But
where could they have come from in the first place? Perhaps
from the beer and burger he had eaten the night before. He
closed his eyes and summoned up an image of these toxic
emanations—animal fats, sugars, alcohol—percolating out
of his skin, swirling into the air, and then wafted away in
unseen waves toward some unseen outtake vent. Toxins.
Wafting. Waves. This was helping.

Dylan slapped Nicolo's shoulders, once, twice, deliberately, pulled the sheet up to cover Nicolo's back, and then
reached and folded the bottom half of the sheet up toward
his waist, uncovering his legs and shorts. Nicolo's heart
lurched. Could any evidence of his condition be seen?

Dylan began to push against Nicolo's thighs, with enough
force that Nicolo was rocked back and forth on the table. He
was now a stew of intensely contradictory feelings: pleasure,
horror, apprehension, anticipation and terror.

"Strong," said Dylan.

"I lift weights," said Nicolo. This was much worse than
before, and painful enough that he was forced to consider
what it might imply.

"Ummmm," said Dylan. "Very nice." He had made his way
downward and was working now on Nicolo's calves.

This went on for another half-hour. Nicolo felt as if he
were being forced at gunpoint along a precipice in the dark,
but every time he thought he might fall, he managed to pull
himself together.

"Other side?" asked Dylan after he had completed Nicolo's

feet. He motioned to Nicolo to flip over on to his back.

"Oh. No. No. Any more and I'll be sleeping on you," said Nicolo. Heat flooded his face. "I mean—it felt great, though. You're very good."

"I do personal appointments too," said Dylan. "In your room if you like. They don't have to be here in the spa. Some of my clients ask for more personal, one-on-one sessions."

Eyes closed, Nicolo tried to discern what might be intended in Dylan's proposal. Was this what Patrick had had in mind all along? An experiment to see what Nicolo might be tempted into? He could not come to any conclusion except this: that if he held his eyelids sealed together for long enough, Dylan might believe that he had fallen asleep.

Seven waves broke on the beach in succession, seeming to increase each time in their intensity.

"If you like," said Dylan.

Nicolo considered. Was this what he wanted?

Five more waves surged and then ebbed.

"Or not," said Dylan.

Nicolo waited until Dylan had gone before he trusted himself to sit up on the table. He felt a bit unsteady, but exhilarated too, as if he had passed a difficult test. He remembered Zoe's advice, in the guise of non-advice, which had been that he should try to learn from everything, both good and bad. What he had learned, he thought, was that he would have to make choices in life, and that one choice was to set himself on a path that did not have Dylans on it.

Late that afternoon Nicolo grew bored and went up to the eleventh floor where Patrick's team was still at work. Patrick had divided everyone into two subgroups, and had assigned them both the same task—reordering the lineup of songs in Frankie's performance. They were to work independently at opposite sides of the room and present their conclusions at the end of an hour. The group working near the window was loud and argumentative, their discussion punctuated by derisive comments about one another's ideas and suggestions. The other group, near the door, huddled intently and their voices were so low and complicit that little could be heard. "*Coloratura,*" one of them repeated several times, in an intense tone. "Shading," suggested another.

"You are so completely full of crap," someone in the window group said loudly.

Patrick sat in the middle of the room with his head in his hands, staring down at the reflective surface of the table. He glanced up and saw Nicolo. "Hey," he said. "It's still pumpkin. The performance, I mean. In case you're wondering. Although Timothy's still pumpkin too, as it turns out. Who was it who turned a pumpkin into a golden carriage? Not me, it seems." He sat up straighter. "Now you're here you might as well sit in. Maybe you'll stimulate some new ideas. I've heard everything this mob has to suggest nine times over. What do you think? Pick a group, although I have to say I'm not sure there's really any choosing between them."

"I can listen if you like," said Nicolo. "I don't think I'll have much to add." The group beside the door looked too tightly huddled to break into, so Nicolo went to sit in an available chair next to Leesa, at the far end of the room, near the window. With her were Claudia, one of the Stevens, Tatiana, Steph and Marlene.

Steven had been speaking when Nicolo came to sit down. He pursed his lips and straightened his shoulders, unconsciously asserting his territoriality within the group, and then cleared his throat. Leesa, mediating, patted Steven's arm.

"Go on," she said. "You were making a point."

Nicolo admired how she achieved this—Steven was reassured and encouraged, but also oblivious to Leesa's intervention.

"What we need to strive for, strive for, is a connection," Steven said. "Something direct, unmediated, personal. That's what I think."

"How can we do that when we're talking about a venue with, like, four thousand seats?" Tatiana objected. She said this from within a tangle of curling, vine-like blond hair, and she spoke each word distinctly, coating each syllable with disparagement.

"It might be that the best we can hope for is to create a sense of *false* intimacy," said Leesa. She had the clear, rational tone of a level-headed woman.

"Audiences are too sophisticated these days for smoke and mirrors," said Steph. "They'll see through it. They need to be convinced to suspend disbelief."

Steven persisted. "An overall sense of genuineness. Is that too much to ask? Is it just too much to bloody ask?"

"Have you even *met* Frankie?" Tatiana said, shaking her yellow head so that her hair coiled and recoiled against her cheeks and chin and shoulders. "He's been singing since he was fourteen or something and by now there's nothing authentic left to him, not a single bone of his body, not a molecule or an atom."

"Have we worked anything out here?" Patrick pulled a chair up to the table, between Steven and Leesa. Leesa moved her chair sideways, closer to Nicolo's.

Each person presented a perspective. Steven argued that he, or someone else, should spend time with Frankie, talking to him, listening to him, in a dialogue, working at getting to the core, to something close to his "essence." Tatiana took the view that more dancing would help. Marlene thought the show should include more of the old classic songs, "The ones people most identify with. That builds closeness, or a sense of closeness anyway. Prior knowledge and all that. People always confuse familiarity with understanding." Leesa agreed overall with Marlene. Claudia and Steph had come up with a lineup that started and ended with new music. "That great Portuguese *fado*," said Steph. "And that a cappella thing from Quebec."

How opinionated they all were, Nicolo thought. How confident in themselves. But then a Zoe-like second thought occurred to him. Was it possible that the force with which they stated their views masked hidden doubts? Possibly, he concluded, it was some of both—confidence and doubt—and that the motivations didn't matter so much as the debate, which generated ideas to which they all contributed and for which each could take credit.

"The other group more or less concluded that we should raze the theatre and tear up the contract," Patrick said. "You guys may have been louder and more divided, but you're certainly more constructive."

Patrick stopped Nicolo at the door and put a hand on his shoulder. "What did you think, Nicco? What would the old lady have to say about this one? We've got to report out tomorrow."

"*U bisognu 'mpara la via*," said Nicolo. "That's the one that comes to mind."

"Meaning?"

"It translates as: Necessity will teach you the road to follow."

"That's not very much help, really, is it? When you get right down to it. Has it ever occurred to you that most of these sayings are variations on Doris Day? You know, *que será, será?*"

"Maybe, but I'm beginning to see why she uses it so often." Nicolo paused, but he decided to give Patrick his own thoughts. It seemed that this is what people did. They offered up their opinions and felt lighter afterward, shed of the burden of holding on to a point of view. Once the opinion was given, then it was up to the recipient to decide what to do with it. You could control what you suggested, but you could not control how or whether the suggestion was taken. There were some situations in which giving counsel was dangerous. Even sound advice in the wrong time or place could lead to unintended results. Here, however, there was little risk. Advice was thrown around as heedlessly as coins were dropped into a slot machine.

"Here's what I think," Nicolo said. "Frankie may not be as natural as you'd like, but he really can sing and it could be that that's what the people who buy tickets are coming for. Maybe you could work with what he is, instead of fighting it. That's what I try to do, with the people I train, even you.

I have to work with the people I get. There's no point trying to get you to do a Pilates class, for example."

"I could do Pilates."

"That's all I have to suggest. And faith. Maybe you have to have more faith in Frankie. There was a guy they taught us about in high school, one of those Greek philosophers. I forget his name. What he said was that the fox knows many things, but the hedgehog knows just one big thing. I didn't understand it then, but I think I do now. Frankie's like the hedgehog. This thing he does, singing the way he does, that's his one big thing. I don't think you're ever going to make him into a fox." Nicolo was thinking as he spoke of himself and Zoe, how he was more like Frankie while her mind was more like the mind of a fox. He didn't know if this was fatal or not to whatever might be built up between them. He felt it might be, but he wasn't sure. He thought of his mother and father, his brother Enzo and Mima, Mario and Angie. The men were each hedgehogs, he was pretty sure of that. But the women were, all of them, much more like the fox. Their minds were divided more intricately, with facets that it could take a lifetime to understand.

CHAPTER TWENTY-ONE

Although Nicolo was gone for only three days, Filomena had been unsettled with him so far away from the house. She had not fully understood where he had gone or why. She had been told that he had gone to the United States, for work, somewhere warmer, drier, and she had formed the impression that he was in Florida. When a satellite image of Florida's jutting peninsula appeared on the screen during the evening weather report, she tried to interpret what the depiction of air systems eddying above the state portended—storms or sun or showers. She raised her right hand in a benediction that she believed had the power to diminish any spiralling storms because the strong North American God of the television set would see that it was so important to her, and this act eased her fear that Nicolo would be beset or harmed in some way.

A few nights after Nicolo returns home, after everyone is asleep, Nonna rises from her bed at three in the morning, goes along the hall and opens the door to his bedroom. She gazes at what she can make out of him in the darkness, a large recumbent form, breathing steadily. She imagines that she can perceive the steady workings of the thoughts underpinning his dreams like the foundation of a well-built house.

In the dark and silent house, Filomena manoeuvres by sound and by feel. She can see in the dim light only enough to avoid the stairs and other hazards. She has to take extra care, though, because she is subject in these hours to aural and olfactory hallucinations. Wandering from room to room she hears, distantly but distinctly, the tones of the church bells of Arduino's three churches—Sant' Agata's twin bells, which were poorly cast and clanged like cowbells, San Giuseppe's, which were sonorous, dense, deliberate and measured, and Santa Catarina's, which were cracked in the fire of 1911 and so warbled and echoed like roosting doves.

At midnight, in the first half-hour of light sleep, she had started from her bed, hearing the voice of her stepmother, Annalaura, calling to rouse her to fetch wood for the stove. A car passing outside in the last slushy puddles on the street leaves in its wake the soft sound of her father's footsteps on the dry dirt path. She turns to rise and in the fabric of her sheets she smells her husband's neck when he came in from the fields—salty, dirty, musty. The husband who came to her from Monte di Dio, one village over, a village you could see from the road that led out of Arduino, on the crease of a fold of the landscape eight kilometres to the west. She had hoped to marry someone from far away, she had longed for a true *straniero*, but Peppino was the one who came along when she was twenty and most wanted to get out from under Annalaura's thumb.

She sits on the edge of the bed and rubs her temples. She had taken her chance, a leap of faith, and had learned to love him over the twenty-seven years of their marriage, a little more every year, a steady increase, like coins accumulating in a bank. He had no extra words and few stories, but he was more solid than the earth. He rose in the morning to work and went to bed only when darkness prevented him from working any longer.

She brushes her knuckles across her eyes and smells the bread in the village's central oven, and then comes the memory of the village moon, which was entirely different in her youth from the moon of today: its surface was the round face of a woman baking bread, a visage streaked with flour and ashes and glowing with the reflected heat of the sun's oven. All that bread. All those women. Cousins and friends and aunts and grandmothers and godmothers. So many opinions. All that advice, almost none of it any use to her here, where she, untethered, is forced to imagine herself into being over and over every moment. It is exhausting. There are no reference points. She was wise in Arduino, but poor. Here she is rich, and unneeded. Even she can see that passing on the old ways to her grandsons is a waste of her breath. So little of it will be of any use to them. Not to piss into the wind. When to plant and when to reap. The portents of the sun and moon and stars. How to mollify wolves and overlords and priests. She is worse than Father Bem in his enormous church addressing his ever-dwindling flock. They are both passing on the old stories to people whose ears are blocked by their complicated, modern lives. Except Nicolo. Nicolo listens. More than that, he understands—some of it anyway. She has felt him reverberate in the way she intends, like a bell first absorbs and then sends out the message that the ringer conveys up the rope to the top of the steeple. The other two mystify her. They are so out in the world, and just what they do out there baffles her. Nicolo is more straightforward. A good boy. A good man.

After she has inspected her sleeping grandson and is satisfied, Filomena feels her way with her hands along the walls back to her room. She lays her head on the pillow and tries to imagine that her husband Peppino's head is on the pillow next to hers, that the faint throb of her blood in her temples is his heart beating as he sleeps. She twists her body in the bed to find a position that has no pain or loss in it, and makes of her many thoughts a kind of quilt to draw over herself— the scent of anise, the way Peppino's laundered shirt smelled when he pulled it over his head, her love for her grandsons and her great-grandchildren—and then she falls into sleep, notwithstanding the recollection of a random scrap of Annalaura's sour advice—*Si cientu anni vò campare i fhatti tue t'ha de fhare*—If you want to live a long life, don't poke your nose into other people's business. Annalaura is thus reduced to this, a small perforation at the edge of Filomena's letting go of consciousness. There is satisfaction in the fact that she has always found a way to do the opposite of whatever Annalaura advised.

Nicolo was awake, but he took care to keep each breath deep and slow so that Nonna would be reassured, and would return to her bed to sleep. He heard her sometimes, wandering through the rooms of the house at two or three or four in the morning. He had guessed that she more fully inhabited these small, easily overlooked hours than the daytime hours when the rest of the family was up and active. Nonna's world was as small here as when she lived in a village of fewer than six hundred souls. Smaller, in fact. In Arduino, Nonna knew everyone, and their history, talents and relationships besides. She knew the language and its intensity and nuances. She was known in return—that slender, headstrong girl with her fine head and untied hair, daughter of Italo and poor Rina, bane of Annalaura, a hard worker but only when she put her mind to it.

Nicolo took several minutes to fall back to sleep, and he filled this time thinking about what he needed to do to navigate the days ahead, which held, in addition to a return to work, a wedding, an important meeting, an examination and then another wedding.

The wedding of Monica's ex-husband Gordon to Hayley would take place on Saturday. The meeting—Enzo's hearing with the dean of the law school—would take place at the law school on the following Monday.

The examination would be the final in his psychology class. His study group included Carla, who was funny and bright but disorganized and so tended to pull the group off track, and two others, both of them keeners as Enzo had recommended. The group had met and dissected the exams from several years past, turning them inside out to determine how they were constructed so that they could see where it would be possible to slot in the facts and concepts they had learned. Many of the problems repeated themselves in different guises from year to year, which was helpful, but this could also be a trap because each year subtle and deceptive changes were introduced that could easily be missed.

The final exam would be closed book and multiple choice, and Professor Werner had spent the final hour of lectures giving the class advice.

"Remember, I will include a number of alternative but wrong answers, which I will nonetheless strive to make as appealing and plausible as possible. You must deeply understand your material, not just learn it, but understand it, in order to resist being seduced by the incorrect answers." Professor Werner wrote UNDERSTAND YOUR MATERIAL on the blackboard and underlined the words twice.

"When the time comes, you may want to work through the exam and answer all the questions you can answer readily, and then come back to the ones you couldn't answer on the first go-through. If you really do not know the answer, remember that, unlike in what is often quaintly referred to as 'real life,' you won't be penalized for being wrong. Even a guess has a twenty-five percent chance of being right. For every wrong answer you are able to eliminate, your chances of guessing the correct answer from among the remaining choices goes up. You should try to eliminate as many as you can so that you can make your final guess from among as small a number of alternatives as possible. Once you do decide on an answer, think twice about changing it. Many people believe that you should avoid changing an answer unless you have a good reason to do so. Sometimes, it is thought, our first instinct that may be our best."

Enzo's lawyer, Salvatore, would go with him to the meeting with the dean, and Nicolo would go too, but he'd been told that he would have to wait outside the inner office where the interview would be held. Any job offers had been withdrawn and the matter of discipline left to the law school. The accused students had been allowed to attend classes while evidence was being gathered, opinions and legal and quasi-legal demands and questions exchanged, and the governing processes determined. This part of the proceedings was finally complete and the hearings would determine the next step—and only just in time. Enzo's final exams were two weeks away. With misgivings but without much discussion, he and Enzo had decided not to tell their parents about the problem. Mario had brought up a news article about the investigation over coffee the Saturday morning after Nicolo returned from Las Vegas, but Nicolo had deflected him by turning the topic to the hockey playoff chances.

Nicolo had, however, told Zoe, whom he had seen almost every day since he got back. She had not provided any opinion about the matter. She had a habit unfamiliar to Nicolo of keeping her assessments to herself.

"Maybe you're just not a judgmental person," Nicolo suggested, a statement that he realized might apply to himself. They were walking south on Beta Street, from

Nicolo's parents' house, where they had eaten lunch, to the Trapassos', a distance of five kilometres, an inviting walk in this last week of April.

"Oh, I judge, all right," Zoe said. "I have some fairly strong views on things. You just haven't heard them."

"So what do you think, then? They could expel him, you know. His lawyer says that's within the range of options."

"I can't say. I only know his side of the story and how it has affected him. Obviously I'm on his side, but even if I weren't, I'm not in any position to weigh all of the factors. The people who run the law school, for example, they have something at stake too. They need to protect its name and reputation."

"So they might take a hard line."

"Didn't your guy, the lawyer your brother hired, say that it will be a question of balancing the interests out?" Zoe reached for his hand and squeezed it. "I think that's what they'll do. Everyone will want to find some reasonable middle ground."

Nicolo had kept her hand in his. He hoped she was right, that middle ground would be secured, and that it would be a place from which Enzo could take his next step forward.

Nicolo heard the creak of Nonna's weight sinking into her mattress, and then another series of small sounds as she settled. He turned from his right side to his left, drew three descending breaths and fell back into sleep.

Nicolo had put the Fells out of his mind over the past few days and so the sight of the brother and sister waiting for him at the gym on Wednesday morning at the usual time and in their usual place, hovering moistly in a dim corner at the far side of the room, caused him mixed feelings, all of them negative. Mainly he felt frustrated that they hadn't after all switched to a different instructor, someone better matched to what he had come to see as their somewhat obsessive needs—as, he realized now, he had hoped they might do. He was also anxious: the last time he saw them, it had occurred to him that they might take some step to express their disapproval of his absence.

"Why don't you tell me what you did over the last week instead of our sessions," he suggested as they walked along the corridor toward the smallest and least frequented of the exercise rooms, the one they preferred.

Bella opened her mouth. "Busy at work—" she began, but Phil scowled and made an abrupt downward, chopping motion through the air, interrupting her.

"We find it to be advisable to keep our personal activities private," he said.

Nicolo pressed his lips together, nodded, and led them into the otherwise empty room and over to the mats.

"Let's begin with one of the stretches that we were starting to work on last week," Nicolo said. He rose up on his toes, raised his locked hands over his head and then reached with one hand back toward the wall behind him. "Push your right hand against the wall and turn your body like this, to the left, keeping your arm slightly bent. This will help to open up the muscles of your chest." Nicolo straightened, walked around Bella and positioned himself between them.

Bella craned her neck around him to see what Phil was doing.

"Very good," Nicolo said, turning to her. "A neck stretch. Phil, can you see how Bella is reaching up and out with her neck. We can easily modify that into a complete neck roll, like this. First, lift your head up and then let it drop around and down and up, and then back."

Both Fells made sharp, dipping, darting motions with their chins.

"Well, that's a start," said Nicolo. "Why don't we leave that for now and come back to these stretches later. For now I think we should give the balls a try." He corralled and rolled two of the largest exercise balls, one pink and one purple, over to the brother and sister. "These will allow us to work on both our stretches and our balance at the same time. These are also excellent for strengthening isolated muscle groups."

Bella made an anxious moue, but arranged herself gingerly on top of the purple ball, leaving the pink one for Phil. He stood with his hands at his sides and gazed at it balefully.

"It is ridiculouss," he said.

Bella bounced her narrow bottom cautiously on the top of her ball. "Try it, Phil," she encouraged. "It is more comfortable than it looks."

"Come on, Phil," said Nicolo. "See how well Bella is doing?"

Bella gave her ball another couple of experimental jounces and began to slide off toward Nicolo. "Oops," she said, and righted herself again. She spread her legs and planted them firmly on each side of the ball, and then put her hands flat on the ball between her legs to control it if it suddenly started to buck or roll. She kept her eyes turned downward, watchful against any unexpected movement.

Phil turned around, bent his legs and lowered his bottom toward the pink ball. His aim was flawed, and he slipped off and landed on the mat.

"Imposssible," he protested.

Bella jolted herself on the ball again, an inch or two up and down. Her mouth stretched into an uneven smile.

"Try it again," she urged.

Phil stood and contorted his body into an exaggerated Z shape. He jutted his rear end over the ball and bent his legs slowly. At the moment of contact, his speed increased and the ball rolled and squirted off to the side. Phil landed heavily on his side on the mat. He lay there breathing rapidly and blinking. Nicolo knelt down beside him on one knee to make sure he wasn't injured.

Bella allowed herself a deeper bounce into her ball. Rebounding, and with her close-set grey eyes open as wide as she could force them, her pale mouth formed into an almost coquettish oval, and her tongue extended, she was thrown from her ball and landed fully on top of Nicolo, who was forced in turn to fall face down onto Phil.

"Oh," said Bella.

Her entire weight sank down on Nicolo. She was unexpectedly heavy—like a sack of hammers, Monica would have said—and her shoulder, hip and knee were very sharp.

"Oh," she said again, almost dreamily.

She seemed to descend again, more solidly, almost deter-
minedly, so that the length of her body pressed down on
Nicolo, who felt Phil begin to writhe and twist underneath
him. Someone's hand reached out, grasped Nicolo's upper
inner thigh and squeezed very hard. Nicolo grabbed the hand
and tossed it away, and then they all three surged upward,
disentangling, sorting out legs and arms.

Nicolo didn't know what to say, and neither Phil nor
Bella said anything at all. Nicolo herded them to the elliptical trainers, which was the equipment they tolerated best,
and allowed them to spend the last half-hour of their session
working on cardio. They skipped the final cool-down and
stretch entirely.

"Hour's up," he said at 7:59, and Phil and Bella evaporated
from his view.

In the change room later, when he pulled off his shorts,
Nicolo saw the shape of reaching fingers forming a bruise
underneath the skin at the top of his leg, reaching almost
to his groin. He thought with distaste of the hand he had
held for less than a second—cold, damp skin over a shifting
assembly of sharp bones. He caught himself scrubbing at the
bruise in the shower as if he could wash it away. It reminded
him in some way of Vito, someone who had worked at his
father's barbershop years ago when he was a boy. He hadn't
thought of Vito in years. He must have shaken hands with
Vito back then; he could almost sum up a memory of Vito's
long, cold fingers and moist unpadded palm.

"Whatever happened to Vito?" he asked his older brother
Enzo the following Saturday afternoon. It was the day of
Gordon's wedding and Nicolo had dropped by to borrow

Enzo's shoes. His brother was on his knees, searching in the back of his closet.

"Jeez. Don't ever mention that name to Dad," Enzo said. He turned around and looked at Nicolo. "Or Ma. He's the only person Dad ever had to fire from the shop and it just about killed him."

"Why did he have to fire him?"

"I don't know. Something like stealing, I thought. Nonna told me once that he was a very bad man. What I remember was that he was there one day and then gone the next, and no one ever spoke about him after that. I remember seeing his station cleared out— Here they are. They're dusty and they could use a polish but they're good shoes. They'll look good on you. Greco. That was his last name, remember? Vito Greco."

CHAPTER TWENTY-TWO

"When we got the divorce, he kept the club member- ship and I kept the kids, which seemed more than fair to me. He always preferred golf anyway. That's when I went out and joined Caruso's. I needed somewhere new I could go to work out where there'd be zero risk of running into him and Miss Chantilly Lace. The kids are over in the reception room with the happy couple getting some pre- event photos taken."

Nicolo and Monica were in the broad, bright, gold- carpeted lobby of Gordon's golf and tennis club, where the wedding and reception were taking place. Nicolo was wearing a new dark grey suit, bought with younger Enzo's help, a blue and white striped shirt, a navy blue silk tie with a repeating design of linked red and gold circles, and his older brother Enzo's good pair of shoes.

"What do you think?" said Monica.

She opened her arms wide and turned around slowly. She had managed to come within an almost satisfactory seven and a half pounds of her goal. Her stomach was flat, her upper arms solid. She was wearing a purple silk sleeveless sheath dress, size eight petite, cut low at her chest and tight across her bottom, which looked just a little bit packed in, like ice cream in a tub. That last seven and a half frustrating pounds would have made all the difference, she pointed out to him; she might even have achieved that inward slope of flesh above her pelvis and between her hip bones that was the hallmark of serious self-deprivation. She opened her purse, brushed a fresh sweep of bronzing powder across her nose and cheeks and cranked her lipstick tube to reinforce the wide pink swath on her lips.

Nicolo was surprised at how protective he felt of Monica, balanced before him in her high heels, and by the realization that he also felt sorrowful for her, although this wedding was an ordeal that she had set for herself. He leaned down and brushed his cheek against hers. Monica smelled like lilies of the valley, the spring-flowering plants that grew in clusters along the walls of his family's garage.

"You'll be all right?" he asked her.

Monica breathed so that her breasts puffed like the chest of a bird above the lilac trim at the top of her dress, and then nodded. He reached for her arm and tucked it under his, and they walked together into the Mallard Room, then up the centre of the room to the front where two rows of chairs had been labelled "Reserved for Family and Special Friends."

Monica nodded to friends from her days with Gordon. She squeezed Nicolo's arm and looked up at him through her lashes. He was, after all, a very sweet guy. Not her type, of course. She liked them older and hapless, but he was a sweetie, especially for seeing her through this ridiculous wedding. She chose seats at the end of the second row in front of a supporting column that provided some shelter from scrutiny.

Within a few minutes, Hayley, plump and pink and dewy in a cascading confection of princess-cut eyelet lace and with her grandmother's long silk veil fastened to her blonde head by means of golden butterfly-shaped pins, made her procession up the centre space between the rows of chairs to the front of the room, where she was joined by Gordon. The bald spot on the back of his head had grown larger over the past year, Monica observed. And it was shaped almost exactly like the hole-in-the-ozone satellite shots over Antarctica that her son Noah had glued to bristol board for his science project this past winter. What did sparkly little Hayley, not twenty-five yet, want with an ozone-headed man in an outgrown tuxedo with two kids he never wanted to see and a selfless but sardonic wife so freshly but not yet completely excised from his past? Nicolo wondered. And did Gordon believe that some magic would be achieved through these new pledges, some alchemy that would transform him into someone else entirely, someone who would cleave forever to wife and hearth?

"Today I gladly and with my entire heart take you for my spouse," they each intoned, Hayley first and then Gordon a beat behind. They continued through the promises in turn.

"I promise to love you without reservation."

"I shall bring you flasks of wine, comfort you with apples, and never tire of love."

"Let our love be like bread, made new with fresh yeast every day."

"Our love will be the morning and the evening star."

"I will share your burden in times of distress, laugh when you laugh, and cry when you cry."

"I pledge to grow along with you in mind and spirit, always be open and candid with you, and treasure you for as long as we both shall live."

"I take you now, before these witnesses, and pledge my love."

Nicolo felt Monica's shoulder shaking against his elbow.

"So stupid, I know," she whispered when he inclined his head toward her. She batted at her nose with a crumpled salmon-coloured tissue.

Nicolo reached out for Monica's hand and squeezed it. "It'll be all right," he said into the thick wave of pinned hair that concealed her ear.

"No," she whispered back, her voice raspy with suppressed exasperation and sorrow. "It won't be all right. Not really. They think it's a game. Like those rides at Disneyland that just keep on going, and you buy the kind of ticket that lets you get on and off and on again whenever you like. I married him for life. For better or worse. That's how it is with me. You shouldn't commit until you know for sure, but once you commit, that's it. For life. Like those parking lots downtown. No in-and-out privileges. It's a game to them, but to me it was serious."

Nicolo nodded. He put his arm around her shoulders. His chin pressed against the top of Monica's head.

"It's too late for me; I won't do it again. But you, you shouldn't go through life alone. Marriage gives you ballast. Having someone else there every day balances you. When we first met, Gordon had a motorcycle. On our second date he bought me a helmet and taught me how to ride behind him. At first, when he took a corner, my instinct was to pull away from the turn because I was afraid that the bike would fall over. But what you have to do is sit as close as possible and lean together. I fell in love with him when we were out on that stupid bike. I thought that was what our marriage would be like, leaning together. That's what a marriage *should* be like. When you find a good one, whoever it is, grab them. Take the chance. Hold on tight. No matter what, it's worth it, it really is."

"Do you know what this is?" Broad-beamed James stood, legs planted wide, in the middle of the hall on Monday morning when Nicolo arrived at Caruso's, holding out several pieces of paper stapled together. James jerked his thumb over his shoulder, gesturing for Nicolo to follow him into the office. He kicked the door shut behind them, dropped into the chair behind his desk and signalled for Nicolo to sit. Then he pushed the papers at Nicolo. Sarah came from her adjoining office, really a rectangle of space between a row of filing cabinets and the far wall, and positioned herself behind

James. She observed Nicolo closely, worrying with her teeth at a few strands of hair that she pulled across her cheek.

Nicolo remained standing and picked the papers up from the desk. He read the heading and scanned the first page silently. "It's the harassment policy," he answered. He could see from the multiple staple and pin marks that this was the copy that usually hung on the bulletin board at the main entrance to the gym.

"Read the first part out loud," said James.

"'Caruso's will not tolerate, ignore, condone, allow or permit workplace harassment and considers harassment to be a serious offence, which may result in disciplinary action up to and including dismissal,'" Nicolo read.

"Go on," said James.

"'Workplace harassment can include a single or a series of incidents involving unwelcome or offensive behaviour, gestures, comments and conduct directed specifically at an individual.'" Nicolo paused. "It goes on after that for pages. Five pages. What's up?"

"There's been a complaint," said Sarah.

"Against you," said James. "Sexual touching. See here?" He pulled the papers out of Nicolo's hand and flipped the top page. "Like it says right here. 'Unwelcome physical contact, intentional or unintentional, such as touching, kissing, patting, contact or pinching.' That's prohibited."

"And discrimination," added Sarah.

"'Refusing to work or cooperate with a member of the public or fellow employee because of their ethnic, racial or religious basis,'" James read again from the policy.

"Me?" said Nicolo. "Discrimination against who?" He was thinking, however, of the Fells.

"See?" said James. His voice, always high pitched, soared into falsetto range. He pointed at Nicolo's face and gestured with his chin toward Sarah. "See that? That look right there? You know what we're talking about, don't you, eh?"

"We're supposed to let him tell his side of the story," Sarah pointed out. She stepped around James so that she stood closer to Nicolo. Nicolo and Sarah were the same height. She fixed her eyes on his. "Do you know what this is about?"

"The only thing I can think of is what happened last Thursday," Nicolo said, and he described the sequence of actions that had led to him tumbling on top of Phil and underneath Bella. "Was that it? I can't think of anything else. But it wasn't intentional. It was awkward, but just as much for me as for them."

"You should have reported it," said Sarah. "Any physical contact, intentional or unintentional, by a member of a staff with any client has to be reported immediately."

"If that's even what happened," said James. "And I can tell you right now, Nicco-boy, that your version of events isn't at all the way we've heard it."

Nicolo closed his eyes. Exactly what had happened on Wednesday? The experience had been as much dispiriting as humiliating and he had tried to put it out of his mind. In any case, even at the time it hadn't been entirely clear how he had ended up in a pile on the floor like the filling of an unsavoury sandwich with the Fells on either side of him. Being forced to consider it now brought a shot of bile into the back of his throat. He didn't like the Fells and—it occurred to him for the first time—they didn't like him.

He opened his eyes and in an instant of clarity, perceived that James disliked him as well, and very probably for the same reason. Nicolo was one of the world's blessed. He had been provided with sufficient resources, more than sufficient in fact. He was healthy, well-adjusted, well-housed and well-guided. He had always had people who loved him, and as a result he had always had at the ready the confidence—doubtlessly naive—of someone who expects to be liked and generally is. James and the Fells must have begun life as deserving—what infant can possibly be born unworthy?—but the workings of the world, whatever they were, and however it worked, had been stinting with them. The world had provided them with miserly doses of many of the advantages that Nicolo had been allotted in abundance. It could be no consolation to them that Nicolo was both aware of and grateful for this plenitude. And Nicolo realized that part of his fortune had been to live in a manner uncircumscribed by rules. His own moral system was enough of a rudder; the rules were almost all superfluous. James and the Fells would struggle for their entire lives with the question of what and who and whose rules should have authority over them, and who they could dominate in turn.

"Just what did they say?" Nicolo asked James. He remembered how Salvatore had asserted charge over a set of difficult facts. He sat down, pulled his chair close to the desk, took the pages of the policy in his hands and straightened them by tapping their edges on the desk, first the long side and then the short.

"That's for us to know," said James. "None of your business at the present time is all you need to know. Our investigation is ongoing."

"But I'm entitled to know the facts. In fact, I need to know them in order to respond to them, isn't that right?"

"Yes, of course we've asked for a written description of the exact allegation," said Sarah. "We'll give a copy to you as soon as we have it. I'm sure it can all be—"

"Are there any witnesses?"

"No. But it's two against one." James folded his arms across his chest. "Only your word against theirs. Two *paying* customers." He wore the satisfied expression of a professional torturer.

"So you have nothing in writing at all. All you have is a complaint against someone who's worked for you for five years so far with no problems?"

"What we have is an allegation that you engineered a situation in which you had contact of a sexual nature with both of the Fells."

"Both? At once? Here in the gym? In a workout room that anyone could have walked into at any time? That's quite a story, don't you think?"

"You've already admitted to the incident and you've also admitted to failing to file a report about it as soon as it happened, as required by the gym rules."

"I have described to you a *collision* that was not my fault and in which no one was injured. There was nothing even remotely sexual about it. If nothing happened, then there was nothing to report. Is that all you have? An allegation? No injury and nothing in writing? Do the Carusos know about this?"

"There is in fact an injury."

"Who? What kind of injury?"

"We have a picture of it, Nicolo," Sarah said.

"Let's see it, then."

Sarah pulled a large photograph from a file folder and passed it across the desk to him, dodging James's obstructive reach. The photograph showed a long blue-white thigh with a bruise almost identical to Nicolo's, but lower down, just above the knee.

"Bella?" Nicolo asked.

"No," said James. "This is a picture of Mr. Fell's injury. He came to see us this morning alone, without Ms. Fell. She was apparently too upset to come in."

"Who took the picture?"

"I did." James rattled his desk drawer. "I keep a camera in case there is ever any need to document an incident. The insurance company makes it a requirement of our liability policy. I keep the batteries charged and fresh film in it at all times. Just in case. The Carusos rely on me to play this kind of thing entirely by the book."

Nicolo closed his eyes and flexed the muscles in his shoulders. He could feel his pulse surging underneath his skin. His fingers clenched. What he wanted, he realized, was to reach over and pull James's head from his neck. He could feel the veins in his forearms inflating. His jaw and temple ached. He took a slow deep breath and then unfolded his hands.

"Well then," he said. "You might as well take a picture of

this for the record too." He was wearing grey sweatpants over his gym shorts. He stood up, pulled his sweatpants down to his knee and placed his leg up on the desktop under the bright, overhanging light for James and Sarah to see.

Enzo slept in on the morning of his hearing. He had worked at the factory until midnight and had been in bed before one, but he hadn't been able to fall asleep until after two. Just before nine o'clock the sound of a door closing somewhere in the house woke him up. He showered, dressed and went into the kitchen. The coffee pot was upside down on a towel beside the sink. The breadbox held a heel of bread from a loaf made several days before. He called out.

"Ma! Nonna!"

No one was home. His father would have gone to work, and his mother must have taken Nonna out shopping with her.

He got his keys and wallet from the top of his dresser and drove to the Vaughan Bakery, the file that Salvatore had prepared for him to review on the passenger seat beside him. The day was cool and blustery. A dry urban wind carried with it scraps of dust and paper and invisible streams of sharp pollen molecules that invaded his nose and eyes and made his tear ducts itch. He parked and walked into the store, and saw with some annoyance that there was a long lineup at the coffee counter. He joined the back of the queue, quelling his natural, type-A impatience. Nicolo had convinced him to start going to yoga twice a week at the gym, and he thought that this might be helping him maintain his composure in general.

The woman in the line immediately in front of him—medium height, indeterminate age, straight hair that reached to her shoulders and gleamed brighter than her complexion and so likely was dyed, rumpled navy trench coat overtop a gold sweater, and red wool, kilt-like, knee-length pleated skirt—spun around so abruptly that at first he thought she must have suddenly remembered that she had left the tap running or the stove on and been about to run from the store. But she didn't step away from the line. Instead she addressed him directly.

"I'm never going to see you again, am I," she said.

"I guess not." Enzo was unsure what answer she was hoping or expecting to hear.

"You look like the kind of person that someone could say just about anything to," she said.

"Yes, I think that's true," said Enzo.

"And it doesn't really matter what I say, since I'll probably never see you again."

"I guess it doesn't."

"You don't look as if you'd be easily shocked or judgmental or anything like that."

It didn't seem that any answer was required. Enzo glanced at the woman's face covertly. He noticed that her purse and hands were small. She might be deranged but there was no sign she was dangerous.

"Because I've just worked it out. Standing here. I think I've finally figured it out."

Enzo inclined his head in a neutral way.

"See that woman over there, behind me, at the table in the corner, in the yellow coat and thick stockings and ugly shoes?"

Enzo looked and saw, waiting at one of the bakery's round tables, a woman who fit this description. She was bent over the tabletop, engrossed in a tabloid.

"That's my mother. She's waiting for me to bring her her coffee and her toast, lightly spread with margarine, but only if it's Becel, otherwise it has to be butter, but only if it's unsalted, otherwise dry, okay? And it has to be whole wheat, but failing that rye or sourdough but never multigrain because multigrain hasn't got any taste or fibre." The woman paused and drew a breath.

"So, what I realized, right now, standing here, is that I'm never going to make her happy, am I? I'm never going to be able to do it. It's a mug's game, right? It's just not possible. I'm going to fail. Each and every time. It will always be the wrong kind of toast or the wrong margarine or the coffee will be cold or the cream will curdle. Because she's the kind of person cream curdles *for*, see? That's just the way it is. And, see, the thing is, I'm forty. I don't feel forty, and I don't even think I look forty, because when you think about it, nothing has ever happened to me and so I don't have as many wrinkles as I probably should have if I'd done all the things I was supposed to have done by now, and I'm not getting fat, but it's snuck up on me anyway, forty, even though I think I really thought deep down that it wouldn't happen to me. It's always that way, isn't it? You don't think it will happen to you but then it does. Your friends grow up and get married and move away and have kids and send you letters, you know the kind, the newsletter kind, and they hand-write something personal in the corner at the bottom, and they still mail them to your *mother's* house because they know that that's where you still live, and no one even asks any more what your plans are because it's pretty obvious really that you're just going to moulder away, and *she'll* make sure no one wants you notwithstanding all of the *hints* about grandchildren. She lets them fly, like missiles, when you've got your guard down and might even be starting to like her. And then, *kaboom,* like that, she explodes some comment like a bomb in your face. Grandchildren. For God's sake."

The line was moving very slowly. There seemed to be a problem with the Gaggia, behind which three of the staff had gathered with their heads together over a spiral-bound manual.

"So, it's up to me, right? Because why do I put up with it?"

"I'm not sure."

"I don't have to do it. I'm forty years old, for Christ's sake. I can do whatever I want. What's stopping me? And, you know, I do know what I want. I've always wanted the same thing and it's not so hard. It's not too much to ask. It's doable in fact."

"What do you want?" Enzo was genuinely curious.

"I've decided that if I'm not going to be married, and at this point, let's face it, it's not very likely—like lightning it would have to be for that to happen now, if you see what I mean. If lightning isn't going to strike, then I want to rent one of those small apartments above a store down on St. Clair. It could even be a studio. The smaller the better. A kitchen or kitchenette that I can clean in five minutes flat. A room with a rug and a couch and a table and a bed. A dresser and a closet for my clothes. And the kind of window you can lean out of. That's the important part. You can lean out the window and you're not so high up, only on the second storey, so you can watch the people walking by underneath and you can really see them, you know, and if they're talking loud enough and the traffic's not too heavy you can hear what they're saying to each other. The best would be over top of a coffee shop that's open early in the morning but not too late at night, you know, the kind that everyone comes to. And a corner grocery store a block away where you can buy everything you need, fruits and vegetables and canned goods and cereal, and even things like yogourt if you check the date to make sure it hasn't been there too long because those kinds of places don't go through a lot of yogourt. And a dry cleaner where they know that this is your *favourite* pink sweater, and not just some woman's sweater that isn't important to her, and so they take special care. They take special care because it's mine and they know that I live down the street in the apartment over the cafe, the one with the window. And when they walk by on Saturday afternoon they know that they can wave up at me and I'll wave back. That's what I want. That isn't too much to ask, is it? I have the money. It's not a question of money. I have my job and they pay me enough to have my own apartment. How much can they cost—the small ones down on St. Clair?"

"I don't think they cost that much."

"Right. So what I realized is that if it's going to happen, I need to do it now. Right now. And if I wait for the coffee to be ready and the toast to be toasted then it will be too late and it will keep on being too late until either she's dead or I am and in either case it's still going to be too late."

Enzo nodded. "That sounds right to me," he said. It was true. He was convinced.

"So, is it okay if I give you this money?" The woman handed him a five-dollar bill. "Would you mind? Because it seems as if I have to go, and I know I'll feel guilty, but I'll feel a little bit less guilty if she's at least had her coffee. Just ask for medium with double cream for here. You can keep the change or put it in the tip jar, whatever you like. Don't worry about the toast, because if you order that for her you'll only get it wrong. Trust me, I know."

Enzo closed his hand around the money. The woman didn't check his face for assent. She seemed to have assumed his complicity, and her mind had already moved on to the next step in the logistical course that she was unfolding in front of herself like a map. She snapped shut her purse and walked away from the queue, which had at last started to advance, and out through the glass door of the Vaughan Bakery. The pneumatic mechanism closed the door slowly and quietly behind her.

Over at the transfer station, Paola and Filomena were taking their first steps as part of a wobbly oval of people forming in front of the main truck entrance. Each participant hoisted a sign stapled to a short wooden stake. WE WON'T TAKE ANY MORE, Paola's sign read. On Filomena's, in her own hand, was the single word BASTA!—Enough! A call had been made to Paola the night before. Sonia Zhu, a woman who lived a block and a half from the landfill, had been collecting names and telephone numbers at each of the information sessions and she was the one who had put out the summons.

Over the weekend, a methane-fed fire had flared up in several inadequately compacted portions of the southeast quadrant of the landfill, deep under the more recent surface layers, and, despite the combined efforts of five surrounding fire stations and an expert flown in from central New York State, and notwithstanding the declared elimination of various hot spots, the fire continued to smoulder under layers and layers of debris, emitting smoke and occasionally shooting up flames in areas the fire specialists had announced were under control. Who knew what toxic substances were being released into the surrounding air, infiltrating homes and the tender growing lungs of children and babies, contaminating homes and gardens and streets and schools? Sonia asked. Officials from the Ministry of Environment had been seen coming and going, ferried in and out of the front gates in their efficient little cars, and there were heavy equipment operators too, wearing white hazmat suits, working around the perimeter of the problem areas, digging trenches with large, cantilevered machines. "It's past time that we made our views known," Sonia had said on the phone.

Paola had hesitated. Massimo and the boys were out and could not be consulted. Nonna, however, insisted that they go. She put on her sweater and shoes and brought Paola the keys to the car.

The sign was much heavier than it looked, particularly when the wind caught it and tried to wrest it from Filomena's hands or flatten it into the ground. The rough wooden stakes bristled with splinters. Filomena, two paces in front of Paola, gripped her sign tightly and she turned around every few minutes to make sure that Paola was holding hers up high enough. Filomena brandished her sign upward with each step. "*Basta!*" she cried out with perfect timbre and timing. The cameraman sent over from the local Italian news station had just started to roll his film and a news reporter was picking her way closer in her high heels, her head inclined into the swirling wind, which carried in it dust and scraps of paper and dried leaves. Paola gulped at the brisk air and stepped up so that she strode abreast with her mother-in-law. She allowed her sign to flutter diffidently alongside Filomena's.

"*Forza,*" said Filomena encouragingly, and then again more loudly, "*Forza.*"

"*Forza!*" cried Paola. "Enough. We've had enough!"

CHAPTER TWENTY-THREE

It wasn't until Nicolo was driving to the law school that he realized he should have met Enzo at the house and brought him to the interview. On the highway, he passed two cars at the side of the road. There had been some sort of minor collision and the drivers had pulled over to exchange licence numbers and insurance information. Enzo's situation seemed to him somewhat like theirs—a short span of inattention, a brief departure from the rules—but with much more serious consequences. Because of abstract notions of justice and fairness, decisions that would affect Enzo's life profoundly would be made without regard to his background and circumstances. No one would think to ask questions about his mother or his father, about where they came from, what the implications for them might be. Wouldn't a humane system manage to take all of this into account?

He stopped at a gas station and phoned, trying to reach Enzo at home in case he was running late and hadn't left the house yet, but no one answered. Nicolo got back in his car and drove quickly the rest of the way downtown. He followed Pietro Salvatore's directions and was able to find a parking spot a few blocks away, and then navigate the quiet halls of the law school to the dean's office without too much difficulty. Pietro was already in the waiting area, which appeared to have been carefully staged as if for a drama, with a cluster of chairs and tables and table lamps, a floral arrangement of outsized red and orange blossoms on spearlike stems, and legal magazines and journals arranged in a precise fan on a polished sideboard. The furniture, the walls and doors, were all glossy with paint or polish, and solidly made. The upholstered chairs were of different sizes but each had carved wooden armrests and ornate legs. They reminded Nicolo of chess pieces.

Pietro was wearing beige slacks with a perfect crease, a navy blue polo shirt and a jacket. He stood beside a broad window that looked out over a view of rooftops and a small courtyard in which students walked back and forth in pairs and alone. Nicolo greeted him and sat down on one of the chairs. The interviews had been scheduled at least two hours apart to minimize the risk that the impugned students would encounter one another coming or going, but the earlier interview must have started late or run long. Five minutes after Nicolo arrived, a young woman emerged from the inner office, pale and red-eyed, flanked by her parents, both of them looking stiff with worry, and a woman in a tailored suit who seemed to be her lawyer. The student pressed her lips together and shook her head at Nicolo while her parents and the two lawyers conferred.

"They're brutal," she said in a husky voice. "I warn you. They'll tell you that you should be open and honest and forthright and all that, but don't believe it. They twist everything you say against you."

Her lawyer came across the room and placed a hand on her shoulder, and then the group moved out to the corridor.

"Where's Enzo?" Nicolo wondered aloud.

"He'll be here."

Pietro didn't sound anxious, and it occurred to Nicolo that at least part of the lawyer's fee was earned for exactly this—the calm set of his muscles and his measured tone of assurance.

Several minutes ticked past, each one punctuated by the audible click of an ornate wooden wall clock with a long pendulum. A thin young man, assistant to the dean, came out twice to ask whether Mr. Pavone had arrived. At ten minutes after the appointed time, Enzo came through the door.

"Sorry," he said. "Something came up that I couldn't get out of."

Nicolo's eyebrows pulled closer together. He hadn't expected to see Enzo looking so unperturbed.

"You're ready?" Pietro asked.

"Yes. Absolutely. Are you?"

Enzo and Pietro knocked and were admitted into the inner office, and Nicolo sat and waited while the clock consumed the successive minutes of first one hour and then most of another. He had planned to use the time to study for his psychology final, and he had brought the textbook and his notebook with him, but he was unable to switch his attention from the process that was unfolding inside the dean's office. No sounds could be heard through the heavy door. He practised a meditation technique that he had learned at the gym. Sitting as straight in his chair as possible, he concentrated first on slowing his breathing. When he had achieved a steady in-and-out rhythm, he summoned up an image of weights stacked in the weight room in a sturdy pyramid stand. He pictured himself reaching out and lifting each one in turn, from the lightest two-kilogram weight up to the heaviest. He imagined the muscles in his body moving together flawlessly and he saw himself clearly, picking up ever heavier weights, each in a single, smooth motion, starting with a crouch, shifting his feet and pressing the weight upward, and then shifting his shoulders, bending his knees and pulling his body under the weight, catching it with locked arms overhead while squatting, and finally locking his arms and standing up with the weight raised overhead.

When Enzo and Pietro finally came out, Nicolo could feel the strain in every muscle.

"They'll make the decision quickly," was all that Enzo told him. "Within a few days."

Nicolo could read nothing in Pietro's expression.

"It went well enough," Pietro said, and then, enigmatically, "I suspect that your brother will have to decide what it is that he really wants to do."

After they left, Nicolo followed Enzo's car north through the streets. Enzo kept a steady pace and hit a green light at almost every intersection. Nicolo stayed close behind, cruising through a few late yellows. At home Enzo pulled up into the driveway and Nicolo parked on the street. They met at the front door.

Both felt, as they entered, the unexpected emptiness of the house. They heard none of the sounds that a house with people in it contains, no rustles or creaks or any of the subtle rhythms of purposeful movement, of tasks and conversation. There was no sign that their mother, father or nonna had been there since early that morning. Enzo checked the garage: his father's car wasn't there. Nicolo dialled their older brother Enzo's telephone number. No one answered. Nicolo and Enzo met up again at the front door.

"Hospital?" Nicolo suggested. They were both thinking of Nonna.

"We might as well check. We can take my car."

They drove in silence to the hospital and parked at a meter near the emergency room entrance. In the triage area a dozen people waited to be seen, most of them enduring the delay resignedly. At the far end of the room, a television flickered local news. No one seemed to be watching it. One man wearing jeans and a denim shirt, with a rope laced through his belt loops and tied in a loose knot at this stomach, was pacing the length of the room gesticulating and muttering anxiously. "Barry Bonds, Barry Bonds, Barry Bonds," he repeated. "Miller Park, Miller Park, Miller Park." He wrung his hands together, spun on his heel, swung an imaginary bat through the air and then turned to stride in the other direction.

Nicolo dodged the Barry Bonds man and asked the nurse at the front desk whether any Pavones had been seen or admitted. She pecked at the keys of her computer, compressed her lips and shook her head. "I'm sorry. We have no one by that name," she said.

Nicolo turned toward Enzo, who was in the corner, watching the television. "They're not here," Nicolo told him.

"Look," Enzo said, directing his gaze to the screen.

"That's . . . Nonna," said Nicolo. "And Ma. What are they doing?"

"Exercising their democratic right to peaceful protest is what it looks like. Over at the landfill."

"Are those *police officers* behind them?"

"It looks like it. We'd better go over and find out what's going on."

They were forced to park on a side road several blocks from the landfill and walk the rest of the way. The main street was lined with parked cars, and traffic was filtering in slowly, some cars trying to get through, others slowing to see what was happening, still others looking for a place to pull over. People on foot were making their way along the sidewalk that ran along the north side of the street toward the commotion at the landfill gates. A sweet, skunky compost-like smell grew stronger as Nicolo and Enzo drew closer. A queue of garbage trucks stretched from the gates back into the street. The truck motors had been left idling and the drivers leaned against their front bumpers or gathered in groups of two or three discussing the situation.

"This is bullshit," one was saying loudly to his colleagues as Nicolo and Enzo pressed past. "I haven't got all day here. It's not as if I don't have a job to do and a wife and a kid to get home to. Does anyone stop to think about that? Garbage isn't pretty, but until people stop making it, it has to get picked up and hauled away. Where do they think it's going to go if it doesn't get brought up here?"

The gates were blocked by about two dozen protestors, almost all of them women, stretched in a line from one side of the entrance to the other, arms linked. Their signs lay at their feet. Nonna was in the middle and their mother was to her right. Nonna's hair was windblown and her coat was misbuttoned so that the left side drooped at the hem. She glanced short-sightedly about her and appeared impatient. Beside her, their mother was neatly dressed in slacks and a zippered coat that ended at her hips. A filmy kerchief was knotted at her neck. The corners of the scarf fluttered around her face in the wind. She looked embarrassed but determined. Behind the line of protestors a smear of greasy-looking smoke rose into the air from a distant zone of the landfill. The wind tugged the sooty streak across the sky, away toward the west. Massimo was off to the side of the gate, in a cluster of husbands, all inclined toward each other, conferring. He shook his head when he saw his sons approaching.

"They say they aren't leaving," he said. "The police have talked to them, and then the manager came out, but they won't go. Some of those guys with the trucks sound like they might start something up, you know, to get something happening. It sounds as if a woman who handles public relations is coming over."

"Can't they get those trucks to turn off their motors?" said Enzo. It was difficult to make himself heard over the noise.

"*Hell no, we won't go,*" the band of protestors called out.

A ponytailed woman wearing a navy skirt and a short-sleeved white cardigan approached the blockade at a brisk pace. She held an orange megaphone. Lifting it to her mouth, she called out something that could not be heard. A man in a brown suit sprinted to her side and flipped a switch on the side of the megaphone, and the woman tried again.

"Most of you know me," she began, addressing the picketers. Although her voice was amplified, her tone was warm and direct, almost intimate. "In fact, I hope that all of you, or at least many of you, would agree that we've established a relationship of trust, or at least, we've built up some rapport, I like to think, over the past weeks and months. In any event, what I would like to say is that I have a few things I'd like to share with you and I hope you will hear me out.

"We at the Vaughan transfer station would like you to know that we have some messages, some key messages, which we want to pass on and that we hope will help to clarify the current situation in which we find ourselves, and ensure that everyone's needs are understood. The important thing, I think you will agree, is not to lose momentum. We already have a positive dialogue going and the dialogue just needs to be given a chance to continue. I have no doubt that with goodwill on both sides—"

"It's a dump!" someone on the line called out—a broad-hipped woman wearing a print housedress tied around her waist. "It's a *dump*. It's not a landfill, and it's not a transfer station, and it's not a recycling plant, and it's not a goddamn pie. It's a dump. Let's start out by all agreeing to call it what it is. It's a dump. Okay? A garbage dump."

The woman with the ponytail took a slow breath. She chewed her lower lip and then her upper lip. "Okay," she said, finally. "It's a dump. A state-of-the-art dump. Does that help? Will that help us get back to engaging in a positive and meaningful dialogue?"

"It's only a dialogue if you *listen* to us. You have to pay attention to what we have to say. You can't just tell us what to think," someone else said. It was Paola. Her voice was loud, but unsteady. Nonna nodded emphatically at her side, and Paola took a deep breath and began to speak again, but she was interrupted.

"Okay." The ponytailed woman held up her free hand, palm forward in a gesture of capitulation. "We'll listen. We agree to listen. We'll engage in a two-way dialogue."

"And you have to take sign."

This time it was Nonna who had spoken. She unlinked her arms from Paola on her right and the woman in the dress who had spoken first on her left, and she stepped forward. She bent down, proud, stiff-backed, and selected a sign from the pile at her feet. She handed it to the young woman with the megaphone.

"Here," she said. "You take."

The woman took the placard in her hands. In order to do so, she tucked the megaphone under one arm and it responded with a loud *squawk*. A few people in the crowd of onlookers laughed.

Seeing the breach in the line, and perhaps sensing a change in the overall mood, the driver of the nearest truck leapt into his cab. He engaged the gears, and with a loud grinding noise the truck began to move slowly, at a walking pace, toward the demonstrators. Most of them took a step backward, spreading farther apart, and the line began fragmenting near the open gates. The driver honked his air horn, producing a deafening claxon sound. He pressed on the horn again, and it felt to the observers as if the earth shook slightly under their feet under the mass of the advancing truck, which was so heavily loaded that garbage spilled out of its sides—coffee grounds, plastic margarine tubs, cereal boxes, carrot scrapings, crumpled tissues, the spilling electronic innards of a radio or other domestic machine. Two or three people at the margins of the line frayed away.

Massimo, Nicolo and Enzo pressed forward and began to push through the crowd ahead of them.

"Come," said Nonna, and she seized the near hand of the ponytailed woman. Paola took hold of the woman's jacket, and she and Nonna pulled her around so that the woman stood between them, in the path of the looming vehicle. NO MORE EMPTY PROMISES, read her sign, which was now turned forward and could be read. Nonna kept a firm grip on the woman's hand, and Paola on her jacket. Their captive turned her head away from the bright lights and lifted her sign to shield her eyes. The rest of the people on the picket line cheered and regrouped. Seeing the sign hoisted higher, they linked arms so that again they formed a single unbroken chain.

The truck came to a halt less than a metre from the tip of Nonna's nose. The roil of its engine made the bones of her chest shudder, and she felt herself shaken and then fully awakened, everything coming sharply into focus, like the picture on the television when one of the boys would come to adjust it for her. It was her first true wholly rounded conscious experience since coming here all those years ago.

She looked to her left, and saw Massimo and the boys out of the corner of her suddenly clear vision. On her right was steadfast Paola, who had loved her and protected her and understood her for more years than had her own mother. She had traded a country and a language for a family. Things of such different sizes and significance. Filomena thought of the words from the book of Ruth that Peppino had recited to her when he returned from Ferramonti, to show her what he had learned. She remembered how he had lowered the pitch of his voice; he had wanted his knowledge to remain a secret between them.

Ma Rut rispose, Non insistere con me perché ti abbandoni e torni indietro senza di te: perché dove andrai tu andrò anch'io; dove ti fermerai mi fermerò; il tuo popolo sarà il mio popolo e il tuo Dio sarà il mio Dio.

Dove morirai tu, morirò anch'io e vi sarò sepolta. Il Signore mi punisca come vuole, se altra cosa che la morte mi separerà da te.

And Ruth said, Entreat me not to leave thee, or to return from following after thee: for whither thou goest, I will go; and where thou lodgest, I will lodge: thy people shall be my people, and thy God my God.

Where thou diest, will I die, and there will I be buried: the Lord do so to me, and more also, if aught but death part thee and me.

Paola reached behind the rigid back of the woman between them and held tight to Nonna's hand. Nicolo suddenly appeared. He turned and inserted himself in front of them, facing the truck. He held himself straight and reached his arms wide against the glare of the headlights and the noise of the engine.

CHAPTER TWENTY-FOUR

Nicolo and Zoe arrived at St. Francis of Assisi parish church at the same time on the day of Mario
and Angie's wedding, a few minutes after eleven, but they
entered the church through different doors and so did not
see each other. Zoe came in through the front door, in the
company of her sisters Emma and Stephanie. They had the
job of setting out the flower arrangements and attaching
white paper flowers and pink pleated garlands to both ends
of each pew. Angie was still at home, being dressed by her
mother and her bridesmaids.

Nicolo, Paul, Frank, Angie's brother Joe, and Angie's
cousins from Vancouver, Nick and Guido, came in from the
parking lot through the vestry door, into the small red-

carpeted room where Nicolo and Frank had robed as altar boys a decade before. This time they were carrying wooden hangers on which hung their tuxedos, zippered into black covers. Nick and Guido, who were older by three or four years, and more experienced, had brought sustenance—a bottle of *vin santo* and a tin filled with hard *biscotti di Prato*. Frank found some glasses in one of the cabinets and persuaded Mario to drink down two glasses of the *vin santo* right away, one after the other, for courage and for luck. Nick and Guido toasted Mario and began to throw out scraps of advice for Mario's life ahead.

"Have your kids young. That's what my father said."

"Wives cry a lot in the first year, my uncle said. Just ignore it and it'll stop eventually."

"They like to get flowers even after you've been married forever. I don't know why."

"You'll need to watch out for your stuff. A friend of mine couldn't find his hockey stick for a game and it turns out his wife used it to stake the tomatoes."

Nicolo kept mostly silent and listened, laughing with the others when they laughed. If only it were really as easy as that, a few simple rules and guidelines—say, no more than ten or twelve—advice like fresh eggs in their neatly divided container. There would be no mistaken marriages, no separations or long-term grievances or divorces. But as it was, nothing was simple or clear between the sexes, and maybe that was how it had to be for the fascination to have been sustained over so many years. Look at how complicated Zoe was, although she appeared as clear and simple as a pool of water. Ideas and past joys and losses flashed in her like fishes. It would take a lifetime to understand her. She had told him that most of what she had learned so far in life was provisional and untried. She had the pale, unlined skin of the untested. She said that she found it inexplicable how readily some people jumped into the concerns of others and offered solutions to problems, when answers eluded them in their own lives. Her life so far, and her visits with her mother on the west coast, had left her with an apprehension of acting impulsively, without careful, reasoned thought. Nor did she like to judge the behaviour or mistakes of other people. She felt that there were always unknown, mitigating circumstances.

At twelve-fifteen, Nicolo walked his parents and Nonna and Enzo and his family to their seats on the left side of the church. At almost half past the hour, Enzo arrived, with Nandita beside him. She wore an orange and pink sari with a gold-threaded border and her dark hair was loose on her shoulders. None of the family had seen Nandita before. It meant something that she was here: a change in Enzo, a change that each of them interpreted differently. Massimo perceived that it signalled a switch from Enzo's single-minded devotion to his studies. Older Enzo thought that his brother might simply want to display Nandita's beauty. Nicolo understood that Nandita's presence represented an unspoken announcement to the family. Nonna searched Nandita's face for the signs of a pure heart, and was satisfied. Paola approved of Nandita's glossy hair and the way she held herself, with her back perfectly straight and her head tipped forward attentively, but she thought that Nandita's outfit might signal something showy or stubborn in her. When she herself had arrived in Canada it had taken her only a month or two to adopt the habits of the people around her, as much as she had been able to decipher them. She thought that it might be seen as self-regard to try to keep up distinctions in a country in which everyone was supposed to be equal.

Enzo stepped to one side and Nandita slid along the pew to sit beside Paola, with Enzo following to sit on Nandita's right. Paola read into this arrangement that Enzo might intend for some sort of approval to be extended. She placed a hand on Nandita's arm and whispered into her ear, a comment on the bride's beautiful dress, because Angie had now begun her procession down the aisle, on her father's arm, toward the altar, where Mario waited, flanked by his handsome groomsmen, her own Nicolo among them. Everything was well done—the rich white flowers, gardenias, masses of them, the long silk dress perfectly cut, a plain piano instead of the organ. The Trapassos were experts at this kind of ceremony. Paola closed her eyes against an odd effect of the soaring music and warm, closely packed bodies. She felt as if her brain and her stomach were sloshing like sea water inside her. She thought with a sudden, acute distaste of her morning cup of coffee. It had tasted bitter. At the reception, she sent Massimo in search of a piece of bread to settle her stomach.

"My client at the gym gave me tickets to the Frankie Donato opening in Las Vegas. Do you think you could go with me?" Nicolo asked Zoe.

"So it came together after all?"

"Apparently. They made a few changes. Irony. That's what did it, Patrick said. They made it more ironic. I thought they should just let him sing, but they went with something different. What do I know anyway?"

"If you're like most people, you probably know more than you think."

They were in the queue at the buffet table. Zoe frowned at the salad, which was principally composed of white wedges of iceberg lettuce, with pallid tomato slices among them. Then she turned to look at Nicolo, and her expression took on the kind of lustre that Nicolo had seen, his entire life, in the faces of his mother and his nonna, a gaze of interest and mindfulness.

"Irony," she said. "Will that make the show better or worse?"

"Worse, probably. But would you come anyway?"

"Yes. I'd like to. Yes."

Zoe took hold of Nicolo's arm, and it seemed as if the next words she spoke had been tucked away for another purpose entirely, but were brought thriftily to use, without forethought.

"Couldn't we simply start and see how it goes?" was what Zoe said. "What's stopping us?"

Nicolo felt as if, with these words, a seed was planted in his chest. No, more than a seed—a sapling, already started, already on its way to becoming what it would become. He set his plate down on the long table, on the white tablecloth with the lines of the folds still on it, and he put his arms around Zoe and held on to her for so long that the long line of patient people began to flow around them.

"How did your exam go?" asked his older brother later on in the day, as evening drew around them.

"I didn't study as much as I planned to. I had too much on my mind toward the end. I had to guess at some of it."

"You always do well. You and Enzo. You have the right head for tests and things. Remember you were asking about that guy who used to work with Dad?"

"Vito Greco."

"I asked Dad about him and he said that Nonna took a dislike to him and wanted Dad to fire him, but then before he could decide what to do, Vito quit, just stopped coming to work. Later they heard that he had turned up downtown, at one of those places that's more of a salon than a barbershop. Pop said Vito was a good worker, just quiet. And then Len came along, remember, and rented the other chair, and Dad said he almost never thought about Vito again after that."

Nonna was walking behind the boys, holding a plate from the buffet table, when, through all the noise and talk, she thought she heard Enzo utter the name of that *furfante*—that scoundrel—from when the boys were small. She had gone to the shop on a Saturday afternoon with a mop and rags and detergent to clean it from back to front. She brought Nicolo with her to push the broom and get at dust and hair in places she couldn't reach. He tried hard to dissuade her from opening Vito's cupboard, stood in front of it with his back to the doors, and was almost tearful when she insisted that it would have to be put in order like everything else. The cabinet was filled with *sporchezza*—dirt—that spilled out when the doors were pulled open, and she questioned Nicolo closely about what he knew about its contents. He knew more than he told her—that was clear. His expression was locked, evasive, and his answers were mumbled toward the floor. Who knew what the boy was hiding or covering up? She felt her blood surge like fire inside her veins.

Later that day, she extracted the address from Gianna and took a bus to Vito's apartment, carrying Vito's comb and scissors and vials of cream and salve loaded into two plastic bags. These she threw on the floor at his feet and told that *disgraziato* that he had better be on his way, that he had no business contaminating with his presence the homes or businesses of honest people.

Poor Vito, who had never got around to removing Guido's stash of magazines from the cabinet behind his chair, believed that Massimo had been so undermined by Vito's challenge to his skills that he had been reduced to sending his mother to effect Vito's dismissal from the store. Never mind. Vito had saved a bit of money and knew his way around the city. He wanted to work somewhere that had music playing and a bit of style, where the clientele spoke English and might want something more than long at the front and short at the sides.

"I talked to Pietro and he thinks that where this is all going is that some of the students will have to sit out next year as a penalty. The group may or may not include me. Pietro said it could go either way in my case, but I've decided that I don't want to wait. Whatever they decide, I'll take next year off school and do something else. I don't like the idea of letting someone else make decisions for me."

"But what would you do?" Nicolo remembered that before Enzo had been accepted into law school he had talked about getting a master's degree. He imagined Enzo at the same university, but in a different building, wearing jeans and a sweater and studying systems of governments and the uses of international diplomacy to settle trade disputes. What Enzo said next forced him to erase this quick mental sketch and replace it with an entirely different one.

"The Vaughan Bakery is up for sale. The Gerussis are going to retire and their son doesn't want to run it. I'm thinking of buying it from them."

In his imagination Nicolo pulled Enzo out of the classroom and put him back into a business suit. "You mean, as an investment?"

"No, I'm thinking of running it myself. I can do it if I get a loan for the setup and a line of credit to cover the operating costs. I've been over there a lot in the last few days, and I have some ideas about how I can improve it. The wire shelves need to go, and the menu could be expanded and updated. The staff wants to stay on. It's not a bad setup. Most of it's marginal. The coffee is where the profits are, the lattes and cappuccinos. Good markups. And what you want to do is arrange it so people don't stay too long, taking up tables."

Nicolo mentally replaced Enzo's suit with jeans and a black shirt and dropped him behind the counter of the bakery. "What if a Starbucks opens up across the street?"

"That doesn't worry me. Not everyone likes the chains, and I can offer a better product. The old machines will need to go. There's a distributor from Italy who's willing to give me an exclusive for the area on these new machines that make a better coffee. It's a science as much as an art. The right beans, the right water—it's got to be filtered—the right temperature and pressure and extraction time. Even though they're more complicated, these machines are easier to operate, and they're more reliable. The manufacturer will fly over and train the staff if I make a commitment to their products. It's a good location and the store's already got good turnover. With a few improvements, I think it could do very well."

Nicolo tried to imagine how his parents would react. They might be slower than he had been to accept his younger brother's move from law school to coffee shop. Enzo anticipated his concern.

"Don't worry about Ma and Pa. Nonna said she'd talk to them."

"You told Nonna?"

"Yes. You know, you don't give her enough credit. She understands a lot more than she lets on."

"What did she say?"

"*Fai l'arti chi farai. Si non ricchisi, campirai.* Do the craft you were meant to do. If you don't grow rich, at least you'll live."

"Good advice, eh?"

"Yeah, good advice."

"I could go in with you, and Enzo too. Both of us need a change. We could try it and see how it goes. What's stopping us?"

The café, renamed Café Fratelli, was very much like other cafés where the owners have no taste for trends or fashions. The Fells, the one time they came to see it, out of curiosity, after they had become very rich, thought that it was somewhat shabby, and very inferior to the coffee shops they frequented in the centre of the city.

"Very common tables and chairs, nothing out of the ordinary. Not much of a business," Bella whispered into Phil's small, grey ear. But in spite of these deficiencies, the wishes, the hopes, the confidence and the predictions of the three brothers who ran it over many years to come were fully answered in its success.

ACKNOWLEDGMENTS

Thank you to my adopted Italian family and in particular to Gilda, Josephine and Maria for their stories and *proverbi*; to Pietro Calendino for assistance with the Calabrese dialect; to the men in my life, including Don, Tony, John, Joseph, Nicholas, Sandy, Paul, Alex, Patrick and Lawrence, for helping me consider the world from a different perspective; to Sofia for her sense of humour; to Allyson Latta for her excellent copy edit; and to Jennifer Lambert and Noelle Zitzer at HarperCollins, for their thoughtful work on this book. Any errors are mine alone.

P.S.

Ideas,
interviews
& features

Author Biography

BORN IN WESTON, Ontario, now part of Toronto, and raised in Toronto and Ottawa, Anne Giardini was, in her words, a blend of her "gentle and creative mother," acclaimed Pulitzer Prize–winning novelist Carol Shields, and her "resolute engineer father." The second of five children, she was a dreamy child who lived in two places, she says, "the real world and inside the stories I scrolled out in my head."

Giardini liked to tell stories to her three sisters, whom she remembers as "the most attentive and astute of audiences." And she thought for a time that she might become an actress—until she realized she "had absolutely no talent for it." After high school she started a degree in economics, by accident, at the University of Ottawa. A registration clerk recommended she try "poli-sci," meaning political science. Giardini thought she meant "poly-sci," meaning many sciences, and so agreed. The clerk then suggested that people who took poli-sci also often took economics, and Giardini signed up for that too. "When I showed up for my first political science class, while I was wondering at the absence of Bunsen burners, the professor held up a book called *Anatomy of a Coup* and said, 'I'm going to teach you how to overthrow the government of a small country.' I remember leaning forward in my chair and thinking, *This is all I ever really wanted to know.*"

After finishing her degree, Giardini was drawn to the study of law, with its "rigour, challenges and creative use of language, and its many stories." She went on to obtain her

Anne Giardini

STACCIE BRACKEN-HORROCKS

LLB from the University of British Columbia, and her LLM from Trinity Hall, University of Cambridge, in England. She was called to the bar in British Columbia in 1986 and in Ontario in 1990.

She is not surprised at all, she says, that so many lawyers she meets want to write fiction, because the law is all about stories. "It contains thousands—millions—of individual narratives, and it creates from all of these narrative threads a good part of the cloth, the stuff, that we call society."

She says it is inescapable that her mother would be the greatest influence on her writing. The first time Giardini realized that her mother was a writer, Shields had just won the CBC Young Writers Competition. "Her winning poem was read on the air. I was about four or five and I was lying on my back on the kitchen floor. She was standing up and we were both listening to her words over the radio. It just seemed like absolute magic."

Among Giardini's many writing projects was a 1996 collaboration with her mother, a paper they delivered at a meeting of the Jane Austen Society of North America. Entitled "Martians in Jane Austen," the paper applied archetypes from John Gray's *Men Are from Mars, Women Are from Venus* to the characters in Austen's novels. Also, for three years in the late 1990s, Giardini wrote a column for the *National Post*, which she describes as the best possible writing experience.

In "Still Life with Power," an essay Giardini wrote for the collection *Dropped Threads* (2001), edited by Carol Shields and Marjorie Anderson, she explored some of the themes that would feed her future novels. Giardini ▶

In 'Still Life with Power' . . . Anne Giardini explored some of the themes that would feed her future novels.

wrote about power and how surprising it seemed to her that it was assumed and wielded so differently by men and women. She had begun a novel, called *Assiniboine*, and was startled to discover that her central female character kept being pushed aside by a male character, who insisted on taking up the narrative. "I marvelled at this, and concluded that my subconscious, aware in its peculiar way that I was striving to write a 'serious' novel, was seeking to ensure that it be led by a serious protagonist, and that a male would perhaps be more likely to be taken seriously than a female. I spoke of this with my mother and these discussions made their way into her last novel, *Unless*, and into my first novel, *The Sad Truth About Happiness*. Norah, the daughter in *Unless* who is so dismayed at the state of the world, shares both some of these concerns and my birthday."

Sadly, Shields, who died in July 2003 after a five-year battle with breast cancer, never had a chance to read her daughter's first work of fiction. *The Sad Truth About Happiness* (2005) went on to become a bestseller and was shortlisted for the Amazon.ca/*Books in Canada* First Novel Award and the 2007 Audie Award, honouring excellence in audio publishing.

Since 1994, Giardini has worked for the Canadian subsidiary of Weyerhaeuser Company, an integrated forest products corporation, and she is now president of the Canadian company.

Giardini is a frequent speaker on legal topics, and on issues affecting girls and women. She was recently a member of the

> " She had begun a novel . . . and was startled to discover that her central female character kept being pushed aside by a male character. "

BC Law Society's Retention of Women in Law Task Force, is chair of the Vancouver International Writers & Readers Festival, and has been appointed to the Board of Governors of Simon Fraser University.

Anne Giardini lives in Vancouver, British Columbia, with her husband of more than twenty years, Tony Giardini. They have three children, two in university and one still at home. Giardini is at work on her third novel.

৻৶

A Conversation with Anne Giardini

What incident or observation inspired you to write *Advice for Italian Boys*?

Over twenty years ago, I married into an Italian-Canadian family. I was somewhat surprised to find that this new family of mine was a fountain of advice of all kinds—advice on career decisions and clothes, on pregnancies and child rearing, and on health, wealth and happiness. At first, I was taken aback. So much advice! Over time, I grew more used to it, but I know that I resented, to a slight extent, the assurance and intrusiveness of the advice I was given. When, finally, some of this surplus counsel became the foundation for *Advice for Italian Boys*, I realized how fortunate I was as a novelist to have this wonderful material—given to me for free!—for this book, and perhaps for a sequel. I am writing a different novel now, but I may come back to the three Pavone men in a future book.

How different would the novel have been if you didn't have the insights derived from your personal experience with the Italian-Canadian side of your family?

The novel could not have existed if I hadn't married into this family. The Giardini family have simply enfolded me, and have shared with me feelings and experiences and stories that I could not have known in any other way. I am certain that I would have had other experiences, and that these would have led to

❝ The Giardini family have simply enfolded me, and have shared with me feelings and experiences and stories that I could not have known in any other way. ❞

6

a novel, but that novel could not have been *Advice for Italian Boys*.

And I could not, without my wonderful mother-in-law, Gilda Giardini, have learned enough of the Calabrese dialect to begin to understand the strength, good sense and peculiar world view of the Calabrese *proverbi*, or sayings.

What's the most surprising aspect of marrying into a Canadian-Italian family? What's the best part?

Most surprising has been the loyalty that this adopted tribe has among them, and has extended to me. The best part is the love, of course, but this is followed closely by the food. In some ways, I have come to understand, the food is the love made manifest.

Your protagonist, Nicolo, is faced with some bewildering life choices. Do you believe that being part of a family that comes to this culture from another makes such choices harder, or easier?

I think being part of a family that comes from a strong culture like this one makes most choices significantly easier. I mean by this the normal choices we all must make: whether to marry and who, what studies to take, what work to do, how to raise one's children. However, a strong cultural base can make it more difficult to make unusual decisions because the patterns of how one should live are more entrenched, and so can be harder to break from. ▶

A strong cultural base can make it more difficult to make unusual decisions.

A Conversation with Anne Giardini
(*continued*)

Did the writing ever take you in unexpected directions?

Advice for Italian Boys was a gift. Almost the entire plot came to me in an instant one morning on a rainy day in Vancouver, as I stood in a queue at a coffee shop waiting to order my daily caffe latte. The story did take some unexpected directions when I sat down to write it. I had been determined to send Nonna back to Italy during the course of the book. She was even more determined not to go! I was also surprised by Nicolo's sexuality as it unfolded. He was more complicated than I had imagined. And he had a firmly fixed moral core—I wasn't expecting this in such a young man.

What surprised me most, though, was that this book wanted to be about married life, as well as about Nicolo. There are many scenes of marriage in *Advice for Italian Boys*, and I have come to believe that marriage is in some ways a constant giving of advice from one partner to the other. A well-functioning couple comes to decisions, and stays on or shifts course as a result of subtle signals from one to the other. Most of this is silent and almost invisible. I wonder sometimes, with the divorce rate being what it is, if this is a skill set that has been lost or whether relationships may have become too charged with concerns about power and equality. In the best marriages, I think, this giving and receiving of advice is done tacitly, in kindness and trust.

> ❝ The story did take some unexpected directions when I sat down to write it. ❞

8

Advice for Italian Boys has been called a "quiet, reflective novel," but there's humour as well. I am thinking, for example, of the quirky characters that frequent the gym. Which writing comes most naturally to you?

Some of the advice that made its way over here from southern Italy relies on humour to bring home its point, and this sense of humour made its way into *Advice for Italian Boys* quite naturally. But I don't think of myself as a humorous novelist. I like to think that my writing reflects people as they are, in all their iterations and all their moods. This makes my writing reflective, but also makes it funny: humans never cease to amaze and amuse us.

Nicolo's nonna's dream memories of her life back in Italy are incredibly evocative. How did you render these so convincingly?

I have spent time in Italy, and so know how it looks and smells and tastes, and so forth. But what I really strove to capture in *Advice for Italian Boys* were not my own experiences but rather the memories of, and a kind of longing for, an Italy that no longer exists—the Italy that I have heard about when speaking with my mother-in-law, and her brother Rudy, who died fairly recently, and her niece Josephine.

Is there a particular scene from the novel that characterizes the book for you, or that lingers in your mind? ▶

> " What I really strove to capture … were not my own experiences but rather the memories of, and a kind of longing for, an Italy that no longer exists. "

A Conversation with Anne Giardini
(*continued*)

I often think about the scene in which Nicolo experiences an unusual sense of dislocation when he goes to the theatre with Zoe. He feels himself flowing into her, as if she has become permeable and he is able to move into her skin. For the shortest possible moment, he feels her body from the inside, sees through her eyes, hears what she hears, breathes as she breathes. He understands that she is both knowable and unknowable. Ultimately I think that it is this knowing, coupled with a sense of ongoing mystery as a counterpoint, that keeps a relationship strong.

This is echoed in another scene between Nicolo's parents, Paola and Massimo. Massimo has come home somewhat upset after an incident at work, but he is a proud man and doesn't tell Paola about it. Later, they are in bed, "as close together as a single sheet of origami paper folded cleverly into two nested figures: sleeping husband, sleeping wife. She felt her eyes fill, so concerned was she for this man, for his hidden sorrows whatever they were, and she thought of a rhyme from her youth. *Se vai' a lettu non mi pidghija sonnu. Pensu a' l'amuri e mi ment' a ciangiri.* If I go to bed, I won't be able to sleep. I'll think of love and start to weep." Paola strokes Massimo's hair. They make love and then fall asleep, so close both physically and emotionally that any secrets harboured can only be minor and can do them no harm.

> **❝ I think that it is this knowing, coupled with a sense of ongoing mystery as a counterpoint, that keeps a relationship strong. ❞**

10

What is the most important wisdom you hope you've passed on to your own children—your version of Nonna's *proverbi*?

I don't think I give my children advice in the form of axioms or adages, the way that Nonna does in *Advice for Italian Boys*. Nonna is *analfabeta*—illiterate. She comes from a culture that didn't have encyclopedias or libraries or Google. The sayings she passes on to her grandchildren represent a method of storing and passing on wisdom that we don't rely on anymore. Having said that, I do like to pass on a piece of my mother's advice, particularly to young women, which is this: always be as intelligent as you are.

What did you learn—about the craft of writing, or about life in general—through the process of researching and writing *Advice for Italian Boys*?

I discovered that my inner lode of love and respect for the family that I married into is wider and deeper than I had realized. About writing, I learned to trust my characters— once they are fully imagined, they will act as they will and I can have faith in them to lead me into and through their stories. About life, I learned that advice freely given is sometimes worth having, and that the best forms of advice are often not so much spoken as shown; the manner in which someone we love and respect chooses to live is the very best advice, if we are alive to it.

❧

> " I do like to pass on a piece of my mother's advice, particularly to young women, which is this: always be as intelligent as you are. "

Thoughts on Writing, Advice, Freight Cars and Clotheslines by Anne Giardini

I grew up in a house in which books were read and written, and so for me, the jump into novels from journalism and short stories did not feel like an enormous one. Finishing and then publishing my first novel, *The Sad Truth About Happiness*, felt to me like the next logical step in a writing life. I do think it is an advantage (although not essential) to grow up in a writing house if you want to be a writer, and I compare it sometimes to being the butcher's child and becoming a butcher yourself in turn. If you grow up around a particular art or business, there isn't as much mystique in it. You know generally how to go about what needs to be done.

I began to write *The Sad Truth About Happiness* when my mother, the writer Carol Shields, was already quite ill. She died from complications of breast cancer before it came out, and so I missed the chance to ask her for advice. However, as I wrote that first book, I kept in mind something that my mother had said, that it had been important to her "to write in the most intimate way possible, as if I were whispering into the ear of someone I loved."

I am starting to turn my attention to a third novel, one with a name that was suggested by my second son and middle child, "Anguish Pie." Each of these books has a theme. *The Sad Truth About Happiness* is about happiness and unhappiness. *Advice for Italian Boys* is about the advice that family members and friends

> "As I wrote that first book, I kept in mind something that my mother had said, that it had been important to her 'to write in the most intimate way possible, as if I were whispering into the ear of someone I loved.'"

12

give us as we make our way through our lives, advice that can sometimes be as baffling as life itself. "Anguish Pie" will be about death and what I believe happens afterward.

I had other kinds of guidance from my mother, not delivered as counsel or warnings the way that the Italian-Canadian characters in *Advice for Italian Boys* deliver theirs, but instead as the kind of instruction you soak up by watching someone else doing something well, like the butcher's son watching how his father separates the filet from the sirloin with a sharp knife and a careful hand.

I knew, for example, that my mother always had a structure in her mind before she began to write a book. She referred to this structure as "a very physical image that I can call up, just the way you would call up an image on your screen." An example is the way that her first novel, *Small Ceremonies*, is organized. It is divided into nine chapters, each representing a month of an academic year—September and on through May. "And in my mind," she said, "those chapters looked like the cars of a freight train, and I just lined them up, nine of them, and I knew I would have to fill those freight cars, and that was the image, and it helped me keep things together a little bit."

I feel the same need for an organizing principle when I set out to write. *The Sad Truth About Happiness* has as its framework the idea that the main character, Maggie Selgrin, is taking a visitor on a tour around the house in which she lives. *Advice for Italian Boys* has a very different shape—I thought of it as a backyard clothesline, with the advice that the characters give to the central character, Nicolo Pavone, a twenty-four-year-old fitness ▶

> **I knew, for example, that my mother always had a structure in her mind before she began to write a book.**

coach, as the pegs that secure his life to the line.

I have always been interested, as my mother was, in the lives of others. "A human life, and this is the only plot I think I'm interested in, is this primordial plot of birth, love, work, decline and death," she said. "This is just life working away toward the end of life." I was the kind of child who liked to stare at other people and try to overhear their conversations and imagine their lives. I suppose I still do this, although now that I am older I try to be a bit less obvious. I look at someone in the queue at the coffee shop and wonder, *Who are you fundamentally? Do you feel as real to yourself as I do? Do you harbour secrets and longings and wishes, or are you entirely contented? What would you blurt out if I caught you in an unguarded moment?* And I often speculate about personal details such as, how does it feel to have the build of a professional wrestler, or to be enormously fat, or to have a yellow braid that you wind up and pin to the top of your head. I absolutely long to ask these questions, but we generally aren't allowed to bother strangers with this kind of enquiry, and so the next best thing is to put the character in a novel and work it out by fully imagining them for a period of time.

In *Advice for Italian Boys*, I gave myself the licence to be a young fitness instructor, an Italian grandmother, a law student who has made a mistake with potentially serious consequences, a woman I saw in a coffee lineup who wants to strike out on a life of her own, and many others, none of them like me, all of

> **❝** I was the kind of child who liked to stare at other people and try to overhear their conversations and imagine their lives. **❞**

them human and interesting, each clamouring for their story to be heard.

I have new goals now that I am working on my next book. I want to use the first-person voice again, and I want to try to follow more closely one of my mother's principles for writing, which was to write exactly what she intended.

When she was writing poetry in her late twenties, my mother said that she began to want to achieve something different in her writing. "At the end of each poem," she said, "I asked myself, 'Is this what I really mean?' and it was the first time I felt I took myself seriously. I was not thinking of [the] reader.... I think we can never think about that. That's like thinking about market.... I put that question to myself very sternly, and it often resulted in the rewriting of the poem to make sure I said what I really meant. Now this is a piece of wisdom you would think I would have absorbed at once, but in fact, it seems I'm one of these people who has to learn the same thing over and over again. So there have been many times in my writing life where I've had to remember that."

This is as good advice about writing as I have ever heard. Why write at all if not to set down exactly what you mean, to come as close to the truth as words will allow?

Reprinted with permission of The Globe and Mail

❝ Why write at all if not to set down exactly what you mean, to come as close to the truth as words will allow? ❞

Further Reading

*Some of Anne Giardini's
Favourite Books*

There are so many! Here are a few that come
early in an alphabetical list. I haven't included
my mother's books, each one of which is a
favourite. I keep a changing list on my webpage
at the Writers' Union of Canada:
*www.writersunion.ca/ww_profile.
asp?mem=305&L.*

A Room of One's Own by Virginia Woolf
This powerful essay has been life-changing
for me and for many thousands of women.

Black Dogs by Ian McEwan
This book is McEwan's best—a short, dark
novel about how narrative is created.

Black Swan Green by David Mitchell
This book absolutely nails adolescence.

Enduring Love by Ian McEwan
A comic mystery of how little we know and
understand each other.

Enigma of Arrival by V.S. Naipaul
This book is about the unfolding of self-
discovery and seeing the world.

Excellent Women by Barbara Pym
Pym is Jane Austen's truest successor, and this
is the best of her slim, razor-sharp novels.

Gilead by Marilynne Robinson
A novel of visions, conflict and love.

The Girls of Slender Means by Muriel Spark
A flawless and macabre book about young
women in London in 1945.

Guns, Germs, and Steel by Jared Diamond
This non-fiction book changed my understanding of the damage we do to each other
and to the world.

Middlemarch by George Eliot
Enormous, wonderfully and confidently
written.

and . . .

Any and all of Alice Munro's stories
These stories are always about two things:
the way people actually live their lives, and
the other, possible lives that they glimpse but
almost never attain.

Web Detective

Here are a few of Anne Giardini's top website picks.

www.carolshieldslabyrinth.ca
This website is about the real and wonderful Carol Shields Memorial Labyrinth in Winnipeg.

www.carolshieldslabyrinth.com
This interactive labyrinth is a virtual walk through Carol Shields's life and work.

www.freerice.com/index.php
Online quizzes test your vocabulary and knowledge of languages, art, chemistry, geography and mathematics. For every correct answer, the site sponsors donate rice through the UN World Food Program.

www.writersfest.bc.ca
The Vancouver International Writers & Readers Festival is one of North America's most important literary events. This site includes "Literary Links" that are useful for readers and writers across Canada.

www.writersunion.ca
The Writers' Union of Canada is a not-for-profit organization that supports and advocates for Canada's authors and Canadian writing.

To receive updates on author events and new books by Anne Giardini, sign up today at *www.authortracker.ca*